Julia Helen Watts Twells

The Mills of the Gods

A novel

Julia Helen Watts Twells

The Mills of the Gods
A novel

ISBN/EAN: 9783337031640

Printed in Europe, USA, Canada, Australia, Japan

Cover: Foto ©Andreas Hilbeck / pixelio.de

More available books at **www.hansebooks.com**

MILLS OF THE GODS.

A NOVEL.

BY

MRS. J. H. TWELLS.

PHILADELPHIA:
J. B. LIPPINCOTT & CO.
1875.

SHOULD THIS BOOK HOLD A WORTHY THOUGHT,

A NOBLE SENTIMENT, OR A TENDER TOUCH OF FEELING,

I BEG LEAVE TO DEDICATE THEM ALL

TO THE LARGEST-HEARTED OF WOMEN, THE KINDEST OF FRIENDS,

THE MOST DEVOTED OF MOTHERS,

MY OWN.

THE MILLS OF THE GODS.

BOOK I.

CHAPTER I.

IT was the last night of the Carnival in Rome.   During the past eight days the fantastic Harlequin of Mirth had disported himself on the Corso, amid the rainbow-decked balconies, where laughing-eyed women displayed their beauty in coquettish, flowery warfare; at every window of the high, dull houses, which broke out all over in smiles, and ogles, and vari-colored streamers; and down in the narrow street, with its contrary flow of carriages,—flower- and frolic-laden,—and its jostling crowd of *masques* and *confetti*-intoxicated roysterers.

And now the evening of "Mardi Gras" rides rollicking over the boisterous waves of humanity, which had roared and rolled high in the fury of condensed excitement all through that sunny day which ushered in Ash-Wednesday.   The riderless horses had run, cheered to the echo; the last bouquet had been thrown; arch glances were deteriorating into weary leers, the revelers and the confetti had become exhausted, and the carnival of flowers and bonbons, of poetry and sentiment, was giving place to the carnival of reckless debauch, of unrestrained license, of frantic excitement, which hides no blush under the shadow of the darkness, and cries, "Let us eat and drink, for to-morrow we die!"

Half the world, the adventurous and the *canaille*, were making night a Pandemonium in that ingenious device of the devil,—the struggle to extinguish each other's torches.

Ye gods! when one contemplates so much fierce energy being wasted upon a senseless sport, one is tempted to wonder why a portion of that frantic zeal is never brought to bear in rekindling an illumination in this darkened land, which would once more put out the lesser lights of the world!

The other half of the Roman population were preparing to array themselves in fanciful garb for the concluding *bal masqué* of the season.

For it is to be an early ball, both at palazzo and theatre, —though fast and furious, for the chime of midnight, like the writing on the wall which disturbed the serenity of Balthazar's *convives*, will startle into a sudden sobriety these wild-eyed Mænads, these laughing rioters, with its solemn—"Peace,—be still!" And then the laughter of these maniacs will terminate in groans, their flashing glances will be quenched in tears, while their confetti-soiled hands will beat the breast from which shall issue one cry, *Mea culpa!*

Throughout those gala-days, in the balconies where the fairest of his countrywomen dazzled the passers-by with their blush-rose charms, Dyke Faucett lounged and lingered, serenely unruffled as a lake under an August moon, amid all that wild uproar of sights and sounds, supplying with lavish hand, flowers, bonbons, compliments, ad infinitum, to one and all about him with impartial liberality. He took no active part in the bombardment of friend or foe, feeling that he had done his part (by far the least exhausting), in supplying ammunition for his fair friends, and the lazy lids drooped occasionally over his handsome eyes, as if the whole thing bored him—and, he would fain have been elsewhere. Of the countless fragrant missiles which rarely missed their mark and which fell at his feet, aimed from all directions with a persistency of fire which showed more ardor than discretion, Dyke took not the slightest cognizance, save when they struck him rather too obtrusively in the face, when his eyebrows would elevate themselves, and he would murmur in the ear of the lovely woman who stood beside him, "Shocking bad form in that girl opposite to bombard a man as inoffensive as myself; pray send her two or three bonbonnières with a flag of truce,—*de ma part.*"

"No, no; you must defend yourself," laughed Lady Jane St. Maur, who had spent six out of seven of those latter days striving assiduously by hook or by crook (a good deal by *crook*) to force that cool *insouciance* to betray by some little galvanic start that blood flowed through those tranquil pulses, and life glowed under that blonde, delicate-tinted epidermis. But for Dyke Faucett, the javelins of all the Becky Sharps in the big Vanity Fair of the world were blunted for the present against the breast-plate behind which his heart was shielded,—the fierce infatuation which had taken possession of him, to which he had, after many ineffectual struggles, surrendered himself. Before the innocence and purity of Dora Fairfax's white soul, he had thrown down his weapons of worldly wisdom, and acknowledged himself defeated. Had her fascination for him been one whit less powerful, or her soul one shade less clean, the cynical callousness which had stood Dyke Faucett's friend on many similar occasions would not have deserted him now. But through all the varied experiences of his former life, he had never encountered such combined attractiveness and power as this little girl possessed, who first drew his eyes away from a saint's face in the Vatican which she was copying, to rest in undisguised admiration upon her own; and then, so deftly weaved her net about him, after a fortunate accident had thrown them together, as to give him but one object in life to pursue, which he did unremittingly, and, for the first time in his life, almost hopelessly, until within a fortnight of to-day.

But Lady Jane St. Maur had not despaired; she had not gained her pre-eminence in London drawing-rooms, and Parisian salons, and German spas, without much and arduous labor, and she did not dream of withered laurels at eight-and-twenty.

"*Fi-donc, mon ami!*" she cried, gayly, as Dyke daintily dusted the confetti-powder from his coat-sleeve. "Your indolence is itself provocative, and challenges attack! You set yourself up as a target, and—there are six feet of you, remember;" and she laughed musically. She was right; six feet of comeliness, dressed by Poole, and surmounted by that Antinöus head, where the sunlight brought out the gold in the curly, chestnut chevelure, could not escape disaster through those gala-days, when every woman's heart rioted in a little tumultuous orgie of its own.

But Dyke Faucett was tired of it all; there were few things which would not pall upon him now; some weeks ago he would have averred that there was *nothing* that would not turn to ashes on his sated lips; but that was some weeks ago.

For this man, in the flower of life, with the beauty of a god and the digestion of an ostrich; with money in his purse, and the world before him, had joined that noble army of martyrs whom the demon of *ennui* claims as its very own; and after years of delightful travel, bronzed by tropic suns and bleached by northern frosts, having plucked the fruit of the knowledge-tree, and eaten thereof in every clime under the sun, he had begun to taste the bitterness of the lees lying inevitably at the bottom of the pleasure-cup, and to groan out that it was all "vanity and vexation of spirit;" or that "life would be very tolerable were it not for its *pleasures.*"

And now all this noisy rabble had begun to bore him unutterably, therefore he suggested to Lady Jane the delicious tranquillity of an inner salon; and she, nothing loth, allowed herself to be seated therein, in the most comfortable of *causeuses*, placed at precisely the correct angle for the display of her faultless profile, which Dyke compared mentally with that of little Dora, to the detriment of the one before him.

Of which fact Lady Jane—making the most of this blessed opportunity which the gods had thrown in her way—remained in blissful ignorance.

And Dyke Faucett simply endured the slow-crawling hours until the moment arrived when, with the plea of an imperative engagement, he freed himself from the toils which this young lady flattered herself were strengthening momentarily, and, at nine o'clock, after a hasty dinner and a careful toilet, he sprang into his cab with the first sensation of pleasure he had felt that day.

With a domino thrown carelessly over his brilliant courtier-dress of the Elizabethan days (having ordered his man to drive to the Via Babuino), he leaned back on the cushions with a smile of satisfaction, picturing to himself Dora's surprise at his novel appearance. Poor Dora! during all these merry-making days and nights she had not left her father's side, who, suffering from an attack of rheumatic gout, which crippled him, was pitiably dependent upon her tender nursing and companionship.

A*

The long, monotonous days held for her but the couple of hours of delight when Dyke Faucett could tear himself away from the claims of his friends and acquaintances, and in the interval between dinner and ball seek the unfashionable Via Babuino, where Dora watched and waited for his coming as the one great gladness of her day. For she loved this man unselfishly, devotedly, seeing only in him the incarnation of her own love-dream; thanking God with tears for the blessing of his love, and praying to grow worthier of it.

And thus another problem was cast forth, which will not know solution until the dawning of that day when we shall learn the answers to many vexing questions; among others, why Desdemonas wed with Moors.

When Sardyx, of mythical memory, went forth to battle armed with the magic javelin which never went foul of the mark, pressed into his hands by the beautiful Aglaia, wet with her tears and followed by her prayers, did a vision of the triumphant return of the victor accompanied by a newer, not fairer, mistress, cast its long, drear shadow over all the days that parted them?

And when within a few miles of his native city, Aglaia rushed forth to meet her hero with wide-stretched arms, did the sight which greeted her pierce less murderously her faithful heart, than the fatal javelin hurled by the hand of him she loved, as the surest and speediest method of ridding himself of an incumbrance? Was it the stirring of this legend in her brain, or was it only the hope deferred of lonely waiting in the sad, still twilight through two long hours, which has given that downward curve to Dora's sweet mouth to-night, and the far-away, prescient gaze out into the gathering darkness? Or is her guardian angel drawing aside the veil from the future years and showing her the gaunt spectre of that life into which the beautiful present has been transformed? I know not; but true it is, that in the pose of the slender form, white-robed and fragile as a lily, there was a certain pensive listlessness as she leaned against the railing that guarded the window, with her graceful head bent in a despondent curve. How exquisitely lovely she looked standing thus, with her slender, white hands clasped before her, while the round arms gleamed like polished marble through the transparent muslin! No ornament detracted from her pure loveliness, a fragrant bunch of double violets closed the lace frills across her white throat, and a knot of the same love-breathing flowers nestled among the rich braids of her sunny hair.

Against the dusky background of her little sitting-room, with its paucity of furniture, its wealth of pictures, books, statuettes, its harp in one corner, and its little hired piano in another, its white-shaded lamp not yet lighted, and its wild flowers everywhere, Dora offered as fair a study of "Il Penseroso" as any artist, however ambitious, could desire.

So thought Dyke Faucett, as, opening the door noiselessly, he stole upon her unawares, to watch her surprise and wonder at his fanciful garb.

She was so absorbed in her reverie that he stood and watched her silently for a moment, and then advanced. With a faint cry she sprang aside, and it was not until he had removed quickly the pointed beard which belonged to the era he represented, that she recovered from her alarm. "Did I startle you, my little fawn?" cried Dyke, caressing her hand with his, after he had bent and kissed her lightly on the cheek; "did you not know me at all?"

"Who are you, pray?" she laughed, while the color came back to her cheek and the gleaming joy to her eyes. "Are you the beloved Essex or the gallant Raleigh?

You are very gorgeous, whoever you are; I feel a great want of court-train and jewels at this moment.''

He laid his hand upon her shoulder. "Court-train and jewels would not add royalty to that gracious head or this perfect form, *ma mie*. I would not have you other than you are at this moment. Ah, if you only knew how sick unto death I am of satins and gems, pearl-powder and rouge, and how divinely sweet you seem to me in your white gown and violets. Oh, Dora!'' he exclaimed, with the nearest approach to passion he had ever before allowed to thrill in his voice,—"Dora, I am growing tired of waiting for you. My love, why can you not come into my life now and make it perfect?''

His arm stole about her, and for a moment she simply existed, nothing more. And then she roused herself. "Dyke, I have talked with my father to-day, a long, long time, and he is opposed to our clandestine marriage. Wait, darling,'' for Dyke was about to interrupt her impatiently; "he says I am very young,—not nineteen, you know,—and we can wait; that no good ever comes of secret marriages, and——''

"That is all arrant nonsense,'' commented Dyke. "My guardian cannot live forever, and after his death there is no one on earth to dictate to me. I know, Dora, that he has other views for me, and would never consent to this marriage. Oh, my darling, do not start away from me like that! I resent his narrow-minded injustice as much as you possibly can, my peerless pearl, but would you have me wait for you through all the long years which may intervene before his death? Can you thrust me away from you,—say, Dora, *can* you do this thing?''

Her face grew very white, but she answered, in a clear, firm voice, "Yes, Dyke, I could thrust you away from me forever, and pluck my love for you out of my heart by the roots, before I could consent to live under the foul cover of deceit and falsehood which this secret marriage might entail, through years and years of hopeless self-contempt.''

'' No, Dora, that need not be. Were my guardian to see you in your winning beauty, with your many gifts, and know that you were *irrevocably bound to me*, he *could* not then refuse to sanction and bless our marriage. Ah, you are but a child, and *I* know the world, and my guardian above all; can you not trust to me?''

'' How long would it be necessary to keep it a secret?'' she asked, her tears falling fast.

'' Perhaps a couple of months; only until I could go over to England and prepare his mind for your reception, dearest, and then I should come for you and your father, and, oh, Dora, my perfect one, can you imagine our happiness and still turn from me ?''

'' I will do whatever you say, Dyke. I will trust you to the end !'' Her last words were smothered in frantic kisses. As he clasped her to his heart a pang of remorse shot through him,—the *last*,—it was the death-sigh of his conscience, which died that night forever in this world.

It was after eleven o'clock when he left her ; and she had promised to meet him two days hence, in the early morning, outside the '' Porta del Popolo,'' where the English Chapel stood, to ratify by sacred vows the trust she had promised to place in him. He could scarcely tear himself away from her, so fearful was he that his prize would elude his grasp; so more than beautiful she looked, in the full rays of the moon, which bathed her in its mystic gleams. and made her almost too spiritual in its glory. Her cheeks were flushed with happiness, her eyes shone like stars, and her scarlet lips showed the tiny pearls behind them in a divine smile. '' Oh, Dora, turn away from me, else I cannot leave you,'' pleaded Fawcett, com-

pletely intoxicated.   She smiled more bewilderingly than
ever, and stretched out both hands to him; but, choking
down an exclamation, Dyke, without one other word,
turned to the door and fled.

Dora stood amazed; what did this mean,—this abrupt
flitting, this disregard of her last good-night?   She sank
into a chair, and mused until the light faded out of her
face, and—

> "The soft, sad eyes
> Set like twilight planets in the rainy skies,
> With the brow all patience and the lips all pain!"

bore more likeness to the fair, doomed Iphigenia, than to
a young bride-elect, standing with trembling but joyous
feet almost on the threshold of her wedding-day.

For two hours, in that ghostly moonshine, she sat, shifting her fate from hand to hand.   It was not yet too late;
her promise had been wrung from her, it is true, but could
she but convince herself that this necessary deception was
unjustifiable, even as the price of such unutterable happiness, she would not hesitate to retract her weak words;
and then,—Dyke Faucett, unwilling to bide the time in
that far-stretching future which seemed so illimitable to
her childish gaze, they must part, part forever; he going
back to his world of fashion and beauty (ah, what lovely
faces she had seen with him in the galleries of art! where
he only acknowledged her existence by a courteous raising
of the hat, which generally drew upon her the lorgnons of
his companions, and more or less audible critiques on her
rare type of beauty), and she,—well, the light would have
been put out of her life forever, and there would be nothing left for her in the dreary, vacant years to come but
her father, whose life was well-nigh spent, she remembered
with a pang,—and—

> "The coiled memory numb and cold,
> That slept in her heart, a dreaming snake,"

that would

> " Drowsily lift itself fold by fold,
>   And gnaw, and gnaw, hungrily, half awake."

And who was this guardian, whose narrow prejudices were to crowd back into the green bud all the full-expanded glories of this gorgeous tropic flower of love, which had absorbed even her vital forces in its luxuriant growth? Not even had he claim of blood, or kindred, upon this man whom he hoped to sacrifice upon some Mammon's altar, whilst his heart beat only for *her.* And what objections could this arrogant, selfish, wicked old aristocrat bring forward against her, when she should appear in his stiff, mildewy old castle as his adopted son's bride? She was certainly well born; was not her mother's name one of the proudest in the peerage? And her father? Well, she did not know much about *his* people; but who could look at him and doubt his blue blood? Surely Dyke's guardian could not fail to acknowledge that? (Himself, perhaps, merely a wealthy old cotton-spinner; she had read of the aristocracy of the spinning-jenny far overtopping, in intolerant haughtiness, the quiet good breeding fed from the *sang-azur* of centuries.) " Personally, he could not object to me," she dreamed on, with a slight flush of conscious vanity dyeing her cheek in the moonlight. " Surely I am as good-looking, and better mannered than those hoyden English girls, who *would* rattle on so, during service at St. Peter's; and I am well educated! Ah! but I am poor,—and this guardian would like to marry Dyke to a great, big-footed, red-cheeked daughter of some old money-bags, who cannot spell his own name, —and hasn't one to spell, if he could. Fancy Dyke, my refined, fastidious, purely artistic Dyke, chained to such a monster!" A dimpling smile broke out over the sweet face, and long before her father's voice, calling "Dorothea! Dorothea!" disturbed her reverie, she had fully decided the subject of the "Porta del Popolo;" for her love once given, she felt was—

> "Like water spilt upon the plain:
> Ne'er to be gathered up again."

And what did those four words, "for better, for worse," mean, if one were not willing, in joining hands, to confront fate, for weal or woe?

CHAPTER II.

"DOROTHEA, you are not looking well; you are pale, and your eyes are heavy, my patient little nurse! What have you done with the roses you brought home from our summer trip in Switzerland, my child, and the glad, bright eyes?"

Dora, sitting in a low American rocking-chair, with the frill she had been hemming lying in a white heap upon the carpet, rocked herself gently, with arms upraised and hands clasped at the back of her head, whilst her eyes looked dreamily beyond the figure of her father in his dressing-gown and easy-chair, with each wretched foot swathed in flannel and occupying separate foot-stools (little thrones of exquisite pain these were to him), answered, in a far-off voice, "Yes, dear; did you want something, papa?"

"Dora," began her father, leaning slightly forward, but immediately drawing back again with the wryest face, the least movement causing a twinge of agony. "Dora, you are vexing yourself about this young Faucett. Now, don't contradict me" (she had not moved or spoken); "and I have made up my mind to put an end to the affair, for good and all, as soon as I am able to put my feet to the ground!"

Down went Dora's arms; the rocking-chair was arrested at an angle. "Papa!" was all she could exclaim.

"Yes; I am quite determined. Since Mr. Faucett has no power of choice in his selection of a wife, and declines to take the trouble to obtain the consent of his guardian (who is he, by the way? I will write to him myself), I shall not sit quietly by and see him take the sunshine out of my life, and fade my little Dora into a colorless snow-drop."

"What will you do?" she gasped.

"I shall just give up this little home, where we have spent four happy years, and go back to see how the beeches have grown about our old English homestead. I feel that I will not be with you long, Dora, and I must look up some trusty friends to leave about you before I go; and" (in a low, tender voice here) "I should like to kneel at my darling Marian's grave once more, and maybe, if it please God, to be laid at rest beside her."

Dora's arms were about his silvered head now, and her tears falling fast upon it. She could not speak. A great fear mingled with a great joy and stifled her. Could this day pass without her innocent heart and face betraying her now fixed purpose of taking destiny by the horns on the morrow? If he pressed her with questions, she must tell him all, and throw herself on his mercy and love.

"Papa, you break my heart when you speak of leaving me. Ah, what sad thoughts have come to you since this cruel pain has tortured you! But you must not think such things; you will soon be well again, and able to go into the sunshine, and to see your friends, who have been so kind since your illness. Papa, Major Goodwin called again, yesterday, to inquire for you, and he asked if you would be able to have him come and read to you to-day or to-morrow.''

"Surface-friends!" sighed Mr. Fairfax; "very kind, no doubt, but friends of an hour, or a fortnight, at longest, who turn their backs and forget you utterly. Did you say he might come?''

"Yes, to-morrow." Dora's cheeks burned, but she was standing behind her father's chair, gently stroking back the fine white locks which waved thickly over his handsome brow.

"Ah, that is well, for I had intended, Dora, sending you and Annunziata out on an excursion to-morrow, to try to coax back some of the pink into those pale cheeks of yours. You must go out of the city and its noisy bustle of this foolish Carnival, into the country; to those fine Borghese grounds, or for a stretch on the Campagna. You will take a closed calèche,—the one we usually employ on the Via Condotti; the man is trustworthy,—and old Antonio will keep within call and serve my dinner; so you must make a long day of it, and come back able to sing once more for your poor old cripple.''

"Shall I sing now, papa? I feel the sweet flower-scented air of to-morrow blowing over me already! What shall I sing for you?''

He looked at her surprised; her whole appearance was suddenly changed,—she drooped no longer; her face wore a rosy flush; her great amber-tinted eyes seemed to brim with joy. She smiled with the old winning brightness, for she felt that in obeying his command on that dread morrow, she would be spared half the humiliation (possible prevarication) of her promised complicity in deceit; so sophistical is the devil's reasoning, she almost felt that her father sanctioned her action by this fortunate coincidence.

She sang unweariedly song after song, and her father lay back contentedly in his temporary freedom from pain, inwardly congratulating himself upon having discovered an infallible remedy for the drooping spirits of his singing-bird. She had been too long caged up in that sick-room, and needed air and light; *voila tout!*

CHAPTER III.

THE night was wet and wintry, rain mingled with sleet, and the icy breath of January, in Rome, struck through the toughest top-coats, into the marrow of the bones of those unfortunates who happened to be exposed to their disheartening influences.

"Pile more wood on the fire, Antonio, and then step around to the post-office; there may be letters from my daughter by the late post." And Mr. Fairfax settled himself down comfortably in his luxurious chair and drew towards him a London *Times*.

A marked change for the better has taken place in the old gentleman's surroundings since we last looked in upon him some ten months ago; a change which, in its beneficent effect, seemed to have added ten years to his declining life. Whether this was precisely the result anticipated, or desired, by Dyke Faucett when he drew the father of his bride away from the small, dingy apartment on the fourth floor of the Via del Babuino, and inducted him into the comfortable and more accessible suite on the Via Sistina, *au premier*, our imagination alone can divine.   But Mr. Fairfax was one of those happily-constituted mortals who accept life as it comes to them : make no loud moan in adversity, and revel in the smile of that fickle wench, Fortune, with a range of vision mercifully limited to the bridge of their own noses.

Mr. Fairfax, in his cozy rooms, with an excellent cook and the factotum of the Babuino quarters (habited in decent guise, and with a new strut of pomposity, appropriate to his altered circumstances, though somewhat at variance with his honest, child-like expression of face) to wait upon him exclusively, with Dyke's choice books to linger over, and his choice cigars and fine wines put entirely at his disposal, Dora's father was not mad, wicked, or ungrateful enough to repine, or to allow the disagreeable thought to intrude and mar the harmony of the ensemble (and his digestive organs), that Dyke had not yet taken that trip to England to break the news of his marriage to his guardian, who still remained in blissful ignorance of the fatal frustration of his plans, and who occasionally wrote kindly letters to Faucett, which were duly and affectionately answered.

When Dora had returned to her father's side on the evening of her wedding-day (for Dyke had carefully arranged the programme, and after the nine o'clock morning service in the English chapel, Dora and he were made man and wife, with all the solemnity of the beautiful marriage-service, by a bona fide parson, and in the presence of one other witness,—Annunziata, Dora's maid, a brown-faced, bright-eyed Italian girl, who worshiped her mistress next to the Madonna) ;—when she came and knelt at his side, with her happiness glowing all over her, and half whispered, " Papa, Mr. Faucett and I were married this morning !" without elaboration or circumlocution, he was simply stunned at a *coup d'état* which had scattered to the winds his plans and projects. And then, for one moment, he covered his eyes with his shapely hands, and swiftly there spread out before him a vision of his youth. The love he had borne for a woman from whom parents wished to separate him; her pleading face, his high-handed venture, and then afterwards, the long, happy married life together,—one continuous courtship until the very end.

"Dora," he said, looking steadily at her through two tear-dimmed eyes, "are you *sure* you love him?"

"Oh, papa!"

"And are you equally sure *he loves you?*"

"Why else should he have married me, dear papa? Ah, tell me you have forgiven me for doing as I have done without your consent, and I shall be perfectly happy!" She laid her cheek on his hands and kissed them.

"God bless you, my own ewe-lamb! May you be as happy as your mother *was*, thank God!" And they wept together, not unhappy tears.

The following day they were transplanted to their new quarters, which Dyke informed Mr. Fairfax he had leased for three years, and which he was to look upon as his home, as well as his daughter's and son-in-law's, when they would be in Rome. For the present, the happy pair intended running up to Paris to choose Dora's very simple trousseau and hear the new opera. ("It was really too much to ask of a man to leave his bride and rush over alone to England; that can be postponed, my dear sir, until after the honey-moon at *least*," remonstrated Dyke, in reply to Mr. Fairfax's innocent query, "When do you start for England?")

Money is the axis upon which the world turns, therefore it is not surprising that, having lavishly employed that powerful agent since the hour in which he left his betrothed dreaming in the moonlight, the very day after the ceremony all things were magically in their places, and the softest and easiest of conveyances carried Mr. Fairfax to his handsome rooms in the new apartment, in which a French cook, Dora's maid, Faucett's valet, and old Antonio metamorphosed, were already in their respective stalls. Mr. Fairfax could not conceal his delight ; and the fact of Dyke's having observed his preference for the forlorn-looking, hybrid maid- and man-servant of his four-years-old home, touched him deeply.

That same night Dyke Faucett and his bride occupied a coupé of a railway train en route to Civita Vecchia, while the faithful Giles entertained, in a second-class carriage and in broken Italian, Dora's dark-eyed little maid, Annunziata.

Dora felt that she had never seen Paris before, after some weeks of the enchanting diversion which that city afforded to a well-filled purse and a man not destitute of *savoir-faire*. It was one long fairy-tale to her, and her eloquent letters full of fêtes, tours of palaces and galleries, theatres and the opera, of Dyke's lavish generosity in his costly contributions to her trousseau and jewel-case, of his devotion to her in all ways, patted to sleep the last remaining scruple in the mind of her doting father, who, in return, wrote cheering letters of his restored health, and of his hope that before their return he would walk as well as ever.

He walked before their return !

After a couple of months of Paris, the advanced spring rendered Italy dangerous and Switzerland desirable. The old gentleman was advised to go to the lakes in the north of Italy, where his considerate son-in-law had already engaged rooms for him, paid in advance. ("As they are included in my suite, you understand ; for Dora and I mean to join you later," wrote Dyke, to soothe any ruffles

on the pride which never died out of the old man's blood.)
But he occupied the suite in lonely grandeur, and if he
missed his singing-bird, and the luxuries of life seemed at
times a poor exchange, he never pained her by such a
confession. He made friends everywhere, and led a sweet,
tranquil life, grateful to God for the comforts of which he
had never mourned the absence.

Only once during those long ten months had he seen
Dora, and then for a brief week's visit after his return to
Rome, in September. "It was only to give him a glimpse
of his darling," Dyke assured her father; "for they were
en route to Naples, and would return to Rome for the
Christmas festivities." And when Mr. Fairfax's material
organ of sight had fully satisfied itself that Dorothea's
eyes had gained in lustre, and the oval of her cheek was
unimpaired, that the willowy figure had rounded into fuller
curves, and her voice deepened in its richest notes, he was
more than content, thoroughly assured that her soul was
full-fed, and that the tendrils of her heart, clinging to a
firm support, were flowering all over in luxuriant profusion.

The subject of the still-postponed trip to England was
not mooted. When all the sky was serenely blue, with
not even a cloud the size of a man's hand to awaken
doubt or dread, why should *he* raise a mimic thunder, or
force discordant elements to agitate the moral barometer
which was set so fixedly at—"*fair*"?

And Dora had certainly not a corporeal wish ungrat-
ified; and although Dyke's bank account had not been
over-weighted by a paul, the money which had ever flowed
like sand through his careless fingers was now concentrated
upon one object, in place of many, the one only, long-
lasting passion of his life. For Dora still held him captive, though ten moons had risen and waned since that in
which he had left her in her slight, girlish beauty, glowing

in the conscious triumph of having woven the last link of the chain which bound him to her feet.

A closer association with her, so far from bringing to him the customary *désillusionnement*, only served to unfold to his view charms of manner and graces of character which had never before come under his observation. The *beau-sexe* had long been a study to this man, but it was always from the same potter's-clay they were formed, however delicate in form and coloring (and frailty). Those Sèvres bits had ornamented his table to perfection, but they never changed in form or tint through all the many costly courses in which they served, and after awhile they wearied the pampered eye, and gave place to another set of a newer pattern and a rarer shade, but bearing the same manufactory's mark under the exquisite enamel.

But here was a woman, guileless as a child, and yet possessed of that innate power of fascination which springs from infinite tact, unerring good taste, art-culture, and a sweet, sunny warmth and brightness of temper, united to a purity of thought and dignity of character which enforced his respect, and which, through almost an æsthetic admiration, he would not have desired sullied any more than he could have restrained his disgust should some Vandal mutilate the Venus of the Capitol or plunge a knife through the canvas of a Titian. And the secret of her power was this: she never bored him for one moment, and yet, strange to say, she loved him. For love, being blind, is ofttimes selfish, and in the insatiable hunger of a *loving* woman's heart, even her arms may weigh heavily, after a time, on the most ardent lover's shoulders.

Young bride, beware! the first, faintest sigh of satiety is the first tremulous sound of the death-knell of your power. Before the orange-blossoms crown your bright tresses, chain your beloved by heavy-forged links of gold or steel, an you will; but after the golden circlet clasps *your* finger, let your victim breathe freely in bonds flower-woven and lightly worn.

Instinct teaches some fine, artistic natures many things; vivid perception and a keen psychological eye see breakers ahead before the dull, half-closed optic of a coarser nature, or the distorted vision of a more sin-clouded soul, would see aught but the sun-glinted waves of the present enjoyment.

And Dora understood the art, more difficult than winning love, of keeping it, and never allowed, through her own weakness or craving, the ineffable charm of novelty, the exhaustless resources of her versatile mind, the ever-increasing charm of her rare beauty and her entrancing voice, to pall upon his taste, or his over-stimulated nerves, or his *blasé* epicureanism. Whether this near communion with her idol had robbed her of some illusions and lowered his pedestal to the level of humanity in general, she had not confessed to her own heart, for she loved Dyke still absorbingly, and, as long as that love lasted, she exercised over him the spell which won his absolute devotion. It was only long after, when her respect became undermined and the whole beautiful fabric of trust and belief in his honor tumbled piecemeal to the ground, that she, through weakened love, relaxed her vigilance and carefully-preserved fascinations, and he slipped gradually his neck from beneath the yoke which had only just begun to weigh even lightly upon him.

But we must go back to poor old Mr. Fairfax, whom we have left so long, wading through that stale *Times*, and who has now been repaid for his perseverance in sending every three hours to the post, by a few lines in Dyke's beautiful calligraphy, announcing the birth of a fine little girl, with the assurance of Dora's welfare at that writing, etc., etc.

Mr. Fairfax put down the letter with an audible sigh of relief. This, then, accounted for Dora's long silence and the neglect of Dyke's promise to bring her to Rome for Christmas; he had not suspected such a *dénouement*, and he was delighted with its plausibility in excusing their evident forgetfulness of himself.

"A little daughter! Dora with a baby! Oh, it was too ridiculous! She never had held an infant in her arms in her life; and born down there in Naples, with not an English-speaking Christian about her; Annunziata was faithful, but she was ignorant and inexperienced. Ah, how I long to see her,—my little Dora,—and—the baby! Ha! ha! ridiculous! too absurd!" And he rang the bell to confide the joyous intelligence to the devoted Antonio (who had known Dora as a slim girl of fifteen, and would have given his life for her at any moment), with the additional information that Mr. Faucett would bring his *family* ("Ha! ha!") to Rome before Easter, and then Antonio should dandle la Signora's baby!

CHAPTER IV.

The tender crocus had peeped forth, followed by the shrinking violet; the orange-trees had blossomed and scented the air all about Rome with heavy delicious fragrance. And now—all spring was spreading full bloom over everything; even the lazzaroni forgot the stereotyped expression of woe frozen into their countenances by the cold blasts of the winter through those dark, narrow streets, and chatted and laughed and sung in the revivifying sunshine.

Dorothea had rejoiced her father's eyes during the last six weeks, and had witnessed, without an apparent pang, the complete transfer of that pink, dimpled, golden-haired cherub Marian to the pedestal which she herself had occupied for so many years, before which her father had bowed in abject idolatry.

And Antonio! Never, save on canvas, had he seen anything so fair and blue-eyed, and with such tender rose-tints about it; it was comical to see these two old men gaze at and discuss gravely together the entrancing wiles and absurd grimaces of the wonderful baby. Dora too, while she laughed at them both, found secret store of blissful enjoyment in the little frail life unfolding day by day under her loving eyes.

Dyke was in England,—at last he had determined to avoid a possible fracas with his guardian by paying him a visit of a fortnight. The fortnight had lengthened into two months; they had left Ellingham and gone up to town; for it was the third week in May, and Dyke had not enjoyed the "season" for some years, and it had novelty enough now to attract him.

His letters to his wife were not frequent, but they were affectionate enough, veiling with plausible pretexts his desire to remain longer than he had at first intended.

Not one word, however, did they contain relative to the divulgement of his secret marriage, and Dora's heart sank like lead within her. She could not fail to remember how guarded Dyke had been during their bridal trip and their sojourn in Naples to prevent the fact of his marriage, by any possibility, being reported in English circles,—how, when in their rambles they stumbled upon parties of acquaintances, Dyke invariably passed hastily with a cold bow, or, hustling her into the carriage, bade the coachman drive home, whilst he turned and joined his compatriots with smiles and hand-shakings.

Through all these twelve months and more, he had never introduced a single person to his sweet young wife, with the exception of a few men who were unavoidably presented just before they sat down to dinner, and whom she never saw after the meal had ended and cards and decanters occupied the table; but the laughter and cigar-smoke mingled reached her in her little sitting-room beyond, where she sang to herself, or sketched, or read a little, wondering if they *never* meant to go and let Dyke come to her.

And then towards the small hours, when her *répertoire* had become exhausted, and she had watered her flowers and buried her face in their fragrant blossoms, feeling that in them she found some strange, sweet sympathy, she would betake herself to her bedroom with its windows looking out upon the beautiful bay. There Dyke, coming in softly, would sometimes find her enveloped in her flowing white *peignoir*, with her luxuriant hair unbraided and falling about her like a cloud, out of which the pure face and great eyes gleamed with almost supernatural beauty. A gentle reproach from Dyke for losing her beauty-sleep, a loving caress, and her loneliness was forgotten, her sadness dispelled. The next morning was sure to be sunshiny, and they would drive along the shore of that magical bay; or often, as the fancy seized them, would take their places in a barciolina, belonging to a fisherman, who was ready to throw aside his net at the prospect of *buona mano*, and lend all the energies in his brawny arms to the swift speeding of the tiny bark over the blue waves. And then Dyke, lying at her feet, would tell her the story of the Æneid, while she, breathing in the golden air of that exquisite climate which makes it a joy to live, with one white hand idly toying with the blue waters over which they glided, listened with unabated interest to the musical voice which had not lost one whit of its charm. Then they would draw in to shore, and would stroll into the cave of the Cumæan Sibyl where Æneas consulted the oracle, or into the Temple of Apollo, where Dædalus retreated after his flight from the island of Crete, and make a festive day of it,—a sort of improvised picnic, *tête-à-tête*, without one jarring element or moment of ennui to mar their entire enjoyment. Or else they would drive to the Castle of St. Elmo, winding through the heart of Naples, and spend hours of delight in the ole-ander-shaded arbor on the edge of a cliff, overlooking the myriad gems set in the sea stretching beneath them ; while Vesuvius towered high above groves of orange, lemon, and citron trees, myrtle-shaded walks, classic ruins, and lovely villas, half buried in acacia-blossoms, on the other hand.

And sometimes they would join the stream of gayly-dressed idlers on the promenade which leads to the Villa Reale, that charming chiaja, which is certainly one of the brightest and gayest in Europe. But this was very seldom, for it was a rare chance at that season that, cosmopolite as he was, Dyke should not meet among that gay throng one or more acquaintances, and this *contre-temps* he avoided religiously when Dora was with him.

And Dora was not sorry : she cared only for Dyke ; his society was her world, his voice a complete orchestra, filling every want to *her* ears ; his approval of her appearance the only flattery she craved, and in their solitary ramblings she found perfect joy.

During those early days of her married life the thought never intruded, like a snake in her paradise, that perhaps Dyke was just a little selfish now and then. She never questioned for one moment his right to dispose of her and of himself as he saw proper or agreeable *to himself*, and on those evenings when he dined out, and just "looked in" afterwards at the San Carlo, for an act or two, she was undisturbed by doubt or foreboding, thinking it all very natural, and rather pitying her husband, who looked so bored as he drew on his light gloves and kissed her good-night, begging her not to sit up for him; he would get away as soon as he decently could, however, etc.

And sometimes when he had taken her to the theatre and she, sitting slightly behind the curtain according to his suggestion ("For, my darling, yours is too lovely a face to be stared at by these brutes of Italians," he assured her), and she would see him in the boxes of the elegantly-dressed women and *distingué*-looking men, evidently English, chatting familiarly, and sometimes with an *empressement* too marked to be unobserved by one keenly interested and with an excellent lorgnette, detained (*pour causer un peu*) in the little saloon attached to each box, a thought would cross her mind that some of these fair dames should have done her the honor to call upon her, as they seemed such old friends of her husband. But she never put her thought into words, and—they never called.

And then came into her cup of joy another drop and caused it to overflow; she cared no longer for the San Carlo or the promenade; she troubled herself with no further questionings of the why or wherefore of the world about her; she never felt lonely or sad when Dyke did not return as early as he promised, for she carried in her heart a blessed hope, the sweetest of all a pure woman's entire life,—the budding promise of a first maternity.

She kept her secret jealously to herself, gloating over it as a miser over his gold, building dream-castles on its frail foundations, singing of it in gushing, caroling notes of very happiness; and Dyke saw her whole expression of face change from that of gleeful girlhood to the sweet serenity of dawning matronhood, intensifying the eloquent eyes in an extraordinary degree, and wondered at her ever-increasing charm.

But I fear when, with blushes and tears and stammerings, the great news was broken to him, his delight was not entirely unfeigned, and if his candid opinion could have been educed, it would have been something after this fashion, "A deuced bore! Hang it all! What's the use of it?" etc., and straightway forget all about it until the next mention. But Dora dreamed naught of this; if she was a little chilled by the calmness with which he received her communication, she consoled herself with the reflection that he was *only a man*, and could not be expected to soar heavenward on the wings of such bliss as hers; could not understand or appreciate it, in fact; but Annunziata could, and did, for *she* wept genuine tears of joy over her young mistress, and was so enthusiastic after her tears subsided, that Dora became quite impatient for the grand finale; and they talked and plotted and arranged the programme of everything, after the manner of women, quite unnecessarily prematurely, and then cried a little more, and ended up in a cheerful and patient frame of mind, both looking a little more consequential than usual, and stealing eloquent glances at each other full of a mute sympathy.

I think the happiest hours of Dora's whole life were those spent in sunny Naples, and yet the time came when she could not look back upon those days without a spasm of pity for her own helpless blindness, so treacherously betrayed.

And Naples was marked in her memory by the loss of her faithful Annunziata, to whom she had become much attached.

Two months after little Marian's birth the poor girl had been seized by fever, and in spite of the most careful attendance and the best medical advice she became delirious, and did not recover consciousness until the end. Dora was deeply grieved, and, as soon as a suitable nurse could be provided in her place for the infant, they left Naples and the flowery grave which had saddened every thing for her, and returned to Rome, Dyke leaving almost immediately for England.

CHAPTER V.

"YES, Dyke, I will go to this ball if you desire it so much." And Dora, standing at the window gazing out upon a street with its shifting panorama with unseeing eyes, sighed a little tremulous sigh, which expressed the struggle it had cost her to accede to Dyke's request, and attend a great ball which was to be given for charitable purposes, patronized by the *élite* of the English residents in Rome.

"You need not sigh so profoundly over the prospect, Dora, my dear," yawned her husband from the depths of his easy-chair. "Most handsome women would be enchanted at this opportunity of exhibiting themselves; there are any number of foreign potentates to add lustre to the——"

"Oh, Dyke," interrupted Dora, reproachfully, "you are only discouraging me. I have never attended a ball, a *real* ball, you know, in my life, and," she concluded, dreamily, "I scarcely think I am fitted to shine in festivities on such a grand scale ; they do not attract me."

"Ah, my dear, you do not know yet; taste the cup before you abjure it. You are dwindling and pining for a little excitement, and as for me, well, I am sick of Rome and—everything." He yawned again, shook himself, and, without a word of adieu, started off for his club.

Dora looked after him with tears in her sad eyes; but there was an unwonted flush upon her cheek as she turned hastily and pulled the bell. Giles appeared immediately.

"Tell Clémentine to prepare Miss Marian to drive with me, and order the coupé at once, if you please," she commanded.

The color had not faded out of her sweet face, when, half an hour later, she stood discussing with feverish animation the rival merits of satin, silk and velvet with Madame Massoni, the most fashionable and expensive *couturière* in Rome. Madame was in raptures; with such a face and such a form she would accomplish a *chef-d'œuvre* which would outdo her rival, Madame Borsini Duprès, and quench her for evermore. And when Dora, becoming weary, and dazzled and confused by the masses of color exposed for her selection and the volubility of the artiste (who was taking in every detail of her visitor's beauty, dress, and appurtenances; for Marian, a three-year-old mass of embroidery and lace, cushioned on Ernestine's Parisian-clothed lap in the neatly-appointed coupé at the door, had not escaped her observation), had at last exclaimed, in despair, "I cannot decide; I leave everything to you. Spare no expense; but make me beautiful; do you understand?—beautiful!"

"Ah, madame, nature has spared me that trouble; but trust me, we shall find a fit setting for such a face as yours even; I understand perfectly. And it is for the ball at the Opera on Wednesday evening? Give yourself no uneasiness, Madame shall be satisfied."

B*

And Dora departed, while a small devil invaded the tranquil depths of her nature, stirring up rebellion at last, and whispering, " We shall see whether love is dead in his heart; if there is *one* spot left which can feel pain, it shall be pricked into suffering as surely as I live."

Thus it will be seen that the years have borne fruit of thistles, which was far from the toothsome fig; and in the inevitable estrangement which had grown up between Dora and her husband there was bitterness as well as disappointment.

After Dyke's return from England, more than two years ago, he had volunteered no explanation of his extended visit, no mention of his determined continued reserve towards his guardian on the subject of his marriage. Dora had pondered long and wonderingly on this strange, to her unaccountable, deception, and at last had timidly broached the subject to him.

She was answered by a cool nonchalant query, " Are you not content, Dora ?   Is there anything more I can do to contribute to your happiness or your father's comfort? If so, only mention it to me, and consider it accomplished ; but do not fret yourself or annoy me by any heroics on the subject of my guardian's blessing upon our nuptials. I fancy we can get on without it, my dear."   And then he kissed her and lounged away, and she knew a seal had been placed upon her lips which it would not be wise to break.

But from that hour her faith in her husband's nobility of character wavered ; her respect for his truth and honor was shaken ; she never loved him quite so idolatrously afterwards.   But still she loved him, and still her fascination was paramount with him, although not all-absorbing as at first.

There were days passed in pleasures of which she knew nothing, save the one grim fact that they took Dyke away from her side; there were dinners and balls and card-parties, to all of which he went reluctantly, but inevitably; and there were visits to England each spring and autumn, in which she did not participate, and there were occasional trips to Paris, and in the summer to the Lakes, in which she did. And now the smooth run of pleasure was beginning again to pall upon Dyke Faucett. The novelty of a wife had worn off at the edges; the flirtations interspersed through these last three years were becoming tame, and he felt that he must stretch out in a new series of experiences or he would perish.

> " With pleasure drugged, he almost longed for woe ;
> And e'en for change of scene would seek the shades below !"

But in vain he strove to shake off the last remaining influence which Dora possessed over him. Other women, when he had grown weary of them, he had been able to dispose of very quietly; some with a few low-spoken decisive words,—many more by heavy drafts upon his bankers; but Dora's great luminous eyes turned full upon him always checked those quiet words before they were formed into syllables. And this was the last vestige of her power over him; he dared not wound her! And this fact irritated him beyond endurance. Caligula, when he clutched his wife Milonia Cæsonia by the throat, shriek-ing at her, " Tell me, thou fascinating devil, what poisons thou hast put in my wine, thus to bind me against my will? Make confession! or the torture shall wring it from thee!" no doubt expressed from the black depths of his cruel heart the same passion which Dyke Faucett, under the controlling influences of the social amenities, whispered only to his own soul.

But who has forgotten that when this Roman monster was assassinated, this wretched wife implored the conspirators to slay her also, "which, in pity for her wild grief, they did"?   And can we wonder that Dora still clings to the first love of her life, though trust, respect, hope, and faith are dying all about his image?

In the sort of moral syncope which had become Dyke's normal condition, he dreamed not of the warring of love and pride and despair in the heart of the woman he had sworn to cherish until his life's end.   And after he had grown used to her beauty, grown weary of her repugnance to certain choice entertainments, in which his male friends participated and from which his lady friends were rigorously excluded, he resented a purity of heart and tone which was a constant mute reproach to him ; and finding his efforts to draw her down to his level unavailing, he grew to feel her a shackle upon his freedom, morally; and the feeling chafed him more and more as he saw her eyes grow sadder and the color in her cheek vary with every emotion through the delicate transparency of her skin. He sought a new device to arouse her: she should know what it was to be admired, courted, flattered ; perhaps she would not prove insensible to the incense which intoxicated all women, and her old charm would return with a knowledge of her power.

He would try it; anything is better than this stagnation ; and he should like to compare her, in a ball-room, to others,—to the beautiful Marquise de Courboisie (the "Pauline" of his Spanish tour, who, with her aged spouse, was spending the winter in the Eternal City, and finding therein unlimited delight in the devotion of her *preux chevalier* of other days).   But to his amazement Dora had declined, gently but firmly, "exhibiting herself," as he had expressed it ; and it was only after the very worst little quarter of an hour of their marital experience that she had yielded reluctant consent.

And then, all at once, an inspiration possessed her: she was to be exhibited, compared with others, perhaps exposed to ridicule or censorious comments on her lack of style, her provincial manner, her timid shyness. Ah, well, she would soon settle all that. Dyke should not be ashamed of her; and perhaps—well, perhaps she would *just stir up a little* the embers of that dead love in his heart.

Hence her order to Madame Massoni, and her inspection of her jewel-case later, and the wild glee in her voice as she burst out into song, for the first time for months, that evening, and delighted her father's heart.

CHAPTER VI.

"Can this be Cytherea, born of the sea-foam,—or Aphrodite herself, just risen from the waves?" asked the young Earl Elphinstone of an officer in Her Majesty's Rifles, as Dora swept into the ball-room on her husband's arm, looking a very sea-nymph in her pale-green robes, lace-shrouded, and her crown of sea-shells composed of many-tinted pearls, from the dark-gray to the delicate rose, of priceless value. This crown was her sole ornament; but the snowy shoulders and small, rounded arms needed none to enhance their loveliness. Her bronze hair rippled above the pure child-like brow, her glorious eyes were brilliant with a new triumph, her cheeks were delicately flushed, and she entered the ball-room amid an audible buzz of admiration, with the proud composure of a queen. Dyke felt gratified in spite of himself, and a little nervous; he must get himself away from her as quickly as possible : people would be pressing for introductions.   Even as the thought crossed him, the Prince · di R—— approached, and entreated the honor of a presentation.   As soon as Dyke had performed the ceremony he vanished, leaving his wife chatting with the most dissolute man in Roman society.   After a few inane platitudes, he branched off into nauseating compliments, fixing poor Dora with his piercing black eyes, and noting her embarrassment with delight.   As he became more and more obnoxious, Dora looked out over the sea of human beings, like a cornered fawn, fascinated under the glaring eyeballs of a tiger ready to spring, hoping to see Dyke's tall form among them; but Dyke had gone into the refreshment-rooms with *la belle* Marquise, and she was not thinking of relinquishing her prey for many an hour to come. Dora, in despair, attempted to freeze the little reprobate with a sudden accession of hauteur; she looked over his head in icy indifference,—and he·drew nearer to her. She replied in curtest style to his florid flattery,—his breath almost fanned her cheek.   She drew herself away and desired him to do her the favor of looking for Mr. Faucett.   He declined courteously but positively,—" it was impossible, in such a crowd, to move, far less possible to find any one; would not Madame waltz? she must waltz divinely."   Dora was on the point of bursting into an hysterical fit of tears when—oh, thank Heaven ! an English voice—a voice she knew—spoke just behind her. " Miss Fairfax !" called out glad tones ; and, as she turned, her hand was seized tightly and the handsome, frank face of Reginald Trelawney—one of the few friends of her childhood—smiled into hers a joyful recognition.

" Ah," cried Dora, " I am so glad to see you again !" (She was.)   And as he slipped the hand he still held through his arm and moved away with her, I fear her ignorance of good manners deprived the indignant prince of even the slightest bow of farewell. "And how you have changed; and yet I should have known you anywhere, in spite of that luxuriant moustache and those fierce whiskers!" And she laughed merrily—the Dora of old—once again.

"Surely you are not beginning already to chaff me, are you?" asked he, with a lingering look in her beautiful face. "You had no mercy upon me in those other days; but may I not hope that I have outgrown now the age at which a man is fair game to a woman?"

"Who outgrows that age? Methuselah himself would find a Delilah to turn his old head were he here to-night. Look at that couple in the cotillion to the right!"

He laughed. It was a picture of Spring and Winter,—a young, pretty girl bestowing all manner of blandishments upon a white-haired, decrepit old man, whose breast was covered outwardly with decorations ·and inwardly with the mildew of age.

"This is my first ball, Mr. Trelawney, and, do you know, I quite long to dance. This delicious music almost bears me off on its wings; but I have not been asked to dance, and I do not know any one," she laughed.

"Excepting the Prince di R——, who was devouring you when I rescued you, and myself. Will you dance with me?" Almost the same pleading voice and bashful manner with which he had implored her years before, when he was a mere boy, to accept his life's devotion.

Dora hesitated. She had never danced, save in those *petit réunions* of artists and their families, before she had met Dyke Faucett, and—well, that valse was really too much for her remaining scruples. She laid her hand on Reginald's shoulder, and in a moment they were whirling away in the delirious delight of perfect music, perfect time,

and perfect step.   Trelawney suited her, in height, in
movement, and in accuracy of ear, and that first real
waltz marked an epoch in Dora's life.   What Reginald's
feelings were, one can imagine ; he had never been so perfectly, unutterably happy in his life.   The desire of his
soul through those long, dreary years in India had at last
been gratified : he had seen Dora once more, and she had
been "so glad to see him !"   What more could earth
grant of bliss ?

After they had danced, rested, danced again, until they
could no more, they sauntered out into the cool lobbies,
where camellia-trees and myrtle formed shady nooks, in
which ices were served to refresh the dancers.

"How have you come to Rome,—are you on leave of
absence ?" asked Dora, sipping daintily her ice, and looking more exquisite than ever under the green drooping
branches of an acacia in full flower.   Reginald could
scarcely tear his eyes from her face.

"Yes; I am on leave.   The fact is I grew tired of Indian service, and longed to get back to England for a
while; so I exchanged into the Rifle Brigade, and here
I am !"

"But this is not England," quoth Dora, maliciously.
"Ah, you wanted to idle about, travel, and see the
world,—to '*do*' Paris, and Rome, and Vesuvius !"

"No ; I came straight from Southampton to Marseilles,
thence here.   Rome is the whole world to me."   His
earnest eyes gazed straight into hers ; she colored slightly.

"Ah, do not say that if you have not seen Switzerland
or Naples, or——"

"And what can Switzerland or Naples, or any other
spot under heaven, bring me of happiness more than I
find in Rome to-night?" he interrupted, with the old impetuosity.   But Dora *would* not see.

"You remind me," she laughed, "in your contempt for the beauties of Nature, of Lord Byron's disgust at passing, on his way to the Castle of Chillon, a traveling-carriage in which lay a lady asleep. 'Fast asleep in the most anti-narcotic spot in the world—excellent!' he exclaimed, *satirically*, Mr. Trelawney. Now can you tell me that Mont Blanc or the Jungfrau could not arouse your enthusiasm?"

"I never tried them," he replied, smiling; "and indeed I do not mean to leave Rome,—at least during your stay, Miss Fairfax."

And then Dora felt constrained to deal her blow. "I reside in Rome, Mr. Trelawney: it is my home; and, I am not Miss Fairfax now." She did not look at him, but she *felt* the white, shocked pain in his face.

"*Not* Miss Fairfax?" he stammered. "Who, then? Oh, surely——"

"My name is Mrs. Faucett," interposed Dora, with gentle dignity.

He did not speak again. This was bitter,—hard and bitter, and utterly unbearable. Never had man more thoroughly, more egregiously, deceived himself; never had man been stunned by so sudden and sharp a blow! For weeks he had haunted every street, every church, every gallery in Rome; run over every visitors' book at each hotel, spent hours watching every face that passed on the favorite promenades; worn out the rims of his lorgnette at every theatre and opera, looking for this girl, who at last burst upon his vision doubly beautiful; and in her shy, sweet, graceful manner (in which nothing of the matron could be detected), had filled his mind with hope and his heart with overpowering happiness.

Reader, do you not know women, of mature years even, who have borne many children perhaps, in happy wed-

lock, who still glide through the world, mutely denying
the marriage estate by a certain girlishness of figure, shyness of mien, wistfulness of expression in the eyes, which
are timid and modest as the eyes of Una herself; just as
you have seen in little girls of ten, sometimes, the square,
set figures, the steady eye and resolute lip of the embryo
Cornelia; and after the mystic ring is slipped over the
plump third finger, it seems as if it had grown there forever; and the rest of her spreads out all over everything
in a motherly embonpoint, which reminds one of nothing
so much as an overgrown cabbage or cauliflower?

Alas! there was nothing of the vegetable about Dora;
the wild rose blooms on her cheek, and her slender figure
suggests the lily; and the violet itself is not more shrinking from the careless gaze than she, or more suggestive
of ungathered sweetnesses.

> " Its loveliness increases; it will never
> Pass into nothingness."

Dyke Faucett's voice broke in opportunely, and put an
end to a silence which was becoming embarrassing to
Dora; and Trelawney was obliged to shake himself together, and shake hands with this man (whom he longed
to take by the throat, then and there), and after a few
more words, to see him walk off with Dora on his arm to
the cloak-room; not, however, before Dyke had handed
Trelawney his card with his address upon it, and begged
him to look in upon them often.

Dora did not echo this invitation by word, or look, or
wish.   She bent her head gravely and turned away, leaning with *empressement* on her husband's arm.

" Were you much bored?" inquired Dyke, during their
homeward drive, "and did that cad di R—— make himself disagreeable?"

"I was not bored, and that cad di R—— *did* make himself disagreeable," replied his wife, concisely, and a little resentfully. If the man was known to be a puppy, why did her husband present him to her and leave her at his mercy? Dora flashed out (inwardly) at this, and at his continued neglect throughout the evening.

"I caught a glimpse of you occasionally, waltzing; do you like it?"

"Yes," slightly mollified (he had watched her, then). "I do like it with a partner like Mr. Trelawney; he dances exquisitely, and oh, the music was divine!" And she hummed a bar or two of the last valse, smiling to herself.

"I thought you did, *with Mr. Trelawney*. He seemed to like it pretty well too."

"Ah, yes, he did," Dora answered, rather sadly. "Dyke, I wish you had not asked that boy to call." Her voice was tremulous and hesitating now.

"Boy! you are ridiculous, Dora. Trelawney is no longer a sentimental boy, but a man who has outlived all that absurd nonsense. Why, you don't fancy that he is spoony about you now, Dora? Really, I thought you knew men better than all that."

"I do not know much about men, you know, Dyke. My father and yourself are almost the only ones I know intimately and perhaps you are right, *I should have known love could never survive so many years.*" There was an indescribable pathos in her voice, and Dyke—changed the subject.

"Have you retracted your opinion on the subject of balls? Are they not all that I painted them?" he asked.

"I do not know. I shall never go to another one," Dora answered, wearily, and then closed her eyes until the carriage stopped and Dyke handed her out, and then, re-entering it, drove to the club for a half-hour or so.

Dora locked her door after her maid left her, and, sinking into a great easy-chair drawn up before the open wood-fire, pondered on many things. And out of the chaos of disturbed thought stood forth in startling distinctness, Dyke Faucett's selfishness and Reginald Trelawney's un-abated devotion; two figures who were destined to war with each other in her tender heart for longer than that night.

Before she slept, she prayed for strength to bear the pain which each day now brought to her, in the conviction that her husband had wearied of her, or been lured from her by distractions outside his home. And then she slept and dreamed that she was back in the Via Babuino again, copying pictures and singing in the church-choirs for a support, with a heart as light as her purse, and the bright smile of her girlhood rested once more on her lips. The dream-angel is the most merciful and the dearest of all the white-winged choir.

———

CHAPTER VII.

" But you could make so much of your life if you chose. Why not give up the army,—it is only ' playing soldier' in these peaceful days,—and take up a new career? Surely there are many open to you where you might win a name, and never-failing incentive to draw forth your powers."

They were sauntering along one of the terraces sur-rounding Monte Pincio, Dora with Reginald Trelawney —her constant companion now,—followed by Clémentine and little Marian with grandpapa in an open carriage.

All over the beautiful Pincian Hill swarmed equipages, from the cardinal's coach to the small, hired voiture de place ; equestrians on thoroughbred steeds, nurses with their laughing charges, men and women pedestrians in holiday garb, thronging the garden on the summit, among its glittering fountains, its gleaming statues, and charming walks flower-bordered.

Ah, what a view of the "City of the Soul" stretched out from beneath that point !   Queenly still in her aged desolation !   Rome !

> " She who was named Eternal, and arrayed
> Her warriors but to conquer ; she who veiled
> Earth with her haughty shadow, and displayed,
> Until the o'ercanopied horizon failed,
> Her rushing wings,—oh, she who was almighty hailed !"

and who now stands unequaled in majesty, crowned with her immortal monuments of art, throned on her seven hills !

Looking out over the vast sweep beneath them, with the great dome of St. Peter's, and the Vatican, standing in bold relief against the background of the Campagna ;—with the Eden-like Borghese grounds stretching their masses of foliage and flower-decked allées under their eyes ; with the Antonine column towering in the distance, and that grim obelisk of the Nile,—and the great round roof of the Pantheon, pride of Rome !—

> " Shrine of all saints and temple of all gods,
> From Jove—to Jesus,"

standing erect in majestic grandeur, as when some two thousand years ago the last touch was put to its simple, massive state under direction of Agrippa, before Christ was born.

But Dora had raised her eyes from the great city with its everlasting monuments, and was gazing beyond, where fair Soracte stood out clearly against the blue enamel of the sky, whilst she strove to stir up, in the young heart beside her, the smouldering ambition which exists in every nature worthy of a name. But in that heart lay a slow poison which was spreading through every vein and numbing every aspiration, all energy, all hope. So he answered, a little contemptuously, "A name! What is it after all? A whole life devoted to the winning of it, and then—a puff in the newspapers,—an epitaph, and—oblivion! The *greatest* men in these days are the *successful ones*, and you know a certain member of Parliament once said, 'I hear a great deal said here about *posterity;* but let me ask frankly, what has posterity *ever done for us?*' I think he was about right," Reginald concluded, moodily, while Dora could not restrain a smile.

"Mr. Faucett tells me you have had your leave extended; is this so?"

"It is; don't be vexed. I know I promised you to get away to some forlorn spot in the Alps where I could devour my own heart in a solitary unselfishness, but I could not do it, and, unless you send me away, I shall stay just here until——"

"Until you have utterly, irretrievably lost my respect and your own; until all that is fine and noble in your nature grovels to the earth under the influence of a mad infatuation, a madness which must end, Mr. Trelawney, sooner or later, and which, with my consent, shall not last another day in my presence." Dora spoke in a low tone of concentrated feeling; pity, contempt, and the all-forgiving sympathy of her woman's heart contending in one wild tumult.

During the last three months Trelawney had been ever at her side; morning, noon, and evening he was sure to be at hand, to chat with her, to drive with her father and herself, to escort her to the theatre, where Dyke looked in upon her and begged Reginald to see her safely home (safely!). In her morning strolls with her sketch-book and little Marian, in her evening rambles, Reginald was always at her service, with his gentle deference to her faintest expressed wish, with his sunny temper and his keen enjoyment of everything, boyish still in its pure zest. And Dora—a little recklessly perhaps,—a good deal thoughtlessly—allowed it all. Could she resist it? Her days were empty—he filled them delightfully; with inventive ingenuity, planned excursions; arranged picnics in the environs of the city, was indefatigable as a guide-book in the galleries, and palaces, and churches; supplied her with flowers enough to turn her salon into Paradise, with music of the newest selections, with books, and all that made up her dearest enjoyments now. Her days were empty and he filled them, her heart was desolate and he cheered it, her mind was going to sleep and he awakened and stimulated it anew.

For there are natures so delicately strung that

> "Should their days
> Melt to calm twilight, they feel overcast
> With sorrow and supineness, and so die,
> Even as a flame, unfed, which runs to waste
> With its own flickering——"

And Dora, with all her sweetness and power of self-renunciation, was *not perfect;* and in the slow, torturing process which robbed her of the last blessed hope of re-animating the dead, callous heart of her husband,—in the last departing flicker of a blindness to his true nature which had so enveloped her mental gaze from the very first,—she had been *more* than woman, if the sweet balm of Reginald's pure worship had failed to comfort her. Alas, she could not go back to the happy days when her father held an unfailing fount of sympathy for every sor-

row of her life ! She could no more satisfy her questioning soul, or calm her aching heart on that loving breast,
than she could go back and be once more the merry,
joyful, singing-bird of old. What wonder, then, that she

> " Grasps at the fruitage forbidden,
> The golden pomegranates of Eden,
> To quiet its fever and pain?"—

recking little, in a new selfishness, that *peace* for her may
mean utter wreck and ruin to the man who loved her "too
well." For she never felt for him more than tender pity,
an earnest affection and admiration, won by his many admirable traits of character; never more than this, though
he poured the whole wealth of his heart and mind and
soul at her feet. If she had felt deeper interest in him
than this,—if his devotion had won her love in return,—
the words spoken then on the Pincian Hill would have
been uttered long before, and to more purpose, let us
hope. For weeks rolled on, and the warm June days
drove them out of Rome to the hills, and still Reginald
lingered in their wake.

For Dyke Faucett insisted that they should not part
company now, just when he could be more with them
and enjoy Trelawney's society, too. It was all nonsense ;
he had six months' leave, why not spend it with their
party? they would not bore him more than others, etc.
And Reginald being in love, and weaker than the reed
swayed by the wind, yielded, and remained.

And his love grew and gathered strength in their moun-
tain rambles and through long days of summer idling (in
which Dyke rarely joined), through long twilights, throbbing with the music of their mixed voices (for Trelawney
had learned to sing, whilst in Rome, of Dora's old maes-
tro). He was happy in a sort of ecstatic bliss which was

half pain; and she, looking forward with unceasing dread, feeling to her heart's core her helplessness, and a frantic sorrow in looking on that wasted life, wondering at Dyke's blindness or—his cruelty (which was it?)—

> " Stretched abroad her trembling arms
>   Upon the precincts of this nest of pain.
>   The Supreme God
>   At war with all the frailty of grief,
>   Of rage, of fear, anxiety, revenge,
>   Remorse, spleen, hope; but, most of all, *despair !*"

CHAPTER VIII.

ALBANO, that favorite resort of the Roman nobility during the " villeggiatura " season from June to October,—the Hampstead or Highgate of Rome,—celebrated for its beauty of scenery and purity of air, was the spot chosen by Dyke Faucett as a temporary sojourn when the heat became oppressive in the city.

Dora was pleased, in a calm, undemonstrative way, very different to the enthusiastic delight which she would have expressed two or three years ago,—she lived outwardly then as well as inwardly; now her inner life was all-absorbing, and all outer demonstration checked and subdued.

She took pleasure in rambling over the ruins of the ancient Roman villas and of the great Amphitheatre, erected by Domitian, which had been, in those glorious days of barbarous magnificence, the scene of the most revolting cruelties under order of the last of the twelve Cæsars.

Dora was becoming very fond of perching herself upon a remnant of ruined wall, moss-covered, and losing herself for hours in idle dreaming, while her eyes wandered over the broad plain of the Campagna or rested on the blue, dancing waves of the Mediterranean, stretching out more than twelve hundred feet beneath her.

Or, with her father and little Marian,—always accompanied, too, by Reginald Trelawney,—she would saunter along the Via Appia, under the blooming ilex-trees, to beautiful Lariccia; or, mounting donkeys, they would ride slowly through exquisite scenery to the lonely Lake of Albano, lying in placid beauty in the crater of an extinguished volcano.

Dyke rarely joined these excursions. Where or how he spent his days and nights, Dora was supremely ignorant.

It was his custom to breakfast late, and then, mounting his horse, to ride off, with a careless " ta-ta" to Dora and perhaps a pat on the golden curls of his child. He seldom returned to dine, and often not before midnight. Little conversation passed between him and his wife,—never a word of wrangling; she was too proud to upbraid, he too diplomatic to attempt to offer excuses or explanations. Mr. Fairfax looked on—and saw *nothing*. Dora was well, and seemed content. She had her child and every comfort of life. It seemed to be the fashion for married people to hold no more than ceremonious intercourse together, and there was no jarring. He and his Marian had not lived together after this fashion; but then, he had married nearly fifty years ago, and half a century brought changes in everything, manners and customs included.

Yes, Mr. Fairfax, in everything save flesh and blood; a woman's heart can ache as keenly now as in the days when the "Lily maid of Astolat" crooned forth her wailing ditty,—

> " Sweet is true love, though given in vain, in vain ;
> And sweet is Death, who puts an end to pain. . . .
> Sweet love that seems not made to fade away "—

before she paid that ghostly visit with face as white as the lily in her hand, and the letter holding her heart's last moan lying on the marble breast.

But Dora, less happy than Elaine, could not die. As she saw slowly unfolding before her a long, loveless, lonely future, she braced herself to meet it at least with composure and tranquil patience. "I cannot struggle to recover what never existed ; he *never loved me* from the very first,—for love never dies. I have just wrecked my life, and must bear it without complaint. Ah, me !—

> " ' None know the choice I made, and broke my heart
> Breaking mine idol ! . . .
> I broke it at a blow, I laid it cold,
> Crushed, in my deep heart where it used to live.
> My heart dies inch by inch ; the time grows old,
> Grows old, in which I grieve.' "

But she smiled and even sang sometimes,—though her song was sadder than weeping,—and believed that she completely deceived her father and all about her. But she never laughed ; that sweet, rippling, girlish laughter, which had been one of her rare charms, never welled up from her heart again.

And there was one pair of eyes which watched her with ever deepening tenderness, that marked the slight but eloquent change in her delicate features and coloring. The eyes were softened by a violet circle about them, the pure oval of her face was less perfect in outline, the skin looked waxen in its whiteness, while the full red lips curved sadly downward faintly rose-tinted.

Reginald Trelawney did not lose one sigh, one sad look, one pang of disappointment which wrote itself upon that expressive face, and in garnering these up, he built thereon heart-ache for himself. . . . And she had still another friend, if an humble one. The piercing gray eyes of faithful Giles fastened themselves upon her with a keen, respectful interest, awakened by her never-varying gentleness, and his knowledge of his master's character. Slowly, surely, was that aroused pity and interest undermining his dog-like fidelity to Faucett, a fidelity which for ten years had never wavered, and which Dyke prized highly; but now he was to stand by and see a cruel wrong done, a crime beside which paled all the numerous unscrupulous deeds of evil which he had known his master to perpetrate without one pang of self-reproach? For Dyke's sake, and because in his slavish ignorance he believed it to be his duty, he had transformed himself into an active machine, a man of indestructible sang-froid, of good judgment, and infinite tact. But under the crust of custom, stirred still a heart, and, after some late confidences wrung from Célestine, the marquise's maid and confidante (when will women learn to burn their letters and hold their tongues?), he had resolutely determined that he would not stand by and witness this crowning wickedness of a bad career.

For Célestine had divulged (being herself completely under the thrall of a serious passion for the masterful Giles), that her mistress, weary of waiting for the old man's death (the marquis had promised by outward appearances to die long ere this, and failed to abide by his promise), had determined to leave him, with *"ce monsieur Anglais, aussitôt que possible."* (They were then stopping in the neighborhood, on a visit to Prince Doria at his villa near the Roman Gate, within an easy ride of Albano).

When the visit had drawn itself out to proper limits according to the code of etiquette, the fair Pauline decided to breathe the air of Switzerland, and, after a week in Paris, she would hope to see her *cher ami* Dyke in Geneva.

Dora was requested to prepare to accompany her husband, while Mr. Fairfax and little Marian would remain at Albano until their return. This was a bitter trial to Dora, for her child had never yet been separated from her. She remonstrated, but "We have taken the apartment in this stupid place for the summer; somebody must occupy it; Marian is doing very well here; traveling is misery to children; come, don't fret about such a trifle," etc., she was mute; but another stone rolled to the door of the sepulchre where her dead love lay, and the tears she shed through the long, silent nights for her baby's arms about her, would have made any mother weep from sympathy.

CHAPTER IX.

"You must pardon my obtuseness, but really, Dora, I *cannot* see how Mr. Trelawney's stay or departure can affect your happiness. If he bores you, avoid him; he is too well-bred to persecute you; if not, and he amuses you, why should he not remain?" And Dyke stretched himself into an easier position on the lounge in Dora's dressing-room, at the Hotel Métropôle, Geneva. They had just arrived, and Trelawney, still in their suite, had been again earnestly solicited by Faucett to take up his quarters in their hotel, and postpone his trip to Chamounix, and ascent of Mont Blanc, until they all could go together (Dyke, having promised to meet some friends in Geneva, awaited their arrival). Dora had at last determined to speak very plainly to her husband, and show him clearly to what this fatuous indifference on his part was inevitably pointing. It was a bitter, painful task for her, as it must ever be to a sensitive, high-strung woman, to tear open the eyes of a man willfully blinding himself to his own dishonor. For there was no mistaking Reginald's utter self-abandonment to the madness which was fast depriving him of even a show of regard for appearances. He was very nearly reckless of consequences, and did not care to conceal it always. As his contempt for Faucett increased, seeing farther into the depths of that cruel, selfish heart, than Dora, his pity and love gained in strength, until they mastered every other feeling of his nature. He felt almost as if his duty was involved in remaining with them constantly, that he might be at hand to protect and shield this fragile, unsuspicious, broken-spirited woman from deadly danger, oblivious of the fact that danger the direst lay in the very protecting influence he offered as a shield. And now Dora had determined, at all costs, to end this feverish, daily increasing infatuation of poor Trelawney's, and through her husband's interposition, for she had failed hitherto in convincing him, unsupported by Dyke's concurrence.

"It is not that he bores me," she said, after a moment; "indeed, it is because *I am beginning to feel that I can scarcely do without him; I shall miss him so sorely*, that I think it better that he should break off from us——" (she waited expectantly; Dyke yawned.) "Do you realize," she continued, "that he has been incessantly at my side during the last six months? Do you realize that he is a man without ties, young, capable of feeling, capable of suffering?"

"And that he is in love with you?" put in Dyke.

Her color deepened. "Yes, if you will have me say it; that he has loved me since the first day I met him" ("Bah!" ejaculated her husband, incredulously),—"who has loved me," she went on, steadily,—"and will love me as long as he lives."

"Well, that does not hurt you, does it? I am not afraid of him or any man; why should you excite yourself about such rubbish as this?"

She left her seat in the window, looking out over the peaceful lake, and came quite close to him. "Because it is not rubbish; it is *sin*, and *pain*, and *grief*,—and perhaps remorse or despair;—who knows? Because *you* have wearied of me, and seen fit to starve to death every loving fibre of my heart, do you think that it is *quite* impossible for any *other* hand to touch my heart-strings? Ah, Dyke, take care! I may seem numb and dead to you; but there is life beneath the surface yet; if you have no pity for him, have at least some care for me!"

She paced the room with uneven steps after that last wail escaped her, and then stood again at the window, awaiting, yet dreading, his reply. None came; was his indignation, his wounded pride, at length aroused? Was he gathering strength to launch calmly at her the bitter sentence which would prove that love was not entirely extinct even yet, and that her cry of despair had touched one vital spot? Oh, would to Heaven this were so! Anger, contempt, curses, blows even, would have wounded less cruelly than the sound which now caused her to raise her drooping head to listen, and then she crossed the room swiftly and stood looking down on the cold, cruel, handsome face. The eyes were closed, the jaw relaxed (the sound she heard had been something between a groan and a chuckle), and *Dyke was sleeping profoundly!*

For one instant Dora gazed at him while her heart seemed to contract with sharp pain, and then, with curling lip and head erect, she swept out of the room.

On, along the corridor, until she gained the door of her salon; and there entering, turned the key and threw herself, face downward, on the couch in one corner of the room and burst into an agony of tears.

Ah me! hope had died forever; the last blow had been dealt by that ruthless hand—to faith, and trust, and love. Alone she must stand for evermore; alone, defenseless, in the hands of a man as unscrupulous as he was heartless, to whom she could never look again for affection, comfort, or protection.

"Oh, Dyke!" she sobbed, "if you had only killed me at one blow! Oh, Heaven pity me!" Heart-breaking was the convulsion which seemed to rend her frail form in its fierce agony (what grief so bitter as the tearing from one's heart the idol which has proved unworthy of its sacred shrine?). But there were dregs still in the cup of her anguish which she had not tasted yet.

Reginald Trelawney, smoking on the balcony upon which these windows opened, was startled out of a sorrowful reverie by the sound of suppressed weeping, and the moaning cry which burst irrepressibly from Dora's lips reached him as he stood irresolute a moment on the threshold of the window, with eyes fixed wonderingly on the prone figure of the woman whom he had learned to worship above all else on earth. One moment, and then a swift stride or two brought him to the couch, where he cast himself on his knees, crying wildly,—

"What is this? Dora! Mrs. Faucett! Oh, what has happened? Speak to me; tell me. I *cannot* bear to see this grief!"

His arms were about her, his voice strained and harsh, his face grown white with sympathy for a sorrow of which he felt the cause. But Dora only raised her hand and motioned him away, creeping closer into the shelter of the cushions on the lounge, weeping no less bitterly at this additional trial.

"I *will not* go!" cried Reginald, answering her movement. "My place is here at your feet; you would not spurn a dog away from you; and I am not less faithful. Oh, Dora, raise your dear head and speak to me; let me help you if I can; even by going away from you forever, if I in any way have caused this pain. Do not fear; I am strong enough to leave you, but too weak to see you suffer." And he bowed his head upon the back of the couch, and tears trickled slowly down his cheeks.

Dora raised her head with an effort. "Oh, Heaven!" she cried, "do you care enough for me *to weep?* Are there tears, then, in some men's hearts? Are they not all stone, hard and cruel, and cold?" Dreamily she spoke, while her face was wet with tears; and her great, sad eyes turned wistfully towards Reginald, recalled forcibly to his mind that incarnation of passionate yet child-like sorrow, the Beatrice of Guido. He trembled from head to foot as she passed her hand caressingly over his fair, wavy hair, murmuring as she did so, more to herself than to him, "A woman is such a pitiful thing,—such a trailing, twining, weak-spirited thing, that when she is torn from a support she has grown used to, she must needs grovel and lie in the dust and wail. Oh, my friend, you may well pity me; but your tears would give me more pain if my heart were not all numb and cold."

C*

She sank back now wearily; the storm had passed and left exhaustion.

"But, why," Reginald urged,—"why have you been so grieved? Who has been so wicked as to hurt your tender heart? Who has dared to make you so wretched? Oh, in pity tell me what has caused this!"

She answered nothing, but lay back pale as a lily, with violet shadows under the large eyes, while Reginald, still kneeling before her, caressed her hand, lying limp and motionless in his. She scarcely knew he was there; her thoughts were straying back to the burial of her dead love; she mourned in her soul over the grave of her most treasured hopes,—over the long, desolate, worse than widowed future which stared in her face in its emptiness; and then the vision of Dyke asleep in heartless unconcern stung her again, and she moaned aloud.

Reginald could not bear suspense quietly; he started to his feet, and strode rapidly up and down the room, Dora following every movement with dreamy, unseeing eyes. But she was aroused from her apathy when he stopped suddenly before her and spoke in a husky voice, and with an expression she had never seen before on his young face.

"You will not tell me your sorrow? Well, I know it; I have known it all along: since the very first days when I met you in Rome; indeed" (with a short, harsh laugh), "who does *not* know? But let that pass; the present is what we have to look to,—and the future. What do you mean to do, Dora? Do you dream of living on in this ghastly fashion,—a wife and yet no wife; bearing your husband's name, and yet unacknowledged, denied, repudiated!—neglected, exposed, unshielded?" Dora gazed up at him, silent, under a horrible fascination; he went on: "And he, is it not enough that he thus forswears himself, and breaks every vow which binds him to you? But he must make his story a by-word in the towns wherever he moves; he must flaunt his devotion to the Marquise de Courboisie everywhere. She it is, he awaits here, she it is who enchained him in Rome, in Paris, even in the hills where you rusticated and enjoyed your simple, primitive life, unconscious of her proximity. Ah, what it has cost me to keep silent! What pangs of self-abasement to touch that man's hand, to sit at his board, to breathe the same air he breathed! And yet, what could I do? Could I leave you, poor lamb! in the fangs of this wolf? Could I go away from you knowing well that *this* day must dawn soon; that you would have to bear the bitter pain which wrings your heart to-day, —alone? No; my life is not worth much, but to its very last breath it is *yours;* yours to use, to be *sure* of, to trample upon, if you so please, but still yours forever. As long as I live my arm shall protect you, and my heart shall come between you and any pain which it can shield from you." He sat down on the edge of the couch, and looked straight into Dora's eyes. "Answer me one question!" he almost commanded: "is your love for this man quite dead?"

"Yes," she answered, in a strange voice; "quite,— quite dead!"

"Then you can bear to hear something from me?" he asked.

"Oh, yes; I can bear anything." Still in that odd, constrained tone.

"This man you call your husband has plotted to get rid of you,—this sounds cruel, but I *must* say it,—and failing, through your angelic purity, he has resolved to leave you. His plans are well laid, and I hold the key to every move. He means to elope with the Marquise de Courboisie and leave you in *my* charge. All this has been divulged to me

by a man who was devoted to him, body and soul, until
he learned to know *you* and your gentle sweetness won his
heart.　Oh, Dora, you may imagine what a night I passed
after this man Giles came to my bedroom door last night
and implored *me* to interfere to save you, telling me the
whole vile plot, and all the circumstances of your secret
marriage.　Heaven help me !　I should have shot that
villain like a dog, had he crossed my path last night.　But
that would leave you more defenseless still ; I *must* be
patient.''　He resumed his pacing back and forth, and
Dora watched him as before ; but in her white cheeks
burned now two spots of crimson, and her eyes had the
cold glitter of steel in their depths.　When Reginald came
near again his voice was very low and pleading, and his
eyes were soft with tenderness.

'' Dora, you must come away with me ; there is nothing
left for you to do ; nothing will come amiss to this man
if he once desires an obstacle removed.　I cannot leave
you in such terrible danger, and I can no longer meet
that devil face to face without telling him my thoughts.
You will come with me, my darling,—you and your father
and little Marian,—home to dear England, where the law
will soon free you from this wretch?　Oh, Dora, I am not
pleading selfishly.　I know there is not a *shadow* of hope
for me ; you never even pretended to care for me, and
I do not think you ever will ; but you will give me a
brother's right to protect and help you in this sad moment,
will you not ?''

Dora slowly rose to her feet ; not one word had escaped
her of all that he had said ; each one was an arrow
shot straight into her heart ; she was quivering all over
with pain and horror as she stood before him, looking up
into his honest, manly face.　Then she rested her two
hands lightly on his shoulders, and said, with incomparable

sweetness, "God bless you; you are very noble. Oh, I *do* trust you, my brother!" And, as he quickly bent his head, she touched his cheek with her lips, and in a moment he was alone.

As Dora sped along the passage to her own apartments she encountered a party of new arrivals; shrinking behind a pillar, she saw them pass: a decrepit old man supported by a valet, followed by a stylish little girl about five years old, and her maid; behind them, the beautiful Marquise de Courboisie, leaning on Dyke Faucett's arm, and speaking in low, confidential tones in French, close to his ear. Just as he closed the door upon the party in their handsome suite of rooms, a cry from one of the house-maids at the other end of the corridor attracted his attention. He was about to turn away in an opposite direction, when the woman perceived him, and called out, "Ah, Monsieur, voilà Madame qui s'est trouvée mal, venez vite, je vous en prie;" and Faucett, advancing, had the felicity of figuring in a *coup-de-scène*, and carrying his insensible wife to her bedroom.

Dora recovered her consciousness only to fall into high fever, which showed symptoms of serious illness, and over which the medical man, who had been hastily summoned, shook his head gravely.

That night, as the impassive Giles laid out his master's evening dress and inserted the studs in the delicate embroidery under which his bad heart held its secrets, he made a vast effort, and, gulping down the last spasm of reluctance at breaking old bonds, spoke out,—

"I desire to give warning, sir, if you please."

"Hey! what!" ejaculated Faucett, turning sharply round from the mirror with one side of his face covered with lather and his razor upheld in his hand. "Did you speak, Giles?"

"Beg pardon, sir; but I said that I desire to give warning. This day month, sir, I should wish to return to England."

Dyke looked at him fixedly. "Hem! you have been offered higher wages, have you?"

"Oh, no, sir. You have been most liberal," answered Giles, delicately sprinkling his master's inner vest from an arrosoir of violets and giving a "légère teinture" of the same to the exquisite handkerchief.

"Ah, you are in love, then; there is some Mary Ann in the case; you wish to marry?"

"Ah, no, sir; I have no thought of marrying."

"What the deuce do you leave me for, then? You suit me. Have I found fault with you? Come, what is it?"

"You have been a kind master to me, sir," answered poor Giles, in trembling tones; "but still, sir, I mean to leave you,—this day month, if you please, sir."

Dyke turned around again, this time pale with rage. "Not this day month, but to-night; there!" throwing him a handful of napoleons. "I paid you up last week; there are a month's wages; begone!"

"Oh, sir!" began Giles.

"Leave the room!" thundered Dyke. And the door closed softly on the retreating form of the best servant man ever had.

CHAPTER X.

It will scarcely be necessary to assure those who have correctly gauged the profound, callous egotism of Dyke Faucett's moral nature, that, however reckless and unscrupulous he became in regard to the future welfare of others, he had always been able to hold in leash his desires when they threatened wreck to himself. Only in one instance—never to be sufficiently deplored—had he allowed his passion to overtop his calculating reason,—in the case where Dora's exceptionally powerful fascination, against which he had struggled in vain, caused him to succumb at last, feeling that when the inevitable weariness supervened, his ready genius of evil would furnish an avenue of escape for him.

For in the early days of his courtship and marriage he laid no subtle plot to give form and feature to his subsequent dastardly wickedness; the idea of making his marriage as private as possible, and keeping it as secret, with the distinct possibility of being able to repudiate its claims when they became irksome, had not prompted his action at that time. To plan would have involved some deterioration of the sentiment, which, false as it was, absorbed him,—and would have cost him some labor of invention and thought,—was *work*, which he shifted aside as much as practicable.

And the years had brought out the realization of his anticipations. He had won Dora, and wearied of her; and without the least effort or the slightest ruffle on the surface of his equable life, he had given her to understand this; and they had just drifted apart, and soon would stand on either side of a fathomless gulf. For, judging her nature by his own, and that of the many women he had known (all being of one type, in different degrees), he never doubted for one moment that, sooner or later, she, driven by loneliness and the bitterness of disappointment, would—in the futile vengeance some women grasp with the avidity of despair—cross that gulf. That he gave her every opportunity; that he strove to the best of his ability to point out to her the way; that he found in Reginald Trelawney's self-abnegating devotion the very weapon at his hand wherewith to slay her soul, only proves that the way of the transgressor is sometimes smooth enough to excite one's wondering awe!

But that he intended to expedite matters by doing violence to the world's opinions in eloping with a married woman, and thus at one blow cutting off from himself his guardian's respect and affection (with their abundant fruit, his princely income), and burdening himself anew with a woman who loved him and was destitute entirely of that fine, sensitive pride which Dora had no lack of, did not enter into his calculations for one moment. In the fervid brain of romantic Célestine, and perhaps faintly suggested as a remote conclusion by her impetuous mistress, alone was such self-sacrifice as this dreamed of.

The marquise and Dyke Faucett were certainly on terms of intimate friendship,—rather more implied than expressed on his side, for he rarely committed himself in words, *never* on paper; but he was always gallant, elegant, handsome, and ready to admire her coquetries,—and she loved him. If the future held some shadowy hopes for her, built upon the rickety life of her aged spouse, she kept them for her solitary hours—and her maid's delectation.

Therefore the last blow, which bowed poor Dora's

head to the earth, and lost Dyke a well-trained servant, was dealt, by fate through the agency of a silly woman's prattle.

And is not the world full of wrecks which have come to grief in those same babbling shallows?

Dora lay ill for weeks, fighting with helpless hands, in the delirium of fever, the spectres of her broken life and shattered hopes, wailing out her plaints in the uncomprehending ears of a Swiss nurse, who watched her carefully and pitied her wretchedness, in her stolid, matter-of-fact fashion.

And Dyke, making inquiry through his new valet each morning and evening, found she was making slow progress towards recovery, and consoled himself for that fact in throwing a faint *tendresse* into his customary *insouciant* manner with the beautiful Pauline, who was totally unaware of the existence of *a wife*.

True, she had seen Dora once or twice with Dyke—in his box at the opera, veiled by the drapery,—but, when questioned, Dyke would eloquently shrug his shoulders, raise his eyebrows, and dismiss the subject. The marquise formed her own conclusions, and, frowning outwardly, smiled inwardly.

During these weeks of Dora's illness, I fear Trelawney suffered most of all. He spent his days lounging about the corridors, waylaying the physician, the nurse, the servants, who entered or came from Dora's rooms. His nights were weary wanderings along the lake border, within call from the Hotel Métropôle—for, by liberal donations, he had won from the Swiss *garde-malade* the promise that, should her patient develop new symptoms or sink into the lethargy which would be the precursor of death, he should be called to her side immediately. He was intolerably wretched; and Giles (whom Reginald had at once engaged in his own service) was as anxious and nervous about his late mistress as a well-trained servant dared to be.

He it was who, seated on a chair outside her door, watched during those three fearful nights, when the doctor acknowledged that he dreaded the dawning of the morning, ready at a moment's notice to fly to Reginald's room ; which he, dressed, haggard, wild with grief, paced in impotent anguish.   He it was who, during Dora's slow convalescence, scoured the country far and wide for fruits and flowers, and delicacies of all kinds, to tempt the capricious appetite of the invalid.   And on those occasions,—very seldom they were, when *Dyke* approached to inquire himself of her welfare,—Giles would rise to his feet from his seat outside her door, and stand motionless before his former master ; Dyke, completely ignoring his existence, would tap upon the panel of the door, and inquire of the nurse, in languid accents, how her patient fared ?   Then Giles, girded in spirit, years of slavish devotion, of unfaltering fidelity, could be obliterated in the heart and memory of this hard, cold man by one single act of self-assertion, one effort to be true himself, to his better instincts.

Dyke never met Trelawney now ; the latter avoided him with a horror which was almost a mania ; he felt that if Dora died, *he must kill this man !* and, I fear, in that ghastly anticipation he found his only solace.

But Dora did not die ; there was tugging at her heart-strings when that deathly weakness which is the twin-sister of Death followed the fever and pain, and was almost tempting in its restful promise of oblivion, the tiny hand of little Marian.   "I *must live* for her, my little one, — poor, helpless orphan baby ! what would become of her without me?   *I will live !*"   And she gathered strength daily, to enable her to get back to her darling and her father, whose anxiety was but slightly veiled in his letters.

Dyke, fearing his father-in-law would follow them, had written concisely from time to time of Dora's illness, and always from the most sanguine view, promising as soon as she was able to travel, to return to Italy, or take her to some quiet place, where they would expect him and little Marian to join them.

CHAPTER XI.

IT would be difficult to decide which face had changed most perceptibly during the last three weeks,—Dora's or Reginald Trelawney's. As she raised her eyes, and stretched forth a thin hand to greet him, she could scarcely repress a cry of surprise and sorrow at the marked alteration of his features. The healthy bronze had all worn off his fair skin, and a white pallor had superseded it, void of ruddy tinge; his frank gray eyes looked larger than she had known them, and had a strained look of habitual pain in their expression; and there were lines about the mouth which told of sleepless nights of anxiety and suffering.

He came forward and took her hand silently, fearing to trust himself to speak, and then sat down beside her great easy-chair, and covered his face with his hand. Dora, looking at him and noting the changes in his face and figure,—for his coat hung loosely now on those square shoulders,—felt sorrowful compassion, knowing full well whence this change had been wrought; and, when he raised his head, he saw the tears steal down her white face,—tears of weakness and profound pity. Every effort to control himself vanished. In a moment he was standing before her, imploring, entreating, commanding by turns; his eyes wild; his haggard face lit up with hope; his heart throbbing, so that he almost feared she would hear it.

"Oh, Dora, you must not let him take you away; you shall not *trust* yourself with him again. I can no longer endure this anguish; I cannot leave you in his hands; oh, have pity, have pity!" And he cast himself down again at her side, shaken with the passion of his last appeal from head to foot. At last her sweet voice broke the silence,—

"I have been very close to death, Reginald, and almost on the threshold of the other world; things which before seemed obscure and clouded to my eyes grew clear, and pointed out my path to me. Reginald, I am a wife in God's sight and my own, whatever the world chooses to call me, and it is not right that you should come near me with such words on your lips, such feelings in your heart. I have sent for you to-day to tell you this for the last time, and to ask you to return to England, and not to add to the grievous burden of my life,—your wretchedness!" She paused, exhausted, and he rose up again and took her hand.

"*I will not;* trust me. I shall spare you all further sight of my sorrow, only tell me this: Should you need me; should the day come when a brother's love could shield you,—*will you send for me?* Will you promise to do this?"

"I will," she answered, simply.

He took from his pocket-book a card and laid it on her lap. "This address will always find me. I shall return to England as soon as you leave Geneva, and I shall not stir out of it until you call me. D) not grieve," he entreated, as her lip quivered, "do not; I cannot bear it. I will do all that I know you would wish. I will leave here to-night for Chamounix, and—Dora, say 'Good-by, Reginald.'"

Dora raised her streaming eyes, and tried to smile through the tears. "Good-by, dear Reginald," she said.

He bent and looked into her face a look of such wild hunger and despair that her heart sank within her, then pressed his lips to her frail little hand, and the sound of his step along the passage told that he had gone, gone, and left her truly desolate.

A few days later, Dyke started with his wife and the Swiss nurse for France, where they settled down at last in a neat, small apartment in Tours, and were joined immediately by Mr. Fairfax, Marian, Antonio, and Clémentine.

Dyke had scarcely established them, and Dora, still prostrated from her recent illness, had just grown strong enough to creep out for an hour or two in the little garden which inclosed their pension, when a sudden shock felled her once more to the earth.

The *Galignani*, and one or two other journals, had been ordered by Dyke to be sent regularly, for the air was full of rumors of war, and the papers of thrilling interest. Sitting in the rustic porch, with Marian playing at her feet, Dora glanced carelessly over the columns of the *Messenger*. Mechanically she began to read an article headed,—

I

"Distressing accident on Mont Blanc. A party of English and American tourists lost in an avalanche. No recovery of the bodies possible, etc. etc."

She read on, without feeling the actuality of the occurrence, until she came to the following paragraph:

"We regret to record among the lost, the only son of

a highly esteemed officer in the British army, General Winstanley Trelawney.   He was also an officer in Her Majesty's service, and said to have been a most promising young man.   The bodies of Mr. Reginald Trelawney and his servant, Giles Humphreys, have not been recovered.''

With a faint cry Dora slid off her chair to the ground, whilst Marian rent the air with shrieks of terror.

On being carried to her bed, she revived, only to experience a relapse of her first attack.   Fortunately, her nurse was still with her, and an able physician in the neighborhood, but it was a close wrestle once more with death.

Dyke had been on the point of starting for a few weeks of Paris when this fresh exasperation occurred and detained him.   He felt sure that she would not survive this relapse, and waited.

But life gained the victory once more, and Dyke, after a few words of cold congratulation to the wan ghost who smiled a feeble glimmer of a smile when he entered her sick-room, told Dora that the next day he must run away for awhile (where, he did not state), and that he had left orders at his banker's to furnish her with all she required during his absence.

Dora merely smiled again and bent her head in acquiescence; but that night, in the temporary absence of her nurse, she arose and, throwing over her a dressing-gown, glided down-stairs to the sitting-room where Dyke was consuming innumerable cheroots in solitude.

He gave a perceptible start as she stood suddenly before him, having glided in unheard in her velvet chaussure, and asked, with irritation, '' What under Heaven are you about, Dora?   Do you want to be ill again?   I should think you had had about enough of it by this time!''

She sank into a chair, breathing heavily; presently she

spoke. "Dyke, I came here because I could not sleep to-night without telling you what is tormenting me. I feel that you are not going away to-morrow for a few days,—or weeks. You have other plans which you hide from me, but I do not care to know them, only I *must* know that which will affect myself and my child. Tell me only this." She fixed her eyes, bright with fever, upon his face; he moved uneasily.

"You are raving, Dora, positively raving; you had much better go back to bed and quiet your nerves; there is no reason for this excitement."

In an instant she was close beside him, looking down into his calm face with her burning gaze. "Is this true?" she asked. "Is there indeed no reason for my fears and suspicions. Have I been doing you gross injustice all these months? Are you faithful and loyal to your wife? Do you care for the welfare of your child? *and am I mad?* Have I not lost your love, your protection, the name you gave me in good faith? Oh, tell me that it is the fever in my veins which has conjured up this misery! Tell me that I shall awake from this horrible nightmare in time, and feel that I have not lost *everything!* Oh, Dyke, my heart is nearly broken!—have pity upon me!" She swayed forward and would have fallen to the ground had she not caught at a projection of the carving of the chimney-piece and held it with the nervous grasp of fever. Dyke pushed his chair back impatiently, and laid his hand on Dora's shoulder, while he said, in tones as cold and clear as ice, "During the five years of our acquaintance, Dora, you certainly have formed some idea of my character; have you ever seen anything which would lead you to believe that I would alter my intentions or change my opinions at the instance of any such tirade as this with which you have just favored me?" (the shoulder upon which his hand rested shivered and shrank.) "Would it not be far better for you to leave the development of my plans to the future, and accept *facts* as they stand at present? I leave you for a time, amply provided for, in your father's guardianship. I am tired of tears and reproaches, *garde-malades* and *caudle.*"

"In sickness or in health, until death do us part," came slowly, solemnly from Dora's lips; unheeding, he continued:

"You can have every comfort here: this is an excellent physician; your nurse is faithful——" he paused suddenly, for a ripple of hysterical laughter broke forth, startling him far more than a burst of tears.

"Yes," cried Dora, wildly, "my nurse is faithful and my doctor devoted and death near at hand; what more can I desire? In a few short weeks,—or days,—all that is left of me will be put out of sight in a nameless, dishonored grave, and you will be free once more! I understand many things to-night which have been mysteries to me for years: *why* you have never acknowledged your marriage to the world; why you have hidden me from sight, and forbidden me to wear your name. But there is one thing which I cannot yet comprehend:—*why you married me !* Tell me that, too, that I may not have one doubt left in my soul of your perfidy!"

"Why, indeed?" echoed Dyke, striding back and forth through the room, casting his cigar into the fire. "God only knows! I suppose most men make fools of themselves once in their lives; but it is the 'repenting at leisure' which I cannot manage. I have not been brought up to it, you see; it bores me !"

For a few moments there was silence after these words; the candles, with their wicks grown long, flickered and sputtered, the green wood in the tiny fireplace crackled and smoked—to Dora's eyes the room grew suddenly darker, dingier, more sordid in its homeliness; the green paper on the walls looked sicklier than before; the black horse-hair covered furniture more funereal than ever; the waxed floor felt cold and comfortless to her feet. Her eyes wandered about over every object in that dreary room, and then unconsciously fastened themselves upon the tall figure pacing to and fro at the extreme end of it.

He stopped abruptly and asked, "Why do you glare at me, Dora? Go to your room at once; this comedy is over for to-night!" He approached the bell to summon her maid, but before he reached it she cried, "Stop! Dyke," she went on in a lower tone, full of concentrated excitement,—"Dyke, *where is Reginald Trelawney?* Where is that boy that you have murdered *as you will murder me? Where have you hid his body?* tell me; I *will* know!" and she caught his sleeve with one thin hand, while her eyes blazed into his with delirium.

"Bah! mad woman," exclaimed Dyke, drawing his arm away from her clasp roughly. Again she swayed forward, and, before he could catch her, fell with outstretched arms, face downward, at his feet. Dyke lifted her gently, and carried her with swift steps to the room above, where he laid her on the bed, whilst he sharply reprimanded the alarmed nurse for her neglect of duty.

All that night the doctor hung over Dora's bed with hopeless zeal; the nurse, weeping sorely, reproached herself bitterly for carelessness; and old Mr. Fairfax sat tearless and stricken in the little sitting-room below.

When morning dawned, and the household was all astir, the news sped from lip to lip—that the poor young English lady was dying.

At last the doctor felt it a duty to inform Mr. Fairfax that there was no longer a vestige of hope to cling to:

life was ebbing away so fast; and the heart-broken father, mad with grief, sought Dyke's room with what frenzied intent God alone ever knew.

For—the room was empty; the bed had not been occupied. Inquiries were made, and then he learned that Dora's husband, the man who had sworn to cherish and protect her until death parted them, had taken post-horses to an adjacent town, to enable him to catch the midnight train to Paris, in order that he might not see Dora die!

The old man knelt down beside the bed where his darling lay so white and still, and strove not to curse the hand which had robbed him of his one ewe-lamb—his little Dora.

> " The light upon her golden hair,
> But not within her eyes;
> The light still there upon her hair,
> The death upon her eyes."

BOOK II.

DEAD-SEA FRUITS.

"But France got drunk with blood to vomit crime,
  And fatal have her Saturnalia been
  To Freedom's cause, in every age and clime;
  Because the deadly days which we have seen,
  And vile Ambition, which built up between
  Man and his hopes an adamantine wall,
  And the base pageant last upon the scene
  Are grown the pretext for the eternal thrall
Which nips life's tree, and dooms man's worst—his second fall."
BYRON.

CHAPTER I.

THE war-cry re-echoes throughout the land! The first blow of the Teuton fist had been dealt right vigorously, and France, the invincible, reeled under its scientific potency!

Sédan has fallen; the emperor is captive; chaos, anarchy, confusion,—a terrible triad,—reigns in his stead.

Gay, beautiful, laughter-loving Paris, mad Bacchante that she was, had danced and sung more wildly than ever during the reckless carnival which preceded the sackcloth and ashes of this fatal 4th September, 1870.

For Paris, drunk with the purple vintages of years of prosperous peace, pressed down and running over under the master-heel of the man who had made her the idol of the world, snapped her rosy fingers in the grim face of fate, crying gayly (*en trinquant*), A Berlin! à Berlin!

But the 4th September has dawned; the thunderbolt has fallen; Paris is sobered at last! "Une Madeleine dans l'impuissance de son pouvoir," she plucks the fading garland from her brow, and robes herself in penitential serge, prepared to eat the bread mingled with tears, of a retributive chastisement.

For over the field of Waterloo was drawn the veil of Time, and, seen but dimly by the eyes besotted by victory and vain-glory, the warning written there in blood failed to deter the grand-nephew of the hero who paid so dearly for *his* lesson, from following in his footsteps in the lust of gain. Perhaps the result of the *plébiscite* had unsettled the brain of the modern Achilles (whose vulnerable point lay in his self-conceit), or he hoped, armed with this ostensibly-flattering tribute of his people, by a brilliant victory to steady the fluctuating tide of his ebbing popularity—and so cast down the gauntlet which Prussia was not loth to take up, whilst all France rang with the bugle-call, "To arms!"

When Brutus, undeterred by Cæsar's spectral warning, lay gasping with spear-pierced side on the field of Philippi, he sighed with his last breath, "*It is well!*"

But Napoleon III., free from other wound than the death-blow given to his arrogance, with drooping laurels and lowered crest, in the retirement of Wilhelmshöhe wraps himself in the mantle of a consoling philosophy and murmurs, "*It is fate!*" For, like his illustrious relative, he despised not the "black art," and held firm faith in auguries. What availed example or warning to him whose destiny was already writ amid the stars? In vain stretched forth a prophetic hand from far-off, sad St. Helena, where

a greater man had chafed away life in bitter anguish, as
he watched day by day the

> " Bleak shores beat back
> The ocean's foamy feet"—

in a remorseful solitude !   For about *his* forehead also had
the aureole grown dimmed through the storm of fate, and
those same "rifts within the lute" of *his* great mind, of
superstition, callous selfishness and vanity, had silenced
all music in the sordid soul which repudiated Josephine !
So naught was left to either of these demagogues after
their worshipers fell off from their allegiance, but the fate
of Prometheus, with the vulture of despair gnawing at
their vitals until Death, that "*unanswered Greek question,*"
released them.   For the people loved them not; it was
their prestige, their success, the glory they achieved
which created the nimbus about their heads, and compelled a worship, a terror, a fanatical admiration for the
beings who owned such gigantic self-confidence, such unscrupulous ambition, such belief in their invincibility.   It
was *Napoleonism* which crossed the bridge of Lodi ; it
was Napoleonism which forced the Austrian government
to sign the Treaty of Campo Formio by simply smashing
a priceless porcelain vase during an audience with the
ambassador, to emphasize a threat as idle and bombastic
as the wind ; it was Napoleonism which marched triumphantly to Paris after Elba, which has carried the tri-
color victoriously over scores of battle-fields, and which
has brought weal as well as woe to France.

And these two men, who each possessed

> " That mystery of commanding,
> That birth-hour gift, that art Napoleon,
> Of winning, fettering, wielding, molding, banding
> The heart of millions till they move as one,"

stood at last stripped of their laurels, forsaken by their worshipers ; the one like a chained eagle beating his wings in impotent wrath on that rocky, desolate shore, the other imprisoned apart from wife and child, broken in health, with spirit crushed, and the curse of his betrayed people ringing in his ears until the last hour of his life !

All foreign visitors to the gay capital had been warned by the chiefs of the various legations to "flee from the wrath to come," and in every direction people were flitting, some gayly, carelessly, taking no thought for the morrow, or what that morrow might bring forth for the fair city which even then had something tragic in her smile; others slowly and sadly departed, bearing their Lares and Penates they scarcely knew whither. English men and women were turning joyfully homeward, glad to be *forced* back to something like comfort and respectability. Americans, with many a backward, tearful glance at the dazzling Danäe, whom that millinery-loving people grow fond of contemplating through a golden shower, embarked sorrowfully for those benighted lands where the indigenous heathen invest not their "wampum" in the vagaries of Monsieur Worth, and bow not the knee to Pingât. Farewell to thee, beloved, lotus-eating Paris ! to thy wealth of art, of taste, of luxury, thy Longchamps toilettes, and thy savory flesh-pots ; thine adorers must hie them away to the Western world, lest they be crushed in thy fall ; but rest assured, never shall they cover their chignons with a home-made bonnet, or *croquer une praline*, without a retrospective sigh for the beguiling city whose glory has departed ; and verily, if there is possible constancy in the feminine heart, they will never cease to mourn that there should be a limit, not to dynasties, or to the ambition of a Napoleon, but to the capacity of that ship's hold which carried their luggage safely over.

Alas for the sluggard who procrastinated his visit to Paris during her palmy days, the days of the luxurious empire and of the gracious Eugénie!

Of the "cakes and ale" of futurity there may be no scant measure, but to the palates grown used to their flavor in those gala-days of prosperity they will be flat and savorless for evermore.

Surely when the flames died out, and the smoke cleared away from the plains of Sodom, there were few hearts stout enough to build upon the site of the scourged city another such monument to commemorate the vices of man.

Already the "abomination of desolation" was marking the deserted boulevards, the empty shops, the half-filled theatres, and the anxious faces gathered about the doors of the cafés, where usually one or more red-capped patriots harangued their fellows with an eloquence born of idleness and absinthe. A few foreigners still lingered, from interest or expediency, or—because life bored them; the curtain was about to roll up, and the play to begin. Why should one not remain and criticise from before the footlights this "piece" which France had determined to exhibit to the gaping audience of the world?—this bloody tragedy ending in the pitiful farce, of which Paris and its environs are the old stock *mise en scène.*

It was not an every-day experience this, in the calmly-ordered, geometrically-measured humdrummery of the lives of those loungers whose spice of life had lost its pungency; and since the beginning of all things, pity for *others'* woes has never been known to bleach the hair white, nor write itself in legible lines upon the human countenance.

Wherefore then should we avert our eyes from the sight of France in her despair? The sight of a queen dethroned and dragged through the mire of her own selfishness and rapacity, must always have something of dramatic éclat to interest one ; and the sad mockery of a disheveled, mud-bespattered goddess of Liberty, with tears of blood upon her famine-wasted cheek, striving to cover with the folds of the *drapeau rouge* the rags of the ermine her rival wore right royally but yesterday, has a unique attraction for the spectator !

Poor prodigal Paris! Will she emerge from this trial by fire, and sword, and famine, after aching and groaning and being glad to fill herself with the swine-rejected husks, repentant, humbled, purified? And shall not all the nations, seeing her afar off, fall on her neck and kiss her with the kiss of a loving compassion ? . . . Who shall answer? The grooves in which Paris ran so smoothly to destruction were deep, and velvet-lined. Would it be surprising that after a trial of the flint road of self-sacrifice she should, after a season, begin to slide gently back into those seductive furrows? Let not the fatted calf be prematurely killed.

CHAPTER II.

IN a luxurious *appartement au premier* on the Rue Royale, Dyke Faucett lounged at mid-day over a scarcely-tasted breakfast, glancing idly over the *Figaro* and the *Journal Officiel*, each charged with the electricity of the coming storm.

Six months had passed since that night when the net had been so tightly drawn about him that he began to doubt the possibility of ever being free again—the night in Tours, when he had lifted the insensible form of his wife, who, driven mad at last by his cold, cruel treachery, had so poured out upon him the pent-up vials of reproachful bitterness, and when he had felt convinced that no other resource remained to him—but flight.

Six months spent in Paris, in those dear, delightful haunts of former bachelor-days (only excepting a few weeks when the heat of mid-summer had driven him under the cool shadow of the Jungfrau). Six months, during which he logically reasoned himself *free*—free from the woman whose bloom had faded under the withering frost of his neglect, whose moral rectitude and pure soul had for him the monotonous aspect and blank vapidity of a sheet of white paper;—for, after the scales fell from her eyes and she realized for what manner of man she had sold her birthright of freedom and the power to live her life out to its grandest proportions, Dora failed undeniably in supplying that piquant incense which her first idolatrous devotion had furnished his unsated vanity. And now he was once more free !

Free from the mute reproach of her white face and heavy-shaded eyes (for she had not rated him with the vituperative eloquence of a discarded shrew, or treated him to the hysterical paroxysms of a brainless idiot ; he must do her that justice);—free from the incubus of a doting father-in-law, who, of late, had been continually trying to button-hole him into a confession of his intentions in regard to his darling child.

Free to loiter in the boudoir of the Marquise de Courboisie, who had so gained in bloom and curve, and had reigned in the choicest circles of Roman society that last winter, an acknowledged queen ; free to divide his allegiance to her, if he so minded, with the great singer of

D*

the day or with any coryphée of the ballet who happened to charm his eye for the moment, without being called to account, or having his slumbers disturbed by the sound of suppressed weeping.

Free some day,—in the far-off future,—when the savor has gone out of everything, when he has come into possession of the estate of Ellingham, and an heir would be desirable,—to choose in the choicest pasture of the sweet English "garden of girls" one fit to be his bride, one in whom beauty, rank, intelligence, and fortune should combine to make a creature worthy of so noble a mate.

For Dora *must be dead;* perhaps even in that moment when she had fallen at his feet, with a last despairing cry, her heart may have ceased to beat! And even had this not been so, the shock which greeted her return to consciousness—of his entire abandonment of her and the child—would, without doubt, have snapped the frail thread of life!

How else construe their silence? The fact of his banker's assurance that no demand had been made upon the allowance awarded them, and the additional information that *no* one had called to make inquiries for Mr. Faucett's present address, all gave solidity to his conclusions. Yes, Dora was certainly dead; and Mr. Fairfax was *trop gentilhomme* to touch another penny of her destroyer's money.

When we wish ardently that a certain thing *should be*, are we not apt in the end to believe that it really *is?* And how often is our belief, our judgment, and *our taste* bolstered up or alloyed by the "trifles light as air" of circumstance or the opinions of others? We bow to hyperbole and the "vox populi"!

Do we not all go to Rome and yield up a devout admiration to the ox-eyed, small-mouthed Raphaëlized conception of the Virgin Mother, knowing all the while that we each hold in our hearts a fairer ideal of sad, *awe-shadowed* loveliness, with a suggestion of the coming anguish seen dimly through the present glory, without that eternal simper which fits the lips of *the baker's daughter*, or the plummet-line of exact regularity of feature? (Was Mrs. Browning ever satisfied with the Madonna of the galleries, I wonder? Her great poetic soul could not warp itself to the meanness and narrowness of this art-apostasy which would sacrifice her dear, heaven-born conceptions to the autocratic, well-thumbed opinions of—the guide-books and the marginal platitudes of the *ubiquitous* tourist!) Oh, that *bête noir* of the art-lover, *the tourist!* When a passage can be taken to the moon, shall we not strive to emulate Americus Vespucius, that we may travel once, at least, without the restricting Murray or the didactic Bradshaw, and form our *own* conclusions, untrammeled by the friendly tourist—on the lunar wonders?

In the mean time we shall continue to ejaculate, with mechanical precision, "how wonderful!" "how beautiful!" "how exquisitely proportioned!" whether we gaze at the Venus of Medicis or the leaning tower at Pisa! Although we continue to prefer, in the silent recesses of our souls, to the finely-calculated, classic measurements of the former, that mutilated fragment of Milo, which touches us more naturally and deeply, perhaps, *because* of its *marred* perfection! and see in that hair-breadth-escape-looking tower nothing but a monstrously ugly index of the moral obliquity of the people over whom it leans threateningly.

For we belong to that well-brought-up class whose ideas are taught to run in grooves—to that class which never raises its glass to its eye to see *anything hung above its own level!*—whose religion is bounded by " Burke's Peerage"

on the north and the "Landed Gentry" on the south, on
the east by the opinions of Her Grace, and by His Lordship the Bishop on the last remaining avenue of escape!
The class which dares not admire a sunset by Millais
without the authority of a titled precedent! or a moon-
rise by—*the hand of God,*—because enthusiasm is vulgar
and Nature commonplace!

Yes, to my unutterable grief I confess it, our ancestors
existed long before William of Normandy *was thought
of,* and in the *crème de la crème* we exist like *flies in
amber!*

And why should *we grieve?* you ask; why should we
not be content in this sea of golden transparency?

Because—we want to buzz!

When, forsooth, we gather up our velvet skirts for fear
they brush the faded finery of the mendicant Magdalen
at our carriage-door, and seat ourselves by the side of
the gorgeous, "dear creature" of a duchess who has not
been "*sans reproche*" (though assuredly "*sans peur*")
since her infancy, we dare not cry out against the injustice
of things, but must e'en stifle our remonstrances and clog
our wings in that yellow sea of inanity!

But all this is not interesting to you, dear reader.
Pardon me!   Even if it were, by chance, would it not be
vain to attempt to solve the psychological puzzles which
madden one, in a digression which *must* be thoughtful,—
and therefore as inadmissible in a novel as in the perfumed
atmosphere of your ladyship's boudoir?

"Yes; I shall certainly stay and see the game played
out," concluded Dyke Faucett, after pondering the matter
over during the space of half an hour.   "There is nothing
doing in England just now, and Pauline is certainly charming."   So resolving, he drew towards him a pile of letters
and dainty notes, which lay upon a salver close at hand,

and, selecting one written on large paper, sealed with wax bearing a coat of arms, in the good old-fashioned style before the vulgar days of self-sealing envelopes, he leisurely opened and perused it.

"ELLINGHAM, Sept. 2, 1870.

"MY DEAR DYKE,—It appears that France is determined to make a fool of herself, as usual; and from last accounts, we understand that before many days it is apprehended that Paris will be in a state of siege.

"Under these circumstances, knowing well how averse you are to privation of every description, and how more than ordinarily unpleasant that city will become, I feel no hesitation in urging your return to your native land, which, during the last ten years, you have almost forsaken.

"When three years had expired, which you considered necessary to spend in travel for the purpose of perfecting yourself in foreign languages, and obtaining that polish which the gentlemen of my day were able to acquire at home, I had hoped that you would be content to settle down and take to yourself a fair English wife; that I might not spend the remnant of my days in solitude, and that I might welcome a boy of yours in the old place before I went away forever. But after a hasty visit, you have contrived upon one pretext or another to cut England almost entirely. It may be that I erred in a too lavish indulgence towards you in your boyhood, when you came to gladden my lonely hearth, and so fostered in you that germ of selfishness which is inherent in all human nature.

"However, I have no desire to reproach you, my dear boy, and will simply add that you have now an opportunity of proving the gratitude and affection of which you have often feelingly written to me. Come home; give up this Bohemian wandering; marry and be respectable. It is quite time, and you know my unconquerable aversion to foreigners.   Take these suggestions into consideration, knowing that I have rarely made a request of you, and will not, in this case, be likely to pardon a refusal.

"Very affectionately yours,

"PHILIP STANDLEY."

Over the blonde, impassive beauty of Dyke Faucett's face a scowl settled loweringly, as he brooded with ever-increasing displeasure over this letter, which recalled him to England at the moment when Paris began to be interesting to him.   His will, for once, must bend to that of another; the meaning of those last few quiet lines he well understood.   Between himself and those vast possessions stood a life,—not a very vigorous one, to be sure, but which held fire enough still to resent ingratitude and disobedience, and he was not even heir-presumptive.   To understand fully the position, we must go back some forty years.

Sir Philip Standley, the only surviving member of a good old Kentish family, had loved, "not wisely, but too well," a woman whose heart and mind gave the lie to the fairest face that ever smiled sweetly in assumed innocence, as she dealt the death-blow to the dearest hopes of a man's whole future life.

In these moral murders, which, since the days of Delilah, have brought worse than *blindness* upon men, by the subtle sophistry of a woman's reasoning, she exculpates herself in a way which cannot but excite our admiration, if not our unequivocal concurrence.

That she foresees the conclusions a man forms upon the ground of blushes and sighs, half-averted looks, and low-toned whispers, she denies; that she can hold in thrall with soft glances and softer hand-pressure a dozen men about her footstool, while over their heads she shoots far and away arrows of deadlier aim, drawn from the quiver of the heart,—she claims as one of the prerogatives of her sex.

Is it not always thus?

Out of the shadows of past ages, are the names which stand glorified immortally, crowned with great men's love, the purest, the noblest, or the *best?* Is Trojan Helen, or the swarthy enchantress of the Nile, or even the self-abnegating Heloïse, the type of what should be God's last, best gift to man? Alas! since the Philistines fell upon betrayed Samson,—since the fiery sword barred the gates of Eden,—have not the desire of the eye and the lust of the flesh waged ceaseless war against the higher aspirations of our very human nature?

There was no repulsive glitter of steel about the *lettre de cachet* (that dread weapon of the Inquisition and the "Reign of Terror"); no blood-marks stained its fair surface, yet it did its murderous work swiftly and silently, and very surely. In the silence of night the waters opened, and closed over the victim's head, and the sleeping world recked not that the light of another life had gone out forever.

On the day when Constance Dyke, feeling the catastrophe of a proposal, which she could not accept, to be imminent, breathed into the ear of the man whom she had beguiled through many months of dalliance into loving her, the fact that she had been affianced for three years to a young lieutenant then on foreign service, she killed at a blow all future possibility of trusting love, in the heart of Philip Standley.

He did not turn cynic and wax bitter against all his kind; his nature was too sweet at the core for that; he not only loved her to the last day of her life, but he formed a warm friendship for the gallant young officer, who, as soon as he had won his epaulettes, came home and claimed his bride. ·

Only, the first fruits of his heart had been gathered, and never again did bud or blossom bloom into promise where the lightning had fallen scathingly.

During six years of happy married life, Constance Faucett learned to value thoroughly the noble nature of the man whom she had unwittingly (?) injured; for, although the wound had never once been laid bare to her eyes, by the aid of that sixth sense with which a woman learns when a man loves her she guessed the existence of a scar.   And when, in the last hour, they stood beside her, the devoted husband and the true friend, it would be difficult to determine which man's heart was more bitterly wrung, or to which the beautiful eyes, fast glazing in death, bade the tenderer farewell.   ·

There seemed to be need for few last words between the two men, after the green sod had been laid over what they loved best on earth; and for Captain Faucett to go out at once with his regiment to active service, and for Sir Philip to take to his aching heart the motherless boy, seemed the only possible way to make each man's life endurable.

In the strong hand-clasp and steady look into each other's eyes, as they stood on the deck of the steamer which was to bear one of them away to danger, possibly to death, there was an eloquence born of strong emotion. They parted silently; and when, after awhile, the news came home that Lionel Faucett had fallen at the head of his regiment, in the thickest of the fight in the Indian mutiny of that year, no one grieved for the strong, brave life so suddenly stricken down, more deeply than the man whose rival he had been.

Throughout the childhood of the spirited boy, who had

inherited the fatal gift of his mother's beauty; through the boisterous Eton holidays, when the irrepressible glee of a perfectly healthy boy, who feared no reprimand, however demonstrative he became, made the old Hall ring again, where the echoes had been silent for more than forty years, Sir Philip found unceasing pleasure and solace for his lonely hours. Through his Oxford career, as well, he had watched the son of his dead love with unabated interest and affection; and, when he returned after graduating,—not without honor,—a remarkably fine specimen of manly beauty, Sir Philip's admiration and pride knew no bounds.

He consented readily to the grand tour which was deemed *de rigueur* to "finish" a man's perfections, but rebelled in spirit when he found that his protégé had become a victim to the travel-mania of the day, and could not be persuaded to pitch his tent on his native soil for more than a month or two during the hunting season, or a fortnight of town in June.

It was a grievous disappointment to the old gentleman, who, perhaps, might be excused for believing in the existence of gratitude won by such boundless kindness,— for he was a true-hearted man himself, and trusted with the charity which "hopeth all things" in the sincerity of others' professions.

And Dyke was invariably courteous and affectionate, in an indolent, graceful way, treating his guardian with a deference which, while it partook of sycophancy, had nothing of its cringing manner; and, during his brief sojourn at home, he managed so to fascinate the kind old gentleman, that it was not difficult to win his consent to another prolonged Continental visit.

The possibility of Dyke's having deceived him, that it was something more than the excitement of foreign travel which lured him, time after time, back to the other side of the Channel, never crossed Sir Philip's mind.

That a man could be so base as to requite unwavering kindness and liberality by deception, or to abuse the unrestrained liberty awarded him in an implicit confidence by the treacherous acted lie of years, he could have believed possible in a romance or a newspaper, but never in the heart and mind of the son of the woman he had loved.

For Sir Philip Standley was a man of a clear and upright nature and the kindliest feelings. Simplicity, frankness, and integrity of principle were his prominent traits. In politics, he was an honest and inflexible conservative; in social life, a genial and hospitable host, a promoter of all good works, a whole-souled dispenser of charities, a man of a too generous nature to be suspicious of evil.

But now, looking out over the troubled aspect of things in France from the quiet retirement of his country home, noting with the wondering eye of an Englishman, to whom such mad folly as threatened that fair land with destruction seemed incredible, Sir Philip felt the time had come when Dyke might be safely recalled to home duties at last.

"Surely he must have grown weary of this incessant knocking about the world,—satiated with pleasure, tired of the unending round of excitement and variety of his restless life. It is time he should marry. I wonder he never thinks of that; and I should be glad to resign my seat in Parliament to him. For I am growing old,—yes, seventy years is the allotted time,—and I may go to my darling soon now, very soon." And on the old man's face, as he thus ruminated, broke forth a smile of joyful anticipation, which lit up his fine hazel eyes with a happy light, which was as radiant as any gleam of youth.

And then, having written his letter of summons to Dyke, he carried his *Times* out on the velvet lawn to his favorite seat under the grand old cedars, and plunged into a fresh recital of the horrors which over-shadowed the French nation, from an Englishman's point of view.

The facts were not more garbled than might have been expected. The fall of Sédan, the capture of the Emperor, were supplemented by other reverses which had not yet befallen the doomed people; and the escape of the Empress, in male attire, was announced prematurely, as well as the death of the Imperial Prince. Enthusiastic were the accounts of MacMahon's glorious death on the field of battle, whilst that wily son of the Irish kings, wounded only slightly in the thigh, was quietly nursing his opportune scratch, in strict seclusion, waiting for better days!

That poor General Wimpffen was obliged to shoulder the responsibility of defeat at Sédan, and, crushed by the execrations and reproaches of the nation, resigned his sword, smarting under unmerited disgrace, did in nowise disturb the equanimity with which the "late lamented hero" hearkened to the pæan of praise which sounded throughout the country in his honor.

I doubt if, even in that proudest hour of his triumph, when President Marshal MacMahon, in the grand chapel of Versailles, robed in gorgeous attire, crimson, violet, and gold, amid an assemblage of ministers of war, of the marine, of foreign affairs; of officers in gold lace, and bedecked and bejeweled women (the *élite* of the peerage); while priests in superb vestments swarmed about him, some of whom he crowned with the scarlet hat of the cardinal, under the direction of the Pope of Rome;—I doubt if, even in that moment, a thought of poor Wimpffen's fate crossed the mind dazed by the smile from the Vatican, intoxicated with the adulation of the people, who *but for that fragment of shell would have held him accursed!* And we scoff at *fate!*

That timely wound just saved the quick-witted soldier from delivering up the sword which he had carried on a score of battle-fields, and following the lead of his sovereign to Wilhelmshöhe; saved him from a like obloquy and condemnation to become the instrument for restoring peace, order, property, in the second siege of Paris. Later, when a seven-years' dictatorship was conferred upon him and he held in his hand the destinies of thirty-eight millions of Frenchmen, he blessed the wound which laid him low at Sédan and shielded him from an odium worse than death!

"*Le roi est mort; vive le roi!*" thought Sir Philip, as he concluded the various articles translated from French journals and the editorial in the *Times*, all bearing upon the disasters of their neighbors across the Channel. "The French must always have something to madden themselves about, and now it is '*liberté, égalité, fraternité,*'—three hoots of the night-owl which have never boded aught but evil to France. Down with the Empire! up with the mob! What a country it is to be sure!" And he looked out over the fair fields of grain and soft emerald-green turf, stretching for miles in peaceful beauty below him, and thanked God he was born an Englishman!

The worn-out hackneyism that no two nations are so dissimilar as the Saxon and the Gaul of to-day requires no astuteness to discover its veracity; but during this last frenzied struggle, during the maniacal, suicidal crisis of the *Commune*, England stood aghast, looking on with uncomprehending horror at a display of passion and recklessness for which her phlegmatic temperament held unbounded contempt. Alas! the fair lilies of France have been smirched more than once by the fierce hands of this hot-headed rabble!

The shadows were lengthening when Sir Philip, after a solitary ramble through the park (during which he had stopped to inquire for a disabled game-keeper who had been ill for some weeks, and to say a kindly word to each gardener or dependent whom he chanced to meet; failing not to stroke the yellow curls of the gate-keeper's little one as he passed the lodge), re-entered his comfortable home, greeting all about, only servants though they were, with his genial smile, as was his custom.

And this is the man who has loved and trusted Dyke Faucett; this man with his large, benevolent soul,

> "Whose nature is so far from doing harm
> That he suspects none."

Alas! if he could look into the heart of this moody Dyke, whom we have left so long chewing the cud of his rebellious reflections! Would his faith in human nature ever recover its equilibrium?

So profound is Dyke's reverie that he does not hear the smooth tones of poor Giles's successor, who announces a visitor and then stands motionless.

"Shall I show her up, sir?" he ventures at last, in despair of attracting his master's attention by the slight cough with which he has endeavored to arouse it.

"Show her up? Who? What? Yes, certainly; and ——" Recovering his customary *sang-froid* and languid drawl: "Simpson, take away these things." He pointed to the elaborate gold and silver service which held his unfinished breakfast. In a trice the dexterous servant had removed the tray, placed the still unread letters on the table before his master, and disappeared.

"Confoundedly early hour to make a visit," muttered Dyke, as he glanced complacently in a mirror opposite and arranged a straggling lock of the chestnut hair which had a way of becoming ruffled in his meditative moods. "Can Pauline be so imprudent? These Frenchwomen are so impulsive ! I wonder how she will take the news of my departure?   Ah, '*che sara, sara!*'" he sighed, impatiently, "I am to go back to England, to orthodox respectability, and—to wedlock; no, not that; *I cannot marry*, unless, indeed—— Good God! Dora! You here!" He started back, with face blanched and eyes distended, as through the velvet *portière* passed the fragile figure of a woman, clothed quietly in some dark stuff and with her veil thrown back.

Had a ghost suddenly arisen to confront him, Faucett could not have been more utterly amazed, so firmly had the idea of her death obtained possession in his mind.

Dora, seeming scarcely to observe his agitation, approached the table, and, taking up one of the letters from the pile lying there, said, in a low, sad voice, "So you have not read my letter, Dyke; you did not expect me, then ?"

He wheeled forward a *fauteuil* for her before he replied, in his usual tones, "Expect you? No. How should I expect you—*here?*"

"And yet," she replied, "I *am* here. Strange, is it not, that the woman you left for dead,—the woman you hoped would die,—yes, Dyke" (as he waved his hand impatiently),—"there must be no more dissimulation between us,—the woman you *hoped* would die has conquered death and distance, and obstacles of all kinds, and—and herself? Not for your sake, Dyke, nor for the hope of any possible happiness between us in the future, but for our child's sake ; and for her sake"—she drew herself up proudly, while the soft hazel eyes flashed with sudden fire—"I mean to follow you to the end of the world, until you consent to grant to me the right to bear your name." She ceased, panting slightly, and leaned back in her chair as if exhausted.

"My dear girl," drawled Dyke, "pray spare me another scene; I have not yet recovered from the last. Compose yourself, and we will talk the matter over quietly." He poured some liqueur from a crystal *carafe* standing on a *console* at his elbow, and placed the tiny glass beside Dora. "Calm yourself," he repeated. "Taste this; in the mean time I shall read your letter."

He sank into a chair opposite her and deliberately opened her letter. He read on steadily for a few minutes, gently stroking his long moustache, with no perceptible change of expression.

Those words wrung from her heart might have been the whine of an over-pampered spaniel for all effect they had upon him. Dora, without noticing the cordial at her side, watched Dyke anxiously.

Seen against the violet velvet of the *fauteuil*, her face looked like Parian marble in its transparent purity; the great golden-brown eyes looked larger from the violet shadows beneath them, while the hand from which she had removed her glove was white and blue-veined as the Mareotis lily.

"Ah!" Dyke exclaimed at last, laying down the letter, "so you refuse to allow me to provide for you and the child. Is not your pride running away with your judgment, Dora, my dear?"

She sat up straight now, and leaned a little forward as she said, "Dyke Faucett, were I to accept from your hand now the alms you offer me, would not I go on through all the miserable future a pensioner on your bounty, an unknown, dishonored dependent on the charity of the man who for five long years has deceived me and tampered with my faith in him, and who will deceive and tamper with me to the end of his life? Oh, my Father in heaven!" she cried, piteously, raising her clasped hands, "is there no truth in this man? no honor, no manliness? nothing but the beautiful face, and the bad, cruel heart?" She covered her face with her thin hands and rocked herself to and fro. Dyke Faucett never wasted his eloquence, therefore he sat quite silent until the storm should be past. Her next words almost startled him.

"Dyke, where is the old man—Foster his name was—who married us?"

"Dead, I understand from a recent letter from Rome; he died two years ago," he replied.

"A *recent* letter?" she looked fixedly at him, and then the moan broke forth: "*Dead!* is it not ominous that all connected with that sad ceremony should be dead? Annunziata, my little maid, and the dear old man who loved to talk of his English home to you,—both dead, and only you and I left to tell the story!" A little ghost of a smile rested on the sweet mouth.

"Don't, Dora, don't get pathetic, I beg of you," entreated Dyke; "all that sort of thing does very well on the stage, but in real life, 'pon my soul it's—ridiculous." He opened his cigarette-case and proceeded to roll for himself some little consolation.

Dora looked at him curiously, and then said, "Dyke, do you mean to acknowledge me as your wife? do you mean to begin from to-day to undo all the wrong you have done me and my child? Do you remember our wedding-day, Dyke, five years ago next March?" How passing sweet and mournful her voice grew as she looked back with her eyes full of a wistful sadness on the scene of her marriage, through the "tender light of a day that was dead"!

"What a happy day that was, Dyke," she went on, dreamily. "We were married, you remember, early in the morning, so that we might drive out to Tivoli and spend the whole day there, and come home in the sweet, still evening. Oh, how blue the sky was! and how the birds sang that day! and the scent of the violets will haunt me till I die. And you crowned me with wild-flowers, and made me sing for you; and then you told me of your childhood; your home; your kind guardian. And when I grew sad with the thought of my dear old father, whom I had deceived for the first time in my life that day, how gently you comforted me!—for you loved me then, Dyke; you *did* love me then! And when we came home weary,—but oh, so happy!—hand-in-hand under the silent stars, you kissed me, and bade me go in and tell my father of my happiness. Oh, Dyke, is there nothing in all these memories to stir your heart?"

There was no answer for a moment, and then—

"Your father,—he is well, I hope," said Faucett, courteously; "and," a little nervously,—"the child?"

Dora looking steadily at him saw the hands which were rolling the cigarette tremble a little.

In a moment, before he could move or prevent it, she had thrown herself on her knees at his feet, with her arms about him, and her lovely eyes filled with the luminous glow which made her face look too delicate to hold them.

"Dyke, your hand is trembling. You do care for her,— our little Marian; she is so lovable and beautiful. You cannot, *cannot* tear her from your heart!" Passionate tears rained down, and the slight form bent and swayed like a young tree before the blast; but Dyke Faucett had never, since his birth, sacrificed himself for another, and he did not dream of beginning to learn that lesson now.

Gently he raised and replaced her in her chair, and then,—"Dora, if you have quite done ranting, a thing I utterly detest,—in the worst possible taste,—I will tell you why what you ask of me is impossible—at present." The two last words were almost inaudible, decidedly reluctant. "My guardian, the kindest man alive, is the most obstinate of men on some subjects. I have told you so often before that it seems scarcely reasonable to expect me to repeat it, that my marriage,—particularly a clandestine marriage, during the three years in which I had pledged myself to keep free from entanglements—would bring upon me the insurmountable displeasure of the man upon whom I am completely dependent,—who would undoubtedly disinherit me, for he is not the man to pardon deception, and throw me—at thirty years of age, without profession, without the energy to work—upon my own resources; and you know me well enough, Dora, to know that 'I cannot dig, to beg I am ashamed.' Now," he concluded, "if you will be patient and reasonable, and allow me to make suitable provision for you——"

"Why did you not tell me this before?" she interrupted. "I have heard nothing, until to-day, of your promise to keep yourself free during those three years. Why have you, during all our married life, promised, from month to month, from year to year, to take me home with you to England, and lift from my heart and head the burden of a shame which is not mine? And now there is no talk of next month, or next year, but an indefinite waiting for another man's death. And in the mean time I may die; I am not strong, you know; and there is Marian,—is she, my spotless lily, to grow up to womanhood with such a stain as this upon her? Dyke, do you imagine that I will endure this? Do you think that because I have been patient in the past—as long as I had a shred of trust in you to cling to—I will be forbearing in the future? Undeceive yourself; the time will come when the vow of secrecy you extorted from me five years ago shall be broken,—when, for my child's sake, I shall denounce the man who has treacherously forsaken me,—the man who is too cowardly to tell me the whole truth,—which is, that he has ceased to love me,—the toy has lost its charm, the flower has faded in his hand ; it is but one more poor, withered weed, to be flung aside when such flowers as this, and this" (laying down before him two exquisitely painted miniatures of celebrated beauties of the day), "bloom near his hand. Ah, Dyke, I am not jealous of these beautiful women ; I can only *pity* them if they love *you.*"

Faucett took up the pictures and carefully replaced them on the cheffonnier, and resuming his seat, said, irrelevantly, "You should leave Paris, Dora, and return to Tours ; it will not be safe for you here. *I* leave for England to-morrow night."

Her face grew troubled. "Will Paris be besieged?" she asked.

"Assuredly." ·

"Then I shall go. It would be terrible for my father, —he is very feeble now,—and for Marian. Ah, I have left them too long, now ; I must go at once."

With nervous haste she gathered up parasol and gloves. Then she came quietly to his side and said, with winning gentleness, "Dyke, I *will* be patient; I will wait until you have seen and talked with your guardian ; I will wait one month from to day, and"—her voice grew firmer here—"if you do not then send, or come for me, I shall stand up and proclaim myself your wife, my Marian your child, in the face of the whole world."

His face hardened into stone; a slight sneer disfigured the beautiful mouth: "I had hoped you had done with histrionics, Dora, when you perceived how utterly they failed with me; and now, as you have seen fit to threaten me, may I ask *how you mean to prove the truth of your assertions in regard to our marriage ?*"

His voice was quite as sweet and low as when, under the sunny skies of Italy, he had wooed her with loving words and promises; and, for the credit of human nature, let us believe that this was merely said as a taunt; but it struck like a sharp knife into the already bleeding heart of the woman before him.

"Do you, then, deny me?" she cried, in a voice faint with pain. "Is this your plan,—to cast me utterly away? Oh, my child! my child!" And groping with her hands before her, like one suddenly struck blind, she passed away out of his sight.

A drizzling rain was falling, as she emerged from the *porte-cochère* and turned her steps mechanically towards the Rue de Rivoli, faint and giddy with the blow which had not been unforeseen, but which had fallen none the less heavily for that.

CHAPTER III.

HEEDLESS of the shower, Dora moved slowly along the Rue Royale, seeing nothing, hearing nothing,—numb with pain,—until, as she turned into the Rue de Rivoli, a horrible noise aroused her, and she became conscious of a shouting, surging, excited mass of human beings, bearing down upon her from an opposite direction, gesticulating wildly, brandishing clubs, armed with stones, shrieking imprecations, dragging along in mad fury an almost insensible wretch, whom they suspected, justly or unjustly, of being a spy. "To the Seine! to the Seine!

Shoot him! Drown him! Chien de Prussien! Vive la République!" A piping voice: "Vive Trochu!" A stentorian voice: "Down with Trochu!" etc., etc.

Dora hesitated, turned to fly, and encountered a band of five hundred "Gardes Nationales" marching to join their comrades on the Place Vendôme, with colors flying and drums beating, and supported by the usual accompaniment of blue blouses and ragged *gamins*.

In a moment they would be upon her. Stunned, deafened, wild with terror, she darted hither and thither among the maddened crowd, when suddenly her foot slipped on the wet pavement, and she went down, down under the brutal feet of a French mob.

Fortunately, the cry, "A woman! a woman! is she killed? is she hurt?" created a diversion, and caused a momentary lull, while a pair of stout arms drew her forth bruised, bleeding, inanimate, as if truly dead. Holding her cradled in his brawny arms, the man, wearing the blouse of the *ouvrier*, elbowed his way out of the crowd, already dispersing before the advance of the National Guard.

He glanced at the white face, with its closed eyes, and the long lashes lying on the waxen cheek, and at the thin crimson thread of blood which issued from between her pale lips, and a thrill passed over the giant frame of the strong man, who a moment ago was hounding a fellow-creature to the death. "My God!" he muttered, "*she is dead*, and *I trod on her!*"

He darted with her into an open door of a pâtisserie at the corner of the Rue de Rivoli and the Rue Royale. The shop was deserted; but, without releasing his burden, he, with his elbow, pushed towards the edge of the counter a huge glass jar of *marrons glacés*, and let it fall with a crash on the marble tiles beneath.

"Ah, mon Dieu! what is this? are the Prussians in

Paris? are we all to be murdered in cold blood?" screamed a woman's voice at the head of the staircase opening into the shop.

The workman needed no further invitation; gently, very slowly, he mounted the stair, guarding Dora's head and limbs from contact with any object which might jar her. The shrieks redoubled, and were echoed by infantile voices in the shrill treble of frantic fear.

"Ah, what cowards you are, all of you!" panted the *ouvrier*, depositing his burden tenderly on the nearest bed; "and you call yourselves Frenchwomen! Sacre-bleu! you are not the women of the last Revolution! Is there anything in that dead girl to terrify you so?" He pointed to the insensible form; and the frightened women, who had covered their eyes awaiting the final shot, removed their hands and ventured to approach the bed. The children ceased their wailing, and crept on tip-toe to their mothers' sides.

"Ciel! comme elle est pâle! Is she dead, do you think, Ernestine?" asked the younger of the two women.

"God knows," answered the other, who was busily occupied in taking off the crushed bonnet and loosening the fastenings of her dress. "Marie, run to No. 10 Rue St. Honoré and send Dr. Dubois here—if he should chance to be at home—immediately,—fly!"

"Oh, I dare not, Ernestine; I am afraid to go into the streets to-day! There are great doings at the Hôtel de Ville, and they say there will be trouble before night, and——"

"Bah!" interrupted the workman. "Where is this doctor? I will fetch him, whether he will or no. What number did you say?" He was off like a shot.

Meanwhile, Ernestine was sponging with cold water the poor, soiled face, and sprinkling cologne over the hands and head. Marie was busy in preparing a glass of eau sucré and orange-water, to be ready on the recovery of the patient, that concoction being considered a specific by the Parisian for every ill that flesh is heir to.

Presently there was a struggling sigh, a gasp for breath, and Dora opened her eyes, and closed them again instantly with a shudder.

"Elle est encore évanouie," whispered Marie, approaching with her eau d'orange. "Oh, elle va mourir; ah, mon Dieu, comme elle est jeune et belle, et quelles petites mains qu'elle a! et quels pieds, ceux sont des pieds d'enfant, véritablement!"

"Ah, taisez-vous donc, Marie; elle revient."

Again the white lids unclose, and the eyes, gazing into Ernestine's good, homely Breton face, ask mutely, "Where am I?"

"You are safe, mon enfant," answered the good women, in a breath; "lie still, the doctor will be here presently, and you must not move until he comes."

"But have I been ill?" she whispered in English; "and Marian, where is she,—oh, where is she?"

"Tiens! c'est une Anglaise," pronounced Marie. "Mamselle no spick Franch?" she asked.

(The pâtisserie window below boasted a card, "Ici on parle Anglais!")

"Oui, oui," answered Dora; and then eagerly, in their own tongue, she prayed to be taken home at once to her child,—her old father,—who knew not what had become of her.

"Mais oui, certainement; you sall come back to the house,—bientôt,—de suite—when M. le Docteur say. Tenez, Mamselle, buvez donc, une toute petite goutte!" She attempted to raise Dora's head, but a cry of pain arrested her.

"My shoulder! it is broken; it is out of place," moaned she, and then lay still with closed eyes.

Heavy footsteps on the stairs announced the return of the *ouvrier.*

"He has gone, your doctor; escaped yesterday to Boulogne; afraid of his skin; and I have not been able to find another. What can be done? Has she spoken?"

"Ah, yes," replied Ernestine, gravely, "but I fear she is very badly hurt; her shoulder seems displaced; some brute must have put his foot on her!"

He shuddered. "It may be she fell in the crowd, and we were punishing ce pauvre diable Müller, so we had not time to be gallant;" he smiled grimly, and then said, sadly, "There will be many such scenes before these troubles are over. The streets are full of madmen now, and I have promised to meet some friends at the Café du Rhin, for to-morrow I am to be enrolled in the National Guard,—Jacques Toquelet, at your service!"—with a military salute and a smile.

"Oh, *mon ami,*" sighed the woman, "you smile brightly to-day, and to-morrow, perhaps, you may lie as she lies now" (pointing to the bed). "Where is this to end? Is Trochu a fool or a coward, that he accepts not the wish of the people?"

"Both, I fear," he replied. "The fact is, madame," drawing nearer and speaking in a tone of conviction, "the people don't know what they want; they have tasted blood, and they are mad. Trochu was the idol of the hour, but he is not the man to save Paris, unless, indeed, he goes with us of the National Guard. What think you, *ma petite dame,* would he accept the command of the National Guard?"

"Ah, monsieur, do not jest; one cannot laugh with the

heart full of tears. If the Prussians invest Paris shall we not all be slaughtered?"

"*Mille tonnerres! mais non, madame.* Can you breathe such a thought while Jacques Toquelet and thousands of other brave hearts remain to defend you? Let them come (*sacrés chiens qu'ils sont*), they shall not wear out our courage or endurance, and before we yield one inch of our France to the *cochons d'Allemands*, we will not leave one heart beating, or one stone upon another, in our Paris! Do not fear, madame: we have met with some reverses, but a Frenchman never stays beaten."

All this time the poor woman, deriving little consolation from her companion's contradictory assurances, stood close to the window, peering anxiously into the street.

"You don't happen to know my good man," she asked, —"Louis Picot, do you? He has not been in since early morning, when he went with a party to the Place of the Hôtel de Ville, to hear what news from the Assembly. I fear much he has come to harm."

"I regret that I do not know him, madame; should I meet him in the future, I shall do him a service if I can; in the mean time you must not torment yourself with forebodings; as I tell my little ones at home: 'never cry unless your heads are off.'"

"Monsieur," came in a feeble voice from the bed.

He darted to the side of the suffering woman. "Monsieur, I want to thank you," Dora said, and put out a tiny hand which lay like a pearl in the oyster-shell of his great brown palm; "you have saved me from a terrible death, and life is very precious to me, for I have a little daughter, sir. I heard you speak just now of your children: you can then feel for me. Take me home, I implore you. See, it is growing late in the afternoon, and

E*

I *must* go now." She ceased, panting from exhaustion, and the man answered her, promptly,—

"You shall go, instantly, the moment I get a fiacre to the door. I will carry you down, and this good little woman will go with you." He pointed to Marie, who sat pale and trembling in a distant corner. As he disappeared in search of a carriage, she took the children by each hand, and vanished, to be seen no more that day.

In great agony, but without a groan, Dora submitted gladly to being carried down-stairs and seated in the fiacre with Ernestine's kind arms supporting her. Jacques Toquelet, postponing his engagement at the Café du Rhin indefinitely, leaped upon the box as they started.

Dora had just time to slip her purse into Ernestine's hand before she became once more insensible.

At the same hour that the sorry vehicle which held the inanimate form of the woman he had vowed to love and cherish dragged at a snail's pace its weary way over the Seine to the Latin quarter, Dyke Fancett, "curled and oiled" in a way that would have astonished the "Assyrian bull" of scented memory, in faultless attire and most complacent mood, dropped into the magnificent salons of Madame la Marquise de Courboisie, who had secured him weeks ago by a dinner invitation for this evening.

In this princely suite of rooms, dazzlingly lighted by myriads of wax candles, where all that art and taste and wealth could contribute to form a whole gratifying to the senses; in the laughing Pauline herself, a charming brunette, with the air of an empress and the fascination of a siren,—or a Frenchwoman,—one failed to realize the peril and anguish upon the brink of which Paris tottered. The Faubourg St. Germain seemed as far removed from all these horrors as—the moon,—and, after the exquisite dinner, the other guests dropped away one by one to fulfill various engagements, and Dyke, finding himself in the cool, dreamy, green light of the conservatory, with the music of splashing fountains in his ear, and the velvet eyes of Pauline raised with well-counterfeited tenderness in their depths to his, broke to her the news of his departure on the morrow.

No scene greeted the disclosure: she was too *grande dame* for any exhibition of that description. She merely crushed her great tortoise-shell fan in her small hand tightly enough to break one or two of its carved sticks silently, and then smiled up in his face, just enough to show the white, even pearls between her red lips, and said, sweetly, "Ah, you think to escape me thus, *chéri*, and to leave me desolate in this poor, stricken Paris, do you, *méchant?* I have half a mind not to tell you of *our* plans, and to say *adieu* to-night in place of *au plaisir.*"

"Can it be possible, Pauline, for you to be serious for one moment? This parting is too sorrowful a thing to me to be a subject of mockery to you."

"*Point de badinage, chéri.* I am as solemn as an owl. We go to England—to your *triste* London—to-morrow night. *Est-ce que tu vas me bouder à présent, ingrat?*"

"And M. le Marquis—he remains in Paris?"

"*Sans doute;* he must remain to protect the aristocracy; but I shall have a chaperone; the old Duchesse de Languedoc resides in London, and I shall take *la petite*, and nearly all my servants. Imagine me with a dozen of your English 'flunkeys' about me." She laughed merrily,—not a trace of ill-humor about her. What a contrast to that fiery little Puritan, Dora!

And yet, when about midnight the bewitching Pauline retired to her sleeping-apartment, and gave in sudden, sharp sentences her orders for the unexpected flight on the following evening, poor Célestine could tell a different story of her mistress's amiability.

Surely among these lowly hand-maidens there are many "martyrs by the pang, without the palm."

That night's mail to England carried the following letter :

"To Sir Philip Standley, Bart., Ellingham Hall, Kent.

"My dear Sir Philip,—The fiat has gone forth; who shall gainsay it? You have commanded my return to England in requesting it.

" In my ready acquiescence, pray accept the gratitude of my heart, which I cannot otherwise express, for your inexhaustible goodness towards me. Pardon me, however, if I confess that your suggestions of a wife for me are less alluring than the prospect of the siege. As to marriage, I hold but one opinion: it is a necessary evil where an heir is indispensable, but I sympathize with the Athenians when they held but one impracticable desire in the zenith of their power, and cried out, 'Ah, if we could but have children—*without women!*'

" I leave Paris to-morrow night, and shall go at once to Ellingham.

"Always affectionately yours,

"Dyke Faucett."

"Rue Royale, Paris, Sept. 4, '70."

After Dyke Faucett had dispatched this epistle, and sundry other notes of farewell to friends in Paris, he lounged an hour away with his favorite cheroot, reviewing the events of the day. His memory passed swiftly over the unwelcome letter to which he had just replied, and the still more unwelcome visitor who had well-nigh upset his nerves for the rest of the day, and dwelt long and lovingly over the unequivocal demonstration of devotion he had read in the suddenly-developed plan of the beautiful marquise. She had not deceived him; their natures were too sympathetic for any by-play to escape unnoticed. They were equally selfish, and equally unscrupulous; but they were both too high-bred to deal in the common emotions of humanity—outwardly. If their hands were clinched sometimes in irrepressible passion, be sure they were *bien gantées* and the nails never pierced the tender flesh.

Dyke Faucett's slumbers that night were peaceful as a babe's.

Nemesis is ofttimes a laggard in our finite judgments; it is, however, a comfort to reflect that although "*the mills of the gods grind slowly, they grind exceeding small.*"

CHAPTER IV.

PARIS, like the wily Ulysses, "fertile in devices," gathered together from all parts of the world the gay, the frivolous, the learned curious, and—the curious unlearned.

To the average Frenchman, a life that is not *débonnaire* presents a foretaste of purgatory, which his *poco-curante* philosophy does not impel him to anticipate, even when engaged in the sterner work requiring a self-abstraction inconsistent with frivolity. Still, there have been presented specimens of intellectual development in the volatile Gaul which have long won the admiration of their insular neighbors, who are not too over-blown with national prejudices to acknowledge the fact, and to transport their inflated intelligences over the narrow seas to reap what benefits there might be found ripe for the plucking.

Of all the French schools of science, none occupy a higher position than that of medicine.

To the Hôtel Dieu, one of God's own mansions on earth, flocked the disciples of the healing art of all nations, that the talents which had been given them should not rot undeveloped, and, wrapped in the napkin of a supine ignorance, fail to expand under the generative sun of a world-wide experience.

Among the others, came Ronald Buchanan, who, for two years, had imbibed deep draughts from this well of pathology (whose depths, alas! are fathomless), with which he hoped to strengthen the backbone of his future prospects—dependent entirely upon persevering exertion—and establish himself in the not-altogether congenial career of a surgeon in his native land.　However, he was a man who, after once putting his hand to the plow, looked not back.

There was an atmosphere of force about him which impressed all who came in contact with him,—in the clean-cut face there was not a vestige of weakness; and in the eyes,—gray eyes, with the brown iris which could soften into such tenderness at times,—well set under dark, straight brows, which gave a decisive tone to the face when considered in connection with the firm lines of a chin too square for other beauty than that of strength,— one could read the honesty of purpose, the unflinching truthfulness of the man's character.

And yet the mouth was the most expressive feature of a face never to be forgotten in love or anger.

There was singular sweetness in the rare smile, which disclosed perfect rows of white teeth beneath the unbearded lip; but when the Scotch blood in his veins was kindled to wrath by cowardly act, or sense of injustice done, the mouth lost its gentle curves, and in straight lines pointed to retribution.

Such was the head, borne upon strong, square shoulders, and proportionate length of body and limb, which ascended with bounding leaps the flight of stone steps which led to his modest quarters, *au cinquième,* in the Rue de Vaugirard of the Quartier Latin.

"Qu'on est bien à vingt ans," he shouted, in far from unmusical voice, which was immediately subdued as he remembered how harshly sounds of mirth might strike upon some troubled heart in his vicinity. Opening the door with his pass-key, he rapidly divested himself of coat and hat, and, slipping into a dressing-gown worn into comfortable creases, he proceeded to fill a pipe and settle himself down to meditation. There was a knotty point to be argued, and he had left it until after his frugal dinner of three courses and sour wine, that he might take his "familiar," the deep-colored meerschaum of years, into counsel.

It was the question which had vexed the minds of half Paris for weeks, and which now, so far as he was concerned, must be definitely decided.

Should he return to England, to the dear old parsonage, where his happy-hearted sisters made so bright a home for him, and where his reverend father, a hale, ruddy-faced, jovial-hearted Christian, expounded the Scriptures according to his lights through their cheeriest messages of "peace and good will towards men"? Or should he remain in the unhappy city, where there would soon be earnest work for him to do among the suffering and wounded, the helpless and the weak?

The parson's quiver is proverbially full, and the little parsonage had long since overflowed.

The eldest of four sons had, through the influence of a relative, obtained a commission in Her Majesty's service, and had been some years in India. The second was glad to accept a lucrative position in a large house in Bombay. The third is our Ronald, and the fourth, still a boy at school.

Of the four sisters, three were rosy-faced, flaxen-haired, jolly girls, with little distinguishing characteristics, all turned out of the same mould. The fourth, the eldest of the family, a dark-haired, gray-eyed, thoughtful woman, with much of Ronald's strength, tempered by a most angelic sweetness in her face.

It was Lydia who, fourteen years ago, just in the budding beauty of womanhood, took the tiny week-old infant from her dying mother's arms and vowed to consecrate to it, and the others, who were so soon in helpless childhood to be left motherless, the life which stretched out before her so full of fairer promise. For it was only a week ago on that sad, never-to-be-forgotten day, that she had pledged her faith to the young curate, who, wishing to add the crowning jewel to a beautiful life full of good works, had won as helpmeet a woman such as this, who found strength to renounce happiness, and find blessedness in taking upon her young shoulders the burden of another.

And after the promise had been spoken and sealed by a kiss upon the clay-cold lips which could never kiss again, there was no wavering, nor shadow of turning away from the self-imposed duty which the steadfast eyes saw before them in the dim, future years.

Had Paul Wyngate resented the decision of his betrothed, or added by useless repinings to the bitterness of her pain, when she drew from her slender hand the ring he had placed there so short a time before, and sorrowfully but firmly freed him from his troth, he would have simply ceased to be the man she loved above all else on earth.

But he never for a moment doubted the noble heart he had learned to know so truly, and his voice was full of love and faith as he said, gently, " Put the ring on again, my darling ; we need not love each other less if we must wait a little longer before you come to me forever."

" But, Paul," she murmured, " it may be years, ten, fifteen years, before I can leave them, and your life must not be blighted by an almost hopeless waiting."

" It shall never be hopeless, please God, as long as you and I live, Lydia," he answered, with a sweet earnestness which filled her with joy inexpressible even in that sad hour. And, as he replaced the plain golden circlet on her finger, she felt strong to walk erect in the path which she had chosen, and which would never now be the lonely one she feared.

All through those fourteen years—since she first, with a new, sudden-born dignity, stepped into the mother's vacant place—had Lydia found comfort, sympathy, counsel in the faithful friend, who bided his time in patience, uncomplaining.

Little Robert lived and throve ; and when the puny, wailing babe had, under her cherishing care, grown into the strong, hardy lad, who looked up with reverential devotion to the sister-mother of the household ; when the three oldest boys had gone forth to fight the battle of life, each girt with the breast-plate of her gentle teachings ; when the fair young sisters had bloomed into maidenhood, —Grace and Edith and little Jean, the pet of her father, " a wee bit *genty*-looking bairn, with a face no to be forgotten, though I couldna say it was bonnie," as he was wont to describe her in one of those moments of rare feeling, when he always instinctively found expression in the dear, almost forgotten, dialect of his childhood in the old Scottish manse,—then Lydia felt that her task was done, and that the rest and joy which she had promised Paul and herself so many years ago, was won.

There are some silver threads through Paul's dark locks, and the bloom on Lydia's cheek has faded, but in the eyes of both there dwells a light reflected from the peace which passeth understanding.

They are to be married very soon. Paul has a little parsonage of his own now, and Ronald has promised to come home for the wedding.

CHAPTER V.

His pipe had gone out, and still the young surgeon sat leaning, with folded arms, on the window-sill, gazing out in the fast deepening September twilight into the street beneath,—where knots of students and the blue-shirted autocracy of the quarter were gathered together in excited discussion,—or, over the way, at the row of high, narrow houses, with their numerous open windows, very interrogation-points to a speculative curiosity. But his thoughts were far away; he was picturing to himself an *intérieure* of English home comfort, in which a good deal of carpet, and an extravagant open fire, good solid mahogany furniture, and better solid rounds of beef, were prominent features, in striking contrast to the gilt rococo style of Parisian *ameublement*, and the eternal *made-dishes* of which the Briton of the true type soon wearies.

The kindly welcome shining out of his father's genial blue eyes, the wholesome, somewhat boisterous, jollity of the girls, above all, the sweet, tender, more quiet greeting of Lydia, wooed him irresistibly. He determined to return to them, but first he would just step around to the Café du Midi and hear what the prospects were of a quiet night. Resuming his coat, and taking his hat and a stout stick, he sallied forth.

He had not proceeded far, when his attention was attracted by the sound of low moans, which seemed to issue from the inside of a fiacre, drawn up in front of a house nearly opposite his own quarters. Several men and women were collected about the open door of the carriage, apparently disputing as to the best means of extricating a helpless sufferer within.

With one or two strides Ronald reached the group, and, with one or two decisive words, sent the disputatious inefficients to the right-about, saying, simply, to a white-haired old gentleman who stood wringing his hands in impotent distress, "Je suis chirurgien, monsieur."

"Ah, thank God!" burst from the old man's lips.

"And," McDonald added in English, "if you will go before and lead the way, I will soon carry this poor child up for you."

"Where does she seem to be most hurt?" he asked of Ernestine, who still sat in the carriage supporting Dora in her arms. (Jacques Toquelet had not been able to resist rushing to the aid of a brother-in-arms, who was being overpowered by numbers on the Pont-Neuf as they were crossing.)

"I think, sir," answered Ernestine, "her shoulder is out of place and her arm injured."

"Sit quite still, then," he directed, "and hold her shoulders as firmly and gently as possible."

He passed his arm under her, and, with an immense effort of strength, drew her forth without more movement than was indispensable. Then, preceded by the old father carrying a light, and followed by Ernestine, he mounted four flights of stairs, and laid poor Dora softly down on the spotless white-curtained bed in her own neat little room; a room which, even in that first moment of entering it, seemed to impress itself upon Ronald's imagination the childlike innocence and purity of its occupants. There, in a tiny cot, lay the slumbering Marian, not yet undressed, but with tumbled hair and flushed cheeks, in the unconscious grace of sleeping childhood. She had cried herself to sleep an hour ago, poor little tot, when mamma failed to come, according to promise, before dinner, and grandpapa had not been able to invent answers to her ceaseless questions with sufficient rapidity.

"Bring more lights," commanded Buchanan; "and," to Ernestine, "will you procure a pair of scissors, please, at once?" She disappeared; returning immediately with the desired implement.

After he had cut away the dress from the arms and shoulders, he found that the collar-bone was broken and that she was much bruised, but there was no other injury. He ordered Ernestine to lock the door and permit no one to enter (the old father stood at the foot of the bed, motionless), until he could go in search of necessary bandages, etc.

In a moment he had reached his own room, supplied himself with all he required,—including a small flask of very fine brandy,—and returned to his patient. First pouring out a little of the brandy in a glass, he, with a spoon, obliged her to take a few drops at a time until she began to revive again. He then set the bone, bandaged and made her perfectly comfortable, with a dexterity which proved his excellent instruction.

"Une toute petite tasse de bouillon à present," he whispered to Ernestine, who stood by with ready hand and sparkling eyes, watching his every movement with undisguised admiration. She flew to do his bidding, and when she returned with a bowl of delicate soup, Ronald sat on the edge of the bed and fed the rapidly-recovering Dora with spoonfuls of the nourishing beverage. As the last mouthful was administered he asked, with the rarely sweet smile softening his grave face, "Should you like to kiss baby now and go to sleep?"

Ernestine had taken up the little one and inducted her into her little night-gown, and washed the hands and face, and brushed the untidy hair, and was now talking in a subdued whisper to her in a distant corner.

"Oui, chérie, tu vas voir maman tout de suite; elle est là-bas couchée, vois-tu, et si tu es sage, bien sage, tu vas l'embrasser avant de dormir."

A grateful smile broke over Dora's pale face at the thoughtful suggestion of the young surgeon.

"Bring the child, *ma fille; viens, petite, maman*-cannot sleep until she kisses you; gently now, gently; don't move."

He took the little white-robed cherub in his arms and, bending over the bed, allowed the child to kiss and fondle her mother without leaning on her. Tears of delight filled the beautiful hazel eyes.

"Assez, assez," cried the young man. "Couchez-la bien vite, mademoiselle," and he restored her to Ernestine's arms, who replaced her in her cot drawn up close to the other side of the bed.

Then, with a quiet "Good-evening, madame, I will see you in the morning," and a bow to the old gentleman, Ronald departed; but not to the Café du Midi; back to his den *au cinquième*, to indite a few lines to Lydia. In half a dozen concise sentences he informed her that it would be impossible for him to leave Paris before the siege. "Only one thing could deprive me of the pleasure of witnessing your well-earned happiness, my dearest sister," he wrote, "and that is a conviction of the absolute necessity of my remaining here. Fate has decided the question; there is work for me to do here, and no other hand to do it, and I must stay. Some day, please God, I shall tell you all about it; for the present, believe that my heart is with you. Love to my father and the girls; as to Paul—he is too happy to need a message from your brother, RONALD BUCHANAN."

In passing out of the opposite house that night, Ronald had exchanged a few words with the porteress which materially assisted in forming his decision.

"Ah, monsieur," began the voluble old woman, "what a misfortune for the poor lady up-stairs! So sweet she is, too,—a veritable angel I assure you, monsieur; so kind to everybody, with such a gentle way with her, and——"

"Who is she?" interrupted Ronald. "What does she call herself?"

"I know not, monsieur; the old gentleman her father's name is Fairfax."

"And her husband, where is he?" asked Ronald.

The old woman shrugged her shoulders and looked wicked. "Ah, I have not seen him; the husband of a beautiful English girl with such a grand air about her don't bring her to the Latin quarter; and she does not wear the English mourning of the widow; but the little child is hers (*Ah quel ange cette petite!*); and she seems quite quiet and respectable; sees no company, monsieur; and never goes out without the child and *le vieux*, until this unhappy day, when she started early in the morning alone, and came back this evening; thus——"

"And her father,"—Ronald hesitated, and then resumed, "does he seem to have means? her room was very small."

"*Ah, mon Dieu!*" began the old woman, "they are poor, for I have seen the young lady painting pictures in her room, which they take away afterwards, I am sure, to sell; and I have got her lace to mend, too, for *les grandes dames*, who have now all gone out of *ce pauvre* Paris."

Slipping a napoleon in her hand and adjuring her to let the lady want nothing that could be procured, Ronald waited to hear no more.

His mind was made up: he would stay.

CHAPTER VI.

THE next morning dawned bright and clear; and as Ronald Buchanan took his early breakfast of rolls and coffee at the Café Henri Quatre, he gathered from the eager voices about him an indication of the turmoil which the events of yesterday had stirred in the heart of Paris.

Perceiving at a distant table a confrère of the knife, also an Englishman, he gathered up his *Journal Officiel* and made his way through the vociferous throng to his side.

"Ah, good-day to you, my dear fellow," joyfully exclaimed Richard Ogilvie, rising and drawing a chair to the table for his friend. "'Gad, it's as good as a bottle of champagne to a thirsty soul to see your face here still; I thought you meant to get back to the paternal rooftree."

"I have changed my mind, Dick, and intend to stay and see how you bear starvation. You remain, do you not?"

"Of course; wouldn't miss it for the world; it's just the sort of thing for a man to look back upon and yarn about to his grandchildren, you see; and, *du reste*, if harm comes to me, who cares?" This with a pathetic sigh and a comically lugubrious expression, which made Ronald smile.

"What *have* you been doing with yourself, Dick? You have not been at the hospitals for days. Are you growing lazy in your old age?"

"Not I; I have had 'other fish to fry.'" He helped himself to another *rognon aux champignons*, and Ronald asked, "What do you mean to do, Dick? The siege seems inevitable before long, and then Heaven knows what comes next on the programme. At all events, there will be plenty of wounds to dress and limbs to amputate."

"No doubt, dear old boy; but I don't propose to dress any limbs but my own, or amputate any—wounds," cried Dick, confusedly, beckoning to the garçon to settle his bill. "I want to fight, and I *will* fight,—National Guard, Mobiles,—anything, so that I can see the fun; (four francs fifty centimes for a breakfast, and the siege imminent: what do you think of that, you old anchorite?)—here!" spinning almost his last five-franc piece to the obsequious garçon. "Yes," he concluded, "there's time enough for the sawbones when I go back to England,—if I ever do go back" (another plaintive sigh); "one don't meet a chance like this often, and I have had some experience, you know" (he was captain of a militia company at home).

"I am sorry, Dick, very sorry," answered his friend;

"we will not meet often, I fear; and I had quite counted on you as a *collaborateur*, for I mean to do the good Samaritan,—though your prospect *does* look tempting!" This with the genuine sigh of the Briton when he renounces, of his free will, the belligerent anticipations which are so seductive to his nation.

"Not meet often? What can you mean? You are not going into a monastery, are you? And I am certainly not intent upon being riddled by the first fire. Now see here, old man, we will make a standing engagement to dine here every day together, at six o'clock, and recount our adventures. Have you any money?"

"A little. I never have very much, you remember."

"Yes, I remember; and I also bear somewhere in my memory the fact that I rarely have *any*,—but I'll share it with you to the last penny, Ronald, my boy; I will, indeed," quite gravely.

"Thanks; I am sure you would," replied Ronald, with equal gravity.

"I say," burst out Dick, "it's almost too early in the day for champagne, isn't it? but I *should* like to crack a bottle with you later,—I have a napoleon somewhere at home,—just in honor of this joyful surprise you brought me. Really," seizing Ronald's hand and shaking it again vehemently, while every feature of his face beamed with good nature, "this is very jolly, isn't it?"

"Calm yourself, my dear fellow; we will dine here together at six, and you shall have your bottle;—but in the mean time be reasonable. The news to-day is gloomy enough, and there seems to be no little excitement in the streets."

"Oh, it's all *rot*," pronounced Dick. "There was a mob outside the Hôtel de Ville at midnight,—and for what? Because these idiots cannot understand that

Trochu and the other fellow—the war-minister, Palikao—will not undertake the salvation of the city according to *their* judgments; who would? If Wellington, George Washington, and the first Napoleon united in one effort to save Paris, these fools would circumvent them, and destroy it in the way which pleased them best."

"Don't be *too* hard on them, Dick; they can't help it; it's in the blood. They do not understand; and not understanding, they fear; and fearing, they become furious——" ("And furious, they become fiends," interpolated Dick). "Why, early as it is, Belleville and Mont-Martre are pouring their incendiary rabble through all Paris, stirring up the people by the irresistible contagion of their example,—vowing vengeance upon whom, or what, I have not been able to find out."

"Nor you won't be, either; they don't know themselves. They will surround the hall of the Corps Légis-latif and yell their menaces and shout their maledictions, which fall equally on Napoleon and Trochu,—on the Germans and the French army,—on all and everything under the sun,—and then they will shake their fists at the façade of the Hôtel de Ville, and commence again *da capo;* but if they were frankly asked what they demanded, they would only glare at you and howl out their favorite meaningless threat, '*Déchéance!*'"

By this time the café was deserted; everybody having breakfasted and delivered himself of a separate opinion on the condition of things, had gone out to gather fresh subjects for argument before the dinner-hour.

Our two friends separated after a few more words and a renewal of the promise to meet at six o'clock, Ronald making his way back to the old city, and Dick going towards the head-quarters of the National Guards.

As Ronald mounted the staircase leading to the room

where he had left Dora sinking into tranquil slumber the night before, he felt a curious sensation of delight and timidity which was new to him. Indeed, the sweet face and gentle voice had not been absent from his mind, sleeping or waking, during many minutes since he had closed the door between them and himself.

He hesitated a moment at the door, overcome by a strange repugnance, but with an impatient " Bah !" at his unwonted weakness, he knocked gently. The figure of a young woman in the garb of a Sister of Charity, with the white-winged cap of the order upon her head, appeared at the opening. "Monsieur le Docteur?" she asked, softly.

"Oui, *ma sœur*," replied Ronald, to whom the apparition was a familiar one in the hospitals.

"Entrez donc, je vous en prie," she whispered. "Madame est très-souffrante : she has fever, you see, and is quite out of her head."

He approached the bed and looked at her a moment, silently. How beautiful she was, lying with her head thrown back, and the masses of chestnut hair flung loosely over the pillows, with a deep carmine glow in the cheeks and parted lips, and the exquisite eyes brilliant with fever ! She was not lying comfortably, but he dared not touch her.

"Raise her, *ma sœur*, her head is too much thrown back ;" and as she obeyed him, he continued : "When did this fever come on,—how long ago ?"

"About midnight, sir," she answered. "I came home and found my poor friend (for we have been friends, sir, for three months), last evening, about eight o'clock (just after you left her), in such sad plight, and heard of her terrible accident (she was asleep, but a good woman, a Madame Picot, I think it was, told me the particulars), and also that she was obliged to return home for the night, and begged me to watch with this poor child. Of course I consented. I have not worn this dress many days, monsieur, but this is not my first experience in nursing. I shall not leave her, with your permission, until she is quite well again.'' He could not resist taking her hand in his. I think if it had not been for that inconvenient *coif* he would have kissed her in his gratitude.

"Thank you, *ma sœur*, you are an angel of goodness; that poor soul seemed utterly friendless and forsaken.'' He looked narrowly at her; something in her accent had struck upon his acute ear. "Pardon me, but are you *française?*'' he asked.

"No, monsieur; my mother was English, and,'' whispering, with a glance around, as if afraid, "my father was *a German.* They are both dead;'' and she added, simply, "my name is Agnes.''

He was writing a prescription, but looked up here, and said, "You speak English, then, do you not? That will be a great comfort to this poor girl during her illness.''

"Oh, yes,'' she replied, "I always spoke it as a child; but,'' she continued, anxiously, "you do not think there in any danger of serious illness, do you, doctor?''

"I cannot tell yet; I fear there is some nervous trouble. Has she had a shock of any kind, other than her accident? The brain, I am afraid, is affected.''

"Nothing that I know of, sir; she seemed always very sad and quiet, and I know nothing of her history; I only know that she is the very sweetest, purest-hearted woman in the world, and that I love her dearly.'' Tears stood in the bright blue eyes, and the firm lips trembled. She bent over the bed and wet the parched mouth of her friend with some cooling *tisane* to hide her unwonted agitation.

"Will you see that this prescription is filled at once, please?'' He handed her a paper, and she left the room.

Ronald walked to the window and looked out. Opposite he could see the casement at which he had sat dreaming the evening before; how long ago it seemed! He could scarcely believe it possible that such a revolution could take place in a human being in such a trifling space of time. What was it? What was this new life which seemed to course through his veins like liquid fire? He felt suffocated; the window was open, and he leaned out as far as possible in the vain endeavor to breathe more freely.

What had come to him? He, the earnest student, the unimpressionable, methodical, frugal-minded philosopher, the man who had lived two years in the Latin quarter in Paris, not perhaps in exact imitation of St. Simeon on his forty years' pillar of renunciation, but at least exempt from active complicity in the mad excesses and reckless orgies which were wont to make " night hideous," in that quarter of merry Bohemianism. He had not rubbed the bloom off pleasure in contact with men or women, who so often in that process evince a perseverance and energy worthy of a better cause. And never since he had assumed the *toga virilis* of manhood, and taken up cudgels in his own defense against the world, the flesh, and the devil, had a woman caused his heart to beat more swiftly; nor had his sleep been haunted by a vision such as the last night had brought him.

Alas, he had taken the disease in its worst form. They are not the Lovelaces of the world who fall hopeless victims to this fatal malady; they are the Galahads, who, when the symptoms manifest themselves in earnest, rarely recover; never, indeed, without carrying the pit-marks to the grave.

To Ronald's excited imagination the open window of his own room seemed to grin at him with a sardonic sneer; he turned impatiently his back to its mocking suggestiveness, and surveyed the room of his patient.

It was a room destitute of luxury, and yet with that indefinable aroma of refinement about it,—like the odor which betrays the violet hidden from sight in its leafy covert,—which many gorgeous salons lack.

On the white-washed walls hung a couple of fine copies of the Mater Dolorosa and Guido's Magdalen. Under them were suspended shelves of the beautiful Mosaic wood of Sorrento, filled with plain copies of Milton and Dante, with Petrarch's Sonnets in Italian; of Goethe, Schiller, and the divine Jean Paul—in their own tongue; of Racine and Molière, of Lamartine and De Staël, with a huge Byron, and a well-worn Shakspeare.

The floor was carpetless,—*cirée*, according to French custom, and scrupulously clean. On the mantel-shelf stood a delicate clock of Genoese silver filigree; and over it hung a faded miniature on ivory, exquisitely painted, of her dead mother's face.

On a little table by the window stood a china bowl of sweet-scented roses, a portfolio of sketches, and a little worn Bible with her mother's maiden name on the title-page. In one corner reposed an easel, with palette hung upon it; in the other, the white-draped cot of little Marian.

Ronald took in every detail of this simple room, and did not fail to draw therefrom some index of the character and tastes of its occupant. He was lost in a maze of conjecture and pitying wonder, when the door opened, and Sister Agnes entered, with that noiseless and elastic step of a gentle but self-reliant nature.

Reader, have you ever observed what expression there is in a footstep? There are women, beautiful women too, who *stamp* through the world on the nerves and senses of their acquaintance, quite unconsciously; and there are others who shuffle through life in an eternal down-at-heel style, which causes one to wax profane when its influence is brought to bear upon one's irritated sensibilities; and again, there are women who glide along by your side with the long, sinuous step which reminds one irresistibly of the old serpent, and causes one to shrink away involuntarily from its deadly fascination.

But there is a step which belongs only to the slender foot with the arched instep, which almost invariably goes in the set with the long, slender, tapering-fingered hand, the small, well-set head, and the delicate-lobed ears, which indicates poetic fancy, keenly perceptive faculties of mind, and tender acutely-sensitive properties of heart; the silent but springy, yet firm, footstep of a thoroughly harmonious woman.

There has been much said in favor of a softly modulated feminine voice; it is no doubt "an excellent thing;" but, reader, when my nervous system breaks down, I fancy I shall go to—Andalusia.

Ronald was not so far lost in his dream that he did not note this peculiarity of the fair Sister,—as she moved lightly about the room, preparing the draught which she had procured, with deft fingers.

After it was administered, and the effect watched anxiously, Ronald, promising to return before evening, was about to leave the room, when, actuated by a sudden thought, he turned abruptly to Agnes and asked, "Pardon me, *ma sœur*, but will you tell me where and how you became acquainted with this poor girl?"

"I met her," she replied, "in the Gallery of the Louvre immediately after she came to Paris; I used to go there frequently to paint. She was copying Murillo's Madonna, so was I; our easels stood side by side; after awhile our hearts touched,—and we have been friends ever since. There has not been a day that we have not met and talked together, and that I have not loved her more and more." She stopped, blushing slightly.

"You did not go alone to the Louvre?" he asked.

"Oh, no; I was still at the Convent of the Sacred Heart, where I was educated, and I had always one of the lower order of nuns, who act as *bonnes*, to go with me; and," she continued, "it was a stipulation of my father's before he died, and left me, a child of thirteen, together with my mother's little fortune, to the good Sisters, that when I became eighteen I should be free to cultivate my taste for art,—which I had, even as a child,—and to choose between the life of the convent and the life of honest labor. I chose the labor!"

He looked at her admiringly. "You are right, perfectly right," he said; "the world is big, and there is always room for you in it, outside that living tomb."

Many times, in the future years, Agnes recalled those words of encouragement and cheer.

"Your father was a German, I think you told me?" pursued Ronald.

"Yes; he was an author, a painter, an enthusiast, and he shared the fate of most of these: he died poor and unappreciated. He had no relatives living who were willing to burden themselves with an orphan child, so I was put in the convent, where I have been very happy,—even though I have held fast to my promise made when my father died, never to abjure his faith, and that of my mother,—for I am a Protestant, monsieur, though I wear this dress as a protection, and a means of doing some good in the hospitals, since I left the convent."

"And where do you live now?" asked Ronald, surprised at the young girl's intrepidity.

She smiled. "I live here with Dora now, since these riots began in Paris, in this dear little room; I spend my days at the hospitals. I have seen you many times, sir; but this screen," pointing to her snowy *coif*, "is useful sometimes, in shielding one from observation."

"It shall not shield you again from me," he answered, with a bright look. "You are too good a nurse to be overlooked." He was watching her at that moment as she raised, just enough, the head of her friend and gave her a few drops of a cool *tisane*.

At that moment the door opened, and the old gentleman he had observed the evening before, entered, leading by the hand a beautiful little girl of four years old.

"How do you find your patient to-day, doctor?" he asked anxiously, but in a whisper.

"She has some fever," answered Ronald; "owing, probably, to the length of time which elapsed before the bone was set, or to her fright; but I trust that the anodyne she has just taken may produce sleep, and she will before this time to-morrow be on the road to recovery."

"It appears," explained her father, "from the woman's account who brought her home, that she was overtaken in the Rue de Rivoli by a mob, and fell under their feet."

Ronald shuddered. "It is probable. These French are very fiends in their fury." With a few more words, and a last look at Dora, now calmly sleeping, he reiterated his directions and went away.

F*

CHAPTER VII.

A FORTNIGHT has passed, a fortnight prolific in events bearing upon the future destinies of the French people. The Emperor, striving in vain to find consolation for his misfortunes in his fatalistic theories, outwardly bore his imprisonment at Wilhelmshöhe with characteristic philosophy. King William, proclaimed emperor, was following up, by other victories, the conquest of Sédan. The Empress Eugénie had fled, and Lord Lyons was again advising all English loiterers to follow her example. General Trochu had accepted the position at the head of the National defense.

Flourens, the idol of the Belleville insurgents, had been placed at the head of five battalions of National Guards, in which Dick Ogilvie held the rank of captain.

The discontent and rebellion in the heart of Paris seethed and bubbled, and threatened to overflow everything, when, on the 19th, the iron cordon was drawn around her,—now passive through despair,—and she was completely invested by the invincible enemy.

At first, people looked at each other in blank dismay; then the blood which had flowed on numberless victorious fields, in the days gone by, rose in frantic indignation at the thought of a foreign yoke; and, with one accord, they rent the air with shouts of defiance, and registered a vow in each individual heart that want, disease, famine should be welcomed before the barbarian horde should march exultantly through their beloved Paris!

Of their indomitable courage, of their Spartan endurance, they made no vain boast. There is something classic in the French character when it rises to the sublime !

Poor Dora, unable to escape from Paris, was just emerging, white and frail as a spirit, from the dread valley of the shadow, where she had wrestled through the last fortnight with the great Destroyer, and now, thanks to Ronald's skill and ceaseless vigilance and Agnes's careful nursing, the fever had left her, and the poor brain was at rest.

Weak and helpless as a little child she lay, watching Marian as she flitted about in the sunshine, which poured its cheering rays into her little room, creating a halo around the golden head, and touching into a silvery glory the white hair of her old father, who sat in an arm-chair by the window, gazing listlessly into the street.

Agnes, with her coif laid aside and her rich, brown hair tucked away behind her tiny ears in many a coil and braid, sat at the bedside arranging, in a bowl, some fresh Provençal roses which had just been presented by the good old porteress.

Their fragrance filled the room, and Dora, stretching out a fragile little hand, took one full-bloomed beauty and pressed it to her lips and eyes, inhaling its perfume with delight.

"How doubly sweet they seem to me !" she murmured. "Oh, Agnes, is not the perfume of flowers the incense offered up to God by the universe ? In the early morning and the dewy evening, after the matin and the vesper hymn, the flowers grow sweetest in yielding up their mute thanksgiving."

"Yes, Dora, you are right ; all growing things, from the noblest tree to the tiniest blade of grass, point upward, and have a solemn significance in so doing. In my opinion, an atheist must be blind, eye-blind as well as soul-blind, to Nature and her eloquent teachings. All innocent things love and understand Nature : old people who are standing on the threshold of heaven, and little children,—and we must become like them we are told. You remember what your favorite, Jean Paul, says,— "Most people cannot *see* the sun, but it shines into the heart of a little child."

"Yes, yes, I know it. Oh, those happy days in Italy, when life seemed one eternal hymn of thanksgiving ; when I sang in those grand choirs with such a joyous, untroubled heart, I used to feel, Agnes, as if I needed only the wings to soar away to perfect bliss ! Ah me !" she sighed deeply.

"You must think only of the sunshine, darling ; let the shadows pass away. You have youth and life, thank God, and Marian and your father left."

"And you, Agnes,—ah, don't forget one of my greatest blessings ; and *you* have no one in all this great, full world but me."

"And God," murmured Agnes, reverently.

She rose to put by the flowers, as the door opened and Buchanan entered.

An angelic smile lit up Dora's wan face as he approached her, as she lay white and delicate as the rose she still held in her hand.

"Are you feeling a little stronger to-day ?" he asked, while his smile answered hers ; "and have these noisy fellows outside disturbed you much ?"

A band of riotous gamins, accompanied by fife and drum, and screaming women, and hooting children, passed under the window at that moment. She waited a little, and then replied,—

"Oh, yes, I am much better to-day. Indeed, you must

not let me be such a tax upon your time while so many need you more. I do not believe you have a moment's rest."

He looked worn and thin. During all those days and nights of suspense, when her life had hung upon a thread, he had not known rest indeed. But now, to see her smile once more, to see the eyes beam with intelligence instead of that fearful vacancy or that gaze of frantic terror, were enough to renew his life within him. In these two weeks of agony his existence had become absorbed into hers. Surely the plant of love grows apace when watered by tears !

"Will the siege last long, sir?" asked Mr. Fairfax, coming forward feebly. "We wish to get away from Paris as soon as possible; indeed, neither Dora nor I could bear a winter here."

"I cannot possibly tell," answered Ronald, "how long we will be shut up; possibly for many weeks. All depends upon the success of the French army outside, and, according to the last telegrams, there has been nothing very encouraging."

"Oh, dear! oh, dear! if we had only remained at Tours! Ah, Dora, it will be terrible for you, my child."

She simply took his hand and kissed it silently; she was thinking of him, not of herself. He smiled and passed his hand softly over her hair once or twice, then drawing a chair forward,—close to Ronald,—he continued speaking in the low, dreamy tone of a thinker who seldom finds opportunity of expressing his views: "It is astonishing to me that France needs this baptism of blood so often; that she *does* require it from time to time is indisputable,—that the plethora which is so rapid in this country should not produce apoplexy, and so terminate the existence of this hot-headed people;—a metaphor borrowed from your experience, doctor," he smiled.

And Ronald answered in the same vein: "So you think that the sword is the point around which cluster the greatness and power of a nation? I agree with you entirely; a little blood-letting is indispensable to the sanitary condition of the world."

"Undoubtedly; did not the Romans understand this when they made valor and virtue synonymous? And when—at the height of their glory, peace reigned and luxurious voluptuousness crept in—the sword fell from their enervated hands, was not their degeneration swift and sure?"

"And," pursued Ronald, "there is no doubt that the warlike peoples—those that are strongest in standing army and ready fleet—are the most progressive, and held in highest respect."

"You are right," returned the old gentleman; "look at the Levant; the Levantines, who know not the meaning of the word war, are they not deep sunk in the sloth of an indolent epicureanism? Even the Alexandrians rarely quit their homes: lapped in a characteristic inertia, they drop into the decay of death before they ever behold the country, the desert, or the sea. Or, dreaming in idle, ignorant content outside the walls of the sleepy city,—on the banks of the lovely Lake Mareotis,—they care not even to penetrate inside. The Delta seems a far-off, inexplorable myth to them, and the mighty Nile, with its gorgeously-fringed banks, a fairy-tale."

"What infinite good would accrue to a nation such as you describe," began Ronald, musingly, "if somebody could be found philanthropic enough to pull Mohammed Ali's nose for him at least once a year, and oblige him to draw his scimitar!"

"Ah, my young friend, when our flag is planted on the shores of the N le. *nous allons changer tout cela.* It is only a question of time; we *must* have a clear road to India, you know. But it is indubitable that when a nation keeps not its hand near the hilt of its sword, it ceases to respect itself, and becomes servile, cringing, superstitious, and degraded."

"It then appears to be the duty of a stronger people to take possession of it and reinvigorate its torpid energies," laughed Ronald. "I wonder if Prussia is being actuated by this conviction in regard to Alsace and Lorraine?"

He rose as he said this, and bade them adieu until the evening,—departing with a brighter face than he had worn lately. Mr. Fairfax accompanied him, with little Marian, as far as the street, where in the sunshine they daily took a stroll together.

"Shall I read to you, Dora? or would you like to sleep a little?" asked Agnes of her patient, when the door closed behind the others.

"I should like you to read, Agnes. No, not that; I am weary of German," as Agnes took up Goethe. "Don't be vexed, only I feel like English to-day."

Her friend quietly took down Byron from the shelf, and began a canto of "Childe Harold." Dora interrupted her: "No, that won't do, Agnes. I hate that arrogant, domineering egotist to-day; he irritates me,— and I want to be comforted."

"For shame, Dora; you do not deny the great poet?"

"Ah, no; but you see I am weak and ill, and I want a wholesome breath of air, not a sigh of sentiment from a diseased, morbid nature! He is very beautiful as a poet to be read in health and happiness,—but—Agnes, read Keats."

"Is Keats, then, so wholesome in his fanciful, tender sensibility?" asked Agnes, smiling.

"I don't know; perhaps sensibility without sensuousness is less Byronic;—and, Agnes, is sensibility a curse or a blessing?" She did not wait for an answer, but murmured softly to herself,—

> "Quanto la cosa è più perfetta,
> Più senta 'l bene e così la doglieza."

Her friend opened the book at the "Eve of St. Agnes," and began to read in a sweet, musical voice with the prettiest accent.

She had not completed one stanza before a voice from the bed broke in: "Agnes, how can you be so unobservant? Did you not see how thin and ill the doctor looked? Oh, what can be the matter? You say he has been here every day since the very beginning of my illness; he cannot, then, be suffering himself." She raised herself on her elbow and spoke in an eager whisper.

Agnes looked at her surprised, and answered, quietly, "Oh, no; he is quite well; but of course anxious, as we all are, about—these troubles in Paris, and the uncertainty of everything. And, Dora," she continued, noting the crimson spots which had returned momentarily to Dora's cheeks, "you must lie down now, and be quite quiet; you will have a return of the fever else." She shut up the book and laid it aside, darkened the windows, and sat down close to the bedside. Dora held tight in hers the kind hand which was so full of sympathy in its pressure, and lay quite still for a moment or two. Then these words of the laureate's fell from her lips,—

> "No life that breathes with human breath
> Has ever truly longed for death :

> 'Tis life whereof our nerves are scant,—
> Oh, life, not death, for which we pant:
> More life, and fuller, that we want."

The last line was almost inaudible, and her regular breathing told Agnes that her weakness was finding strength in sleep.

CHAPTER VIII.

WITH the exception of three or four unavoidable absences, Ronald Buchanan and Dick Ogilvie met daily at the Café Henri Quatre, and generally dined together.

It was approaching seven o'clock on the evening of the last day of October, 1870.

Ronald had waited much later than this, and been waited for, on various occasions during the past month, but to-day he had worked hard, and had scarcely tasted food ; he was much exhausted, and determined to wait no longer.

He had just given the order for dinner, when Ogilvie entered hastily, with uniform bespattered, hands blackened, and appearance generally disheveled.

"Sorry to detain you, dear boy," he cried, after calling for a bowl of water and a towel, and when in a corner apart he made a rapid toilet, while Ronald supplemented the dinner by an additional horse-steak and potatoes. "You see," he continued, drawing his chair up to the table, and speaking excitedly, "this morning after the news came of Bazaine's treachery in giving up Metz, and allowing himself to be taken prisoner, we, that is, a party of our officers, went to the Hôtel de Ville to find out what the government meant to do, as things were looking very serious. Well, we were received by M. Arago—(I say, garçon, tell them to put plenty of truffles about that horse-steak, and bring a pint of Rœderer. Mark my words, Ronald, if we are shut up here until we have to fall upon and devour each other for lack of meat, we will always find truffles, champignons, and champagne to flavor the meal in Paris). Well, M. Iago (or whatever the fellow's name was) bowed and temporized and expostulated, and finally promised to give us an answer at two o'clock. Of course we were on time; were you there?" Ronald shook his head. "The Place was one dense mass of human beings: National Guards, strong in numbers, men, women, and children, shouting, yelling, struggling; Ronald, it was Pandemonium incarnate! Our men were exasperated by the bad news of the morning, and the fall of Le Bourget yesterday; the rumor that the government would proclaim an armistice maddened them. Our banners bore the inscriptions, 'Vive la Commune!' 'No armistice!' and 'Vive la République!' Well, old boy, we waited some time, not patiently, almost deafened by the cries, 'Down with Trochu!' 'Vive Trochu!' and the rest. At last Trochu appeared in plain clothes, with Rochefort and other members of the government behind him, at the principal gate, which was guarded by a company of Mobiles. Trochu looked depressed, and was greeted by yells of 'No armistice! Down with traitors! à la lanterne!' I never witnessed such mad frenzy; his voice was drowned, and, in a few minutes, *how* I cannot tell, we were all bursting into the Hôtel de Ville. Then there was confusion worse confounded; everybody speaking at once,—some threatening to arrest the members of the government should they refuse to resign. One man in my regiment, a fiery Hercules, actually sprang forward, and laid his hand upon one of the members as they sat in council,—his name is Jacques Toquelet,— 'red' to the backbone. If it had not been for the 106th Battalion there would have been blood shed; *they* behaved well. I left them, Ronald, striving to eject my *confrères* at the point of the bayonet, and came here to relieve your anxious heart, and my hunger at the same time. En route, I had a little skirmish with three gens-d'armes, who sought to detain me to hear the news. Fancy the rashness of men putting a spoke in the wheel of a hungry Briton! I soon sent them to the right-about. *Garçon, dépêchez-vous donc.* Gad, I'm glad to see you!" apostrophizing the steak which, smothered in truffles, now made its appearance. The garçon flew about the table : he was serving a national guard !

"The capitulation of Metz seems to have been the spark which has ignited all this gunpowder," said Ronald, who had listened, much interested, to the account of a scene he had been debarred from witnessing through an accumulation of hospital work ; "and yet, why should it? It is not the first reverse ; luck has been against them all along."

"Yes," replied Dick, with his fork poised half-way to his mouth, "as Frederick the Great said, 'Providence always takes the side of the strongest ;' and that old duffer knew something about this sort of things. No, no, it was the taking of Le Bourget yesterday that riled them," continued Dick ; "they don't want much to set them off when the steam is up, you know; great oaks often grow from their tiniest acorns."

"Yes," replied Ronald, "Pliny tells us that the sight of *a fig* caused the destruction of Carthage ; why should not the loss of a village destroy Paris? That Pliny also vouches for the fact that a woman became mother to an elephant, does not incline us to doubt the truth of the other incident.''

Dick laughed, and filled Ronald's glass. "Here's a health to *anybody* or anything that will open the gates of Paris before these madmen butcher each other for lack of somebody or something else to butcher. I hear meat is getting scarce already; how long do you think one could live on champagne and olives, Ronald?''

"*Cela dépend*," answered Ronald. "I have heard of cases where a man subsisted for a long time on shoe-leather; and there are plenty of rats in the sewers of Paris!''

"Pah! don't, Ronald, there's a good fellow,—I haven't dined for two days, you see.''

He was indeed making up for lost time, and Ronald was obliged to leave him, to make a visit to a poor woman who had been frightfully injured in a riot, a night or two before. Agreeing to meet the next day, they separated.

Alas, many days passed before Ronald again looked upon the kindly face of his friend. He saw it then by the light of a horn-lantern, blackened and distorted in agony.

CHAPTER IX.

BEFORE midnight, the 106th Battalion had restored quiet in the Hôtel de Ville, and the National Guards had dispersed by command of Flourens and Mégy, *les oreilles tant soit peu baissées.*

The next day the people of Paris were called upon to decide whether they would recognize the authority of the government for the National Defense.

The majority of the votes were for the government, and

for once the populace of Belleville and Montmartre controlled themselves. Later, they made up for this suppression of their natural instincts, when hundreds of them were killed at Montretout, at Garches, and at Buzenval.

The sufferings of the besieged were increasing daily; mid-winter with its cold rains and frost was upon them; black bread was being rationed out to them in insufficient portions; the famine that they had denied the possibility of, was fast approaching.

General Vinoy had been named commander-in-chief of the army of Paris. Trochu still continued President of the government. Flourens had been imprisoned for inciting rebellion, and released by a mob of his own men. Riots were of daily occurrence.

Clément Thomas in vain issued his pacific proclamations; the people were desperate, the people were defiant, the people were hungry.

The Place of the Hôtel de Ville was often the scene of idle discussion, fruitless argument, noisy demonstration. In the afternoon of the 22d of January, a detachment of a hundred or two National Guards drew up before the Hôtel de Ville, crying, "Down with Trochu! Vive la Commune!" After a few moments, an officer of the Gardes Mobiles approached and tried to say a few words; in vain. Suddenly a shot was fired, and through the great door of the Hôtel de Ville poured forth, as if waiting for that signal, a volley of fire upon the Place, whence the National Guard and idle by-standers fled, shrieking with fury and fear.

Ronald Buchanan happened to be one of the spectators of this *coup de théâtre*, and, as the smoke cleared away, he advanced to investigate the condition of the wounded who lay upon the Place. He first attended to two women who were injured, not mortally, and placed them on two of the litters which were arriving from the Rue du Temple, and then turned his attention to the men. What was his horror, in raising the head of a white-haired old man who had fallen on his face, to recognize the features of Mr. Fairfax, fixed, apparently, in the rigidity of death. He raised him, with the assistance of a soldier who carried one end of a litter, and strove to restore him, but the heart had ceased to beat; he had been shot through the brain, and must have died instantly. Ronald gave some directions to the soldiers who were to bear him away, and turned, with an aching heart, to minister to the relief of the other victims. About a dozen men still lay groaning around him; this man was dead, and could feel no more; he remained, and, with steady hand and unclouded eyes, dressed their wounds, and then went straight to the Rue de Vaugirard, to break the sad news to Dora.

What desolating change has passed over Dora's pretty chamber since we last glanced into it? Where are the roses, the books, the filigree clock? Where the pictures which adorned the blank whiteness of the walls? and where the laughing, golden-haired child, who danced so gleefully in the sunshine of three short months ago?

Who are these pale phantoms, robed in close-clinging serge, with the red cross of Geneva on their sleeves? The one stooping over a handful of fire stirring some miserable broth with an iron spoon, the other bending over the little cot, whose curtains have gone long since to supply some housekeeping deficiency, where the tangled curls, white face, and hollow eyes of a child tossed wearily upon its pillow.

" Make haste, Agnes; she is awake now. Perhaps I can

induce her to take a spoonful. Is it done?" Dora's voice was harsh and strained.

Agnes replied, in her own sweet tones, "Yes, it is done, and I think will be nourishing; that last piece of meat good mother Bénoit brought us has made it quite good."

She cooled a little in a saucer, while Dora took up the fragile form of little Marian, and implored her with kisses and caresses, the cooing tenderness a mother always uses to hush a wailing infant, to take some of the broth which had been so difficult to prepare. But no: Marian turned her head away and closed the pretty little teeth resolutely; she would not taste one drop. In vain Agnes plead; and Dora urged that Marian would surely die if she did not eat something. The child only fretted and wept. "Marian don't care; Marian wants to die," she sobbed.

In despair the mother, motioned away the saucer with the untasted broth thereon, and rocked her baby in her arms, while great tears coursed each other down the thin cheeks. Agnes carefully covered the little saucepan and set it aside for after while; she hoped still.

Marian had been very ill: a severe cold taken one evening, when she had been obliged to wait with her mother at the corner of a street, in a pouring rain, until a mob which had collected around Félix Pyat, and had changed into a riot, had dispersed, settled on her lungs, and for two weeks she had hovered on the confines of the angel-world. After the fever left her, she seemed to sink; insufficient nourishing food, a cold room, and a delicate organization all were against her; she could not rally, and for nearly thirty-six hours had absolutely refused to taste anything. The ornaments of the room, a few trinkets of Dora's, and a little money she had saved of her father's sufficed to provide them with the bare necessaries of life until now. To-night they shared their last meal, Agnes and Dora alone, for the father, who had gone out in the afternoon to apply for aid at the English Ambulance Office, had not yet returned. They knew not, these two forlorn women, where another meal would come from; even Agnes's bright spirit was dimmed: she sat with drooping head, quite silent. How joyful was the sound of Ronald's step upon the stairs! Even Dora stopped crooning, and raised her head to listen; Agnes rose and lit the lamp.

But his step surely sounded differently this evening; it was slower, heavier, and destitute of that buoyancy so characteristic of his temperament.

He came in quietly, sadly, and sank as if weary into a chair near Dora and the child. "Did she seem to enjoy the broth?" he asked, placing his fingers on the tiny wrist,—"did she take any of it?" There was something of alarm in his voice now, for the pulse indicated that the flame of life was just flickering, no more.

"No, she has taken nothing,—nothing," sighed the mother; "but I think she is better, decidedly better. You see she does not moan at all now, or roll her head about in that distressing way; and she has not a particle of fever, has she?"

"No, she has no fever," answered Ronald, "and I think might sleep a little, if you will allow me to lay her in her cot; sleep will strengthen her, you know."

Instantly Dora rose, and with her own hands laid her gently on the pillow. When she returned to her seat she could not help noticing the attitude of deep dejection into which Ronald had sunk. "You are ill," she said, softly, "or something new has happened in this fated city. What have they done now? We know nothing."

He leaned towards her and took her hand in his.
"Dora," he began,—she shuddered slightly at this unwonted style of address, it made her fear she knew not
what,—"Dora, you must be strong and calm; in these
troublous days men and women are called upon to bear
terrible trials. For the sake of your child, who needs all
your care and strength"——His voice broke down, and,
drawing her hand from his, she wailed forth,—

"Ah! why do you not strike the blow at once? My
father! he is hurt, wounded, killed, perhaps!" Her voice
rose at each word, and at the last it had grown into a
stifled shriek.

Ronald knelt on one knee before her, and said, striving
to speak calmly and firmly, "Your father did not suffer
one instant; he has been saved all the tortures of a protracted siege; in his old age he might have starved slowly
before your eyes; he is now at rest, happy, perhaps, with
the wife that he has never ceased to mourn. Dora, it is
for the best. Oh, my friend, look up and tell me that
you feel it is best so." She answered nothing. Convulsive sobs shook her frail form from head to foot. Agnes
was wiping her own quiet tears away, in an obscure corner of the room. Ronald began again: "You will be ill;
you are wringing my heart, Dora; have you no pity for
me?"

"Hush! hush!" she cried, in anguish, "you must not
speak like this to me! Oh, my God, is not my burden
heavier than I can bear?" She started to her feet with
streaming eyes, and paced up and down the narrow room,
moaning at intervals. Ronald sat with bowed head,
wrestling in his heart with the fiercest temptation he had
ever known. To go and take the desolate creature in his
strong arms, to be to her father, husband, friend, all in
one, to hold her close to the heart which was bursting with

G   13

pity and with love for her in her helpless sorrow, the heart which had never held another image than hers, that was true and strong and noble to the core.

But this was not the time; to take advantage of her crushed heart in this hour of grief, when she might turn to him through gratitude or loneliness, or for protection, was foreign to his nature, and his voice was quite steady as he went towards her, saying, "Should you like to see him once more, dear? There is no wound that you can see; he is quite near. Shall I come for you and Agnes in half an hour and take you to him?" Dora bowed her head in acquiescence, and Ronald went away.

He had ordered the litter-bearers to take the body to his own number in the Rue de Vaugirard, and to request the concierge to allow them to place it in the little *salle d'attente* on the *rez de chaussée*. There it lay, covered with a snow-white pall which the good porteress had thrown over it, after recognizing the features of the old English gentleman who lived opposite. Ronald examined the body attentively; there was no drop of blood about it; they had done their work neatly, those carbines of the Gardes Mobiles. On the left side of the head the bullet had entered, and gone out through the right, carrying life with it. A few drops of blood had clotted the silver hair; the good woman had washed these away and brushed the soft locks over the wounds, completely hiding them. The expression of the face was untroubled, almost a smile lingered on the lips, and the eyes were closed naturally. The white, slender, aristocratic-looking hands were folded on his breast; it was an image of rest and peace.

Ronald lingered awhile, giving orders for the burial on the morrow,—explicit orders, paid for out of his own scant purse,—and then went to bring Dora to bid a last farewell to her idolized father.

To his surprise he found her quite calm,—very pale, and with violet shadows under the heavy eyes,—but composed and with an angelic softness about her manner. She wished to go with him alone, she said; "Marian cannot be left without one of us, and Agnes shall go afterwards, if she will."

With the same quiet calm, she entered the little room where all that the world held for her of protection, love, tenderness, lay cold and still in death; then turned and said, almost in a whisper, "Will you leave me here a little while alone, please?"

He went out silently and closed the door. After a quarter of an hour, during which he had heard no sob or moan, his anxiety conquered his will, and he opened the door and entered. She was kneeling beside the litter, with her face buried on the bosom of her father, one of whose arms she had raised and placed around her shoulders, holding it there firmly with one hand; her other arm she had slipped under the head, now, alas! so heavy and unyielding to the tenderness of her caress.

As Ronald came near, she gently drew her arm away and laid the dead hands together on the breast, and rising slowly and painfully from her cramped position, said, quietly, "Thank you very much. I will go, now; and," stooping over the pale face once more and pressing a kiss on the closed eyes, "it has been such a comfort to me to *know* that he is so happy." He took her hand and led her away, his heart too full for speech.

As they entered the little room where the sick child lay, they trembled with apprehension; perhaps the little one had passed, in sleep, away. Agnes's voice, with a subdued but cheerful ring in it, greeted them: "Oh, Dora, I have had Marian up and fed her; and look." She drew her to the table where the saucepan stood, half emptied of its contents. "She seemed actually hungry and enjoyed it, and went off to sleep immediately."

Dora listened eagerly, and then stepped to the side of the cot where her darling seemed to be sleeping naturally. In a moment she turned to Ronald, while a divine smile broke over her pale features. "You see," she said, "God has pity upon me, after all."

That night Jacques Toquelet, who had been one of the litter-bearers of her poor father, brought a note from Buchanan. It ran thus:

"Your father, dear friend, will be buried to-morrow morning. Everything has been attended to; should you feel strong enough, I would advise your going with us. I shall call with a carriage at nine o'clock A.M., and if Marian continues to improve it will do her no harm, well wrapped up, to go with you, if the weather should be fine.

"Be brave, dear friend, and let the smile of hope and faith I saw last in your face, rest in your heart forever.

"RONALD."

Jacques Toquelet also deposited with Mère Benoit, the concierge, a basket containing a fowl, some potatoes, white bread, and a couple of pots of prepared beef for broth for Marian.

Dora, Agnes, and Marian breakfasted in the sunshine which gilded the poverty of their denuded chamber the next morning. At nine o'clock, a dingy fiacre, followed by a hearse bearing a plain coffin, drew up to the door. They were soon all on their way out to Père la Chaise, thankful for the inestimable privilege, denied so many poor hearts in those days, of seeing their beloved dead buried with the sacred rites of the Church.

A simple wooden cross marked the last resting-place of Dora's beloved father, bearing the following inscription:

To the Memory of Vincent Fairfax.

Died January 22d, 1871.

CHAPTER X.

A clear, crisp winter morning, without frost.

In front of the noble-pillared portico of one of the "Stately Homes of England" which Mrs. Hemans sang about, was drawn up a gay cavalcade of fair women and brave men, mounted on fine horses, and moving about in that state of suppressed excitement preliminary to a stunning run and a sure find, on a hunting-day, when the weather is not too gay for the scent, and the pack all that could be desired.

There were half a dozen or more bright-faced girls and young matrons, with sparkling eyes and peachy cheeks, looking their very best in their perfectly-fitting habits and neat hats, with tightly-braided blonde and chestnut hair stowed away somewhere in the crown, and only just appearing beneath the brim.

About twice as many gentlemen,—old, young, and middle-aged, sitting square and firm in their saddles,—to the manner born (if I may misquote), and looking a trifle impatient at the slight delay before the hounds "throw off."

The master of these canine beauties, with the keen eye of a hunter from boyhood, stood a little apart, with one or two other gentlemen, inspecting a favorite leash of thorough-breds, lately added to the pack.

Reclining in an exquisitely-appointed pony-phaeton, enveloped in a rug of sable, velvet-lined, in one of her most *séduisante* Parisian toilettes, lay Pauline de Courboisie.

She was unusually brilliant to-day, in exuberant spirits, and monopolized the tiny carriage, driving herself (the miniature groom was as ornamental as useless), for her hostess, the Countess d'Hauteville, never missed a run with the hounds on any occasion whatever; and the man she had hoped to have with her had resolutely refused to double up his long limbs in her honor, and had ridden to the meet, compromising matters by keeping steadily at her side until now.

But she was not alone. Around her were gathered together, on horseback and on foot, red coats, in all and every phase of imbecility concerning her; and with them all, in sparkling talk and brilliant repartee, she held her own in French and broken English, which she lisped with such beguiling simplicity. There were not wanting women who asserted that, with her own sex, she could speak their language volubly enough, and never wore that delightfully naïve puzzled expression, which arched her brows and made her look so bewitching, as she asked, "Can you not tell me what I mean?" with an appealing glance at the best-looking man in the group. But then these virgins were *turned thirty* who defamed her, and not handsome.

A close observer would have detected, in Pauline's brilliant eyes and coquettish manner, something a trifle overstrained this morning; and, when she occasionally allowed her lace parasol to droop a little between her face and those of her adorers, she shot forth a rapid but keen glance at the cavalier who had deserted her awhile

ago, and who was now absorbed in mounting, and arranging with much deliberation the folds of the habit
belonging to a fair, stately-looking blonde, of a rare and
high-bred type of beauty.

As Lady Florence Ellesmere gathered up her reins, and
thanked the tall, handsome man at her side, with a bright
smile and a few courteous words, granting him permission
to *lead* her in the coming run, there flashed out from the
depths of Pauline de Courboisie's eyes a gleam as deadly
as ever brightened steel.

For the languid Adonis, who now vaulted into the sad-
dle of a superb chestnut, held in waiting by his groom,
was no other than Dyke Faucett, the man for whose sweet
sake she had come to wither in this cold, bleak, dreary
country.

What if she *had* been fêted and courted, and passed
from one country-house to another as its choicest guest,
since her flight from Paris, carrying destruction everywhere, in the arch coquetry and charming *minauderies*
innate in her, and fostered by the exquisitely-polished
genre of the court circles of the Empire; turning men's
heads who might otherwise have gone down to respectable
graves ignorant of the song of the sirens, winning from
thwarted mammas and mortified daughters unequivocal,
and not unexpressed, disapproval: to say nothing of the
maledictions of many a neglected wife, who strove in
vain to attain the willowy grace of attitude and movement, the delicate tapering waist, and that faint rose-
bloom on their own health-colored cheeks, which just
penetrated the polished ivory of Pauline's well-preserved
complexion? And yet they could not see what the men
saw in that over-dressed, affected French doll; she was
certainly not good style,—and her husband abroad, too.
Indeed, they could not understand how the dear duchess

could have taken her up with so much *empressement,* etc. etc.

And she had forsaken her France, and all the delightful chateaux which solicited her presence under the sunny skies of her own land, for this.

True, there were piquant morsels in her daily fare,— but would they not have been equally delicious away from the fogs, and the east wind, and these horrible fox-hunts which formed the staple of the winter's amusement, which took all the men away from the house all day, and sent them home tired and stupid, and red in the face, for the eight o'clock dinner, more inclined for one more bottle afterwards, than anything more stimulating and less sleep-engendering in the drawing-room?

Yes, it was for this,—to sit and chafe inwardly, and suffer in impotent anguish the pangs she had so ruthlessly inflicted upon others,—chatting cheerily, and smiling gleefully, while her heart wept sore within her, as she noted the boundless devotion in every look and move-ment of the man she loved towards a younger, fairer, *freer* rival. Yes, retributive justice had seen fit to smite her at last; and the wily coquette, who had begun the game *pour s'amuser*, went down prone, in the abject idol-atry of a woman who had never learned the lesson of self-control. After she had given up speculating upon the possibility of such a dénouement, she struggled awhile madly to disentangle herself from the meshes of a net which restricted in a great degree her enjoyments, and threatened to bind her down to the inthrallment of a *grande passion;* but finding it hopeless, she resigned her-self to the new experience, and poured into it all the vehemence of her undisciplined nature.

Alas! not only was she willing to come at his beck to these bleak shores of England, but even to the borderland of the great Unknown would she unhesitatingly have followed his lead.

It did not make her pain less keen to know that in the beautiful Florence Ellesmere she saw the woman chosen by Sir Philip Standley as the destined bride of his adopted son; if one drop could be bitterer than another in the cup which had of late been pressed to her lips, it was the galling thought that *one* was free and the other bound, and that Dyke loved himself better than either, therefore he would be lost to *her*.

The hunting-party were all assembled; many, especially the younger members, impatient for the start, when Dyke Faucett rode up to the side of the pony-phaeton to say *au revoir* to its fair occupant. She finished her gay speech to an infatuated major of dragoons (why is the major in a play or a novel inevitably a fool?), on her other side, long after she had *felt* Dyke's approach; and then, as he addressed her, she answered in rapid French, which was the signal for all the other men to disperse, who still hung about her.

"I need not ask you how you have enjoyed the meet," he began; "only to look at you sparkling and brimming over with witchery, and driving these poor fellows mad, is indicative enough of your thoroughly amusing yourself."

"Yes," she laughed, "*je ne m'ennuyais pas trop;* I contrive to exist somehow; but, oh, I do wish I could hunt! You all look so *very* jolly, and it will be so insupportably *triste à la maison*, unless indeed that handsome *sabreur* has returned from town and will comfort me!" She sighed.

"Pauline," Dyke began, impatiently, "you are making yourself quite ridiculous with that American, of whom you know absolutely nothing,—a conceited snob he is

G*

too. Really, how you can spend hours in his society, in a house so full of *bels esprits* as Grantly Manor is at present, I cannot imagine!"

She waited patiently until he had finished speaking; every word was delightful to her ears; he was really jealous enough to be unjust, and a trifle energetic!

"Pardon me, *mon cher*," she rejoined in the sweetest accents. "You are quite wrong; *I do* know absolutely very much about this good-looking colonel. A gentleman who brings letters of introduction to the Duke of L——, and who is received at your best houses with *empressement*, is not unknown—or a snob."

"Perhaps," assented Dyke, ungraciously. "Still, that does not alter my opinion of his priggish impertinence and stupid assumption of superiority. I do not count many Americans among my acquaintance; but I certainly know no other of his stamp."

"Possibly," acquiesced Pauline,—"for he is decidedly the most *spirituel* as well as the most fascinating man in the house, and," she added, maliciously, "undeniably he is the handsomest."

"Yes," replied Dyke, who instantly recovered his *sang-froid;* "he has a handsome face, of the style women affect, I believe; but the man is simply obnoxious to me,—*voilà tout!*"

"Strange!" murmured Pauline, meditatively. "I should have imagined you would have been great friends. He is such a strong, noble, courageous creature; and his manners are simply charming. And oh, Dyke, what a musical, *trainante* voice he has! I have never heard one to equal it!"

"And I am detaining you when you might be listening to its dulcet tones!" cried Dyke, irritated in spite of himself. "I have the honor to bid you good-morning."

As he put spurs to his horse and galloped after the party who had just scattered, as the hounds threw off, and Pauline saw him draw rein beside the Lady Florence, she bit her lip till it bled, while she smiled in her soul, saying, "Yes, he is certainly jealous!" and drove quickly home to transfix with a surer arrow the heart of that *brave garçon*, Percival Tyrrell.

But Madame la Marquise had met her match!

Ah, Pauline de Lénepvue, when you took to your arms the decrepit form of the old Marquis de Courboisie, because his rent-roll and his pedigree were equally long, when you echoed the shameless words of the beautiful and ambitious de Pompadour when she married Lenormand d'Etioles, untouched by his frantic love for her.—"I accept him with resignation as a misfortune which cannot *last long*" (while her eyes were fixed upon the king),—and stifled therein your last spark of true womanhood, you lost forever the power to touch a heart like Percival Tyrrell's!

Had you also, like Madame d'Etioles, sworn eternal fidelity to your husband ("unless his majesty should fall in love with her!"), I doubt even then your being able to blind a man of his quick perceptions to the rigid narrowness of your soul; and, as it was, he saw—and admired, as we admire a conception of Rubens embodied in his inimitable flesh-tints,—feeling through them—the clay!

For, although he was not that most intolerable bore, a pedant, Percy Tyrrell was a deep student, and not only of books but of that mysterious paradox—human nature. With an intellectual capacity of a high order, he was ambitious of acquiring knowledge, both for its own sake and because of the legendary tradition—in which his belief was firm—that it was *power*.

He was a very proud man, not merely in outward development of character, but in the recesses of his heart and conscience; he held his own standard of right and his own apex of honor,—and to both he was willing and believed himself strong enough to sacrifice all that warred against either. For he was that not uncommon antithesis, —a Christian in form, at heart almost a pagan! Reverencing religious faith as something divinely beautiful and harmonious, and regarding its devout followers with a respect and admiration not unmixed with envy, he had not learned to regulate his own thoughts, actions, and hopes by the counsels drawn from divine inspiration.

In manner he was undemonstrative, quiet, and rather cold; one could rarely detect that he was disappointed, annoyed, or grieved; he seemed perfectly self-reliant; it appeared almost absurd to think that love's fitful fever could ever sway the pulsations of that tranquil-seeming heart.

And yet, had he once been able to trust a woman implicitly,—to feel that he was all in all to one whom he could thoroughly approve,—there were depths of tenderness in his nature which would make the "shallows" which "murmur" seem but dry, barren soil. But that woman had grown a shadowy, mythical creation of the brain to his fastidious requirements, and his somewhat cynical insight into human nature furnished no semblance of the ideal he sought; therefore, calmly and a little bitterly, he decided at thirty-five years to live out the rest of his life, as fully as may be, alone.

That he reckoned without the consent of those weird sisters who spend the strength in their bony fingers tangling the skeins of life for most of us, he acknowledged not—until afterwards.

And this was the man whom a Pauline de Courboisie fancied she could bring into subjection by a few glances of her brilliant eyes, a few murmured reproaches for a coldness which repelled while it attracted her. For Percy Tyrrell was a universal favorite with women,—perhaps because he seemed so indifferent to their attractions,—perhaps because all women worship strength and gentleness combined, and these were his chief characteristics.

CHAPTER XI.

As the fairy-like carriage, with its spirited ponies, swept swiftly around the drive shaded by grand old beeches, and drew up before the entrance of an ancient pile, covered with moss and lichens and bearing on its noble face the weather-marks of centuries, Pauline gave a rapid glance around before she threw the reins to the tiny groom and prepared to descend without the assistance she had confidently expected would await her.

I fear her frame of mind was not angelic as she noted the stillness which reigned about the deserted mansion,—no sound save the cawing of the rooks in the rookery and the plaintive moaning of the doves in the dove-cote to break the silence. Not even a servant visible, of whom she could make some inquiries. Ah, this was too much! and poor Carlo, a handsome St. Bernard, who had cautiously approached, received a vicious little kick from a delicate satin boot, which ruffled his sweet, equable temper only for a moment, and he walked away with an eloquent dignity while the marquise pulled the bell energetically.

"Colonel Tyrrell,—has he returned?" she demanded, as the footman threw open the doors.

"Yes, my lady; he returned an hour ago; he is in the shrubbery somewhere, reading; I saw him a few moments ago."

"Reading! always reading!" she muttered, as she crossed the superb entrance-hall, which, by its vast proportions, its high, carved chimney-piece, under which the massive sideboard still stood, with its sculptured boars' heads and wide-spreading antlers, indicated the dining-hall of days of yore, where many a feast had been merrily held, with wassail deep.

Through a second hall Pauline now sped, whose walls were hung with favorite Landseers and large crayon likenesses of certain pets in the earl's stud and kennels, and still she encountered not a human being. "It is like an enchanted palace," she thought. "Where is Mignonne, I wonder?" And she went on through the empty library and into a small circular hall which separated it from the billiard-room.

There, standing in the dim light, filtered into rainbow hues through the magnificent stained-glass windows, whence they fell upon the marble tessellated floor, she had an excellent view of a *tableau-vivant*, of which not the smallest detail escaped her.

Three windows opening to the ground formed the south end of the billiard-room, and in one of these, with the sunshine falling here and there upon them through the flickering leaves of the ivy which hung in festoons over their heads, stood two figures who were worthy of an artist's pencil.

A girl, slightly above the medium height, with one of those lithe, willowy figures which it is a pleasure to watch moving about; with a small head bound tightly with dark braids, the deep-blue eyes, black-lashed, and the rich-colored cheeks and lips which showed her Celtic blood, watched with loving glance a child who flew here and there over the lawn, chasing a butterfly in great glee.

Leaning slightly against the opposite side of the window, with his eyes fixed upon her eloquent face, Percival Tyrrell completed the picture.

A man, tall, slender, wiry,—with not an ounce of superfluous flesh about his well-knit, nervous frame,—with features clear-cut as a cameo, the lower part of the face delicate, the nostrils arched and fine. His eyes, of a clear blue-gray, expressed intelligence, and at times shone with a cold, analytical severity; rarely did they soften as at this moment, and more rarely still did the firm lips curve into such a winning smile under the heavy moustache that screened many a satirical expression which rested there too often—for his own happiness.

And yet there was a languid grace in his manner, and a tenderness towards all women and children, which contradicted his cynical smile and proved an irresistible fascination. Few among the boisterous, muscular Christians assembled at Grantly, who boasted so noisily of their prowess on water and in the hunting-field, would have guessed that this quiet, reserved, gentle-voiced and gentle-mannered American—who gave but lame and impotent enthusiasm to their dances, and smiled at their excitement over the *brush*, and did *not* think the world well lost for any *danseuse* that ever pirouetted—had through three years of hard fighting, during the late civil war in his own country,—leading into action sometimes three regiments of almost undisciplined recruits,—spending the nights of an American winter on the frozen ground, and suffering bitter privation of all kinds without a murmur,—shown nerve and pluck which exceeds even that manifested in the taking of fences in the fox-hunt or the pulling of oars at a university boat-race.

That he had had seven horses killed under him in
action, and that each hair of his head remained uninjured, was duly set forth only in the servants' hall by his
faithful mulatto servant, who went through the war with
him, and worshiped him accordingly, with the steadfast
devotion which is met with in his race.

For Tyrrell did not dilate upon his experiences, and
not even his hostess herself knew that she counted among
her guests one of the most distinguished officers who
figured in the late Rebellion, in the cold, quiet man in
whom she saw nothing more than a scholarly lassitude,
which, by contrast with the rampant spirits and exuberant health of the other men, was delightful to her tired
nerves.

Tyrrell, upon his return from town, had taken a book
and sauntered out under the shade of a great copper-
beech, and tried vainly to resist the temptation to join
little Valérie and her governess, of whom he caught
glimpses through the billiard-room windows. He was
not loth to continue an acquaintance with the spirited-
looking girl, who had none of the depressed, dog-eared
look about her that he was accustomed to associate with
her vocation ; for when she accompanied her pupil to the
drawing-room after dinner, although she always chose the
shadiest corner therein, she did not seem to droop or look
bored. And if any one approached her,—which was rare
indeed, and *never* done by women,—she showed an ease
of manner, and a certain stately grace in holding her own
in conversation, as though the blood of kings ran in her
veins.

And she was only the daughter of an Irish naval officer,
who died poor, and left her at eighteen, with her luckless
dower of beauty, upon the mercy of the world.

She had one brother, whom we have met before, Richard Ogilvie, a ne'er-do-weel, who could just take care of himself—no more—in those early days of his career.

Anne Ogilvie had been well educated, and for three years remained as teacher in the school near London, where she had already spent eight, of joyless life, and then she accepted the position offered her by the superintendent, of governess in the family of the Earl d'Hauteville. For three years she had filled this somewhat trying position with the unequivocal approbation of her patrons.

" She was beautiful, to be sure, but then she was modest and retiring, and she was *a lady*, and that is so desirable, you know, with a child of Valérie's age. Some of these walking encyclopædias are so very objectionable, my dear, have such hands and feet, and dress quite shockingly, it always makes me ill to see them about the grounds of the places where I visit ; and as to having them in the drawing-room, I should think that were quite impossible. Now, Miss Ogilvie dresses like a lady ; always quietly, like a lady in reduced circumstances to be sure, but still, a lady ; and then, her voice is very fine, and she is so obliging about singing and playing accompaniments," etc. etc. So buzzed on her ladyship on those occasions when her governess's beauty wagged the tongues of her acquaintance, and silenced them.

As they stood together in the full glare of day (for Anne's fresh bloom dreaded no sunlight, however searching), Pauline de Courboisie took in the picture from the open door ; and, setting her small teeth together firmly, she registered a vow, in what she was pleased to call her heart, "That girl shall leave this house. Last night Dyke Faucett took her into the conservatory to show her the new orchids, and—now—to-day——" She turned suddenly, and mounted to her own rooms, where she spent the remainder of the shining hours, alternately ill treating and caressing a hideous pug, Bijou by name, and extracting from Mignonne, her precocious six-year-old daughter, the gossip of the servants' hall, which her nurse faithfully retailed to her.

Célestine, standing patiently behind her mistress, benefited by the conversation, whilst she invented a *coiffure* that should out-Venus Venus at the dinner-hour.

CHAPTER XII.

THEY were speaking of the book Tyrrell had been reading, and, as he placed it in her hand, he said,—

"It is Lamartine's 'Confidences.' I have quite finished it. You may like to look over it; pray keep it. You will find some beautiful thoughts there, and I think you told me you knew French?"

"Yes," Anne replied; "I have read Graziella and Raphael in the original; they were very poetical. Is this like them?"

"Yes; all his works are somewhat alike, in that they are each but a beautiful setting for the gem,—*Lamartine*. Even his 'Revolution of '48' is an exquisite bit of egotism."

"Ah," she exclaimed, with a bright look, "then you think with me that, however graceful his images or perfect his ideals, Lamartine never loses sight of Lamartine!"

"Alas, yes," replied Tyrrell; "he is a profound self-worshiper; a man who, even under the influence of the divine afflatus, looks around the shoulders of the muse at a reflection of his adorable self."

Anne laughed. "It is quite true," she said. "One

forgets to admire the poetry of his conceptions in wonder at the sublime ingenuity of a vanity which would be amusing were it not so pitiful."

"Like his compatriot, Montaigne," pursued Tyrrell, "he studies himself more than any other subject. Do you remember where he says, '*I* am my metaphysic, my natural philosophy, my virtue, and my religion'?"

"Yes, I remember, Montaigne always paraded his faults, and he seems to me invariably to make a merit of his selfishness, vanity, and skepticism. What a pity it was!" she continued, musingly. There ensued a pause, during which the little girl came up, and, leaning against her governess, twined her arms about her waist. Anne caressed her mechanically, her thoughts far off, and then asked, "You would not compare Montaigne with Lamartine, would you?"

"No, they are unlike in all things," replied Tyrrell, "save that underlying current of self-worship, which we find in German Goethe, in English Byron, and in our great American giant, Emerson, who is indeed the Montaigne of the New World."

"But without his coarseness, surely," remonstrated Anne, "without that materialism which chains the French skeptic to the earth, even in his most powerful efforts to soar into a purer atmosphere?"

"Ah, yes," asserted Tyrrell; "Emerson is Montaigne refined to an essence, which, while it contains a subtle strength, is etherealized fragrance embodied in exquisite language." Anne listened silently. "It is that," pursued Tyrrell, presently, "which makes him so attractive and so dangerous, to women especially; who would turn away uninjured by Montaigne, but who yield a loving reverence to Emerson, saying, like Frederika Bremer, 'I know he is not faultless; but then,—*he is so lovely!*'"

At this moment Justine, little Valérie's French maid, appeared, to take her young mistress to be dressed for the early dinner which she took with Miss Ogilvie and their young guest.

Anne also sped away to her pretty suite of rooms, carrying with her her precious book, with " Percy Tyrrell" scrawled on the fly-leaf.

That little book became a devoted friend of Anne's during many dreary months of her life, and for many weeks, when the burden of her days pressed very heavily upon her, and when she felt very sad and lonely, Lamartine's " Confidences" were stifled between her cheek and the pillow, and sometimes drowned with tears.   For her lines were no longer cast in pleasant places, when they crossed the path of Pauline, Marquise de Courboisie.

CHAPTER XIII.

THE awful pause before dinner !   When the guests are all assembled, and the rustle of the ladies' dresses and the stifled yawns of the men (who glance surreptitiously at their watches every moment) are the only sounds that break the stillness of expectancy.   It is not worth while to commence a conversation which may be interrupted immediately by the appearance of the portly butler, and, *du reste*, nobody has spirit enough to set the example. A few tittered nothings from the mass of pink and blue, surmounted by blonde, crêpé chignons in the corner, and a laudable effort on the part of the hostess, are at last checked by that most welcome *Deus ex machina,*—" Your ladyship is served;" and they file out, arm-in-arm, in solemn procession, the etiquette of precedence being rigidly observed, towards the brilliantly-lighted, warm, flower-scented dining-room.

As they took their places at the sumptuous board glittering with gold and silver *épergnes* containing choice hot-house flowers and fruits; where the heavy plate was relieved by painted china, equally costly, and glass whose exquisitely-delicate form and tint shed faint flower-like hues over the snowy damask underneath; while the noiseless, liveried footmen glided about observantly, and the pompous butler waved his magisterial wand occasionally, animation seemed to return magically to the exhausted energies of the guests at Grantly Manor.

At either hand of the Countess d'Hauteville sat the Duke of L—— and the Bishop of C——, both men of culture and conversational ability. The host was equally well provided for, and the Ladies Florence Ellesmere, Maud St. Maur, and Jane Evelyn, were supported by Lord St. Maur, the Viscount Aguylar, and Colonel Stanbury, of the Rifles. The Marquise de Courboisie recovered her good humor between Dyke Faucett and Percival Tyrrell, who, on his left, had the sparkling little widow of the gallant Colonel Dundonald, of the 42d Highlanders.

Before the clear soup had disappeared the ball of conversation was rolling smoothly, and the hum of small-talk and the subdued laughter of the ladies mingled pleasantly with the popping of corks and the delicate aroma of the pines and sweet-scented flowers,—not too powerful, however, to annihilate the bouquet of the priceless wines which supplemented every course.

After awhile the small-talk grew into discussion, and in one or two instances into argument, among the graver members of the party. The duke and a *vis-à-vis* were discussing the admission of a new member into the House of Commons,—a mutual friend. This led to a complaint on the duke's part of the engrossing nature of the duties in both Houses to a conscientious member, drawing forth the expression of Macaulay in relation to Horace Walpole, that, "after the labors of the print-shop and the auction-room, he *unbent his mind* in the House of Commons," from his opponent, in a laughing contradiction of his assertion.

"I am afraid," continued Lord St. Maur, who had taken his seat in the upper House at an unusually early age, and promised to be one of its brightest ornaments, "that the pity wasted upon our arduous exertions is something akin to that one instinctively feels for the camel on account of the hump on its back. I have heard that the moment the smallest load is put upon the back of one of these animals, he closes his eyes and bellows piteously, although they can move along comfortably under a well-packed burden of seven hundred-weight."

The duke smiled. "You speak with the ardor and contempt of youth for obstacles of all kinds which beset the earnest worker. To be an accomplished statesman,—to learn the disposition and genius of a people, and the inclinations of his sovereign, diplomatists, and leading minds; to study the meaning of great treaties, the real value and strength of the land and sea forces of all countries,—is not enough! Principles, opinions, and interests change, and one must be ever watchful, patient, and—unimpulsive. To such young blood as yours, my dear Algernon, I should always be tempted to utter Talleyrand's warning to his impetuous friend who was just entering upon his ministerial duties,—'et surtout—*point de zèle, monsieur.*'"

"Ah," laughed St. Maur, "if I were not by birth and training as conservative as your Grace, I should imagine you were pushing me for some daring innovation, you speak so seriously. To my mind," he added in a lower tone to Percival Tyrrell, who had been listening, while the duke turned to answer a remark of his hostess,—"to my mind, the infusion of young blood into both Houses is of the greatest advantage—it reinvigorates them."

"Take care," answered Percival, smiling under his heavy moustache; "you know the fate of the old bottles when new wine was poured into them."

"Combustion? Yes; but our bottles are iron-bound and proof against accident of that kind," replied St. Maur. "Why, earthquakes may swallow up kings, nations may crumble all about us, the Prince Imperial may sit on the throne of France, and the Czar of Russia in the chair of St. Peter, but the houses of Parliament—those two monuments to our wisdom—will be left standing in their gloomy grandeur, breathing defiantly to the world, '*Après nous, le déluge.*'" He stopped, out of breath, laughing with the rest, and turned abruptly to his neighbor,— "Enough of politics; did you hunt to-day? I could not get here in time."

"Yes," answered Lady Florence Ellesmere, "I did, and enjoyed it amazingly. And," she added, with sparkling eyes, "*I have the brush!* I was in at the death, and Mr. Faucett was good enough to secure it for me!"

St. Maur suppressed a smile. "How very gratifying," he said. "I am sure you would not be willing to exchange it for the bay crown of Corinne at the capitol, or even the sonnets of Petrarch's Laura?"

"Most certainly not," answered the beauty, disdainfully. "I consider a good run with the hounds superior to either.   As for Corinne, I cannot sympathize with her morbid sentimentalism ; and, besides, I have an aversion to her because she was an *habituée* of the school-room, and is always associated with copy-books and the ' use of the globes' in my mind.   As to Laura, who knows whether she ever existed ?   She was only a peg to hang Petrarch's fancies on."

"Yes," replied St. Maur, "you are right.   Everything is dubious, and everybody mythical, in those days before the institution of the fox-hunt.   There is nothing certain, any more than new, under the sun, excepting the additional brilliancy and beauty of the fair Dianas themselves this evening ;" this to her, with an admiring glance, and inwardly, "The fable of Prometheus is *no* myth, but repeats itself eternally."

Faucett all this while was languidly laying himself metaphorically at the feet of the Marquise de Courboisie, and, as her neighbor on the other hand seemed absorbed in an animated conversation with the pretty widow, she bent herself to the employment of every art of witchery known to the modern Circe, and had almost succeeded in awakening him to a perilous animation, when the signal was given, and the ladies were obliged to adjourn to the drawing-room.

As she passed through the door held open by Faucett, she murmured one word in his ear, which sent him back to the table with a faint blush on his cheek and a dangerous glitter in his cold, blue eyes.

Pauline was not ignorant of the diabolical poison in the Parthian shaft ; and, as she swept across the hall to the drawing-room, in her rich white silk covered with black *chantilly*, looped here and there with pomegranates as scarlet as her lips, caught with diamond sprays less bright than her triumphant eyes, she whispered to herself, " We shall see. No man ever trifled with me with impunity; *Gare à vous!* Monsieur Faucett."

She endured the purgatory of an hour with the ladies with cheerful resignation, and improved the occasion by a few sweetly-delivered, spiteful speeches on a subject which still rankled.

When the tea-service was brought in, Miss Ogilvie—looking more than usually handsome in her ordinary dress of rich black silk cut square at the throat, with a ruff of rich old lace standing around the snow-white neck, without other ornament than a pair of valuable pearls (her mother's wedding-parure), which she wore in her small ears, and the crown of dark hair which gave her a queenly look—advanced with little Valérie from an obscure corner and prepared, as was her custom, to make the tea.

"What a very handsome, ladylike creature that governess is!" commented the duchess, dropping her glass, after a glance through it in Anne's direction. "She has quite the '*grande air.*' Indeed, she is far too beautiful for most houses, but dear Earl d'Hauteville is so madly in love with his own wife that he has no eyes for any other woman!"

"Ah, really," murmured Pauline, with languid interest; "and yet they say he is quite *épris* of the lovely governess of late, although the dear countess does not dream of it herself."

"Is it possible!" whispered the duchess, horror-stricken already. "Surely some one ought to warn the dear child. What a snake the woman must be!"

"Your Grace has reason," replied Pauline; "somebody ought to unmask the wicked girl. Did you ever see a menial—yes, a menial, for, whatever her services, she is paid for them, is she not?—with that air of the *grande dame* that she did not begin to imagine herself mistress?

I never did. I had a maid once," she continued, "who walked like an empress, and I dismissed her at once, before she could imagine herself Marquise de Courboisie. I regretted her, for she had superb taste, but *que voulez-vous?* one *must* be careful."

"I shall certainly make it my business," said the duchess, "to open this poor child's eyes before things go any further. It is only a duty we owe each other, and I should be rejoiced, if such a thing could be possible" (she drew herself up, while the diamonds in her bosom flashed with ducal indignation), "that any one should warn me under such circumstances."

"My Mignon tells me," drawled the marquise, "that the earl is constantly in the school-room; the little Valérie is such a good excuse, you know."

Her Grace fairly bristled. "It is infamous! the earl in the school-room! Ah, I can scarcely contain myself!"

She contained herself just in time, for the footman approached with a salver laden with cups of the chat-inspiring beverage, and the door opened to admit a party of gentlemen, among them Dyke Faucett, whom Pauline summoned to her side by the faintest possible sign; and Percy Tyrrell, who, after a few words with the duchess, now all smiles and graciousness, advanced to the corner where the tea-maker rested from her labors.

"Has the 'cup that cheers' any attraction for you?" she inquired, smilingly, as he sank into a *causeuse* whose corner touched her table.

"Have you seen me show any marked predilection for the rival cup," he asked, "that you should entertain a doubt on the subject? I have been thirsting for this all day," he added, trying to look in her eyes as he took the fragile wonder in egg-shell china from her hand; and then noting the deepening color in her cheek, fastened his eyes upon the tiny *thumb* which appeared over the edge of the saucer. "Did you know, Miss Ogilvie, that the *thumb* is an index of character?"

"Indeed!" she laughed. "I am not versed in the science of palmology. What does it denote?"

"D'Arpentigny says, 'L'animal supérieur est dans la main, *l'homme dans la pouce*,'" quoted Tyrrell, gravely stirring his tea; "and variety of character and disposition is determined by *its* dimensions. Now, a thumb such as I was scarcely able to distinguish on the porcelain of this saucer a moment since denotes that its owner is governed in all things more readily *by the heart;* while a person with a large thumb, like mine, for instance, governs himself entirely by *the head.*"

"In short," cried Anne, smiling, "the small thumbs point out the amiable idiots among us, and the large ones the Solons and Platos! But is this test infallible?" she asked. "Have you been under obligations to your monstrous thumb for your merciful preservation all these years from the weaknesses of small-thumbed humanity?"

"Love, I presume you mean by weaknesses?" demanded Tyrrell.

"Yes; but perhaps you do not believe such a thing exists. La Rochefoucauld *must* have been *large*-thumbed, for he says, you know, 'True love is very like an apparition; everybody talks about it, but *very few have ever seen it.*'"

"I agree with him," burst forth Tyrrell. "The only love-affair I ever had was *platonic* from beginning to end, and discouraged me from any further attempt."

"Perhaps," rejoined Anne, "your admiration of this man, with whose skepticism on sentimental subjects you 'agree' so completely, induced you to form a compact similar to his own with Madame de Lafayette. Nothing could have been freer from weakness than that faithful friendship."

Tyrrell knit his brows a moment, and then—"Ah, yes, I remember; madame acknowledges the platonic *liaison*, on the ground, ' he gives *me mind* and *I reform his heart.*' Was not that the tie?"

"Yes; very sensible, but unsatisfying, I fancy. A woman's world cannot be peopled by her brain; her affections are her existence; all the poets and romancers are unanimous in that conclusion."

"And you? Do you share their opinion? You seem to live and thrive, and yet I doubt the atmosphere about you being over-freighted with affection or tenderness." He glanced, as he spoke, at the coldly-impassive face of the countess, who seemed absorbed in earnest converse with her Grace, who, panting once more with righteous wrath, delivered herself. Anne's face saddened; with eyes bent upon the hands lying clasped on her lap, she remained silent.

Tyrrell, regretting that he had so clouded the brightness of that face, changed the subject abruptly, and asked, " Did you see the sunset this evening, Miss Ogilvie? It was unusually fine."

"Oh, yes," she answered. "The superb sunsets here compose *my* gallery of pictures; I never miss adding one to my collection if I can possibly help it. I have seen the ' morning hours' called the ' prose of the day;' surely our exquisite twilights are its ' poetry.' Valérie and I generally walk to the ruins of the monastery to see the sun go down behind the hills. Do you know the end of the cloister where the great oriel stood?" He nodded. " We sit there, on that crumbling ledge, and look out, as it were, from the *loge* of a theatre on the great panorama which stretches out from that view. I think," she went on, while a dreamy softness came into the blue eyes, —"I think when that misty veil is drawn over the vivid green of all those billowy meadows, reaching to the very foot of the hills, while the sleepy cattle browse gently, or lie about enjoying the rest and quiet, after the burden and heat of the day, one cannot help drawing a part of that peace and tranquillity into one's very soul. I always come back to the school-room feeling as if I had taken a fresh draught of patience and strength; and sometimes both are needed," she added, smiling.

Tyrrell replaced his now empty cup on the table, and then said, earnestly, "I have been trying to obtain some information in regard to your brother, Miss Ogilvie. A friend of mine, an American, is in Paris at this moment, and I saw some of his people yesterday in town. They are moving heaven and earth to get communication with him, and if they succeed you will have tidings of your brother."

"Oh, how can I thank you?" broke from Anne's lips, as her face beamed with joy. "I have been so hopeless lately of ever being able to discover any truth about my poor Dick. How very good you are! It was for this, then, that you missed the hunt to-day?"

Tyrrell laughed. "It was not a heart-breaking disappointment. There are plenty of foxes in the world unslain, but there are few opportunities of winning such grateful smiles. May I not wear one of them in my memory rather than the brush in my hat-band, if I please?"

That treacherous, quick Irish blood dyed Anne's cheek again with its scarlet signal of distress, and once more Percival came to the rescue.

"Poor Paris!" he murmured. "I fear there is but little hope of her coming out of this fierce fire unscorched. Everything seems against them; continual reverses, treachery, mistrust everywhere. And yet one's sympathy is tempered by the thought that they brought all these disasters on themselves, the madmen !"

"Oh, but that only makes it the more pitiable," urged Anne. "A ship wrecked by a storm, with its crew on board, is sorrowful enough, but a ship wrecked wantonly by the grasping, cruel greed of a mutinous *few*, is heart-rending,—is it not ?"

"You are right. Waterloo was less humiliating than Sédan. I am afraid there is nothing left for poor France now but Oliver Cromwell's *dernier ressort.*"

"What was that ?" asked Anne, anxiously.

"His despairing command to his soldiers: 'Put your trust in God, and *keep your powder dry*,'" answered Tyrrell.

Anne's smile was sad as tears. "Yes," she said, "all earthly trust seems to have been misplaced ; they are undoubtedly *doomed.*"

Before her companion had time to restore the cheerful serenity of her habitual expression by a more successful effort at changing the conversation, the earl had sauntered up to the tea-table, and drawing little Valérie away from Miss Ogilvie's side, where she always nestled contentedly during the hour or two Anne was expected to remain in the drawing-room, he asked, while he caressed gently the golden curls, "What depth of metaphysics or philosophy has Colonel Tyrrell plunged you into, Miss Ogilvie,—you have both looked so solemn during this last quarter of an hour ?"

"Oh, nothing so abstract or so agreeable as those interesting theories," replied Anne, rallying with an effort ; "we were speaking of the peril of poor France, and her sufferings."

"And may I have some tea if I try to demonstrate to the best of my ability that this scourging will ultimately benefit 'poor France,' who undoubtedly needed to be brought to her senses?"

Anne, smiling, handed him his tea, quite cold, but sufficient pretext to warrant the earl's seating himself in the chair Tyrrell had vacated at that moment.

As he stirred the unpalatable concoction, wondering what he should say to this handsome girl *à propos* of France's scourging, now that he *had* ousted Tyrrell, Anne's eyes followed the latter as he lounged across the room and sank with indolent grace into a *fauteuil* by the Marquise de Courboisie, from whom Dyke Faucett had craved leave of absence in favor of *just one little cigar*, and I fear there was a wistful regret in their blue depths.

"What could be expected?" the earl's voice broke in. "Paris was pampered at the expense of the provinces; the police and the press hampered with restrictions; the supremacy of the priesthood daily increasing; and all these things, symptoms of a tottering government, were ignored by the people until too late. The fact is, the French were too completely bewildered by the magnitude of their position of late; they resorted to mean and futile devices to increase it overwhelmingly, and their fall was sure." The earl sipped his cold tea with a pleasant conviction that Anne must be duly impressed by these well-ventilated sentiments. But she only sighed and said,—

"Ah, yes; it is very, very sad,"—as she might have assented to the most commonplace observation delivered by any other than a peer of the realm, and a member of the House of Lords, where his opinions were not denied weight! And then she asked: "Do you think, Lord d'Hauteville, that the siege *can* be prolonged to any greater extent? Are not the people *starving?*" Her voice trembled, and a slight shudder passed over her as the last word escaped.

"I very much fear they are," replied his lordship,—"at least the aged and the children, who cannot exist on coarse food—and little of it. Some of the accounts are harrowing indeed ; let us hope there is much exaggeration, which is most probable." And the kind-hearted earl turned to his little daughter again, and drawing her affectionately to his knee : "Is this little girl all that can be desired, Miss Ogilvie?" he inquired, pinching the dimpled cheeks with gentle fondness.

"Indeed yes," the young governess replied, eagerly. "She is as sweet and good and lovable as she can be. She is improving so much in her French too. Speak to papa in French, darling ;" but Valérie hung her head and was mute.

"How do you manage to keep her so shy and retiring?" the earl asked, well pleased,—"so different from the pert forwardness of the precocious young ladies of her acquaintance, who are only too obnoxiously ready to exhibit their accomplishments——"

"I fancy there is a good deal of the violet in the nature of my little Valérie," replied Anne, coloring with pleasure at the faint word of praise which rarely greeted her best endeavors. "She is naturally timid, and very sensitive,—almost too much so, I fear, for her own happiness." And she looked lovingly at her little charge.

Silence a moment, and then Valérie spoke, drawing closer within her father's arms : "Why do you not go out with us, papa, as you used? It has been four weeks (is it not four weeks, Miss Ogilvie?) since you walked to the monastery with us ! When will you come with us again ? We miss you so much ; do we not?" nodding appealingly at Anne for confirmation.

"It would be far pleasanter were papa to join your rambles, darling, for *you ;* but would it be so agreeable to papa? that is the question," Anne remonstrated.

"'To be, or not to be,' papa?" laughed Valérie, her shyness vanishing before her father's affectionate glance and the loving pressure of his arms about her. "Are we to have you for one little, wee hour, away from all these grand people, in the old jolly way, before they came here, —every evening before dinner? Oh, yes; say yes, dear papa. Do help me to persuade him, Miss Ogilvie; nobody could refuse *you* anything; and Colonel Tyrrell is not half so amusing as papa."

A quick gleam of intelligence shot forth from the earl's eyes right into Anne's, as her cheek crimsoned. "Then you have found a substitute for papa already! Ah, inconstant little girl! How can you expect me to forgive such treachery?"

Valérie's eyes filled. "Oh, papa, it was not I who wanted him; that is, I *do* like him very, very much; but I never asked him to fill *your* place. I love you best, of course, and he shall never go again if you will only promise to come with us; shall he, dear Miss Ogilvie?" Whether Anne would have perjured herself under stress of severe embarrassment is not known; for at that instant Lady d'Hauteville approached, with an unwonted cloud upon her placid brow, and the icy breath of the glacier in her clear, cold voice, which seemed to cut deeper than Anne's ears as these words dropped from her compressed lips: "I should like a few moments' conversation with Miss Ogilvie in the library, if she is disengaged."

The earl, whose practiced ear recognized the bugle-note of danger,—with a pang of sympathy in his heart for Anne,—arose, and, taking Valérie by the hand, strolled into the conservatory, while the poor young governess, struck dumb by this unprecedented summons, followed the countess mechanically from the room.

11*

CHAPTER XIV.

THE library was but dimly lighted, and as her lady-ship sank with an exhausted air into a large arm-chair drawn up in front of the blazing wood-fire, the expression of cold severity in her face was plainly distinguishable, but of Anne's, as she stood by the chimney-piece with one hand resting lightly on its carved surface, nothing could be discerned save that her head was carried rather more erect than usual, and the color seemed to have all faded out of her poor face.

"Miss Ogilvie," began the countess, "I have desired this interview, that I might acquaint you with the fact that for the future your presence will not be required in the drawing-room, or indeed outside your own apart-ments, excepting during those hours when you walk with Lady Valérie *in the grounds,*—outside of them I do not wish her to go."

"Very well," were the only words Anne could force her tongue to pronounce, and turned towards the door. Her hand was on the knob, when with an effort she re-traced her steps, and, coming close to the countess's side, said, gently, "May I not know in what I have offended, or failed in my duty?"

"I have no complaint to make," returned that lady, while her white face, with its pale-colored eyes and straw-colored lashes, and the thin-lipped small mouth, which could smile so sweetly when it chose, and could be so very "firm" where the *convenances* were assailed, seemed to grow colder still in the fire-light. "Towards Valérie, you are all that can be desired; I have nothing further to say." She waved a thin hand, bloodless but begemmed, in token of dismissal, and Anne, bending her head slightly, left the room.

The earl's slumbers were somewhat protracted the next morning, the natural result of having been called upon, in the dead of night, to extenuate his marital probity to his outraged spouse.

Her grace the duchess slept profoundly, and, I fear, snored, for she was a *bonne vivante*, and inclined to corpulence ; and——

Lamartine's "Confidences" received their initiatory baptism of—tears.

CHAPTER XV.

An unwonted darkness brooded over the distorted face of suffering Paris on the night of the 25th of January, 1871.

Rain poured down in torrents; the guards who patrolled the outer Boulevards and the Place de la Bastille were chilled to the hearts, under their dripping water-proof capes, and the soughing of the wind, through the almost deserted streets, sounded like the wail of a lost spirit.

The Communists, since their last defeat at the Hôtel de Ville, had been apparently tranquil; but Flourens, chafing at delay, was biding his time. The people of Paris seemed stunned for the moment by the fact that the enemy was at their very gates, but they soon rallied, and capitulation was as strenuously opposed as ever. But, by whom? The governor of Paris had sworn to die before he would give up the city, it is true, but the National

Guard, stirred up by that eloquent fire-brand, Gambetta, and the starving, wretched, broken-hearted, but not broken-spirited, population of *women*, cried out, "After the forts the barricades, and after the barricades, *we will burn the city;* that resource remains to us!"

All this time the French and Prussian batteries were exchanging fire; mitrailleuse and cannon were stationed before the Hôtel de Ville and the Louvre, on the Rue de Rivoli, and the various Places; battalions of National Guards assembled daily, while regiments of infantry and cavalry, and Mobiles, occupied the other side of the Champs Elysées.

Provisions were almost exhausted; meat, excepting the high-flavored horse-flesh and the succulent rat, had entirely given out; the infirm and the aged were dying as fast as the helpless children, of hunger and cold and despair.

It was close upon midnight, and still the rain came down, and the wind howled drearily, mingling its woeful voice with the occasional booming of the cannon from the forts.

Dora drew her watch from her bosom, and, leaning towards the lantern hung against the wall, murmured to herself, "Midnight, and he has not yet come; what *can* it mean? Agnes!" she called, softly.

It was a long room lined each side by narrow cots, in each of which lay, in the sleep of exhaustion, or tossed in the restlessness of pain, a victim to the *chassepots* or the *nädelgewehr* of civilized warfare. Over the head of each bed hung a little ticket, bearing the number by which its occupant was designated.

Kneeling at the bedside of No. 16, Agnes was striving to cool the burning head of a poor fellow who had suffered amputation of both limbs the previous day, and whom fever was fast destroying. He was a mere lad,—not eighteen,—and had a comely, provincial face, whose honest blue eyes filled with grateful tears more than once, as Agnes bathed his forehead with iced water and turned his hot pillow with dexterous hand.

At a little distance stood another angel of mercy, wearing the Geneva cross on her sleeve,—a French lady of rank, Madame de Bergeret. Her husband, in the army of Napoleon, had fallen on that disastrous day at Sédan, and when the news was gently broken to her, and she was implored not to give way under her bitter trial, she drew herself up, and said, proudly, without a tear, "Give way? Wherefore should I break down? Had my Victor owned a thousand lives they should each have been dedicated to our France! He died gloriously, as the Emperor *should* have done, on the field of battle." If she ever wept her Victor, it was in the dead watches of the night, and the story of his life's sacrifice was recounted, dry-eyed, by her to many a wounded soldier nursed by her unflinching but tender hands. She was invaluable as nurse during operations which caused both Dora and Agnes to grow faint and useless; her eagle eye and strong dark face never blenched where nerve and pluck were imperatively demanded.

"Agnes," asked Dora, in a whisper, approaching the cot of No. 16, "is it not strange that Mr. Buchanan has not been here all day, or to-night? Can anything new have happened in Paris, do you think? and it storms so terribly." She ceased, with a slight shudder; it was chill in that dim-lighted, carpetless room after midnight.

"Nothing new, dear," answered Agnes; "but how pale and weary you look, Dora! Ah, give up to-night, and rest a little. You have no right to destroy yourself; think of little Marian. Where is she?"

"Come and see her," answered Dora; and, after a few words to Madame de Bergeret (Sœur Thérèse, as she was known in the ambulance), they left the room together.

Just outside, in the corridor, was a little "cabinet" devoted to the storing of lint, bandages, splints, etc., and containing a sofa, a table, and a chair. On this sofa Dora had obtained permission to lay her last remaining treasure, wrapped in the woolen cloak (which covered her from neck to heel when she went into the streets), on the three nights weekly which were allotted to herself and Agnes to watch by the bedsides of the wounded. Little Marian slept here very comfortably, and on the alternate nights shared the poor room which Dora and Agnes occupied near by, where they tried to find rest on a mattress of husks, and to warm their half-frozen feet and benumbed fingers over a couple of miserable *chaufferettes*.

But Marian was warm and comfortable to-night, for there was a small stove in the room used for preparing messes for the patients outside. There she lay curled up like a little white rabbit, under the warm folds of the woolen cloak; all her golden curls in disorder, her thin little face flushed with sleep, and the sweet, red lips parted with the soft, regular breathing of health.

"How well she looks," whispered Agnes, "and how lovely! Could you not lie down with her there for a little quarter of an hour? I will watch, and awake you at one o'clock."

"Oh, Agnes, if she had died!" cried Dora, unheeding the last suggestion, and gazing at her idol with love-brimming eyes. "I could not have borne it; indeed, I could not."

"But she did not die," returned the more practical Agnes, "and you must try your very best to get stronger yourself, or you may be called to bear a heavier sorrow than that.''

'' Oh, what, Agnes, what do you mean ? Could *any-thing* be harder to bear than to see her die ?''

'' Yes : to die yourself, and leave her, as I was left,— alone on the charity of the world,'' answered Agnes. '' Now, dear, you will rest awhile, and,'' taking from her pocket a piece of dark-looking bread, '' eat this; I had more than I wanted to-day.''

'' Oh, Agnes, was there ever such an unselfish angel as you on earth before ?''

But Agnes had vanished to her post by No. 16, and Dora, with a moan of real weariness, threw herself on the hard couch beside little Marian, holding fast in her hand the morsel of bread, lest her child should awake hungry, as she very frequently did, poor little dear !

How long she slept she knew not ; but she was awakened by the tramp of many feet outside in the corridor and the subdued hum of many voices. The lantern hung in the centre of the *cabinet* was burning dimly, and a few struggling rays of light through the *persiennes* assured her of the commencement of another day.

It was five o'clock, that hour in winter the most chill and comfortless of all the twenty-four. Dora rose to her feet stiff and unrefreshed, and tottered to the door, for there was certainly a fresh arrival of wounded, and her services might be needed.

As she opened her door, four men carrying a litter, on which was lying a form with a handkerchief thrown over the face, wearing the uniform of a National Guard, passed her. By the side of the litter walked Ronald Buchanan, his face white and rigid. Dora trembled, and a fear shot through her heart born of sympathy and quick intuition.

'' Can it be the friend—his friend—of whom he has

spoken so often to us, who was in the Gardes Nationales, and whom he has not seen for days?" She waited breathlessly, until they had disrobed the senseless form and laid him on his cot; and then behind the screen which was drawn around him, whence only a few stifled moans betrayed that he still lived, Buchanan was tenderly dressing the frightful wound which had laid open poor Ogilvie's skull by an inglorious sabre-cut in the hand of a drunken Mobile. For, amid all the other horrors of famine, cold, and want, the "wet damnation" of drunkenness had crept into the ranks of the soldiery to a fearful extent.

That night a party of Mobiles had demanded entrance at the house of a respectable bourgeois, whose two sons had gone to fight for their country. The old man was suspected of having stored up provisions, and these hungry, absinthe-maddened wretches broke in upon his startled family, devoured all they could get, and frightened the women out of their senses. They were proceeding to institute an orgie upon the relics of some old Burgundy found in the cellar, when two or three National Guards passed the open door. Hearing cries for help, and the sobs of women, they entered unceremoniously, and soon a terrible conflict was taking place in the comfortable sitting-room of the family. The Mobiles were two to one, and well-armed; but, being all of them more or less intoxicated, the contest was equalized. What the result would have been, Heaven knows, had they not been interrupted at the height of the mêlée by a posse of gens-d'armes, whom the incessant screams of the women had attracted to the scene.

The Frenchmen fought like devils; Ogilvie fought like a Briton. *They* fired here, there, and everywhere; slashed with their swords' and *sacré'd* in guttural gasps. Ogilvie used his fists; down went a spluttering Gaul, who was brandishing his sword over the young Englishman's head; down, as if dead at his feet, with one blow between the eyes; down went a second victim to muscular science, and a third would have followed, had he not struck viciously at Ogilvie's uncovered head with his sabre. As the door burst open to admit the gens-d'armes to the rescue, the foremost one received in his arms the senseless form of a man wearing the National Guard uniform, whose face was deluged with blood from an ugly sabre-cut over the right temple.

Buchanan's duties at the hospitals had been unremitting that day, and he had just turned, tired and sick at heart, into the narrow street leading to the ambulance hospital, to refresh himself with a sight of Dora and her friend, when the litter-bearers passed him, and a fragment of their conversation caught his ear. "Yes," they were saying, "he is certainly dead, *ce pauvre Anglais;* he is a fitter subject for a pine coffin than an hospital; *que diable allait-il faire à Paris?* If he had remained in his own country he would have saved his skull." Buchanan waited under the lantern at the entrance to the hospital, and when they approached and he saw lying senseless, under the pouring rain, the ghastly face of the jovial chum of many long years, his heart quailed within him, and his hand trembled as he threw over the poor, drawn face his pocket-handkerchief. His voice was almost choked when he addressed a few inquiries to the bearers of this sad burden, and directed them where to place it.

The day was far advanced before Ronald stirred from behind the screen which still sheltered poor Ogilvie from the gaze of others, and when he came forth he looked wan and ill, and very anxious, for he was very doubtful of the success of the trepanning which had been necessary in this case, and he had conceived a warm friendship for this whole-souled, fearless, generous-hearted man, which he was slow to form, and gave not lightly up when formed.

Dora had been watching for him all the morning, with a heart full of sympathy, and eyes full of pity (for she knew now that it was his English friend whose life was apparently ebbing away); but she was engaged far off at the bed of a convalescent, reading, as she had promised, a page of the *Gaulois* to him.

She saw Agnes meet Ronald as he emerged, and hand him the cup of coffee which they had prepared together, and as she noted the sweet smile which lit his sad face for a moment as he thanked Agnes for her thoughtfulness, a sharp pang struck through her heart. She did not hear Agnes's eager reply,—"It was Dora's suggestion; she feared you would feel faint from exhaustion. Is the poor man's wound fatal?"

"I fear so; he seems sinking. It was a terrible gash; the only wonder is that he lived to get here."

He put down the coffee, untasted, and covered his face with his hands. Agnes stood silent; she dared ask no further question.

After a moment,—"It is Ogilvie; my friend, and Sister Agnes,"—a little effort at a smile,—"I want to put him under your charge until all is over,—may I? He cannot last long, and I should like him to be carefully tended; I will be with him as much as possible."

"I shall do my best; do not despair. Think how many have been given up for dead who have recovered. If careful nursing will save him he shall not die."

Ronald took her hand in his, as he had done once before, when he confided Dora to her charge (how long ago that seemed!), and said, "I thank you; you are indeed a sister of mercy and loving-kindness."

Dora, afar-off, watching this little scene, bent her head

suddenly over the paper, the lines of which swam before her tear-filled eyes.

Ronald gulped down the coffee in three mouthfuls, and then disappeared again behind the screen with Agnes. He lingered there long enough to give her careful directions, and then, with a long breath of relief, turned towards the other end of the room where Dora still sat, reading to the crusty little Frenchman, who commented and criticised every article with the ironical spleen of his bilious little nature, until she was ready to scream with impatience and vexation.

She did not stop reading or raise her head as Buchanan approached, she saw him taking Agnes's hand all over the little sheet of the *Presse;* and, when he came quite near and addressed her, to his surprise she answered coldly, with scarcely a glance, "I am very well, thanks; and you?"

"I am not well," he replied. "I had a most exhausting day yesterday,—I have been up all night. Agnes's coffee has restored me somewhat, but I feel shaky yet."

"Why do you not go home and sleep?" she asked, anxiety getting the better of pique. "You could have a few hours at least to-day."

"I cannot," he said. "I must not leave Ogilvie for an hour."

"Is it——" she began; her voice broke down.

"Yes," answered Buchanan, shortly; "I have done all I can for him, and left him in Agnes's hands; there will be no change for an hour, I feel sure. Could you get out, do you think? A turn in the sun would do us both more good than sleep with anxious hearts."

She rose instantly, and, putting on her black bonnet and cloak, and Marian's little hat and jacket, they turned to the door.

The rain was over, and the clouds were breaking away before the face of the sun. The streets looked clean and bright, and people were filling them in every direction. A long line of women stood patiently before the door of a baker, each waiting her turn to get a little loaf or two of a doubtful-colored bread. They passed a man who had four rats tied on a stick; he was selling them at one franc each. This sight seemed to recall something to Ronald's recollection. He thrust his hand into his surtout pocket and drew forth two new-laid eggs.

"I forgot these," he said. "I brought them for Marian. They cost me an hour's argument and an amputation. Boil them for her dinner; but only one at a time: eggs are very rare."

Dora placed them, with a bright look of gratitude, in the little basket on her arm; she was going to do her marketing for the day.

"Will you dine with us to-day?" she asked, archly. "We are to have '*potage à la printanière*,' '*navets au naturel*,' '*pommes de terre sautées*,' and black bread."

To her astonishment he answered, gravely, "Thanks; I will dine with you with pleasure. At what hour?"

"At five o'clock, in the little 'cabinet,'" she replied, with drooping head (there would not be enough for two, let alone *three*, in her little basket, even with Marian's eggs).

He watched her from under his eyelashes.

"You will not be offended if I supplement your very good *menu* with a *pièce de résistance* I was presented with yesterday by the same person from whom I begged the eggs. He is an old rascal, whose son was hurt on the Place of the Hôtel de Ville a week ago (I was obliged to take off one of his arms, which was shattered by a chassepot), and the old man wanted to pay me in money for my obliging services. But I had heard that in his garret he had a poultry-yard, from which he occasionally sold a fowl at enormous prices; and I suggested, in view of this dinner-party, that he should give me as a fee a couple of good fowls. He consented, and gave me a pair (I have them safe, don't fear). And then I asked for a few eggs; but the old fellow was immovable, and I could only extort two for my little pet. But will you ask me to dinner as long as the fowls last?"

"Indeed, yes. Oh, how glad I am! Agnes has been actually starving."

"And you?" he said, tenderly. "You are not looking as robust as you ought. You are getting so small and frail that the wind will blow you away from us some day, and then——"

"And then," she returned, "you will still have Agnes left, and she is the best nurse, you know, or you would not have given her this important post."

"I gave it her," he replied, gravely, "because it will require unwearying attention, and that you are not able to endure just now, nor would I suffer it to be imposed upon you."

Ah, Dora, keep those golden-gleaming eyes of yours hidden under their long lashes, for they are speaking to the heart of the man beside you in a language which you never more may use.

She was so happy. It was not January, it was surely June, the sun was so bright and warm. Her feet scarcely touched the earth; and, when she returned to her post in the hospital, a lovely rose-color made her face radiant in beauty, and there was a light in her eyes born of the knowledge that she was beloved.

CHAPTER XVI.

To every man who has passed the rubicon of his first quarter century, whether by the *pons asinorum*, or otherwise, there have been presented experiences, however widely differing in tone and circumstance, of the same general character. The tale of our daily life, if carried back a few centuries and clothed in steel and fustian, would appear to knight and yeoman as a specimen, strange only from the extra bloom, forced in the hothouse of civilization, the kernel being always the same.

It will not, therefore, be necessary for me to explain why the frugal repast, cooked and served by Dora's fair hands in the *petit cabinet* at five o'clock precisely, exceeded in delight any banquet of the gods given on the heights of Olympus.

They were all very hungry, to be sure, and this in itself is a *sauce piquante* that Brillat-Savarin could not concoct. The table was laid for four, with somewhat cracked particolored china, and not much table to spare, but the *nappe* was spotless, so were the napkins, and the *poulet fricassée* delicious. The vegetable soup (vegetable *pur et simple*) was delicately flavored and hot (two good qualities for soup, rather rare), and, although it looked *un peu maigre*, the carrots and square bits of turnips bobbed up and down in an effort to look jolly, which was laudable, if unsuccessful. The *pommes de terre sautées* could not have been excelled at Philippe's, and the three hundred grammes of black bread tried to hide themselves behind the soup-tureen in a shamefaced sort of way.

They were very happy, for the critical hour when poor Ogilvie's life had hung in the balance with death, and a straw's weight would have kicked the beam, had gone by and left him conscious, and, although excessively prostrated from loss of blood, restored to a sense of outward events, and on the hope-list of convalescents. Ronald watched by him until five o'clock, and then begging Sœur Thérèse to take his place, joined Dora, Agnes, and little Marian at dinner.

Human nature is an insolvable enigma; is it not?

Here were three people, possessing not one pound sterling between them, who had bartered away, one after the other, every object of value they owned; behind them the past four months, one series of horrors, privations, and trials; before them the future, a great, black, impenetrable cloud of certain calamity; around them the moans of the suffering, and the murmurings of rebellion among the people; beyond these the incessant booming of the cannon in the distance. And yet, these three people, the imaginative, timid Dora, the thoughtful, gentle Agnes, the earnest, provident Buchanan, with baby Marian on his knee, were eating their *fricassée* and drinking their *vin ordinaire* (surely no Falernian ever tasted better), not with long faces and lugubrious sighs, but with cheery words, and soft, musical laughter, subdued from respect to outsiders, but bubbling from the heart nevertheless, while the glow in Dora's face reflected itself in each of those about her.

In the life of almost every woman there comes one interval of happiness as free from taint of earth as that which filled Eve's soul as she gathered in the sunlight of God's smile of all the fruits—save one—during the guileless innocence of her first days in Eden, an hour when the unacknowledged love in her heart finds its reflection in another, and the pure blossom, with the dew still clinging to it, expands into full flower in the exotic atmosphere of a mute reciprocation ; a divine flower, not breathed upon by vows, nor robbed of its bloom by handling, however tender, nor placed on a level with vegetables and weeds by barter, or exchange, or the foot-trampling which is inevitable in the dense crowd of a careless-stepping humanity.

In this spontaneous offering of soul to soul, needing no words or protestations, but stealing into her inner consciousness, an intangible perfume of love, Dora saw no danger, dreamed not of actualities, accepted the beautiful present without a glance back or forward. It was only long after, when life narrowed down to a blank drawing of the breath,—nothing more,—when, while the hands toiled patiently, the soul took its ease in the slumbrous inaction of a dull despair, and the sacred fire was quenched under the ceaseless dripping of the inane platitudes which fell upon her with the stone-wearing persistency of her forced surroundings, it was then that she felt most bitterly the result of having walked, in joyful ignorance, in that rarefied atmosphere which tries too severely human lungs, and leaves them ever after more sensitive to the chill breath of the world-mistral.

Had she known what it was that lifted the sad weight from her heart, that gave the days wings, and made this French ambulance refuge a very heaven of joy amid the shrieks and groans and cries of a purgatory through which she moved like an angel, carrying balm upon its wings, her face lit up with the soft radiance of a loving charity towards all the sorrowing, the suffering, and the sinning, springing from the fount of love within,—had she known whence sprang that fount, she would have plucked out this new life in her heart, then and there, unhesitatingly; for she was pure and white-souled as her four-year-old Marian.

But it is not thus that we are allowed to shape or determine the weight of the crosses laid upon us. Our eyes are scaled, until they assume such proportions as shall chafe sorely the tender flesh, and bring from the heart tears of blood, and bow the head humbly to the eventual crowning—let us pray—of immortality.

And so they dined, and chatted, and shook out the golden dust from the petals of a blissful present over the grim, gaunt realities around them, until they even laughed gleefully among themselves, and found as much pleasure in the chocolate-sticks which served as dessert as could be extracted from the pines and forced grapes of a bloated sumptuousness.

"I do not think I ever shall regret," said Agnes, nibbling at her share of that delicacy, "having been in Paris during the siege; it is certainly an experience which few can count in their lives, and I confess to a leaning towards the unusual in our daily walk."

"How very high the convent walls must have seemed to you!" laughed Dora. "Do you imagine she could have endured them *à la perpétuité?*" (to her *vis-à-vis*).

"I fear not," answered Ronald, smiling. "You remind me, Sister Agnes, of a speech of George Selwyn's after a terrible orgie the night before: 'I look and feel villainously bad; but, hang it, it is life! *it is life!*' You are willing to suffer all things for the sake of adding to your experiences."

"Ah, not so bad as that," she protested, laughingly. "I am not insatiable in search of adventure, though I do soar sometimes above convent walls."

"I cannot help feeling that if one of us *was to be shut up here*," said Dora, "how fortunate it is that we *both*——"

("*Both!* do you hear that, Marian? *We* are not counted in," interpolated Buchanan)—"that we both," continued Dora, unheeding, "should have been prevented from escaping.   What should I have done without Agnes?"

"And what would Agnes have done without you?" she replied.

"And what would have become of Marian and *me* without you both?" piteously cried Ronald, stealing another chocolate-bar for his little friend.   "It was all foreordained," he continued; "you are aware that 'there is a divinity which shapes our ends, rough-hew them as we may' (so the Bard of Avon assures us), therefore the inscrutable hand of fate has brought together these three noble specimens of three separate nationalities; for you call yourself American, do you not?"

Dora raised her head a trifle proudly, as she answered, "Certainly; I was born under the shelter of the great republic, in its noble forest and among its kindly people; surely I can be proud of my nationality, and of that glorious country?"

"Yes," Ronald answered, gravely.   "You own a noble birthright in claiming as your native land this vigorous offspring of dear old England.   America has always commanded my admiration, and of late years my sincere respect ; she has wiped out gloriously the great stain of slavery, which was the only grave blot on her escutcheon."

Dora's eyes shone.   "I do love to hear America praised by an Englishman," she said; "generally they feel it a bounden duty to snub us *à l'outrance;* I was always bristling like a porcupine among the English residents in Rome."

"Really," exclaimed Agnes, "I could not have imagined you would show so much spirit in waving your 'stars and stripes'; it is positively bringing some color into your cheeks.''

Dora laughed. "Let us have some of your 'Ach Gott! mein liebe Vaterland,' from you now, Agnes, and then Mr. Buchanan will sing 'God save the Queen,' and we will disperse quietly.''

"No," answered Buchanan, "you shall have no roar from John Bull to-night; he is in a quiescent frame of mind, not to be piqued or driven into any enthusiastic demonstration whatever: he is simply thankful that he —exists.''

"And yet," said Agnes, "I have heard of people, under pleasanter circumstances than yours at present, regretting that they ever had been born; how strange that seems to me!''

"And," Ronald rejoined, "I have no doubt there are instances on record, of people who would feel grateful if the same extinction of existence were extended to some of their relatives and acquaintances.''

"Oh, how dreadful!" exclaimed Agnes and Dora together; and the latter continued,—

"One who stands alone, without a connection or near relative, feels this almost a blasphemy." She looked sad for a moment.

Ronald regretted his last speech, and returned to the first idea : "Do you not think that there are some people in the world who care little for life? The great host of Buddhists, who are probably the largest religious community on earth, look upon life as the greatest misfortune, and upon death as a blessed release.''

"Ah," exclaimed Agnes, "that is not peculiar to the Buddhists; look at the starved lives in the convents, simply waiting for death.''

"It is all very sad," murmured Dora; "and the world

seems so big, and so full of work to do; and pleasant work, too."

"That is quite true," assented Buchanan; "there is no excuse for idle hands in this vast work-room, and still there is no art so highly cultivated as that of killing time *without labor.*"

"Is it not Auerbach who says that 'leisure is diviner than labor, and the gods leave drudgery to mortals'?" asked Agnes.

"Yes," answered Buchanan, "you have some very lazy dreamers in the fatherland; but their dreams are more effective than our steam-engines sometimes."

"Thanks" (with a mocking bow) "for qualifying that first mild slander. Have not the Rhinelanders proved lately that they *can do something more than smoke and dream ?*"

"Ah, yes, *Fräulein,*" laughed Dora. "You can afford to be magnanimous and overlook home-thrusts now; you think, alas, that the poor French people could not see through your dense pipe-smoke the clinched fist which has struck them to the earth."

"Don't grow melancholy about the result of their short-sightedness, *petite Américaine,*" retorted Agnes. "You know one of your favorites, La Rochefoucauld, says, 'We all of us have sufficient fortitude to bear the misfortunes of others.'"

"Pardon me," cried Buchanan ; "are you not mistaken in attributing that cynical sentiment to La Rochefoucauld? I have no doubt he thought it, but it is our Swift who says, 'I never knew a man who could not bear the misfortunes of others with the most Christian resignation.'"

"I do not know," began Agnes, doubtfully; "I am almost certain I have quoted correctly."

"You have," pronounced Dora, emphatically. "I have often read that passage in La Rochefoucauld, and I have seen it also in Dean Swift's works; and," she hesitated a moment, as if trying to recall something, "is it not Shakspeare who says, 'Every man can master a grief but he that has it'? which is the same sentiment in another dress."

"And who shall deny, after this," cried Buchanan, "that a literary kleptomania existed even among the greatest minds? There must have been dishonesty somewhere; who was the thief?"

"That is a question," laughed Dora, "for graver heads than ours. I should not like to accuse Shakspeare of petty larceny."

They all laughed again at this, and felt rebuked immediately, as a gentle knock sounded on the door-panel. "Come in," was answered by Sœur Thérèse, who begged Agnes to return to her post, as *Chirurgien* Sauter had called for her, in the amputation-room.

Buchanan, handing her the last remaining glass of wine, begged her to be seated, and little Marian pressed upon her acceptance some chocolate.

Agnes had returned to the bedside of poor Ogilvie, whose pale, pinched features lighted up with a faint smile of welcome as she drew near.

"Shall I see you again to-night?" asked Buchanan, as he lingered a moment after Madame de Bergeret had gone to her painful task, of Dora, who was busy removing the traces of their late meal before retiring to her little room across the way, for it was an off-night of her duty at the hospital.

"No," answered Dora, with that hesitating, tremulous intonation which makes *no* more affirmative than *yes*. "We are going home soon, Agnes and I, and baby. I slept last night, but Agnes has not been in bed for two whole nights."

"I am glad," he said (he looked rather sorry). "I will watch Dick to-night, and, after I have just looked at him for a moment, I will come and take you and Agnes home. Shall you be ready in a quarter of an hour?"

"Oh, yes," Dora answered, gladly; she dreaded above everything going into those dark, soldier-sprinkled streets. Indeed, since her father's death she had never been allowed to enter them without Ronald's protection after dusk. Ogilvie had dropped into the slumber of exhaustion when Ronald appeared behind the screen. How changed he looked,—the ruddy complexion so pallid, the genial blue eyes so dim and hollow, the muscular frame helpless as an infant! And twelve hours had done this; in such frail caskets are our souls enshrined.

Ronald observed him anxiously and critically for a moment, and then beckoning Agnes to follow him, stepped outside, and said, in that gentle, yet firm tone which no one ever dreamed of disputing, "I shall send one of the good Sisters of the inner ward here immediately, to take your place until I can see you and Dora safely home. I will watch Dick myself, to-night."

"But," she could not help remonstrating, "you are utterly worn out; you look almost as badly as he does; have you no mercy on yourself?"

He smiled and shook his head. "I am not to be subdued by such a trifle as the loss of a night's rest. I will expect to see you in the little cabinet in ten minutes." And he went away in search of a substitute until his return.

That night, Dora wept sorely on Agnes's bosom after the light was put out, and the three helpless ones were curled up in their warm nest together.

"Why do you weep, my darling?" quoth gentle Agnes, caressing, with a pitying tenderness (for the quick, sympathetic nature had already divined the cause of those tears), the bowed head of her friend. "What is your trouble now?"

"My trouble, oh, Agnes, is that I have been so happy to-day,—so happy!—and the grass is not green on my dear father's grave." And she sobbed afresh.

"Yes, dear," replied Agnes, "that is true; but, Dora, do you not feel sure that your father has smiled *before* to-day, in heaven? Wherefore should you grieve?"

Dora kissed her gratefully, and they slept.

CHAPTER XVII.

"Citizens:

"The enemy has just inflicted on Paris the most cruel insult that she has yet had to endure in this accursed war; the too-heavy punishment of the errors and weaknesses of a great people.

"Paris, the impregnable, vanquished by famine, is no longer able to hold in abeyance the German hordes. On the 28th January, the capital succumbed, her forts surrendered to the enemy! The city still remains intact, wresting, as it were, by her own power and moral grandeur, a last homage from barbarity!

"But, in falling, Paris leaves us the glorious legacy of her heroic sacrifices. During five months of privation and suffering she has given to France the time to collect herself, to call her children together, to provide arms, to compose armies. . . . Thanks to Paris! we hold in our hands, if we are but resolute and patriotic, all that is needed to revenge, and set ourselves once more free!

"But . . . without our knowledge, without either warning or consultation, an armistice, the culpable weakness of which was known to us too late, has been signed, thereby delivering into the hands of the Prussians the departments occupied by our soldiers. . . .

"Prussia relies upon the armistice to enervate and dissolve our armies, and hopes that the Assembly, . . . under the impression of the terrible fall of Paris, will be ready to submit to a shameful peace. . . .

"FRENCHMEN:

"Remember that our fathers left us France,—whole and indivisible; let us not be traitors to our history. . . .

"Who, then, will sign the armistice? Not you, legitimists, who fought under the flag of the Republic, . . . nor you, sons of the bourgeois of 1789; . . . nor you, workmen of the towns, whose intelligence and generous patriotism represent France in all her strength and grandeur; . . . nor you, tillers of the soil, who never have spared your blood in the defense of the revolution. . . . No! Not one Frenchman will be found to sign this infamous act. The enemy's attempt to mutilate France will be frustrated, for, animated with the same love for the mother-country, and bearing our reverses with fortitude, we shall become strong once more and drive out the foreign legions! . . .

"To arms!"

This stirring manifesto from the eloquent Gambetta, like the hot breath from the cannon's mouth, swept the land with increasing desolation. The National Guard had obtained permission to retain their arms from Bismark,—a concession perhaps not so magnanimous as it looked at the time,—afterwards a frightful calamity;—it may be, not entirely unforeseen by that astute diplomatist. May God forgive him!

From the issuing of Gambetta's war-cry, succeeded by more pacific proclamations from the few lovers of order who remained in this bedlam, Paris had been in a constant ferment. Secret societies threw their death-fraught shells from the ambush of incognito; men suspected of treachery, or of being Prussians in disguise, were dragged to the Seine and drowned without mercy; sometimes as many as twenty or thirty thousand persons were assembled on the Place de la Bastille; (fortunately, the police had seized some time previously ten thousand Orsini bombs, and hundreds of others charged with fulminating mercury). There seemed to be but one spirit among this indomitable people,—the spirit of defiance!

At last, on the 1st of March, the enemy fulfilled the threat which had so excited the derision of the French, and which had been their triumphant cry throughout the war, "To Paris!" and kindled their bivouac-fires in the beautiful Champs-Elysées.

Alas! what a sad contrast to the first opening spring day of other years! The leaves of the trees refused to come forth, and the buds of the flowers to blossom, from very shame!

During the three pitiful days of the unwelcome foreigners' visit, the city mourned outwardly, as well as in the bitter hearts of its people. The Bourse, the shops, the cafés were closed; the eight gigantic figures on the Place de la Concorde, representing the towns o' France, were veiled in black crape; from the windows hung black flags, or the national flag draped with crape; few women stirred without, and those wore complete mourning. Ah, it was all as sad as it could be!

1*

The hospitals were crowded with the wounded and the dying; the labors of our three friends unremitting.

Dick Ogilvie, entirely recovered from his wound, had rejoined his regiment, but carried with him that which disabled him for all his future life from rejoicing in that free *gaieté de cœur*, which had never been under the influence of any more serious passion than a momentary flirtation would call for.

A week after his accident he had pulled Buchanan's face down to his pillow with feeble hands, while he whispered, "Who is this angel you have set to watch over me, Ronald? She has the sweetest face and the softest hands I ever felt."

"Well!" exclaimed Buchanan, "for a half-dead man, you do show a surprising amount of energy in your investigations; it's the best symptom I have observed yet. She is a dear, good little girl as ever lived, half English, and with good blood in her veins, I fancy. None of your larks with her, Dick, my boy."

"You mistake me utterly," returned Ogilvie. "I meant no disrespect to her, bless her! But not being used much to women folks of her description, about me (I scarcely remember ever hearing a sweeter voice than hers), I appreciate the novelty, don't you know? Where is she now, I wonder? I do wish you would not drive her away, Ronald," he somewhat peevishly concluded. Into such littleness does the master-weakness of our hearts betray even the sweetest tempers among us.

Agnes was just outside, preparing a bowl of broth for the refreshment of No. 25 during the night. She turned quickly at the sound of Ronald's voice,—

"Sister Agnes, will you just turn this poor fellow's pillow for him, and give him a sup of that *bouillon?* Meanwhile, I will visit my other patients."

No. 25 was smiling broadly when Agnes reappeared at his side armed with soup-bowl and napkin, but pretended to be still too weak to hold the spoon himself. Gravely she pinned the napkin about him, and fed him as she would have done a child. He delayed the consumption of the rather tasteless *bouillon* as long as he decently could, and took more than was good for him, devouring, at the same time, with his eyes the sweet face of the unsuspecting girl, whose thoughts, meanwhile, had strayed to Dora and sleepy Marian, who were waiting for her in the corridor.

At length Ronald returned and released her, and, with a hasty touch or two to the arrangement of a little table containing his *tisane*, etc., and a "good-night," without a glance in Dick's direction, she sped away to join Dora.

"She might have said good-night to a fellow decently," muttered Ogilvie, stung by her eagerness to escape, and turned a moody face to the wall, where he nursed his wrath to keep it warm, until the sun looked in upon him.

During the ensuing weeks of his enforced idleness, although he did not cease to regret the unlucky blow which had struck his sword from his hand at this interesting crisis of the siege, when strong arms and sane heads were in demand, Dick Ogilvie could not deny that he found some compensation for his seclusion in the intelligent companionship of the Madonna-faced, sweet-voiced Agnes.

And when the last day of his convalescence came, and he was pronounced "whole," he came to say farewell to his gentle nurse before returning to the fierce whirlpool which hissed and seethed outside; a spasm seemed to contract his heart, and he could only stammer out a few incoherent words, and get himself away as quickly as possible.

And Agnes, after watching him go forth, pale and thin and weak-looking, to the imminent peril with which the very air seemed charged at that time, went back to her seat beside another poor fellow who had come to grief (and who was no other than Jean Picot, poor Ernestine's husband), and glanced over at the empty white cot of No. 25 with a sigh of genuine regret. "Shall I ever see him again?" she asked herself. "What clear, honest eyes he had, and what a sweet smile! And how disputatious he was!—always arguing for the love of argument, and yet so very good-natured about it. Ah me!" Another sigh, and then a smile, at a folly which was so foreign to her habit of thought. For Agnes was a very little nun at heart, and knew not that through the long silent watches of the night, and the days spent in tender ministration to her patient's suffering requirements,—in those delightful hours of convalescence which she passed in reading from his favorite "Ingoldsby Legends" (a well-thumbed volume, his inseparable companion, and which he had, with a laudable effort of generosity, presented to her as a token of his gratitude before leaving),—she had let her heart slip from her unawares.

And Agnes sighed and smiled, and sighed again, and tended poor Jean Picot with mechanical assiduity, and resisted not the temptation to compare the brown, knotty, toil-hardened paws, which lay in passive weakness outside the white bed-covering, with the comely-shaped, filbert-nailed, large, white hands of her last patient; nor did she fail to wonder how there could be such vast difference between the coarse, black, unkempt crop which veiled the low, sunburnt brow of poor Jean, and the soft, luxuriant silkiness of the wavy brown hair she had brushed with such admiring care every morning, during those past weeks.

And when sleep closed the lids over the beady black

eyes of honest Picot, she drew from her pocket the dog-eared "Ingoldsby," and lost herself in the inimitable humor of its quaint pages. Scarcely a day passed that Dick did not appear at the hospital to report himself doing well, as he explained ; and, on some precious occasions when Ronald was unable to get away, he had the overwhelming satisfaction of escorting Dora and Agnes to their quarters for the night.

Indeed, of late, since the capitulation had stirred up to boiling-point the city, he had considered it necessary to accompany them nightly, even when Ronald was at liberty ; and there existed a tacit understanding among the four that, up to any reasonable hour in the evening, they would each wait for the other ; and Agnes had never been known to offer objection to the plan, although Ogilvie was almost invariably the latest of the quartette, through his imperative subjection to roll-call and muster.

CHAPTER XVIII.

It was the night of the 18th March, when two women with pale faces lined with that agony which ages one in a single night,—suspense,—met for one moment behind the screen which inclosed another dangerous case in their ward.

Neither dared acknowledge to the other, scarcely to themselves, the fear which had drained the life-blood from their cheeks and lips, but in that momentary meeting, two cold hands met and crushed each other in a grasp of pain, while, "God help you !" burst simultaneously from each pitying heart.

It was nearly midnight of that fearful day of horrors which saw the assassination of General Le Comte and poor old Clément Thomas.

Since early morning the cry of the Communists had been echoing throughout the streets; Montmartre had been occupied by some of the National Guards, who had taken forcible possession of the cannon stationed there; skirmishes had been frequent throughout the city; drunkenness abounded among the demoralized soldiers; shouts, menaces, bullets, filled the air.

In the afternoon, the two courageous generals who paid so dearly for their efforts to restore order were conducted by a hundred of the Nationals, supported by the hooting rabble, to the top of the hill at Montmartre, and after a mock-trial, or no trial at all, were shot.

The civilized world blushed at the manner of their death, and their blood cried not to Heaven in vain. Is not civil war with its ghastly train of evils looming in the distance?

This evening the Hôtel de Ville is filled by the National Guard (the government has fled to Versailles), and the Commune is proclaimed!

Liberté! Égalité! Fraternité! Under these three banners, blood is to flow again!

In vain had those who sought to restore order amid this chaos, placarded their proclamations and paraded the streets, sometimes numbering among their ranks as many as three thousand men, cheered by women from the windows as they passed, bearing on their flags the pacific sentence, "Meeting of the friends of order!" always supplemented by the popular "*Vive la République!*"

In vain! The last attempt to organize a meeting on the Rue de la Paix was frustrated by the madmen, who confronted these three or four thousand unarmed citizens by a body of the National Guard, armed to the teeth, under orders from the Central Committee.

A pistol-shot, the usual signal (fired by whom? God knows), was followed by a volley of musketry poured out upon the defenseless crowd, who fled shrieking with horror, leaving killed and wounded behind them.

The Hôtel de Ville, where the members of the Central Committee are sitting, is formidably defended; the Place Vendôme is thronged with insurgents, piles of stones here and there through the streets suggest the barricade; on the Place de la Bourse are glittering piles of bayonets, and crowds of people congregated, gesticulating fiercely.

Lines of National Guards and Mobiles defend the entrance to the Rue Vivienne; the Belleville fire-eaters drag their cannon through the streets, yelling defiantly; more than ten thousand men well-armed, ready for the spark which shall ignite their gunpowder, fill every quarter night and day; cries, groans, and curses, and the hideous sounds of drunken revelry, resound throughout the doomed city,—and the Commune is born!

Three days later, night again,—a beautiful moon-flooded night; an unnatural stillness, an ominous quiet, brooding over the palpitating city, asleep on the mouth of a volcano!

Every hour the muffled sound of many feet is heard passing by: it is the Mobile patrol making its rounds; now and then the butt-end of a musket strikes the pavement, or a cannon heavily rolls by; no other sounds are heard. It is the pause when the wind takes breath before the storm breaks into fury; it is the calm, sultry hour before the volcano bursts into eruption.

The new-made widows and the childless mothers dry their tears and hush their sobs, to listen to the first rumble which will warn them that the hour of ruin has struck.

The morning is breaking; all the east is waking up in a glory of rosy flushes. After the golden serenity of the night, the morning dawns full of a delicious balm, breathing forth the very spirit of peace and good will towards men.

But the eyes of these poor Sodomites are blinded; they saw nothing but the glitter of the sunrise on their bayonets. Who shall see another day dawn?

And this will be the fifth day since either Ronald Buchanan or Dick Ogilvie have been able to visit for a moment the ambulance hospital.

Dick, having been refused a half-hour's leave, in the exigency of an excitement which threatened every moment to become a revolution, had confided sundry billets to a *gamin*, who for a slight consideration had promised to deliver them faithfully, and who, being of that low order of urchins who get more kicks than half-pence, with a conscience long ago seared by the hot brand of cruelty, kept the consideration and dropped the notes in the sewer.

Unluckily, Buchanan, being detained over-night by a press of work, had had the audacity to communicate the fact to Dora, with some directions in regard to the patients belonging to his ward, and to conclude with a quotation in German, and " *Schläfen sie wohl ?*"

He was writing hastily in a *café* which he did not usually frequent,—a nest of *bonnets-rouges*. When he had finished, he beckoned a *garçon*, and, giving him some silver, urged him to fly to the hospital on the Rue —— at once. The man promised to do so, and Buchanan went away.

Scarcely had he turned his back than murmurs arose among the denizens of the café, who were busy imbibing the columns of the *Vengeur*, the *Cri du Peuple*, and the vile destroyer, *absinthe*.

"Who is he? the aristocrat! What does he do here without a carbine? He is a spy! A Prussian! Ah, *sacre mille tonnerres!* Give us that letter," etc.

The terrified *garçon* yielded without remonstrance, and, on opening it, the execrations burst forth afresh.

"Ah, did I not tell you so? Look at this! and he dares to come among us, the *cochon d'Allemand!* Here is proof; this is German!—and this, and this!"

He rose to his feet, a great, red-haired giant, in a uniform of the National Guard too small for him, out of which seemed to overflow his great bony wrists and ankles, his bull-dog neck, and great red beard.

"After him!" he shouted. "Stop him! We want no letter-writers among us! No German dog shall rest in Paris!"

"Follow him! Stop him!" cried they all, dashing down the street. In a moment they came in sight of him, and he, hearing their fierce cries and wondering what it all meant, turned calmly around and waited until they came up to him. He did not look much surprised, but a good deal contemptuous, as they laid violent hands on him; he only said, in excellent French, as he shook them off as a great Newfoundland would a couple of curs, "It don't require a dozen men to arrest one. What is my crime?"

"*A la lanterne!*" returned the fanatics. "To the Seine with the dog of a German!"

"But I am not German!" In vain Buchanan repeated this assertion. Through the increasing darkness of the streets he was hustled on,—on he knew not whither,— encircled by a mob which grew momentarily larger and stronger. The red-haired giant held him firmly by the shoulder; on his other side walked a man with a loaded pistol. Buchanan ceased to struggle or remonstrate: he walked silently, proudly, his head up. They were approaching the Seine; a roar of delight arose from the madmen around him as the glimmer of the water shone in the light of the rising moon. They pressed more closely about him; although this was not an uncommon occurrence—this drowning of suspected men,—it had lost none of its zest yet, and they feared a surprise. One came! As they passed a corner shop, brightly lighted, one of the escort made a sudden movement of astonishment, and ejaculated, catching firmly the right arm of the giant redbeard, "Simon, we are wrong! this man is English! I know him!" He tore back the cape of his top-coat and showed the cross of Geneva on his sleeve. "I answer for him! Pierre! Simon! take your hands off this man!"

But Simon replied, with a hoarse laugh and an oath, "What does he here with a cross on his arm in place of a carbine in his hand? What does your Englishman write German for? To the Seine with him!"

"Not so!" shouted Jacques Toquelet, in a voice of thunder. "You take him to the Seine over my dead body! He is a surgeon, I tell you; he has helped many of our poor fellows back to life; he is a good man and a brave one! He shall not die! Jacques Toquelet has sworn it!"

His voice, his earnestness, carried conviction even to these half-maddened animals. There were murmurs, and the man on the other side put up his pistol and took his hand off Buchanan's arm.

A Mobile, just behind him, proposed that he should be confined in the guard-house until further investigation should be made,—accepted by a majority. In the guard-house he spent the night, and they—forgot him. The guard supplied him his rations during those five wretched days and nights, and then, after repeated efforts, a communication reached the English embassy, and he was set free.

How the flower of love expanded into perfection during those hours of anguish and suspense in Ronald's heart, and in poor Dora's, may be told by those who have loved and suffered.

For forty-eight hours Dick Ogilvie and his men have not slept, and, weary but resolved, have remained on duty in the Place de la Bourse, to which now, however, a fresh detachment have arrived, and these poor fellows will be enabled, after five days of almost continuous duty, to get a little rest.

But Dick prefers to refresh himself in his own way; he makes a fresh toilette, after a plunge in the Seine, and takes a hasty cup of coffee.

At six o'clock he might be seen walking slowly along the quiet Rue de Valois with a slight little figure hanging on his arm, and two lovely blue eyes raised to his with more than a suspicion of tears in their depths.

Both Agnes's little hands were clasped on the sleeve of her companion, and there was a little tremble in her voice as she said, "You will never,—*never* do this again? You cannot think how anxious Dora and I have been!"

"You?" he said, suddenly stopping and turning a little towards her. "Oh, my darling, I can scarcely realize the fact that you did care so much. And to think that that brown-faced imp never brought you a single line from me! Did you think I was dead, little one?"

"I cannot tell you all the fears I had; I was very wretched; but there were few hearts in Paris that were not nearly broken during these last days. Why should I complain?"

"Oh, Agnes," Dick burst forth suddenly, "this is, in

truth, no time for love-making or fine speeches, but if death should be in store for me in the great struggle which is inevitable now, and drawing very near, I think I would die happier if I could feel that you would love and weep for me."

This was a long speech for Dick, and not in his line at all ; but when is a man consistent to his prejudices after he has taken that leap in the dark,—fallen in love ?

All the white purity of Agnes's face and neck crimsoned for the first time in her life, at the stirring of a new-born delight, as she said, timidly, " You will not expose yourself unnecessarily, will you ? Ah, have pity upon those who sit at home and wait for your return ; their pain is deeper than any pang a bullet can bring to you !" There was a ring of passion in her voice which betrayed how great had been her loving anxiety for him. He bent his head suddenly, and kissed the little hands upon his arm.

It was close upon ten o'clock when they parted inside the outer door of the hospital ; in Agnes's hand was a tiny bunch of early field-flowers, bought from a blind old woman, Dick's first love-offering ; in her face was the joy and freshness of the spring.

Ogilvie looked a little graver than usual, as he promised, come what might, to see her once in every twenty-four hours that he lived ; and then, as the flush suddenly faded from her face, the meaning of those words flashing over her, and she broke down for a moment in hysterical weeping, so unusual to her calm, tranquil nature, he folded her in his arms and pressed kiss after kiss on her bonnie brown hair, her tender hands, her snow-white eyelids, and, with a " God bless you, my own darling !" he tore himself away.

From that moment Agnes's peace was gone ; through

all the dreadful days and nights and weeks of terror and despair through which Paris now wrestled for its life, Agnes shared the sorrow of the wife, the mother, and the sister of the soldier, whose life was menaced hourly in the fratricidal frenzy of their own people.

As Agnes hung up her bonnet and cloak in the *armoire* of the corridor, she became conscious that Dora was approaching her from the door of their ward, with a quick, eager step. But, for the first time, she shunned those loving eyes; how could she explain these traces of tears, her long absence from her duties? how breathe the story which was so new yet to herself?

But Dora observed nothing; she came quite close, and asked, in a rapid whisper, "Have you heard where he is, Agnes?—Mr. Buchanan, I mean,—why he has not been here all these dreary days and nights? Oh, tell me; you have seen Mr. Ogilvie; what does he say?" She stopped, breathless, and wrung her hands together. Agnes's heart ached.

"No, Dora, I have heard nothing. Mr. Ogilvie"— her face flushed slightly as she named him—"has not seen or heard from him since they walked home with us that last evening."

A low moan broke from Dora's lips, and she grew even whiter than before. "Agnes," she said, solemnly, "I have killed him,—*I* who would give my heart's blood to save him from harm," she went on, wildly,—"that night I sent him away from me with a cold, bitter falsehood. I told him not to come near me any more. Oh, my God! Agnes, he has only done what I commanded. He has exposed himself to danger, and he is dead, dead, dead!" She sank down on the wooden bench which stood in the window of the corridor, and trembled from head to foot as with an ague.

Agnes was almost stunned by surprise, and pity of an anguish whose bitterness she had never before known. She bent over the bowed figure of her friend, but only kisses and tender caresses seemed possible to her over-full heart and strained nerves. A silent prayer for help, and at last she found strength to say, " Dora, do not moan so, darling ; be brave. He may come in at any moment, and you would not care for him to see you thus. He has been detained—you know his good heart—by some suffering wretch whose pain he alone could relieve. Surely, you would not wish to deprive any of these tortured ones of his skill?"

" Oh, no, no !" sobbed Dora, to whom tears, blessed tears, had come at last; " but, Agnes, it is all my fault, my sin, my sin ! I have let him love me, even after I saw that he cared for me too much. I was so happy, I could not thrust his love away; and, oh, if he knew,—if he knew how vile and weak and wicked I have been ! how cowardly ! he would despise me."

" Oh, no, Dora ; think what you are saying ; he could never despise you, my pure pearl, my true, noble-hearted Dora !"

" Agnes, you are killing me ! I tell you, you cannot guess how wicked I have been, how I have sinned. I am not worthy that your pure arms should touch me, or that my Marian should rest upon my heart !"

" Hush, Dora ! hush ! you are too excited now to reason calmly. Come with me and lie down in the little *cabinet* for half an hour. Should he come, I will bring him to you. Will you, dear ?"

" No, no, he will never come again ; and if he did, Agnes,"—she raised her agonized face and spoke quite quietly now,—" you must not bring him to me. I will never willingly see his face again." She broke out afresh into bitter weeping: "I have deceived him and you, and all who have been so good to me; I am not what you think me, Agnes." She buried her head in her arms resting on the window-sill, and Agnes tenderly smoothed the ruffled hair, and murmured,—

"No matter who or what you are, Dora, I love you, and shall love you all my life; everybody loves you, darling."

At this moment the outer door opened, and a French surgeon, followed by Buchanan, looking pale and depressed, entered the corridor. He caught sight of Agnes at once, and with an almost imperceptible motion of her head, she summoned him to her side. Then, with uplifted finger to enjoin silence, she drew herself away and left him standing in her place, close to Dora, who still wept bitterly.

Ronald stood silently, looking down at the frail figure of the woman he loved with all the intensity of a first and last passion of a lifetime, and a great hunger came into his heart the while. At last Dora murmured, from the shelter of her tear-drenched arms, "But, Agnes, if he had been detained, and not hurt or angry, he would have sent a messenger, or——"

What is this? Has she died, and is she at last in the haven of peace and rest with her dead mother's arms about her? Has her suffering, maimed life cast off its earthly shell, and is her soul free?

For one brief, ecstatic moment Dora lies in those strong arms, and weeps for joy on the broad breast in which the heart beats so wildly; for one sweet moment while anguish flies before supreme bliss, and anxiety and suspense melt away under the blessed certainty that Ronald is here, safe, well, and loves her still! For one moment! . . . .

It was a moment such as this which doomed Francesca

da Rimini to such terrible punishment, and for which from time immemorial men and women have sacrificed not only "all other bliss," but "all their worldly worth." Alas! these moments are not to come within the province of our human experiences; they are not "written in the bond" of our Eve-sullied birthright. Beware of them! For they take the savor out of all lesser moments to eternity. And then Dora drew herself gently but firmly from that restful embrace, and stood before Ronald trembling from head to foot, but strong in her inward purpose to end all this terrible deception and the consequences it involved, at once, and forever. For dependent and clinging as she seemed, this fragile Dora owned a firmness of character and an inflexibility of decision where her conscience battled with her inclinations, or where a question arose which endangered the fair spotlessness of her pure life, that would have led her unflinchingly to the stake in a righteous cause, or would have submitted her to that still more painful martyrdom, a sacrifice of all that makes life other than a weary waiting for death.

She looked so young and weak and fragile, as she stood before him with eyes heavy with weeping and the tender mouth quivering, that Ronald's heart ached for her more than for himself; for he knew, with that unfailing prescience of love, that she was about to pronounce his doom —and her own.

She swiftly readjusted some tresses of golden-brown hair which had fallen about her tear-drenched face, and then, leaning a little against the casement to support her trembling limbs, she said, in a voice husky and almost inaudible from emotion, " I have been weak and wicked, but it is not too late to undo the evil I have done. You say you love me. I believe you do. Don't speak, please, yet." She raised her hand a little to silence him as he was about to interrupt her. "Yes, I believe you do love me, and therefore I dare to ask you to leave me,—now, at once, —and not to come near me again, ever, ever; for between you and me *there is a gulf as deep as death!*"

He was standing now before her, with one hand resting on the window-frame, and a grave, anxious expression on his noble face, but not a sign of weakness in those firm lines of mouth and chin.

"I will do as you wish, Dora, always, should we never stand again on earth together," he said, gently; "but I claim as my right a hearing before we part,—if part we must. On the last evening we were together, I was surprised into a betrayal of my love for you,—a love which sprang up in my heart in the single night after your accident, my darling; the only love of my whole life, and the only one that will be with me in my last hour; and you will remember how you answered me! It was my hope—my intention—that if we both survived these troublous times, in some quiet spot in Switzerland, perhaps, or dear old England" (she shuddered), "I might choose a more fitting time to plead my cause. But these things are not ruled by our wills or governed by our plans; the moment when I must speak has come, and I tell you that there is *no* gulf so deep—*save that only of your own will*—that my arm will not span it and snatch you to my heart. *Once there*, God alone can take you from me. Oh, my little storm-beaten flower," he cried, taking her hands with gentle force in his, "give yourself up to me! let me take you away out of Paris,—to my dear sister's arms, that you may rest at last!" He stopped, wondering at the burst of sobs which shook her whole form in an anguish which only God and his angels should have witnessed.

She tore her hands away from him. "Ah, do not," she

cried,—"do not try to tempt me! I cannot; I have no right; I am unworthy! Ah, if you knew how false and wicked I have been, you would not stand there and plead for a heart that is broken through its own sin!" She made a terrible effort, and resumed, more calmly: "There is no use in prolonging this pain; you will believe me when I say that your hope can *never be realized*, and that I can no longer see you or accept your friendship (and it has been very precious to me), after to-day."

She was turning away when he laid his hand upon her arm,—"Dora, you are mad; you love me, and you are leaving me! What is this mystery which overshadows you? Give me at least a hint of its nature, that I may dissolve it into air!"

"I cannot!" she moaned, "I cannot! It is too late. I should have told you long ago,—before things came to such a pass as this; but I did not, because I was weak and lonely, and your love was so sweet to me; and now, look at what punishment I have brought upon myself; *not my pain only, but yours.*"

"But I will not suffer it," he answered, in clear, ringing tones. "Were I alone the sufferer, you might have found me a marvel of patience; but *you* are grieving; you, who have had so much to bear of late. Can I allow you, then, to take the responsibility of deciding for us both in this question? No, a hundred times no! I will accept no dismissal in the dark. Give me your reasons, and let me sift them for you; otherwise you must submit to my presence, and in time let me take all your burdens on myself."

She looked at him, seeming to devour his words (what a strong, masterful voice he had!), a death-like paleness in her face; suddenly she swayed backward and forward slightly, and as he sprang towards her, sank down on the bench beneath her. She had fainted; the great strain had relaxed; the decisive words remained unspoken; sleepless nights of anxiety and fatigue had done their work. And as he raised her in his arms, Ronald scarcely could restrain his tears from falling on her poor white face.

This was the second time he had held Dora in his arms unconscious; how long ago seemed that first sight of her measured by the growth of his love since then! And, as he bent over his idol, it is characteristic of the man that he did not venture to press his lips to the marble face,—which could not then have repulsed him; it seemed like taking a mean advantage of her helplessness.

He carried her quickly to the little *cabinet* where they had dined together so joyously a few days before, and, laying her on the sofa, sent a passer-by for Agnes.

As he waited impatiently for her arrival, chafing Dora's cold hands, and bathing her temples with water, the while, he could not repress a shudder at the shrill treble of Marian's bird-like voice, as she sang gayly, perched upon the foot of Jean Picot's cot, a little French *canzon*, of which she had caught perfectly the air and words. How many hours had the little ambulance-fairy not cheated out of gloom and despondency for those anxious sufferers, condemned to a trying inaction, by her bright prattle and her sweet little French songs!

Agnes's efforts to restore Dora to consciousness were successful; but when she opened her eyes and looked about her,—hoping and fearing to see Ronald's earnest face,—she met only Agnes's pitying eyes and murmured words of comfort.

He had deemed it best to spare her further agitation, and, after visiting his patients in the ward adjoining, he had gone away to other cases outside. A few words with Agnes before he went showed the deep anxiety Dora's incomprehensible conduct had cost him. "She is laboring under some mistaken sense of duty, Sister Agnes," he said, "and will listen to nothing I can say to change her determination. You have been a faithful friend to her. Can you see any reason for this strange refusal to let me care for her? Tell me, Agnes, do you think she loves me?" She could barely catch the words, so low were they whispered.

"I fear she does, and in that fact lies her reason for denying you any share in her existence." Agnes spoke hurriedly, and as if the words hurt her, but *must* be spoken. "I imagine that it is her *past* which is weighing her down; some fault, perhaps, or treachery, which she had hoped to outlive alone, but would not shadow with it the man she loved. There! I have told you my suspicion, because I love her too dearly to see her suffer, and because I believe you to be too noble to let the *past* come between you and her now!" She bent her head, and the scarlet flush in her face told how great an effort had been made in the cause of friendship.

"Agnes," he said, gravely, "Dora's life can hold no foul sin; her eyes are guileless as a child's; her heart is pure as an angel's. But if it were not so; *if I had to stoop and lift her from the very dregs of crime*, I would do so; for I love her, and would shield her from every evil and danger and pain—in life. Tell her this for me; and also, that should I wait for her until her chestnut hair turns *gray*, I will wait, not patiently, but faithfully, until that time comes."

Agnes caught his hand as the last word fell from his lips, and, with an irrepressible impulse, laid her cheek upon it, crying, "God bless you! Oh, you have a great, noble heart!" and fled back to poor Dora to pour this balm into her wounded spirit.

But, to her intense surprise, Dora only wept and shook her head, and refused to be comforted. What *could* it mean? Surely, such all-forgiving charity as that promised by the young Englishman should banish all doubts and fears and fill her soul with peace! What if her past held one blotted page, as she had undoubtedly confessed to Agnes, here was a love so deep that it could hide in its great trust even such a secret as this, and cover with its wings the penitent head which was bowed upon its bosom. Was it not mad folly to cast away such shelter, such divine compassion, such adoring devotion, as this?

"You will tell him," she said, in answer to Agnes's pleadings, "that *it cannot be.* Agnes, spare me any further entreaties; you are trying me too severely. Have pity; *it cannot be!*"

And after Agnes had left her alone with her bitter pain; with the yearning in her desolate heart which was *sin;* with a wild repining at the darkness of her days, after the sunny brightness of all those former years before that fatal mistake which wrought her woe for evermore,—the question which tormented her, who could answer? Should she betray the secret of her marriage? Was she not absolved from the oath extorted from her by a man so false and base as Faucett had proved himself? Had she not told him that she would force him to acknowledge her claims, if he had not come to do so voluntarily, after a sufficient time had elapsed upon his return to England? Had those last bitter words of his, that well-nigh broke her heart, not sundered all tie between them? Was she, in God's sight, this man's wife still? This man, who had never loved her, who had coveted her, and married her simply because she was pure; who had wearied of her before twelve moons had risen and waned; who had systematically neglected her, exposed her to peril, crushed

19*

her under the heel of his one-idead egotism, and then abandoned her, ill almost unto death, with a heartlessness not less cowardly than inhuman.

Yes, she felt sure that she was absolved from her promise of keeping their marriage an inviolable secret. She would tell Ronald how it was that she seemed so cruel and unreasonable in his sight; and he would forgive her, and love her still, and see that he must go away from her—where? To England, where Dyke Faucett was? And would it be possible for Ronald to live in the same land with that man, who has so wrecked both their lives, and not seek him out, and—then—then—ah, what might not be the result? But she might suppress his name, and there could be no danger of a meeting between these two men. Yes, she would tell Buchanan all; all the trials of those dreadful years when she lived under the shadow of a hopeless disappointment, striving to fill her starved heart with the caresses of her child,—all, save the name of the man who had betrayed her trust in him. "For I must not let him think me vile," she said. "And what did Agnes mean by her 'He is willing to overlook the past and all the pain in it, if you will let him do so?' *Overlook the past!* Ah, Ronald, my past can bear even your eyes into its darkest corners; there are plenty of tears, but no blushes to be found there, thank Heaven!" And so she slept.

CHAPTER XIX.

It was the height of the London season. Half a dozen crushes nightly, in the wake of just a "show" at the opera, now in full-blown glory, which followed in due procession "the horticultural," the afternoon concert, the kettle-drum, or a hundred other *divertissements* in the offering up of sacrifices to Moloch.

The streets smiled under the indefatigable efforts of a regiment of scavengers (masculine and feminine bundles of rags), happy in the rich harvest of coppers flung by the munificent hand of "the season." Shops, gay with their tempting wares, smiled out of their plate-glass windows with the seductive leer peculiar to them. The great casements of the West-End clubs were ornamented by the array of manly beauty which suns itself in yawning luxuriousness there, invariably, in the smiles and shy glances of the passers-by : groups of whiskers, varying little in style, but of an infinite variety of hue ; coats of irreproachable cut ; a glass screwed into the near-eye, the off-eye inevitably vacuous from exhaustion. Equipages of every description, rolling magnificently, or gliding sneakingly, along : the stylish landau, with its high-step-ping, perfectly-matched animals ; the quiet victoria, and the distinguished simplicity of the comfortable brougham, interspersed with the plebeian hansom, or that despised maid-of-all-work, the "growler."

Let us not stand stock-still gaping into those entrancing shop-windows, or into the comical face of the Punch who is sending his wife to the devil persistently, at every corner throughout the London season, exposing by our *naïveté* our country origin, to the amusement of the genuine cockney; and, above all, let us not betray our amazement, otherwise than by a prolonged stare, at the apparition, wonderful to behold, which reclines obesely on the soft satin cushions of an open carriage, passing at this moment.

Not in "purple and fine linen" only, is my lady of the rubicund countenance clothed,—such a combination being too *pur et simple* for the national taste,—but there is a *commingling* of the "*seven primaries*," which would cause actual *mal au cœur* to a Parisienne *pur sang;* the whole surmounted by the favorite sky-blue parasol, from beneath whose fringes peeps forth the deliciously-grotesque hideousness of the inevitable *pug*—rose-ribboned.

The "British matron" is of all matrons (Roman included), the most admirable. Of her virtues, Heaven forbid that I should insinuate a doubt! All honor to her, as a model wife and mother, as social law-maker, as hostess, and as friend! There were only three fairy godmothers forgotten at her christening,—the French *chausseur*, the French *couturière*, and the French *femme-de-chambre*. Those fair daughters of Albion whose youth has been more propitiously attended, and who boast these acquisitions, are unrivaled in the world. The Channel is less wide than formerly. There are many such divine combinations as beauty, health, freshness, well-dressed, well-shod, *coiffée à ravir*, on that deliciously-exhausting tread-mill of London society this season.

Perhaps it is because the Parisians possess so little real beauty, that they have elevated the toilet to a fine art, and cultivate it to such perfection.

And yet taste in dress is an instinct more than an acquired talent. See the Spanish and Italian peasantry, how picturesquely they array themselves; and the simplest grisette in Paris boasts a certain *tournure* in her cotton gown, and in her snowy cap a dainty coquetry, with always a dash of color in her breast-knot, if only a sou's worth of violets, or a pale pink rose. They are never gaudy, the Parisians; even the class which revels in the costliest raiment is rarely "loud" in style; their love is for neutral tints, soft grays and pearls and mauves, or black velvets; and, above all, they adore the *cachemire* and priceless laces. Thousands of francs in a toilette, if you please, but let it be *distinguée* above all things. Rarely is one's eye shocked by vulgar contrast of color on *their* side of the Channel; we must go for that startling experience to sober England, or—to the Comanche Indians.

And there, strolling slowly under the trees, over the velvet turf of Regent's Park, with a golden-haired child on one side and Percival Tyrrell on the other, is an illustration of the theory of an innate, artistic taste in the lower orders.

There is something inexpressibly refined and *élégante* about that tall, willowy figure of Anne Ogilvie's. In her simple morning-dress of fine white cambric, with its neatly-fitting jacket, garnished with crisp, fluted frills, with her white chip bonnet, destitute of other trimming than a careless spray of the wild rose with its buds and tender green foliage, Anne looked the incarnation of a June morning. Between the folds of the lace fichu which half revealed her snowy throat, nestled one great mellow-looking tea-rose, half-blown, whose fragrance encompassed her about as if it belonged to her. She really was "*gentille à croquer*," and Tyrrell thought, as he sauntered by her side, that she looked fresh and fair and sweet as a daisy with the dew upon it.

In the distance stood the brougham which had brought

the little lady Valérie and her governess to the Park for
an airing, as foot-exercise was deemed advisable for the
young lady. It has been their favorite resort for weeks,
and this is only one of many delightful walks and talks
Anne and Tyrrell had partaken of together. After the
prohibition of the countess, which precluded all possibility of meeting Anne in the orthodox propriety of
drawing-room limits, Tyrrell, man-like, had desired all
the more ardently to encounter her in the more uncon-
ventional latitude of the Park at Grantly, to which her
walks were circumscribed.

Therefore he laid in wait for her in the grounds daily,
and never could be persuaded that it might cause displeasure, and bring down upon her the wrath of the auto-
crat who had decreed that she was unfit for such select
company as that which comprised the social circle of
" her betters." At first, Anne could not overcome her
feeling of shyness, and repugnance at being misconstrued
by her employers a second time, for she had soon begun
to comprehend the reason why she had been ostracised.
The countess's manner to her was invariably courteous
and kind when they met out of the presence of others,
after that evening in the library, but if there were wit-
nesses to their interviews, she was chilling, haughty, and
reserved.

Anne was not slow to read these signs ; her intuitions
had been forced prematurely in her solitary girlhood, and
she felt keenly this change in the aspect of her position.
She knew as well as if the countess had spoken, " My
dear Miss Ogilvie, I do not object to you personally, also
I feel sure that your duties are executed conscientiously,
and I would fain extend to you some little kindliness, but
my friends assure me that you are dangerous (you cannot
deny that they are just in their estimate of you), and,

K*

therefore, you must be suppressed. I am sorry, but—*que voulez-vous ?*" I fancy Anne would have liked her ladyship better and respected her more, had these words been audibly expressed. As it was, she trembled and sought to evade the pertinacious attempts of Tyrrell to break through the rigid seclusion which she believed her dignity demanded; but, after a time, his arguments prevailed; she saw through his eyes that there was no harm in an occasional opportunity of conversation, which in nowise interfered with the peace of any inmate of the house of which he was a guest.

I fear she looked for him as eagerly as he for her, and was perhaps more disappointed, when he failed to be found lounging at the foot of their favorite copper-beech with his book, than he would have been had he not perceived the flutter of her white dress among the rose-bushes.

Their talk was of the most prosaic description; no halo of romance or sentiment lingered over a single interview; they might have been a couple of students, or a preceptor and his pupil, so thoroughly void of all coquetry on her part, or love-making on his, was their intercourse. They talked of books, of art, of music, and even of the politics of the nations; of antiquities, and of his postponed journey to the East; of all and everything which could prove how congenial were their tastes, their thoughts, their aspirations; how thoroughly the one comprehended the complex nature of the other; how like a fine instrument under the hand of a master the grand chords of Anne's harmonious character rolled out their deep-toned music; and how all the sweetest, softest melodies in Tyrrell's unstirred silences, vibrated to the touch of Anne's gentle fingers.

And this they both acknowledged in their hearts, although their tongues had never whispered it or their eyes betrayed it all through those months when he had seen her, constantly, even, after his visit to Grantly had terminated, running down from London for the purpose. He had always some plausible pretext for his visits, however; it was a new book which she had desired to see, and he was going fishing in the neighborhood, or, he was *en route* to another country-house in the adjoining county, where he would spend a fortnight and ride over occasionally.

He never came empty-handed; and after a while Anne came to have quite a little library of her own, of which the pleasure was not decreased by the thought that, in the pages of each book comprised therein, she could meet on equal ground the spirit of the donor,—the ground of an intellectual appreciation, the freemasonry which levels all differences of station or fortune,—the fellowship of *mind.*

For it seemed to touch Anne Ogilvie into a deeper humility, the fact that this man, whose rare beauty and fascination, whose fine intelligence and *unexceptionable* introductions, had made him sought after and in request at every dinner, ball, and social gathering where he or his friends were known, should have so singled out and distinguished by his preference a lonely, friendless orphan, occupying the position of a dependent in the house of a great lady, who would undoubtedly have swooned away had any one suggested an equality between her and her hireling governess.

But Tyrrell was an American, and democratic enough to acknowledge that a pearl was a pearl when he stumbled on one. An Englishman often drops the pearl in his effort to open the oyster in an awkward but aristocratic manner. And shall we censure him? It has become such a difficult and hazardous operation, this opening of the oyster. Inexpert hands are often lacerated in the process, and ofttimes, after the shell has at last yielded, the tempting bivalve is just a trifle less fresh than one expected, or the flavor is flatter than one anticipated, or there is a great deal of salt and pepper to be laid on before one can swallow the thing without a wry face. Meanwhile, alas! the pearl worth a king's ransom rolls away, and hides itself in some crevice out of sight!

"What is your name, Miss Ogilvie?" asked Tyrrell, catechetically,—"your Christian name, as, I believe, it is called?" on that June morning in the Regent's Park.

"My name is not an euphonious one," she replied; "it is Anne."

"Anne! Anne!" He dwelt on the monosyllable lovingly. "It is a homely name (I mean *homely* in the real sense of the word; why it should be otherwise used I cannot tell). It is a simple name, full of comfortable suggestions. Anne! It has a ring of royalty about it too; a smack of dignity and command. I like it."

Anne's smile brought into play the dimples on each cheek, where the rose-bloom had deepened perceptibly.

"Few people like their own names," she said. "Mine has often sounded very harsh to me."

"Indeed!" He looked down kindly at her. "It may be that the voice which took your name upon its rude lips lent it harshness; there is much in that."

"Oh, yes," she assented, thinking what a musical caress had sounded in his "Anne! Anne!"

"Now I, on the contrary, have always fancied my name. 'Percival' would have been my choice, had I been consulted, even before I read the legend of the Holy Grail," he continued, smiling. "I always feel like buckling on my armor and going forth to do battle for the right, when I meditate on the responsibility my sponsors laid upon me with this name and its associations."

"Yes, they are certainly very beautiful and fascinating,

in a poetical, visionary way," Anne replied ; "but do you know, had I been a man, I should have chosen something more rugged as my model,—like Oliver Cromwell, or better still, like Martin Luther. Ah, there was a great, fiery soul, if you will ; a strong, fearless image-breaker, as somebody calls him ; a soldier every inch of him, —a soldier of the cross,—brave and strong and noble, and yet with such tenderness and poetic sensibility at times !"

Tyrrell looked at her, a glow of delight in his face.

"You are quite right !" he exclaimed ; "that man was inspired ; it is a grand character. He is always associated with those words of Jean Paul——" He hesitated, and Anne said, softly,—

"Tell me them, please ; I cannot recall which you mean."

"It is something like this : 'When, in one's last moments, all faculty in the broken spirit shall fade away and die,—imagination, thought, effort, enjoyment,—then at last will the night-flower of *Belief* alone continue blooming, and refresh with its perfume the last darkness.' And this precious legacy Luther left to many a benighted soul. Ah, yes, it *was* grand, this sturdy fighting for the great truth of Christianity ! Why did you mention Cromwell ? Did you know that he has been compared to Luther by —— Carlyle, I think ?"

"No ; I had forgotten it. But they *are* alike ; they are both rough, earnest, uncompromising warriors, with the same stern conscientiousness and rigid ideas of discipline."

"Voltaire ascribes 'something of the bully' to both of them," continued Tyrrell ; then abruptly: "How did you come to speak of Martin Luther, I wonder ? He is one of my great ideals. Strange ! Strange that you should creep into the lumber-room of my oldest fancies and uncover them, dusty from neglect, to the light of day.''

Tyrrell had taken off his hat, and was striding on bareheaded, with shoulders thrown back, and quickened steps, as if to the sound of martial music, as was his habit when excited. His thoughts were all with Martin Luther now. He was subject to these fits of silence even with Anne, which she was careful never to interrupt. She was content to wait until his thoughts stretched out towards her again, even after she found that, when he recalled himself to the fact that he was not alone, it was often to ejaculate a farewell and leave her, without further parley.

Ten minutes passed. Little Valérie, walking behind them with a young companion whose mamma had dropped her from one of the carriages drowsing along in the distance, laughed out merrily at some remarks of her little friend. Tyrrell awoke from his reverie, drew a long breath, replaced his hat, and said, whilst he moderated his pace to Anne's,—

"Do you remember his marriage? How characteristic is his explanation of his choice of the ex-nun, Catherina von Bora! He 'wished to please his father, to tease the Pope, and to vex the devil.' No mention of himself or his own inclinations; he had crucified them all long before."

"Not too gratifying to the lady," laughed Anne, "and done very much in the same spirit in which he glories in his obscure origin and poverty. I believe he earned his bread, at one time, singing from door to door; as he says, 'It is God's way to make men of power of beggars, just as he made the world out of nothing,' you remember."

"How true that is!" commented Percival. "The greatest minds of all ages have sprung from the attic or the cellar, the highest and lowest rungs of the ladder of poverty and obscurity, almost invariably.''

"Yes," Anne assented, "genius seems to thrive in poor soil, and a dried herring does not clog the imagination as the *petits plats* of an accomplished *chef* might. I doubt if the 'Paradise Lost' could ever have been written had Milton dined off eight courses and a *chasse*.''

"And yet," returned Tyrrell, "the manuscript only sold, at first, for five pounds.''

"Is it possible? Can you imagine anything more embittering than such a proof of ignorant stupidity? Such a want of appreciation must be maddening to a man of genius.''

"It is so," he answered; "the knife that struck poor Keats and Chatterton to the heart has dealt as certain, if less swift, destruction to many an older and stronger man. Milton was not blinder in his old age than the herd who failed to recognize his godlike gifts during his lifetime; and the adder is not so deaf as the multitude who listened to Beethoven's music, without yielding him the crown of his wondrous genius until his last hour; for Beethoven only knew that one perfectly happy hour in his life, and it killed him.''

"Ah, yes, he had lived so long upon hope, you see, that when the realization of his dreams came, he was too weak to bear the shock. Hope is not a substantial diet, and often grows most shadowy when one feels most starved.'' Anne sighed; she was thinking of her brother, and the peril which she was so weary of picturing to herself.

"I have driven you into melancholy," cried Percival, with a quick sympathy, self-reproachful, "with my maunderings about blighted geniuses and my mouldy recollections of my boyhood's ideals. Even Martin Luther is not worth such a plaintive sigh as that I caught just now. After all, Miss Ogilvie, a later experience has brought to my knowledge the physiological fact that ammoniated tincture of assafœtida is an infallible prescription for people who are inclined to religious enthusiasms and new doctrines. Who knows how far a box of pills might have cooled the ardor of the great reformer?"

"And you are sure," she rejoined, laughing, "that all manias will yield to drugs? If so, what would you recommend to a Romeo or a Juliet? Has your scientific research reached that extreme of madness?"

"Do you call love a mania?" he asked, with one quick glance into the dark-blue eyes. "If it were," he concluded, as she did not reply, "there will be no need for building additional lunatic asylums, for it is a rare type of aberration nowadays." Still silence; and they walked on side by side, but their thoughts on this subject far as the poles asunder.

Can it be expected that the virgin heart of a girl of twenty-three can view the dear, delightful subject through the experience-clouded glasses of cynical thirty-five? Ah, no; to one, it was a very El Dorado of unexplored golden promise; to the other, but a sandy desert where no flower bloomed or fountain bubbled.

"Why did you mention Romeo and Juliet? Do they form your idea of 'love's sweet madness'?" Tyrrell asked, presently.

"You will laugh at me if I tell you that I consider the character of Juliet one of Shakspeare's best conceptions. I do not see in her, as many do, a love-sick, silly girl, misguided and pampered by a doting nurse. She loved with all the fire and intensity of her Italian nature, knowing no restraint or reason for restraint; she loved for the first time in her life, with her whole soul and

strength and mind ; her thoughts were all absorbed with
the one fair picture of her gallant Romeo ; her eyes saw
only his face and form in the whole world ; there was no
vapid weakness in her love, but a fiery energy,—a wonderful courage,—which was able, without shrinking, to carry
out the horrible stratagem that ended in her death !"
Anne stopped suddenly, blushing at her own enthusiasm.

" Yes," Tyrrell observed, quite gravely, "it is a very
beautiful picture of love's tragedy in those days, and
under the skies of Italy,—a masterpiece in its way; but
the love of to-day, in foggy England,—have you any
picture of that in the gallery of your imagination to show
me ? I have a companion picture to yours somewhere in
a far-away corner of my memory, but I am afraid you do
not care to see it."

" You are not treating me quite fairly," she laughed,
blushing still ; " I dare say it is Dante and his Beatrice."
This with a slight scoff.

" No, not half so fine," he answered; " it is only,—on
my honor, Miss Ogilvie,—it is only Schiller's Max and
Thekla. I am very fond of them, and if I ever allow my
thoughts to wander into more than ordinary imbecility,
they fasten themselves upon Thekla. There is something
about the German character which inspires *trust;* a solidity, not graceful perhaps, but which is not devoid of a
certain restfulness, very captivating to the storm-tossed."

Before Anne could answer, the carriage of the Honorable
Mrs. Somers drew up, and, the young girls being separated,
Anne felt that it was time to return to their brougham,
on which the coachman was dozing gently. He was
awakened rather rudely by a sharp elbow applied with some
force in the locality of his ribs: "I say, Markham, wake up !
you'll be 'avin' the nightmare 'ere in this blessed Regent's
Park if you don't mind."

The obese, bottle-nosed individual thus rudely aroused from his slumbers, shook himself up and replied, in gruff tones, "Your imper'ance is surprisin', Thomas; I never was wider awake in my life. Every day I have another investigation of your imper'ant insurance; I won't bear it much longer!"

At this juncture, the governess and her charge were seen approaching the carriage, accompanied by Tyrrell. After they were seated, he lingered for a moment chatting with Valérie, with whom he was a prime favorite. He never tried to make her sit on his knee, or teased her to kiss him, or pulled her long locks and then looked away, as the other gentlemen did constantly; "he just treats me as if I was a grown-up young lady, and not like a doll or a poodle," exclaimed Valérie, when asked why she was so fond of Colonel Tyrrell, and so still and silent with all the other loungers in her mamma's drawing-rooms.

Just before the horses started, with their heads turned towards home, Percival dropped Valérie's little gloved hand rather abruptly, and said rapidly to Anne,—

"Can you not get a holiday—say Thursday—all day, from the rising of the sun to the setting of the same? I want you to go with me on the river, and to the Royal Academy, and, you need an outing, and so do I."

Anne fluttered with delight and dread, lest she might be obliged to refuse. "I will try," she said.

And he answered, with a beaming gladness in his violet eyes, "I shall come for you, then, on Thursday, before the dew is off the grass. Surely they cannot refuse you *one* day in the twelvemonth."

"*I will try*," she repeated, and then they drove away, and left him standing with raised hat under the shadow of the trees.

"I am so glad, darling Miss Ogilvie!" whispered Valérie, laying her cheek against Anne's shoulder. "You *shall* go, and have a whole, long day to yourself."

Anne bent and kissed her silently; her heart was full of singing-birds, and her eyes with the tears of a great delight.

CHAPTER XX.

"CERTAINLY, Miss Ogilvie, I can see no reason why you should not avail yourself of his invitation, if you are engaged to be married to this eccentric Colonel Tyrrell; otherwise, you are, I am sure, aware of the impropriety of going about with a young unmarried man without a chaperon. I imagine there *are* governesses who could do this sort of thing without criticism; but you are far too striking-looking to pass without remark. And really," (bridling a little), "I should not feel as if I could reconcile it to my conscience to leave Valérie in the charge of a person who could subject herself to impertinent observation." This peroration concluded the lengthy argument pro and con,—the projected holiday.

The "cons" had it, and there remained only a bow of acquiescence on Anne's part, and her ladyship sat alone sipping her matutinal chocolate with the self-satisfied air of one who has done her duty manfully. (I am doubtful about the sex of that last word. I fancy a *man* would have looked at the monstrous proposition with a more lenient eye, and from a larger point of view.)

That evening, Percival Tyrrell, enjoying his after-dinner cigar in his rooms at the Albany, and dwelling with a novel pleasure upon the prospect of a long day of summer-idling under the trees at Hampton Court, or on the Thames in a cockle-shell *à deux*, or on the greensward at Richmond, with the handsomest and most intelligent woman he knew, received the following extinguisher on his rosy anticipations:

"DEAR COLONEL TYRRELL,—Lady d'Hauteville has vetoed my holiday. I do not think she knows how great a disappointment it is to me.

"Please accept my grateful thanks for this and all the many kindnesses you have shown me.

"Yours very truly,
"ANNE."

"Oh, the narrowness of these puppets in buckram!" sneered Tyrrell, as he drew his letter-case towards him.

It was then ten o'clock. How many hours he sat there with his head buried in his hands and his elbows on the table, his portfolio open, and the pen ready to his hand, he never knew; but when he rose at last, he was cramped and stiff, and very cold and pale, and a letter was lying before him folded, addressed, and sealed.

Percival Tyrrell had spent those hours in closely questioning his heart and conscience. For many weeks past he had been disturbed by the conflict which had been waged between his feelings and the skeptical opinions, which had become almost fixed convictions, in regard to the truth and steadfastness of woman's nature. That this high-spirited Irish girl attracted him irresistibly by her beauty and intellectual capabilities was not enough; other women had won *so* much from him, but no more. Was there heart underlying these surface-gifts? Heart, pure and true and faithful,—Thekla's heart in fact,—and an honest integrity, which would never be shaken by circumstance, time, or temptation? And then: if, after all, this jewel "more precious than rubies" existed, does he love her as she would deserve, to the exclusion of every other fancy or desire?

Out of the shadows of the past there steals the outline of a head,—a fair girl's head,—with ripples of golden hair and dewy violets of eyes, and the guileless mouth of a cherub; a face, one would say, of an impersonation of Spring, or of the dawn of the morning, so pure and delicate and fresh it looked in its child-like innocence and beauty. And Tyrrell, with closed eyes, gazed inwardly at its loveliness, as he would have looked at a "bit" of Greuze hung up against the background of his memory; seeing its exquisite form and coloring, and feeling to his heart's core that they were but canvas and paint after all.

For that angel face had beguiled him years ago, and when he had looked beyond the fair exterior, deep down into the heart, and seen the rottenness within, his whole nature had received a shock which left it paralyzed for nearly fifteen years; and now, when he had become almost reconciled to a life free from the joys and torments of love, behold the electric touch has reanimated his sapless heart-fibres, and a new, strange life pours into them its nourishing strength. All night he sat with the pale ghost of his past love on one hand, dim and shadowy, and the living, glowing presentment on the other of the woman whose touch had stirred up the smouldering embers of his heart into a blaze in which were fast disappearing all the prejudices, resolutions, fears, and doubts which had stood as sentinels at the outposts during all those years.

The letter ran thus:

"THE ALBANY, June 25.

"MY DEAR MISS OGILVIE,—The Countess d'Hauteville's decision, of which you have informed me in relation to our projected holiday, has only confirmed my impression

of her ladyship's excellent taste and *savoir-vivre*. Pardon
my audacity in thoughtlessly having made the proposition,
and accord me, with her ladyship's permission, the honor
of an interview to-morrow afternoon.

"My servant will await your answer.

"Very truly yours,

"PERCY TYRRELL."

CHAPTER XXI.

"I PRESUME," Anne was saying, in a constrained voice,
as she tendered the precious little note reluctantly towards
the countess, who (with an absence of delicacy perfectly
justifiable towards a dependent), had requested permission
to read it, "your ladyship will not object to my receiv-
ing Colonel Tyrrell,—the man is waiting for an answer."

"A very proper note," deliberately pronounced the
countess, folding it leisurely; "for you perceive, my dear
Miss Ogilvie, Colonel Tyrrell acknowledges the justice
of my disapproval."

"Yes; your ladyship will not forbid me to receive him,
I trust?" ventured Anne once more.

The countess looked pensive. "If he means marriage,"
she said, slowly (Anne writhed), "why does he not come
and talk with me about it? I am the proper person,—or
the earl. But I fear, I very much fear, that such are not
his intentions."

"Madam," began Anne, proudly, "the man is waiting;
will your ladyship be good enough to reply to this note?"

"Certainly not," answered the countess, flushing
slightly. "Colonel Tyrrell has not shown the good taste
which I supposed he possessed, in addressing his note to

you. You alone can reply to it; but first let me warn
you. As a woman of the world, I tell you that man does
not mean to marry you; and one cannot be too careful,
you understand; put nothing on paper to commit yourself. I have no objection to one interview—*one*, remember—in your own parlor. Cécile may be present, if you
prefer it."

"Thanks," replied Anne; "there is no necessity; governesses can dispense with such rigid etiquette. I require
no chaperon for a half-hour's interview."

"You are very self-reliant, Miss Ogilvie, too much so
for your years; but I have warned you sufficiently, and
you are not devoid of good sense. Colonel Tyrrell is a
man of fortune and good family; he can choose a bride
among the best people I know. Do not allow his *pity* for
your unprotected situation to lead to any folly on his part
or your own. You may go and write your note now."

The countess languidly closed the straw-colored fringed
lids of her pale-blue eyes, or she would have been startled
by the expression flashing from those blazing sapphires in
Anne's face and the scarlet flush on her cheeks as she
moved towards the door. She had only time to write
hurriedly on her card in pencil, "Come at four o'clock,"
and inclose it in an envelope, before the flood-gates of
her tears broke down, and she spent her passion in bitter
weeping.

Surely this was but the wraith of the beautiful, sparkling
woman, Tyrrell had closed the carriage-door upon but
yesterday; this cold, proud, pale creature, looking so tall
in her sweeping black silk, and the crown of hair encir-
cling her perfect head. Why are her eyes so heavy and
her cheeks so white, and the hand which lies in his, a
moment, so limp and chill?

And yet never had she looked so attractive. There was a charm in that statuesque repose, in that sad droop of the red lips, in that tearful haze over the blue eyes, which affected Tyrrell more powerfully than all the rose-blushes and dimples of his previous acquaintance with that eloquent face.

All that he had intended to say to her vanished out of his mind, and without preliminary he began, abruptly,—" Miss Ogilvie, I have come to ask you why you were prohibited from accepting my invitation,"

" Ah, surely," she replied, with a weary little smile, " that need not all be gone over again, need it ?" He bent his head, and she went on : " I am only a governess, Colonel Tyrrell, who teaches the rudiments of the French and English languages at so many pounds per annum ; something a little above the lady's maid, and a trifle beneath the housekeeper ; a well-treated, comfortably-lodged hireling, but still, a hireling. Consequently, society does not provide for such as me a chaperon, and should I venture into the light of day without one in your escort, society condemns me ; that is all."

" But do you look forward to a whole, long life of French verbs and black-boards ?" he asked, with a smile. " Is there no possible escape from such a ceaseless grind as this ?"

" Oh, yes," she replied : " I am laying up savings. Do you know what that means ? It means a tiny house, some day, in a neat English village, furnished after my own heart ; plenty of trees and flowers outside, plenty of books and music within, and, if God has spared my poor brother" (a tear trembled in her voice), " there will reside a contented old maid and her gouty brother (for Dick had twinges at twenty-five, and I feel sure will be one trouble to keep me alive), and I shall——"

"In short," interrupted Percival, "you will exchange one slavery for another! Anne! you shall live no such narrow, sordid life! You shall come into my lonely heart, and let me shelter you from all the trials in store for you; Dick's gout not the least," he added, smiling a little. "But, Anne, you are weeping! Why is this? have I so grieved you?"

Anne sat with bowed head, her whole figure averted, while sobs shook her with uncontrollable emotion. Her nerves had been strung up to their last capacity of tension by the warning words of the countess, which found but too sure an echo in her proud heart. The sudden revulsion of feeling tried her too severely; she could not reason or judge, she could only feel, and she felt that it was as the countess had predicted,—this man *pitied her!* She strove hard to control herself, passed her handkerchief over her face, and, rising, stood before him, with her head slightly bent.

"Do you not see that you grieve me, Colonel Tyrrell? You must not mistake me; I am very happy here; they are kind to me, and I love Valérie dearly. *I have no wish to leave them,*" she concluded.

A great fear shot through Tyrrell's heart; could it be that this girl had not learned to love him as he had supposed? True, she had never in words, scarcely in looks, given him any assurance that he was more to her than another,—and *there might be another,*—she was so much admired! Had his self-conceit deceived him, and was he again to blindly offer his heart a sacrifice of no avail? Were they all alike, these beautiful, treacherous fiends, who steal men's souls to make sport of and desolate their lives for evermore? His voice was very cold and his face stern, as he said, gently, "There is no need for distress; *I am going.* I have made a mistake; you will forgive me?" He stood quite still a moment devouring her with his eyes; her head drooped lower; she raised her hand instinctively as though to ward off a blow; had she been turned to stone, all power of speech or volition could not have been more utterly denied her.

Pride, delicacy, a girl's shrinking from a first avowal, each and all paralyzed her tongue, her movements, almost her thoughts. The grace of her attitude appealed even at that moment to Tyrrell's keen æsthetic sense; he felt he must *begone*, or in an instant he would gather her to his heart. He seized her uplifted hand and pressed his lips upon it, almost crushing the slight fingers in his frenzied clasp, turned,—the door opened and swung shut,—he was gone!

It was only after the closing of the door had sounded the knell of departing happiness for her, that Anne started from her trance, and the piteous cry burst from her lips, whilst her arms stretched out to emptiness, "Oh, Tyrrell! Tyrrell! come back to me!" But the silken *portières* in that house stifled all unseemly moans, and Tyrrell was striding along with a curse in his heart and a set anger in his face at the inconceivable folly which had so nearly betrayed him *for the second time.*

As Anne stole along the corridor leading to the schoolroom an hour or two later, she encountered the countess and Valérie, who had just returned from driving. The countess could not resist commenting upon the swollen eyelids and pale face Anne tried to hide, by the usual, "I told you so, Miss Ogilvie. I was quite certain you were needlessly exposing yourself to humiliation. Even these Americans, when they are well-born and rich, are not willing to sacrifice themselves to their democratic ideas, you see. Ah, you will take my advice next time, I fancy."

Anne drew herself up haughtily: "Your ladyship must

pardon me; I decline to discuss this subject further."
And she glided by, leaving the countess stunned by her
audacity.

"That girl will certainly come to harm," she mentally
ejaculated, moving towards her own apartments; "such
pride as hers must have a fall."

Little Valérie was very tender to her "dear Miss Ogilvie" that evening. She put the shades over the lights,
and poured out the tea, and spread the thin bread and
butter herself, waiting upon Anne with a loving assiduity
which was balm to her sore heart.

<hr>

CHAPTER XXII.

BUT when night came, Anne wrestled, in the lonely
darkness, impotently with her anguish, for she knew as
surely as if she had read Tyrrell's heart and the bitter
secret of his past, which had made him so intolerant
of doubt or hesitation, that the cup of joy which had been
held to her lips for one sweet moment would never touch
them again. She knew the character of the man she
loved as well, perhaps, as it is ever given to woman to
decipher the mystic lines of a man's nature, and she felt
that he had not lightly spoken, nor lightly resented, her
apparent indifference to his words. And still, mingled with
her grief was a spark of anger, that he should have been so
harsh, so precipitate. Surely he must have known that
her tears were tears of joy, restrained only by the doubt
which was natural to one for whom life had few such blissful surprises. "Ah, does he not regret?" she murmured,
when the morning came with its cheerful sunshine. "Now

that a night has passed away, and he has had time to think, does he not know how it was that I could neither speak nor stir?"   Her doubts were soon dispelled.

Before mid-day, Toto, a bright mulatto boy who accompanied Tyrrell in his travels as valet (having proved his fidelity and worth incontestably as his servant throughout the war, showing an absorbing devotion to his master which is often met with in his affectionate race), brought and delivered into Anne's hand a letter from Percival Tyrrell.

Anne smiled sadly upon the boy, whose appearance had so often been the harbinger of good news to her, as she took the missive from his hand, and then bidding him await her summons in the servants' hall, she carried it away with her into her bedroom, where, after locking the door, she threw herself on her knees beside her bed, and burying her face on its sealed pages, she prayed that the sorrow which they held in store for her might be patiently borne.   For a presentiment held her heart from hope and its whisperings; the letter was wet and crumpled before she opened it; woman-like, she wasted tears on an uncertainty, and spent in suspense moments that might have been employed in allaying every doubt.

At last she broke the seal !

"I send Toto, my only faithful adherent (who lays aside his banjo with alacrity at my bidding, for I believe *he* is weak enough to love me), with this letter, which must bear to you the burden of my farewell.

"With my orders to leave it only in your own hands the boy will attain to the happiness of seeing you !

"The sight of you in the crisp freshness of your morning toilette will jewel this day for—*him*, an I you will also *speak*—to him ! (I have observed in him a keen sense of the beautiful, and his musical ear is wonderful.)

"And this day, in another but not less heroic fashion, will be always marked for Toto's master.

"For he bids you farewell to-day!

"'Tis thus that Toto gains a smile from you, and so, there appears to be no exception to the rule that in all that you do, joy must come to somebody!

"Adieu! Toto and I withdraw from before you!

"In the cloudy haze of your sublime indifference, can you discern which is Toto and which is—I?

"Anne, I feel as if I were going mad! When I commenced this letter the pride which your own soul has ere this approved, upheld me, and with it a longing for the peace which after fierce warfare comes to men when, life ebbing, they give themselves over to death without a groan; but, it is with me now even as when I am beside you (this talking with you on paper brings you so near to me), and I lose that protecting sense of antagonism which secures one's coolness at the least!

"I am quite undone under the influence of your surrounding presence. I can see you before me; I can smell the tea-rose in your breast. My dream of peace and my pride have vanished! Anne, I love you! I love you!

"You have done so much for me: you have rekindled faith in woman—trusting love, implicit confidence—in a heart which was arid as the desert!

"Was it to slay them all again with your tender, white hand? . . .

"We parted abruptly twelve hours since. I have dwelt upon your look then, your pallor, your reserved manner, your pensive grace! I cannot forget the drooped curve of your unkindly sweet lips, the veiled sadness of your love-denying eyes, the shadow of a grief which *I* was not to know, *in words*, paling the roses in your cheek.

"But you judged me correctly, Anne. I was not so obtuse that I could not read those eloquent signs.

"(In the amazing system to which we poor mortals are bound, why should I not share the common intelligence which reads inconsistencies clearly, and which awards the same weight precisely to a woman's smile or frown ?)

"But I will not pain you by bitter words; they shall lie quiet in my empty heart and disturb you no more. For I have not forgotten the pale, tearful face which, while it told me that you had rightly construed my request for an interview, told me also the pain which it caused your kind heart to wound me by refusing the gift I sought.

"The cold, proud reserve with which you armed yourself against me was not needed, Anne; your averted head, your hand raised as if to ward off my words, were expressive enough of your refusal to hear me. And then, that bitter setting forth of your position, to warn me from approaching nearer; your tears, your altered voice, all, all are written on my heart, else I should not find strength to say —farewell !

"PERCIVAL TYRRELL."

The ecstasy in Anne's heart shone out in every feature as she read the concluding lines of this letter. Pressing it to her lips, she seized a sheet of paper, without a moment's delay, and wrote hastily thereon :

> "And you called me cold ! God knows
> Underneath the winter snows
> The invisible hearts of flowers grow ripe for blossom'ng !"

And, inclosing it in an envelope, with the most fragrant of tea-rose-buds embalming it, she sealed it, and rang her bell. "Send the boy who brought me a letter," she commanded, in ringing tones, with the air of an empress and the smile of a child. A moment later Toto entered. "Toto," she said,—and the lad thought there was music in those two syllables,—"you will give this letter to your master as soon as possible, and—— Well! what is it?" His expression had become suddenly downcast.

"Massa Colonel Tyrrell has gone! I am so sorry; it will be too late to catch him at the train." Glancing at the clock.

"Gone!" Anne cried, faintly,—"gone! Where?"

"To Liverpool. He was took sudden with a wish to go back to America, and I am to join him with his dogs and luggage to-night. Massa Colonel Tyrrell telegraphed for our passage yesterday evenin'. We sail in the 'Russia' to-morrow."

Anne still held her letter; an ashy grayness spread over all the roseate tinting of her face. She crushed the envelope in her hand,—the rose-bud died silently,—and then she said, without a quiver in her voice, "Very well, Toto, there is no answer; and,"—she stretched out a slim white hand suddenly,—"good-by, Toto! May your voyage be safe and pleasant!" And then bent her head in token of dismissal, while a smile, more sad than tears, rested on her lips.

Such a smile as that which curved the tender mouth of the Lady Jane Grey as she bade farewell to her weeping maids of honor before she left the Tower to ascend the scaffold. Toto went out with his head drooping, and his melancholy, big, brown eyes swimming in tears.

CHAPTER XXIII.

FASHIONABLE London was putting itself in kid gloves, —*rose-tendre* and *crême-pâle*,—and that bewitching siren, Patti, caroling like a thrush to the ample shoulders and diamond-besprinkled heads of the nobility and gentry; to the sweet English faces, and less pretentiously-decorated lower social scale of music-lovers,—was packing "Her Majesty's" from pit to dome, on a somewhat oppressive evening in mid-June.

With the exception of the Royal box, in which the popular and lovely Princess of Wales, with her *suite*, smiled graciously on the performance, there were no other stars of greater magnitude in that aristocratic firmament than were diffusing their brilliancy from two boxes almost directly *vis-à-vis*. One of these held the most beautiful *débutante* of the season, the Lady Florence Ellesmere, duly chaperoned by her mamma, a wary and vigilant (not to say unduly suspicious) matron, with a ruddy countenance, a *parure* of priceless emeralds, and an idolatrous devotion to this third and last of her darlings to be disposed of, amounting to fatuity. The opposite *loge* held, robed in one of the most artistic creations of Worth's genius (he does accomplish a marvelously-exquisite toilette *sometimes*), fitly framed in costly bouquets, and backgrounded, as usual, by the faultless simplicity of the male full dress,— Pauline, Marquise de Courboisie. It was only after the eyes became accustomed to the dazzling *ensemble* of that picture, with its appropriate filling-in of fragrant exotics, brilliant light, and the thrilling music of Patti's warbling, that one could perceive, sitting slightly in the shadow of

L.

the curtain (roses whose full-bloom leaves have begun to
grow slightly yellow must not be too prominently placed,
—the shaded light softens outline, and tells no tales of
pearl-powder), the sallow, bright-eyed, terrier-like face
of the Duchesse de Languedoc.

At last, she had lured her restless guest back to her
own roof-tree, and had most sincerely congratulated herself on the inspiration which impelled her to make of this
fascinating enchantress a decoy-duck to fill her daughter-
less house, from morn till dewy eve, with the gayest, the
wittiest, the most *recherché* ineligibles of the society in
which her soul delighted. For although the duchesse had
"had her day" in London circles, time, the inexorable,
had not passed her by ; and from young and entrancing
she had passed to middle-aged and fascinating (*passée*
but agreeable), and lastly, oh ! inevitable conclusion ! to
old and tiresome ! Never handsome, but with intelligent
eyes and a mobile expression, she, like De Staël, had
held in bondage by her sparkling wit and personal magnet-
ism, and cultivated *esprit*, men to whom pink cheeks and
rounded arms would have appealed in vain.

Her "petit soupers à la Régence" were the crowning
point of one's aspirations during the season not later than
ten years ago (for she was loth to abdicate, and the aroma
of her power lingered even after the vase was cracked
and discolored by time); and at her table met only the
harmonious elements of intellect and culture and wit.
Title, however high, yielded precedence to a *diseur de
bon mots ;* the epigrammatic style of her countrymen being
preferred and encouraged ; and dearer to her heart than
lovers or *kudos,* in those early days after her lord duke had
transplanted her (through official exigencies) to England
a bride, had she prized the little suppers, where she often
gathered members from the famous "King of Clubs"—

Sydney Smith, Romilly, Mackintosh—and other *beaux-esprits* of the time, to give stamina and the wholesome bitter to the "flow of soul," which might have palled nauseatingly without them. For the young Duchesse de Languedoc counted lovers by the score, but she was wont to reverse the decision of Sir William Temple, who says, "The first ingredient in conversation is truth; the next, good sense; the third, good humor; and the fourth, wit." The two *last* being *first* in her consideration : good sense and truth might be together at the bottom of the well to eternity, if they so willed, undisturbed by her Grace. But, like her compatriot of famous (or infamous) memory, "she sinned and supped so *delightfully.*"

Just on the outer curve of ivory shoulder—which issued, whiter by contrast, from the foamy, rich, old lace of Pauline's corsage—appeared the blonde, impassive face of Dyke Faucett, who, in sleepy voice and with drooping eyelids, was taking advantage of an "aria" into which Capoul was throwing his whole soul, to whisper,—

"I am going now, Pauline; I shall see you later at Lady Emilie's. You will not stop for the last acts,—shall you?"

"Ah, surely not yet," pleaded the marquise, touching a spring in her bracelet, which disclosed a tiny watch under the jewels; "it is not more than eleven. Why do you go?"

She was not acting now; all the strength of her nature had become absorbed in this ceaseless struggle to keep the only creature that she loved, and over whom her power was not omnipotent, docile in the snare.

"I must say two words to the *grand'-mère* (oh, shades of the past and spirit of *de l'Enclos!* are you convulsed with merriment in the sulphurous regions of your just condemnation, at this *sobriquet* attached to a kindred soul?), and then I shall drop into the box *en face* to observe the effect of your toilette from a better point of view."

Pauline only smiled with her lips,—her heart burned (Lady Florence looked more like a pale pond-lily than ever this evening, but she was unusually lovely),—"*Au plaisir*," she said, with her brilliant smile and glance.

"*Au revoir, chérie*," he whispered. "And your Grace?" he asked, with his winning voice,—"I shall have the pleasure of seeing you at Lady Vivian's?"

"*Sans doute*," replied the duchess, with animation,—Faucett was a favorite with her as with all women,—"the Vivians boast the finest *chef* and the most genuine cellar in town; and *la gourmandise* is the last of my vices I have retained."

Dyke smiled, and Pauline cried, "And pray what has your Grace done with all the rest? I should like to gather some of them up; they were certainly more attractive than other people's virtues."

The old duchess cackled, and showed her still perfect teeth. "Ah, *mignonne*, you do not need them; and," addressing Faucett, "you know your Swift says that 'when we grow virtuous in our old age, it is merely making a sacrifice to God of the devil's leavings,' and that 'when our vices quit us, we flatter ourselves with the idea that it is *we* who quit *them!*'"

"Your Grace is in a moralizing vein to-night; is it in consequence of the dissipation of last evening, or as a preparation for the banquet of to-night,—a taste of vermouth to give you an appetite?"

"No, no," she replied; "I have never habituated myself to the B. and S. of the 'next morning;' retribution never attacks my digestive organs,—a consequence, *mon cher*, of only dining and supping where I know the *cuisine* is safe. Tell me," she continued, changing the subject abruptly, as was her habit, "what do you hear from *ce pauvre* Paris to-day? Has Proteus presented another and more startling aspect? or are they taking breath for a fresh *dénouement,* these Communists?"

"I imagine the Commune has breathed its last," replied Faucett; "the people are chastised sufficiently, and are already hopeful about the accomplishment of the milliards demanded by Prussia as indemnity. Wonderful, their recuperative power!"

"Wonderful indeed," assented the duchess. "I see they are jesting already in that irrepressible *Mot d' Ordre. Ce cher* Lord Lyons figures as '*un vieux polisson*' in one of its articles, through his benevolence in throwing open his hôtel to the Carmelite nuns when other refuge was denied them."

Dyke laughed. "One of Rochefort's illusions, I fancy; nothing more probable. The very air of Paris is full of canards; it is the effervescence of their late excitement. But I shall never get away unless your Grace is merciful; pray reserve me a corner of your *causeuse* later." He brushed with his moustache her delicate glove and, without a glance at Pauline, disappeared.

The view of a swan-like throat opposite, curving itself to bring the small ear of Lady Florence on a level with Dyke Faucett's lips, was not a sufficiently edifying sight to detain the occupants of the duchess's box longer from dropping in at a reception at the Russian Ambassador's, prior to the concluding engagement at Lady Vivian's.

When Dyke raised his *lorgnette* at length to take in the full glow of Pauline's beauty, there were only vacant chairs and broken sprigs of flowers lying about in the deserted *loge.* He smiled sarcastically under the fringe Nature provides to hide expression, and resumed his decidedly lover-like conversation with the beautiful girl, who was less coy than confident, and had long ago mentally determined not to reject the future heir to one of the oldest and finest estates in the south of England. The course of their love ran so smo thly that it almost became wearisome in its sameness; Dyke drifting down the stream, selfishly indolent, Lady Florence gliding gently over the surface without any of those pangs and tremors, sighs and blushes, which we are apt to consider concomitants of the tender passion.

Papa and mamma smiled approval, for although Dyke did not boast a title (titles had been laid at her feet before now), he was in other respects unexceptionable, and Ellingham Hall and Marsden Park lay side by side, and the latter belonged to Lady Florence. "They would form a very pretty property together," mused the old earl, "and Faucett is a man of integrity and principle,—a sterling good fellow;" and he was eager to add, "God bless you, my children!" and have the matrimonial noose securely drawn about them. But Dyke had not yet breathed the irrevocable words; there had not been the faintest allusion to settlements or orange-blossoms. Still, the understanding between them all was clear and well defined, and, with a plunge, he meant to take the final leap that night. For he felt that he could no longer stand off, dallying with her prospects and his own ; other suitors had dropped away, one by one, yielding him place, and papa's affability was overshadowed of late by a surprised coolness ; each time they met now the tall, slender figure of Florence's father assumed more and more the appearance of an exclamation point of wonder at this unnecessary and very embarrassing delay.

That *Dora* flitted like a phantom between Dyke Faucett and the fulfillment of his ambitions, cannot be denied ; but after he had recalled the fact related to him by his *concierge*, on the day before he left Paris, of Dora's accident (that trifling incident when she was no doubt trampled to death under the feet of a French mob), he reasoned logically, and with a sense of relief, that had she not died then, she could certainly not have left Paris, and therefore as certainly had not survived the siege. As for her father,—old, infirm, and idolizing his daughter,—it was most unlikely that he had outlived her loss. And golden-haired little Marian? But he would not think of her; it was the one thought on earth which could pierce through the crust of selfishness which had hardened on this man's heart and draw blood. He put it resolutely away from him, and began of the " funeral-baked meats" of poor Dora's memory "to coldly furnish forth the marriage-tables !"

It was with ungirlish self-possession and without a fluttered eyelash, that the Lady Florence murmured, as Dyke dexterously packed her mamma and herself, with their voluminous drapery, into the brougham, after the fourth act had hinted with the fall of the curtain that the ultra-fashionables might now retire to another entertainment, " I shall be at home at two o'clock, to you alone, to-morrow ;" in reply to his request for a *tête-à-tête*, un-disturbed.

" Thanks," he replied ; " you have made me very happy."

She smiled brightly, and, as their eyes and hands met, they perfectly understood what that interview por-tended. They felt betrothed from that moment, for neither doubted what the result would be.

" My angel Florence !" cried delighted mamma, press-ing an unctuous kiss upon the cold cheek next her, and crushing, in an impulsive embrace, all the *point d'Alençon* ruffles on the bodice inclosing that colder heart, " I con-gratulate you ; I *am* so happy !"

" Don't be premature, dear mamma," suggested the

demoiselle. "And do not forget, above all things, that we are *en route* to Mrs. Somers's last ball of the season; and if there is one thing I prize above another, it is lace which looks bought for the dress, and not crumpled and *défraichie.* I'm not off your hands yet, mamma, so don't rumple me." . . . .

"How late you are!" looked reproachfully from Pauline's soft, dark eyes, as she stood like a queen, surrounded by her courtiers, at the upper end of the ball-room that night, as Dyke sauntered towards her.

"I believe this is the *galop* you have promised to give me," drew her immediately out of the charmed circle; and, as Faucett never danced, they soon wandered off into a cool nook in the flower garden, which had been roofed with canvas and mysteriously illuminated with Chinese lanterns. When they were seated, and Pauline, glancing about, was assured of their isolation from the rest of the world, she drew from her bosom a letter, and, leaning towards Dyke so that the perfumed tresses of her hair almost touched his lips, she whispered, with a beaming joy in her face, "Dyke, I may be free soon ! He is ill,—too ill to remain in Paris, and has gone to our *château* in Brittany. See, this letter is from his physician ; he urges me to return at once to France, and says, 'The excitement, anxiety, and deprivations of the siege have undermined his health so that recovery is hopeless !' *Pauvre vieux !* I should be sorry for him were he not my husband, and—the only barrier between you, *mon ami*, and myself." Dyke suppressed a groan.

"Read me the letter, Pauline,—all of it, every word !" These were the only words that found utterance in this terrible emergency. They were words full of another significance to her. She rapidly, and in glad tones, read the death-warrant of the man who had loved her unselfishly, and given her all the good gifts of life which were in his power to bestow.

By the time the letter was concluded, Dyke had recovered from the shock, and prepared, with the recklessness of a gambler, to play out the game, cost what it might.

"And must you go soon, *ma mie?*" he asked, tenderly. "And you will let me hear from you constantly,—will you not?"

"Ah, Dyke, why do you not tell me you are glad? All through that hateful opera this letter was burning into my heart, I so longed to tell you of it, and now you do not even look glad." She fixed her eyes mournfully upon his, and a cold chill struck through her veins. "Do you not love me?" she burst out, in passionate, low tones. "Have all your protestations and prayers and vows been mere lip-service? and is it nothing to you that soon—very soon, perhaps—I may be *free*,—free to acknowledge to the world the love I have borne so long in secret?"

What could he do but fold her in his arms and hush her with words of endearment?

Before another twenty-four hours had measured another day Dyke Faucett found himself engaged in honor (!) to marry the Lady Florence Ellesmere, as well as the Marquise de Courboisie (for her widowhood loomed forth drearily certain), with the additional piquancy of a possibly-living wife!

This was really becoming diverting; life was not such a sapless thing after all.

Emilia, in looking at this man psychologically, as she regarded Iago after the grand *dénouement* filled her soul with loathing horror, might have been tempted to wish Heaven's vengeance meted out at a more liberal ratio than "half a grain a day."

BOOK III.

RETRIBUTION.

"Vengeance is mine; I will repay, saith the Lord."

"La Vengeance est boiteuse, elle vient à pas lents,—mais—*elle vient!*"

CHAPTER I.

It is the festival of St. John the Baptist.   The morning sun streams down on the assembling multitude, chiefly of women and children (for there are some left yet in France), as they file slowly into the fine old Abbey-Church, which is the pride of St. Denis.

There is the yellow glow of summer in the atmosphere, and the sun-rays, when not filtered through the full-leaved lindens, are somewhat oppressive even at this early hour; whilst the drowsy hum of myriad insects intoxicating themselves in fathomless wells of sweetness among the honeysuckle and clematis, wreathing and flowering every-where in the luxuriant prodigality of June, fills one, even at the church-door, with delicious, somnolent suggestions, and mutinous longings for the greensward and the rippling brook, or the dense-shaded forest-haunt, where one could offer up one's devotions in primitive fashion in a Temple not made with hands, or idle the hours away in a moral

258

paralysis, the result of the over-fullness of life in a perfect summer day.

But, it is a *holiday of obligation* to-day, and one must be happy according to the decrees of the good old man in Rome; therefore, under the sacred arches where the kings of France lie buried, must one bend the knee, and smother one's pagan yearnings for nature's altars and sylvan sacrifices. Therefore airy fabrics of delicate hue compose the toilettes of the *dévotes*, with a touch of summer splendor in their bright diaphanous effect (surely at four miles' distance from Paris one need not punish one's self with "*ce triste deuil*"?) and in every breast-knot, and many childish hands, wilts languidly a festive flower or a tiny bouquet of mignonette (that prized bit of sweetness so dear to the work-people of the sense-fostering nation).

And many are the long wax-tapers interspersed amid the more graceful floral offerings, particularly among the sabot-shod, high-capped peasantry, whose lips move as they furtively finger their rosaries, whilst their bright, shrewd eyes wander about, taking note of everything, from the texture of their neighbor's "polonaise" to the size and quality of the candle which represents their pet sin or most cherished hope.

The entrance to the ancient sanctuary is garlanded with flowers and evergreens, and each representative of "our Blessed Lady" is *éblouissant* with June roses and the fragrant white hyacinth, to which flower she is supposed to be partial; the emblem of purity and sweetness combined fitting her sense of perfection.

For it is the Feast of St. John, and the war is over!

But, spite of sunshine, flowers, and fragrance (and fresh toilettes), an unwonted gravity marks the countenances of these worshipers. There is none of the brisk animation and lively chatter which prevails ordinarily among a concourse of French men and women; even the most coquettish-eyed *brune* among the girls wears a sedate look, which fits her like her grandmother's cap, and there are stern lines about the sallow-faced men, and tear-furrowed cheeks amid the older women, which mark the shadow cast by the recent storm, whose fury had well-nigh wrecked their land.   Paris recuperates rapidly, clears away blood-stains, rouges artistically her horror-paled cheek, and smiles through her tears heroically; but throughout her environs, and in the provinces, heads are bowed yet in shame and rage and grief; for although the white dove of peace broods over stricken France, the wounds it strives to cover with outstretched wings are bleeding inwardly still.

The dim twilight in those lofty aisles is heavy with the breath of incense, through which the consecrated torches twinkle like stars, while the "kyrie eleison" bursts forth, following close on the slow, solemn footsteps of the benediction, swelling in harmonious accord from the great choir above.

The congregation stood drinking in the glorious sounds, which seemed to raise on their airy wings these earth-bound souls to celestial peace and rapture, when suddenly the voices died away and a stillness almost oppressive supervened.

There was a slight rustle of expectancy, and many eyes turned in the direction of the choir, full of surprise at this unusual interruption, when, like a prolonged, mellow flute-note, there pierced through the fragrant twilight a soprano voice of superhuman sweetness and sustained power, filling every corner of the sacred edifice with the beautiful "Gloria," in solo.

The people, motionless, held their breath to listen; never, surely, had such sounds reached mortal ear before.

Was it child's or woman's or angel's voice? Ah, it was enough to draw one's soul from purgatory! Many of those listeners trembled and grew pale with emotion as the words of the wondrous thanksgiving swelled out in thrilling music, while quiet tears stole down some hollow cheeks which had been rarely dry of late. And when the strains ceased, leaving the air still vibrating with melody, the people, with a long-drawn breath, wiped their eyes, and looked at each other as if just awakened from a dream.

Near the entrance, in an uncushioned pew, stood leaning against a pillar, with crossed arms and a look of rapt delight on his sun-bronzed face, our ex-National Guard, Dick Ogilvie, and by his side the figure of Sister Agnes, dressed in black, but wearing no longer on her steadfast arm the badge she had borne so nobly through many months of peril and unflagging devotion,—the red cross of Geneva! Under its merciful banner, how many women during those terrible days showed courage, patriotism, endurance as unflinching as any that ever waved the tri-color in field, while the death-cry, "*Vive la France!*" pierced the din of battle!

There must be heroic stuff in the women of France which might cover with a cloak of charity a multitude of their frivolities. Something heroic and grand even when it trenches upon eccentricity; when it clothes its maiden limbs in armor and sallies forth to battle as Jeanne d'Arc; or when it slays its tyrants *en déshabillé*, as Char-lotte Corday; even when it waxes demoniac in its wrath, and shakes threatening fists in the fatally-fair face of the hated Austrian, hounding her on to death; or drags can-non through the streets to the accompaniment of maledic-tions, or pastes with vindictive leer its "billet condamné," "B. P. B." (*bon pour brûler*), on the doomed sites where the fiend of petroleum shall rage in flames. Something grand and terrible, though horrible, a suspicion of the tigress-blood which shows out so undeniably in the deadly *émeutes*, the wholesale massacres, which have dyed with crimson the streets of their fairest cities!

And yet this anomalous mystery, this woman of France, false, vain, frivolous, cruel, in the moment of her country's agony lays aside velvets and laces, and goes into the hospitals, emptying therein larder, cellar, purse, crying out to the last, "No armistice! no capitulation! We can suffer, we can starve, we can die, but we must *not* be conquered!" And she *did* suffer and starve and die, more than once, as only that joy-loving woman *can die*, during those months of carnage and famine and fire, holding high, undauntedly, their motto "tout est perdu, fors l'honneur!"

Agnes's face had lost the pure curve of its outline, but her expression of sweet repose was born of perfect happiness and sense of rest after "the burden and heat" of a troublous day; and over Dick's genial, ruddy countenance had settled a seriousness which proved that his rollicking, somewhat reckless nature held depths which could be stirred by the scenes of suffering through which he had come forth ennobled. He could never go back and be the *insouciant*, devil-may-care "good fellow" of other days, when he had always been more or less inebriated with that vernal wine of life which is unmixed with the gall of later experience; but if his smile was less frequent, it had a new sweetness in it, and if his laugh was a trifle less ready, it had a truer ring,—and the graceful, careless *bonhommie* of old was not more charming than the quiet dignity which sat so well upon him now.

And Agnes thought him simply perfect, and idolized him, after the manner of her kind.

As the last echo of the "Gloria" died away Dick

aroused himself, and, approaching Agnes, whispered, " Is the story of Orpheus a fable, think you? Would not that voice draw one up—or down—as it pleased?"

Agnes smiled, and answered, whispering also, " Dora's voice, like herself, could only draw one nearer heaven. Listen!" For now flowed forth on the air the soul-stirring words of the " Agnus Dei," with its pathetic appeal, " Dona nobis pacem, pacem, pacem!" piercing every heart with its grief-born pathos.

" Sainte mère de Dieu!" whispered one woman to another, " this is no human voice!" And she hastily crossed herself and muttered an *ave*.

Agnes's eyes filled with tears; it seemed to her *that Dora's heart was bleeding.*

" Have we an angel among us, or one of the *cantatrices* of the opera?" murmured Madame la Baronne de St. Lo to her son, leaning over her velvet cushion to reach his ear, while she strove to pierce with her *lorgnon* the obscurity of the choir from which this mysterious voice issued.

" Mais non, maman," replied the youth, pale with excitement; " it is a miracle, but a human being is the instrument; a young English girl. I have seen her; she is beautiful as her voice, with a face of marble, and the eyes of one inspired, and a——"

" Silence, I pray thee, my son. This is not the place for *persiflage* of this description." And the baroness, becoming uncomfortably red, fanned herself vehemently, while she made a mental calculation of the remaining days which would intervene before this last, only scion of her house should return to retirement and study at St. Cyr, sublimely unconscious that the subject of her anxious meditation, with eyes momentarily lowered from the choir (and growing more unwholesome-looking than before,—

through a combination of concentrated emotions), was vowing in his heart to escape by his window at an unholy hour, and spend that very night promenading before the house which contained this divinity with the statue-like face, and the golden-gleaming eyes, and the voice which had awakened the embryo man in his sluggish soul.

Dick Ogilvie and Agnes stood a little apart from the outflowing congregation after service, waiting for Dora, who, with Marian by the hand, soon appeared, and joining them they hurried homeward, to escape the curious gaze of many enterprising individuals upon whom her exquisite voice had wrought its spell. Turning into a quiet, partially built-up suburb, lined on each side with villa-looking buildings with the square, white bit of information *appartements à louer*, on most of their *étages*, and neat, primly-kept, oblong suggestions of garden in front, into which juts the inevitable balcony with its creeper in a perfect state of preservation, its three iron chairs and round iron table, they moderated their pace somewhat, and Dora threw back the veil with which she had shrouded herself, to the imminent risk of suffocation, on that mid-day of June. Agnes's cheek was quite flushed now from the rapid walking and the heat ; but Dora's was free from the faintest tinge as the snow-drop, while her eyes looked preternaturally large and bright through the attenuation of her features. Agnes, glancing at her, almost trembled, so fragile and delicate she had grown, and so angelic was the expression of

> "That peaceful face wherein all past distress
> Had melted into perfect loveliness."

but into a loveliness so unearthly, so spiritual, that her friend's heart grew faint with fear at the thought of their coming separation, which might be a longer one than either anticipated. For Agnes and Dick were to be married shortly, and Dora had steadfastly resisted their entreaties to accompany them to England, where Dick could obtain a livelihood in the practice of his profession in a country town, and where he now felt that he must make his home on his sister's account.

Dora was unable to think of England without a shudder of horror and grief, not untainted by self-reproach; for she felt now that, however anxious her husband should be to reclaim her, she would rather die than return to his side.

The conviction of Dyke's base treachery towards herself had destroyed all lingering vestiges of love and respect in her heart; but for her child's sake she would have crushed down her aversion and walked steadily on in the path beset with thorns on which she had entered, had not the great, insurmountable barrier of this new cross which barred her with its mighty power from following the line of duty,—her love for Ronald Buchanan, and his great love for her,—forced her to turn her agonized face away from a greater anguish than she had strength to bear.

"I may not even die," she moaned to herself in the dark hours, as she heard Marian's soft breathing by her pillow; but her slight figure grew more slender, and her step slower, and her face resembled an alabaster vase through which the lamp of the soul beamed forth, too luminously for earthly uses.

At those rare times when Agnes found it impossible longer to withhold her gentle reproaches and warnings, and tried to awaken some anxiety for her state of health in Dora, she would be answered by the very saddest of sweet smiles, and words like these: "Never fear, Agnes; I am stronger than I look; as long as Marian lives, God will not take me to himself. Do not let my pale face grieve you, dear; remember—

> " ' I have watched my first and holiest hopes depart
>   One after one;
>   I have held the hand of Death upon my heart
>   And made no moan.'

Why, then, should you reproach me, or wonder that the *laughter* has all died out of me forever?"

And Agnes was fain to be content and watch her silently.

As they approached the cottage where they had all taken refuge after their escape from Paris, the tall figure of Ronald Buchanan arose from an easy-chair which he had drawn through the window out upon the balcony, and advanced to open the gate of the little garden for them. He also bore the impress of suffering upon his frank face, and his left arm was in splinters and hung in a silk scarf, helpless; for it had been broken in two places, a fortnight ago, when he had dashed into a burning house to rescue from a frightful death a bed-ridden man and some helpless children. He bore them all out uninjured in his strong arms, and had just turned away, blackened, singed, burned about the hands, when a wall fell in with a crash, and part of the mansard-roof slipped into the street upon the shrieking spectators.

Ronald knew nothing of what had happened; many were crushed, many more frightfully mangled, and he was drawn out from the smoking *débris* for dead. But, fortunately, a *sergent de ville* took the precaution to examine him before he was cast upon the heap of bodies consigned to the Morgue; and finding signs of life, dispatched him on a litter to the hospital of the English ambulance. There poor Dora had the melancholy comfort of nursing him until so far recovered as to be able to remove outside of Paris, of which they all were weary unto death ; and in this quiet retreat, where all the hideous sights and sounds of the last nine months could be at times forgotten, they all rested.

Ronald Buchanan and Dick Ogilvie had each communicated with their men of business in London as soon as the siege was raised, and had received ample remittances.

Dora also had gone timidly to her father's banker in Paris to draw their accumulated monthly installments from America. The banker, an American who had known her father well, and who had been absent from Paris during the troubles, had just resumed business. He handed her the sum accruing to her without demur, and she went straightway and invested the greater portion of it in a neat trousseau for her little friend Agnes, leaving barely a margin to cover the rent of their rooms and weekly boarding.

The day following their arrival at St. Denis, she offered her services as choir-leader in the Abbey-Church, and a few days later sought and obtained pupils, to whom she undertook to give singing lessons three days in each week. For Dora's was a staunch, sturdy heart,—far stronger to endure than the frail casket which enshrined it.

And Agnes, overwhelmed by so much loving-kindness, spent days, and parts of nights, too, in creating wonders of convent needle-work wherewith to clothe little Marian, who passed her happy days frolicking in the sunshine, without more thought of raiment than the lilies of the field.

How blessedly happy would these five hearts have been, had it not pleased God to weave into the destiny of one of them the dark thread of evil, which could not be unspun !

As it was, both Dick and Agnes felt it almost an insult to their dear friends to let the glory of their happiness shine forth. Only when they were alone together did they cast aside the sadness born of a true sympathy with the sore trial, of which they both guessed the general features.

No common tie bound these four souls together; for months had they struggled, endured, suffered, hand-in-hand. And during those last fearful weeks when the Commune had ruled like the Genius of Destruction in Paris, when the roaring of cannon, the whizzing of shells, the screeching of the *mitrailleuses*, filled the heart with dire forebodings, which the constant ringing of bells and beating of drums served only to heighten, while the cry of despair, "*Nous sommes trahis!*" from the frenzied National Guards, was heard from time to time through their expiring struggle, they had cheered each other. For there was fighting at Neuilly, at Bagneux, at Asnières, and the shells from Versailles scattered death through the Champs Elysées. There, under the trees where children had danced in glee, where *bonnes* had coquetted, and fine ladies peeped from under their dainty parasols at the gay cavaliers and the dashing equipages, on many a spring day passed, lay now, stark and stiff in death, the bodies of Frenchmen, slain by Frenchmen in fanatical fury.

The Royalists and Federals fought like tigers, thirsting for each other's blood; shots were exchanged from window to window; there were encounters on the staircases, on the roofs, in bath-houses,—it was a wild orgie of murder.

The churches were closed, the *curés* imprisoned, the convents emptied; sacrilege and blasphemy flourished in such a hot-bed of crime. The Cathedral of Notre Dame was invaded, the sacred vessels, the priests' robes, the ornaments, handled with coarse jests and impious sneers.

The spirit of Voltaire arose like the phœnix from the ashes of corruption, and the Goddess of Reason, with her saturnalia of blood, menaced France once more.

Buchanan, called upon to attend a prisoner whose soul was nigh escaping through the bars of La Roquette, encountered on one of his visits the reverend Abbé ———, who was allowed to enter the cells of the condemned on presentation of a passport, which bore these words,—"Admit the bearer, who styles himself the servant of *one of the name of God!*"

One could almost see Voltaire's contemptuous shrug, or hear his impatient dismissal of the unanswerable argument of Christ,—"I pray you never let me hear *that man's* name again!" As Ronald returned the passport to the white-haired priest, a shudder of dread ran through him, and he smelt the smoke of the flames already which were to devour this Gomorrah. Not long after, when Archbishop Darbois was dragged forth and put to death without cause, who was surprised? He was only the third Archbishop of Paris who died a violent death at the hands of *his flock!*

Can one wonder that the barricade sprang up magically in the God-forsaken city, writing the word *riot* in each street, or that placards disgraced the walls calling upon the women to take up arms "to stimulate the cowards who hold back!" For the same noble end, no doubt, women old and hideous (the refuse of "La Force" generally), in rags, and with red, Phrygian caps on their disheveled heads, dragged about the deadly *mitrailleuse*, shouldered the musket, hurled forth curses more vociferously than could be possible to man.

In this horrible chaos the National Guard went mad.

Disheartened and disgusted, Dick Ogilvie unfurled the tri-color, and, waving it wildly, called upon his regiment to follow him! They went over to a man to the Versaillais!

In those days Dora and Agnes rarely stirred outside, fearing to leave the shelter of the hospital, where they found plenty of work to do.

How weary they were sometimes of groans and moans, lint and bandages! How they longed for the blue sky and the green turf, and the sweet, untainted air of the forest! And how many an hour of rare rest did each of these friends sacrifice for the other! Many a meal, too, was divided by four to the satisfaction of—none, alas!

They had all been unwearying in sustaining the strength and courage of Dora, who looked so terribly fragile, but they found that she could circumvent their tenderness by a crafty unselfishness, which returned their kindness in equal measure. And now, with life spared, with youth and its quenchless hopes, they must separate, in all proba-bility, forever.

They had talked it all over the night before this feast-day of St. John, and Agnes had plead her hardest to move Dora's heart towards England. "But it cannot be, Agnes. I could walk down into my grave before I could go to—— Oh, my darling, do not urge me; it cannot do good, and it only tortures me."

"But, Dora, I cannot leave you here alone. Have some pity upon me, dear, and tell me what I ought to do."

"I shall not be alone, Agnes; I have Marian, and this widow who owns the house is friendly and seems to be a good sort of woman." ("Oh, Dora!" sobbed Agnes.) "And you *must* go with Captain Ogilvie; he is quite right to return to England and make his home there. You will be very happy, dear; he is a noble-hearted man." And she kissed her tenderly.

Of the keen pang which it cost Dora's sensitive, clinging, timid nature to cut herself loose thus from her only friends, she gave no sign ; it would only mar their happiness, and nothing could be otherwise arranged. What could one pain more signify to her? had not her life become

> "A drear golgotha, where all the ground is white
> With the wrecks of joys that have perished, the skeletons of delight"?

And so without one sigh or tear she set about preparing for her friend's marriage and departure, with a strange, calm serenity which was not natural to her years. One would have imagined it was a mother whose tender voice advised and suggested and encouraged a daughter's manifold preparations for her wedding journey, instead of a young creature of her own age, to whom it all seemed the dreariest mockery.

The wedding-day was fixed for the 28th,—only five days yet to be together,—and then, Agnes with her husband were to start for England, and Ronald with them !

As she passed through the little gate held open for her by the ever-ready hand, Dora could not resist sending one swift upward glance at the pale, sad face of the man she loved, and murmuring, "Have you been in pain? Is the bandage easy? You do not look as bright as when we left you."

"Thanks, it is quite comfortable ; the heat is trying me somewhat, and yet I have not stirred out of the shade of this porch."

He spoke coldly, though courteously, and brought his chair forward for her. But she gently declined it, and, with a sadder expression in her face, slowly mounted the stairs to her room, followed by Marian.

Dora laid aside the child's hat and her own, and then

drew her to her knee, and said, "Marian, look at me; do you love me?"

"Oh, yes, mamma," answered the little one. "You know I love you, dear, darling, sweetest mamma!"

"Then put your arms about my neck and love *me tight.* Oh, my darling, creep into my heart and still its pain!" she wailed.

Marian covered her with kisses, showering endearing epithets upon her, lisping consolation with every breath; and gradually the storm passed,—the sobs ceased, the tears were dried, and smiles and nursery rhymes took their place. And then, at last, Dora yielded to her petition to sing her to sleep, and her mid-day nap was taken while the prayer for peace rose up once more from the aching heart upon which her curly head rested. "*Dona nobis pacem!*" echoed through the cottage, and from the open windows fell upon that other heart below, which would never more know peace apart from her.

When the voice ceased, Ronald arose and left the porch, going out into the acacia-lined road in a fever of unrest, and presently Agnes and Dick sauntered away in an opposite direction.

An hour afterwards, Dora stood at her window looking out over the fields in their spring-tide beauty, with the fair heavens smiling down upon them, and her heart grew calm, and she bade Marian look at the little clouds which lay still "like flocks of sheep, or vessels sailing in God's other deep." "And shall mamma tell Marian some pretty verses about those lovely clouds? and Marian may learn to say them too. Now listen:

> "'Thinned to amber, rimmed with silver,
>   Clouds in the distance dwell,
>   Clouds that are cool for all their color,
>   Pure as a rose-lipped shell.

> "'Fleets of wool in the upper heavens
>   Gossamer wings unfurl;
> Sailing so high they seem just slipping
>   Over that bar of pearl.'"

"Ah, that is beautiful, mamma! Tell me it again," pleaded Marian.

And then came more verses, and some loving serious talk of what lay beyond the bar of pearl; and when Agnes came in shortly after, Dora's smile of greeting was radiant, for the peace she sought had been found, and God had smiled out of the heavens upon her.

CHAPTER II.

"This is the last time that we may ever speak together, Dora; to-morrow at this hour I shall be far away; answer, then, I implore you, the one question I ask you."

They were walking together, Dora and Ronald, for the first time since they left Paris; but it was their last day (to-morrow was to be Agnes's wedding-day), and Dora had not been able to refuse his earnest request.

It was evening, the sun was setting, and the

> "Sweet, calm day in golden haze
> Melts down the amber sky."

They were walking along a country road, and Dora leaned on his uninjured arm. She had laid aside her mourning, to please Agnes, until after the wedding, and her pure white muslin with its violet ribbons, and the bunch of roses in her belt, made her look more like the sweet Dora of the old Rome-days than she could have believed possible.

M*

"I will answer any question you desire answered," Dora said, at last.

And Donald burst forth: "Tell me that man's name, *your husband.*" How bitter the words were in his mouth! "What is he? Who is he? Ah, I thought so. You will answer any question *excepting* the one I wish answered, —woman-like." For Dora had drawn her arm away from his and walked on silently beside him.

"I cannot," she spoke in a constrained voice,—"I cannot tell you; forgive me,—it would fill my days and nights with terror to feel that *you and he might meet.* Oh, spare me this anxiety, if you can!" she plead.

His resolution wavered; he took her hand gently and replaced it on his arm. "I will not pain you again, dearest; and these minutes are too precious to waste in fruitless argument. Dora, will you write to me?"

She thought a moment. "Yes, I will,—not often, and of course not such letters as you would care to receive from me; but I will write, if you wish."

"Thanks; it will not be against your principles to say that you and Marian are well and happy, will it?" smiling down at her. "And, Dora, is it necessary for you to continue these singing-lessons?"

"Not absolutely; but why should I give them up?— they give me occupation, and I *must* fill up the days some-how, you know."

He looked away; he could not speak. There was a pathos too deep for tears in this acknowledgment of her utter loneliness. And then they spoke of Ronald's future, of his plans and prospects, speaking in that flat mono-tone in which no note of gladness, hope, or ambition could be traced, looking forward to it only as something to be lived through,—a patient, hopeless, waiting for the end.

They walked slowly, arm linked in arm, so near in spirit
that the thought of one needed to be but partly expressed
to the quick comprehension of the other, with such perfect
"*rapport*" existing between soul and soul, that their long
silences were more eloquent than speech ; and yet between
them stretched an impassable gulf ! Each realized fully
to-day, as they stood one on either brink and gazed across
with tear-blurred eyes at each other, that on the morrow
that dread gulf would have widened to such proportions
that they could see or touch each other's hands in this
world never more.

And so they talked together, wandering on in the solitary, hay-scented, June twilight, sadly, but with an unselfish attempt at resignation, lest the anguish which lay in
either heart might overflow the barriers of self-control,
and so make endurance futile, knowing the while, to its
uttermost pang, what two poor souls have known, one of
whom was condemned to die before the sun should set
to-morrow.

Dora drew Ronald on to speak of his home, of his
family, each of whom she had known by name long since.
" You will find your greatest happiness with Lydia," she
urged. " Go to her, and let her nurse you back to health
and strength ; the gayety and exuberant spirits of your
younger sisters at the parsonage will jar upon you after
all the pain you have witnessed lately, but Lydia's calm
restfulness will soothe and heal you, I feel sure."

" Yes, Lydia is repose itself; the very soft rustle of her
garments has something of the flutter of angelic wings
about it. But would it be right for me to bring into her
new-born happiness, her bright, sweet home, my wounds
and scars, my broken health and broken spirit ? For,
oh ! Dora, I have felt lately that, morally and physically,
'there is no health in me;' and"—he went on vehe-

mently, unheeding her gesture of remonstrance—"I always seemed to feel, through all former troubles or cares, that God's hand held the thunderbolts of fate which are sometimes hurled so crushingly at humanity. But now all is dark; I cannot understand; the justice of God is incomprehensible. I stumble about in a blind rebellion, striving to find comfort in parallel cases throughout the ages of pain since the Creation,—in history, in the experience of other men; and," he added, sadly, "I have found them, but they do not comfort me. Yes, Dora, suffering has existed since the world began.

> " ' I have seen those who wore Heaven's armor worsted;
> I have heard Truth lie;
> Seen Life, beside the fount for which it thirsted,
> Curse God, and die !'

and it has not made my pain less bitter !"

There was a little pause; they were resting now on the top of a slight elevation, where the *débris* of a broken-up camp still scattered the ground. On that spot, only a few short weeks ago, had the Prussian troops held their orgies, gloating over the sight of fair Paris in conflagration· in every quarter; drinking deep; their most rapturous toast being, *"Paris, cuit dans son jus !"*

Dora, whose strength was soon exhausted, had seated herself on a heap of demolished tent-props, and was gazing now at the western sky, where the sun, just disappearing, left his foot-prints in gold and purple.

"I know so well what you feel," she said, presently. "I have gone through that dark valley before now. I, too, have *doubted everything*, despaired of everything, in a dumb agony of hopelessness. But it has passed away; there will always be a sad, empty pain in my heart,— *always*,—but I shall never rebel as I have done again. Ah ! what avails it to thrust one's self against the jagged rock of Unbelief,—question the mercy and justice of the God who has given us the power to suffer for His own wise purposes? The end of it will come to you, as to me, when, bruised and broken,—

> "'I heard Faith's low, sweet singing in the night,
> And, groping through the darkness, touched God's hand.'"

Ronald, looking in her rapt, upturned face, with its transparent clearness and great, glowing eyes, with the waved nimbus of gold-brown hair above her pure brow, felt a sickening pang shoot through him, which warned him that this was well-nigh the last time his eyes would rest upon that face, which bore even now God's seal upon its beauty.

Instinctively he took the light shawl he had carried on his arm and drew it tenderly about her shoulders, as though by even that trifling action he could postpone the coming of the dread messenger.

"There is one thing more, Dora, you must promise me," he began, huskily, after ten minutes' silence, through which he dared not trust his voice.

"Yes, dear," she said, dreamily, drawing away her eyes with an effort from the western sky, and fixing them, full of solemn glory, on his heart-broken face.

"Should you fall ill, or Marian, should harm come to her, will you have me sent for immediately?"

She answered, gravely, "No, forgive me! I cannot promise this. Ah! my friend, when you look at me like that my pain is intensified so that I cannot bear it;" and tears rolled down over the white face. Ronald's composure was shattered at the sight.

"Then I shall not leave you. No, Dora, no pleading of yours can move me now. I shall stay with you as long as you are spared to me on earth, and then—well, then I will stay with you still!"

A gleam of joy broke out over her sweet face as he spoke, and the deep eyes gleamed through their tears,— tears born of renunciation. So welcome, so dear to the heart of woman is the iteration of the old, never worn-out story, that she would draw back from the gates of Paradise, or linger about the dread shores of Avernus, to hearken once more to its faintest whisper.

"You are not yourself now," Dora said, gently stroking with her cool, soft hand the strong, feverish one which clasped hers like a vice. "You are not the strong, noble, courageous man who would die before he would stoop to dishonor, that I thought, or you would not make my task so hard."

"But, Dora," he interrupted, "can you expect me to look on your face for the last time to-morrow? Is it not bitterly cruel enough to leave you, delicate, unprotected as you are, but I am to be possessed of superhuman endurance?"

"And would it comfort you to see me die?" she asked. "Is that what you wish me to promise?"

He answered nothing, but loosed her hand and bowed his head in his palms with a smothered groan. Then the *woman* in Dora reasserted itself, and she leaned eagerly towards him, whispering,—

"Rest content. I *could* not die without bidding you farewell. I will send for you when the end draws near. *I will have no one by me at the last but you.* Do you hear? Oh, look up, and tell me *you will come to me!*"

He did not move or speak; his face was hidden, and a strong shudder passed over his frame. Her voice broke the silence in tones sweet and sad as the wail of an æolian harp:

"You will be patient and good for my sake. No one knows what the future may bring to you of forgetfulness.

or joy, of which *no* life is utterly bereft. You have much happiness before you; loving hearts await you in your dear home. You have youth and health and energy, and, I hope, ambiti n. How many are there who can count not *one* of these blessings! You will not let *one* sorrow crush you. One disappointment, however bitter, should not wreck a man's life. Why else is strength given one but to overtop misfortune and to conquer fate? One is so tempted to exaggerate one's misery. You know *my favorite* says,—

> "'We over-state the ills of life. We walk upon
> The shadow of hills, across a level thrown,
> And pant like climbers.'"

Still Ronald sat mute, drinking in the sound of her gentle pleading, unable to speak or move from the concentrated anguish which held him in an iron grasp.

When he arose at last, his face was drawn and white, and the sad smile with which he offered her his arm, saying, "The dew is falling, Dora; you must go within now," made her heart ache as it had never yet done through all her sorrowful life.

These were almost the last words which passed between them.

The next day after the quiet wedding—which had been solemnized at the British Embassy, in Paris, Dora preserving throughout perfect composure and even a cheerful serenity—they drove, all four together, to the "Gare" (Marian having been left in charge of the widow, their landlady), where the happy couple and Buchanan were to take the train for Boulogne, *en route* to England.

Agnes, when the moment of parting came, broke down utterly; sobs shook her as she clung to her friend in wild grief, and only Dora's firmness saved her from missing the train. She it was who unlocked the frenzied clasp of

Agnes's fingers upon hers, who whispered, "Agnes, Mr. Ogilvie is pained by this sorrow of yours on your bridal-day. Calm yourself, my darling; I beg you not to un-nerve me. Agnes, let me go, dear; you are killing me!" And she tore herself away, just pressing Dick Ogilvie's hand silently as she passed him, which he as silently returned, and then sprang into the railway carriage, where Agnes had thrown herself back in convulsive weeping.

Ronald Buchanan and Dora stood alone on the platform,—alone in a rushing, scrambling, noisy crowd of passengers scurrying for seats. Dora looked confused, and put her hands for a moment to her temples. Ronald quietly laid his valise on the seat next Dick's and approached her. "I will see you safely to your carriage, Dora; there is sufficient time."

She took his arm, and, trembling violently, turned towards the entrance of the station, before which the hack stood which had brought them. Ronald placed her in the carriage and gave the necessary directions to the coachman to drive as quickly as possible to ——, St. Denis, and then he leaned forward and said to Dora, "Remember, your letters will be my *one consolation*, and you promise to send for me when—if——" His voice failed, he shut the carriage-door and turned away.

"Ronald!" cried a voice piercing him to the heart, and a death-white face, with eyes distended and wild, gleamed on him through the carriage-window. He rushed forward, tore open the door, and seized her in his arms. Then, out of the agony of his heart, for the first time, were showered kisses and tears upon that stricken white face.

Half fainting, he laid her back upon the cushions, with a fierce effort closed the door upon her, and, drawing his hat down over his eyes, he strode away into the station.

There, with a porter's cap upon his head and a porter's barrow in his hand, Jacques Toquelet stood awaiting the incoming train. In less than two minutes his barrow was transferred to a companion, and he was seated, by Buchanan's orders, on the box of the *fiacre* which contained poor Dora.

From that hour Jacques deserted the corps of porters, and became the faithful servant of Dora and the indefatigable slave of little Marian. He found the position far more agreeable, as well as more lucrative, than his former occupation, for Buchanan would have lived on a crust rather than that Dora should be unprotected and in need of a faithful servant.

CHAPTER III.

ANNE OGILVIE sat in a brown study, with two open letters lying in her lap.

Her duties in the school-room were over for the day, and Lady Valérie had gone to drive with her mamma, therefore it was permissible for the young governess to indulge herself with a day-dream, growing out of the astounding news which had just reached her through the medium of the afternoon post.

The first of these letters had come from her brother Dick, and informed her in half a dozen cheery lines of his arrival in England with *his bride!* The letter was dated Folkestone, but they were coming at once to London, where he begged her to meet him the next day at Batt's Hotel, Dover Street.

The other was a lawyer-like document, on stiff white

paper, blue-lined, and written in the stereotyped legal calligraphy. It informed her, on the part of Messrs. Snodgrass and Phipps, that she had come into possession, through the death of her godmother, the Lady Anne McIntyre, of an annuity of five hundred pounds, on condition that she should at once resign her position as governess and take up her residence in a neatly-appointed country-house, which was one of that kind but eccentric lady's many possessions.

At first Anne felt stunned almost, by the shock of such undreamed-of good fortune; falling into her lap, too, just at the moment when she would have greatest pleasure in it. For here was Dick, dear, good, thoughtless, old fellow, having taken unto himself a wife, would be so glad of a home for her and himself, and how happy they would all be together! "I wonder what this Agnes is like?" she thought, taking up the letter and glancing over its hasty lines. "Of Agnes I will say nothing," Dick wrote; "you will love her almost as much as I do when you see her. You must be great chums for my sake," etc.

And then Anne read over again the lawyer's note, and sank once more into musings, over which many a smile rippled. The vivid color deepened in her check as she drew towards her her *escritoire*, and, opening it with a key hung on her watch-guard, she drew from its recesses a letter written on thin foreign paper, and, dimpling into a loving smile, she opened and read it for the sixtieth time.

It bore the American post-mark, and it was signed by Percival Tyrrell. With those three letters on her lap, Anne's cup of joy overflowed in happy tears of thankfulness to the God of the fatherless.

For Toto had gone down to Liverpool that same day when he had unconsciously dealt such a cruel stab to poor

Anne's heart, brimful of sympathy for the chief actors in this drama, of which the pale, sad face of his master and the sharp pang which the news of his sudden journey had perceptibly caused the beautiful lady whom " Massa Percy had been sweet on so long," had furnished him the key. And he had poured out his vivid description of her joy at the reception of Tyrrell's last letter, the ready answer which she had been about to confide to his charge with smiles and blushes, when, like a blow, his information of his master's absence and return to America struck the color from her cheek, the light from her eyes, and "she just crushed up the letter in her little white hand as if it had been a wasp stinging her; and she smiled at me so sad, Massa Percy,—as if her poor heart was just breaking." And the great, big tears stood in Toto's brown orbs and expressed more than his poor words.

How many times throughout the voyage Toto was called upon to dilate upon the scene of that morning need not be remembered, or how often Tyrrell had regretted his hasty conclusions, and longed to be back in England.

Scarcely a month had elapsed since Anne Ogilvie had believed that love and hope and joy had gone out of her life forever, when she received the following communication from Tyrrell:

" Brevoort House, New York.

" Toto tells me you forgot to give him the answer to my letter. May I entreat you to delay no longer the posting of that which will bring new life to one who has been starving for ten days?

"Percy Tyrrell.

" Miss Ogilvie. June 22."

CHAPTER IV.

THE parting between Anne Ogilvie and her little pupil was a painful one on both sides. They had, through nearly four years of constant association, become warmly attached to each other. Even the cold, proud, undemonstrative countess's nerves were somewhat shaken at the thought of the hiatus which would intervene between the exodus of one such faithful servant and the very doubtful possibility of the incoming of an equally trustworthy successor.

It would be unfair to this lady not to mention that she regretted also the withdrawal of the bright young face, and the winning, high-bred manner, which, though the antipodes of obsequious, never varied in its gentle, respectful deference, — that somewhere, even in that narrow heart through which the blood flowed languidly in an admirably aristocratic pulsation, there glowed something nearly akin to affection, differing from that inspired by her pet poodle of years' pampering, in that it was mingled with respect, which the pure tone and innate dignity of Anne's character exacted from all who were associated with her.

Her ladyship presented her, in bidding her farewell, with a handsome watch bearing her monogram in brilliants; and Anne, in kissing the countess's hand, left thereon two crystal drops which all the brilliants of Golconda could not purchase.

The little Lady Valérie would not be consoled by the gift of a new necklace for her dear governess's departure, and wept sorely all that last day, bedewing with her tears each article which she laid in Anne's boxes, and insisting upon embracing her every quarter of an hour.

Her little face was red and swollen with weeping when Anne stooped under the lace and silken curtains of her bed, to kiss her hot cheek for the last time, at midnight, for she was to leave the next morning at six o'clock, and she would not disturb her little friend.

A double dose of red lavender did not compose the countess to slumber, and the earl was called upon, in the small hours, to say how they *ever* could find a person to fill Miss Ogilvie's place; whether it was not *too* unfortunate that she should have had a god-mother; and other conundrums too numerous to mention.

His lordship devoutly thanked heaven when the sun mounted into the sky to sufficient altitude to authorize his adjournment to his dressing-room.

As Anne descended from the railway-carriage which had borne her swiftly up to London, and entered the station, her attention was attracted by a large party of ladies and gentlemen, accompanied by stylish-looking lady's-maids and valets laden with dressing-cases, traveling-rugs, etc., among whom she recognized Lady Florence Ellesmere, on Mr. Dyke Faucett's arm. "Can it be a wedding-party?" she wondered; but no, there loomed up in the background papa and mamma with little Lord Lawrence and his tutor.

Lady Florence was looking very delicate, and at the conclusion of the season, to which she had contributed almost her last spark of vitality, her physician had ordered her to go at once to the Isle of Wight, where she could absorb sea-air without the dissipations of Brighton.

Dyke Faucett, assiduous to the letter of his devotion, was not to accompany them, but had promised to follow them in his yacht, which was a new and all-absorbing toy at this moment, and which was being fitted out in luxurious magnificence at Southampton.

Lady Florence's marriage was arranged for the latter part of September, and was to take place at their house in Ventnor, as town is empty at that season ; and part of the bridal-tour was to be taken in the superb "Io," a yacht of some two hundred tons, furnished with a regal magnificence and at a regal cost.

Dyke had fully satisfied his not-over-sensitive conscience that having failed in procuring any information respecting Dora's existence, through his banker, after the siege had exterminated the weak and helpless in Paris, the danger of becoming a bigamist was so infinitesimal that it was not worth a second thought.

He had, therefore, not a single care upon him, if we may except the occasional violet-perfumed missives which flowed in undiminished ardor from the *château* in Brittany, where the beautiful marquise was saving her complexion, and counting the sands of life which were running swiftly through the hour-glass of her husband's life. "How denced unlucky it would be should the old man step out before September !" ruminated Dyke, after the receipt of the last effusion, in which a P. S. stated that they had been ordered to take the invalid to St. Malo, "as he was becoming daily weaker, and the sea-air *might* prolong his life a *few weeks;* longer they could not hope for." "I very much fear," continued Dyke, addressing the familiar demon in his soul, "that should such a *contre-temps* occur, Florence would be obliged to go to the wall. I am equally engaged to each of them, and—I cannot marry them both." (Why not ? A man of such infinite resources might do *anything.* A triple bigamist is an anomaly, to be sure, *even* in a novel of the present day, but I have no doubt it could be done, and *has been.* We have the assurance of that keen student of moral anatomy, Solomon, that "there is nothing new under the sun;" and in the great menagerie of the world there glide monsters, beside whom the "wolf" would seem a meek household pet, wearing the "sheep's clothing" of Poole and others of his craft.)

"Yes," mused Dyke Faucett, complacently, as he dawdled over his chocolate at mid-day, "Florence would have to succumb to the force of circumstances and the energy of that little *brune*, for Pauline *would* marry me in spite of everything, even were we, Florence and I, standing at St. George's chancel-rails,—she *is* such a fiery little *diablesse*. She wouldn't suit me, by a long shot, as well as the other; she has fallen over head and ears in love with me, and that is so deuced unfortunate —*in a wife*. Her devotion was becoming oppressive when that *Deus ex machina* arrived, recalling her to her post at her lord's bedside. I wonder what he is worth? They lived well, but one cannot always tell. Well," yawning, "I shall just look in at Tattersall's and at White's, and then, ho! for Southampton and the Isle of Wight!" For a telegram had just announced to him that the "Io" was in readiness, awaiting his commands.

CHAPTER V.

"'There is nothing a man knows in grief, or in sin,
    Half so bitter as to think, "What *I might* have been,"'

"LYDIA, and this thought haunts me and troubles me ceaselessly; and even were it not so, can I ever hope for peace whilst that poor child remains in that pestilent land which reeks even yet with crime and rebellion? It is not safe for her, it is not human to allow her to be so exposed, —fragile, delicate as a flower, and *alone* in a strange land." And Ronald Buchanan, lying on a lounge in the cool, shaded library at Woodland Parsonage, with Lydia sitting on a low ottoman by his side, almost groaned aloud.

His sister's tender eyes grew soft with sympathy as she replied, in a sweet, low voice, "It is pitiful, but it is better so. You tell me she has a man-servant with her; is he not entirely reliable?"

"I feel convinced that he is; I have seen his fidelity, his honesty, and his courage severely tested, and those are three attributes of a good servant. I have sent him my address, and bidden him write me each week."

"And Dora,—does she write also?"

"Yes. Ah, do not blame me, I must be able to judge for myself in this case;" for a sadder look had shadowed Lydia's face. She smiled a little now. "Do you think, my boy, that *in this case* you are an impartial judge? Do you not believe that passion may overthrow in a moment the stores of wisdom laid up through years of experience. You must not pride yourself upon reason, when love has made you most unreasonable."

He took her hand and kissed it. "Ah, that is so like old times, Lydia; just a wee bit of a lecture, tempered by your sweet voice and loving eyes. But what would you have me do?"

"Pray!"

"I cannot. There is no answer for such prayers; there is not even hope in the next world, since our lives must be perfected here, or carry the incompletion into the life beyond. It seems to me that there would be but the ghost of our nature left after casting the shell of memory, hope and human love; and there can be none of these in the heaven above, for '*there is perfect rest.*'" He sighed impatiently, and, rising abruptly, paced the room. It was not difficult to see that *rest* and *he* were no longer friends; the calm, phlegmatic temperament had become nervous, irrritable, petulant; the smooth, white brow was wrinkled into a frown; the clear, gray eyes looked strained and sunken in their hollow sockets; the firm mouth was set in the stern lines of an unconquerable grief.

Lydia's heart grew sadder as she watched him, noting the changes which had been wrought, and into her memory stole two lines of French cynicism,—

> " Près des femmes que sommes-nous?
> Des pantins qu'on ballotte!"

For it seemed to her strong, pure nature that love must be void of selfishness, and that although it is surely the sweetest, yet it is not the highest duty of man or woman; and she saw clearly that in this case it should be resolutely stamped out, even though the spark of Ronald's life—or Dora's—should be crushed underfoot in the doing of it. To her upright, uncompromising integrity of character, no half-measures were justifiable. "To dally with wrong which does no harm" had always been an inconceivable paradox to her unclouded reasoning. The demon of sophistry fled before her steadfast out-look, and she never ventured in those crooked labyrinths where wish-fathered thought loses itself irretrievably, and the pale shade of a self-constituted morality is seized, in lieu of the stalwart substance girt about with the law and gospel of one's inner consciousness.

If Lydia felt the tenderness of her affection for her best-loved brother over-weighted in the faintest degree by pity, and its twin, contempt, that so fine a nature should have succumbed in such disastrous fashion to passion for a woman, it was but for a moment, for quickly her sense of justice interposed, and she remembered that he *was a man*, of different quality of fibre, nerve, and a lesser power of endurance than women, and therefore the " mene tekel" of a woman's judgment could scarcely fail to be faulty.

And then all other thoughts were swallowed up in the great wave of sympathy for a trial so bitter as this, and she spoke to him lovingly and comprehendingly, avoiding the platitudes of condolence, which she felt would but chafe him; withholding all remonstrance that in his present mood would prove futile as unwelcome; and though she dared not point at *hope*, and would not hint at the possibility of forgetfulness, so exquisite was her tact, yet, when he left her, he felt that the keenest agony had passed away. Her last words rang in his ears exultantly throughout the long, swinging walk which was to insure him a good night's rest.

> " So we'll not dream, nor look back, dear,"

she had whispered,

> " But march right on, content and bold,
>   To where our life sets heavenly clear,
>   Westward behind the hills of gold."

CHAPTER VI.

" I HAVE nothing further to say to you, sir. You have heard, and thoroughly understand, I believe, my decision; either you give up this mad freak of yours, to go over to France almost upon the eve of your wedding-day, or you cut yourself adrift from me forever!"

Sir Philip's voice was strong and clear as these words fell slowly from his lips, but his face had grown white with the indignation and anguish which was biting "sharper than a serpent's tooth" into his good heart.

Dyke Faucett, perfectly cool, calm, and handsome as ever, indolently lounging in a great bamboo smoking-chair whilst he enjoyed his delicious cigarette, glanced through half-closed eyes at his guardian, who continued, emphatically,—

"The whole course of your life has been a source of self-reproach to me; I have been culpably weak, and because I traced many of your faults of character to that fact, I have been less harsh than you deserved. Of your ungrateful neglect of myself, and the estate of which you believe yourself to be the heir, I shall say nothing, but of your profligate habits whilst abroad, of the stories which are told of your extravagance and recklessness, I am not ignorant as you imagine. You have disappointed and grieved me inexpressibly; but to my knowledge you have not yet brought my name into dishonor, and, by Heaven, sir, you never shall!"

Dyke arose slowly to his feet, stretched himself, yawned slightly, and pulled the bell.

Sir Philip grew a shade paler. Can it be believed he loved this man with a yearning affection still? Mothers of prodigal sons who have killed the fatted calf seventy-times-seven, read me this riddle!

Yet a flash shot forth from Sir Philip's gentle hazel eyes as Dyke addressed the servant, desiring him to send a messenger to the captain of the "Io" to command that all should be in readiness to sail on the morrow.

After the door had closed and Dyke had resumed his seat, Sir Philip, leaning slightly towards him, said, "This is your answer, then; you repudiate my claim upon your obedience, respect, gratitude; with your own hand you sever all tie between yourself and me?"

"By no means," answered Dyke, at last. "I have already explained to you that my temporary absence is unavoidable; were it not so, I should not dream of causing this excitement." He replaced his cigarette and smoked placidly.

"How can it be unavoidable? If it is a question of money,—there is my check-book; if not, *what* could take you away at such a time, at the risk of postponing your wedding-day, or breaking off a marriage which was arranged by me and to which my honor is pledged? Rest assured, Dyke, Florence meant what she said when she told me this morning that you had refused *her* request and might accede to mine, but that she would find it very difficult to forgive a discourtesy of such marked nature."

Dyke raised his shoulders, and his lip curled slightly: "All talk,—for effect; she will not let Ellingham slip through her fingers for such arrant nonsense as this. *I am obliged to go*, and I informed her of that fact. Should she take exception to it, she may, and that is the end of it; she loses Ellingham—and *me*."

"But Ellingham is not yet yours, monseigneur," replied Sir Philip, quietly. "And should you be so unfortunate in wind or weather as to be absent from your post at this place on the 28th—*Ellingham never will be!*"

There was no oath, nor the slightest raising of the voice to emphasize this determination, but any one looking into the drawn, resolute face (the face of the man who had been true to his one love for forty-five years, who had been faithful and trustworthy through his friendship for her, living, constant and unfaltering in his memory of her, dead, who now looked into the heartless, beautiful face of her boy, to whom he had never denied a wish, upon whom he had lavished tenderness for her sake, and read therein the cold, deep-seated egotism, the hollow nature, the false soul), would never have doubted but that he was able, and would be willing, to carry out to the letter his intentions. He was not a man given to idle threats; he never used a mean weapon; his sense of justice was correct and keen, and he never wasted words.

Dyke felt that "the game was up," but he did not relax a muscle, or change his languid attitude, or allow his clear complexion to alter by a shade.

"Surely, sir, you do not imagine that I should so far forget my position as to dispute your disposal of your own property! I am under endless obligations to you already. You have called me ungrateful; perhaps you do me injustice there. I am *not* ungrateful" (a little tremor in his voice here, admirably done). "I will bid you good-day, sir, until the 28th. Farewell."

He bowed low, and when Sir Philip raised his head from his hand—he was alone. The air still vibrated with the melodious, *trainante* voice of his adopted son; he almost regretted having spoken so harshly,—"the fellow evidently had some feeling hidden away under that stoical indifference. How sad his voice sounded, and how it trembled with emotion! Perhaps, after all, he *was* forced to go off at this unseemly time; still, there would be a terrible *fiasco* should he fail to return before the 28th. The earl would have an attack of apoplexy, and the storm would burst upon *my* unlucky head!"

Dyke, alone on the sands, strode moodily back and forth, with hands thrust into the pockets of his shooting-coat and head bent in meditation.

At length he drew forth a letter, in which the Marquise de Courboisie, in her indecipherable French *griffonnage*, shot forth from behind the bulwarks of an inch-deep black-border of grief her last quiver-full of arrows. If they were not poisoned, they were gold-tipped, therefore quite as deadly to Dyke Faucett's peace. For her "pauvre marquis" in consenting to die, at last, had recompensed her for her impatience by several surprises. He died at St. Malo, in his bath-chair on the beach, whilst his wife sat at a little distance, absorbed in the fertile invention of Mons. Balzac, and the sea sang a dirge over him for some fifteen minutes before his servant knew that the weary soul was free.

He had left ample instructions with his physician, who telegraphed at once to Paris to his friends, the Baron de R—— and the Marquis de H——, also to his legal advisers. They, in due course, appeared at St. Malo, and were received by the charming widow drowned in tears and crape. The will was read, and Pauline was compelled to bear a succession of shocks which were far from disagreeable.

She found that her husband had greatly underrated his fortune to her; that instead of being simply large, it was princely. In addition to this was the information that his only brother, the Comte de C——, who had gone out, thirty years ago, to South America, and had amassed a fortune there, had died recently, a bachelor, and bequeathed all that he possessed to the marquis. Papers substantiating the fact of his death, and his will, were shown, and Pauline's dread of the long-absent brother returning a beggar on her bounty, was forever dispelled.

After the reading of the wills and the necessary discussion with the lawyers, the bereaved marquise announced herself too ill to travel. The gallant gentlemen all declared it would be very wrong for her to attempt to make any further exertion after her heroic devotion to her poor husband and the severe shock she had sustained in his decease. They would attend to everything : accompany the remains to Paris and see them interred with all due honor in the family vault. Little Mignonne, whom she had left with a friend in Brittany, should be informed immediately of her sad loss, and as soon as her mourning was completed should meet her mamma *en route* to Paris.

"In a fortnight I shall be quite able to travel, I trust," she murmured, gently, "and better to thank you all, dear friends, for your goodness to such a desolate creature as myself."

And as the "dear friends" kissed the slender hand of the "desolate creature" with an income of one million francs, they, one and all, thought her too divine to be left on that bleak shore *alone*.

CHAPTER VII.

It was wonderful to see how rapidly animation returned to the languid form and face of the widow when the last echo of the carriage-wheels sounded through the *porte-cochère*, bearing away from her sight her obsequious legal advisers and her sycophantic friends.

Springing from her recumbent position on the lounge before an untasted breakfast, and ringing the bell, she ordered a comfortable *déjeûner à la fourchette*, and, flinging wide the shades, opened her windows and stepped out upon the balcony in the broad glare of noon. What delicious, long inhalations of freedom she took in with every breath! How the light came back to her eyes, and the color to her clear, dark cheek, as she stood there gazing out over the illimitable sea!

"Ah," she sighed, "how happy would I be now did I not love this cold-hearted Englishman! With my freedom, my beauty, and my wealth, I could be queen of society in Paris! *Quel malheur* that I ever met you, monsieur; that, spite of all *I have*, I still stand here, straining my eyes and blistering my skin in the sun, gazing across this cruel sea which lies between us! *Quelle fatalité que l'amour!*" And she hummed lightly, as she re-entered her boudoir,—

> " En l'amour si rien n'est amer,
> Qu'on est sot de ne pas aimer !
> Si tout l'est au dégré suprême,
> Quand est sot alors que l'on aime !"

and seated herself at once at her *escritoire*, where she concocted a Machiavellian epistle, which covered its thorns with flower-wreaths and its threats with kisses.

Through the English *Court Journal* she had heard of Dyke's arrival at Ryde with his yacht. (She took most of the English May-fair journals to keep herself *au courant* with the movements of her friends.) She also saw a notice of the Earl and Countess ——, with Lady Florence and her brother, having arrived at Ventnor. She was quick-witted enough to be little surprised when the announcement of the approaching marriage of the Lady Florence to Mr. Faucett appeared in *The Queen;* arranged to take place at Ventnor on the 28th of that month.

Not a moment was to be lost. Dyke should be drawn cleverly out of that net into another more secure in its meshes. The strongest possible incentive had been given to her determination,—*another woman had secured him* (as she thought); that cold, haughty Florence must be taught that she could not poach upon a French siren's preserves with impunity. And so the letter was written: every word weighed carefully in that diplomatic little head; never a hint of any other engagement or a suspicion of the existence of Lady Florence,—only a pathetic appeal in her loneliness, an entreaty that he should come to her in her desolation. With just two lines in postscript, veiled in tenderness, to say that should he not be *able* to come to her, she would find the air of the Isle of Wight necessary to her health, "*and come to him.*"

To this, Faucett, groaning in spirit, had returned an equally diplomatic reply, evading the invitation with masterly adroitness, hoping to meet her in Paris in January, etc.

For once he had miscalculated the power of his opponent. A letter by return post, in which the "griffes" were plainly discernible under the velvet skin, had the effect of proving this fact to his entire *dis*satisfaction.

"You 'hope to meet me in Paris in January,' you say, *mon ami*," (she wrote),—"after the honeymoon has waned, I conclude (for the news of your anticipated nuptials has reached me); but you will pardon me if I find it, for the first time, impossible to agree with you.

"*Ecoutes donc, chéri!* you are a man of the world, and as such I meet you on equal ground; let us be done with sentimentality and be reasonable. You are engaged to marry a woman who does not love you, and who will not suit you the least in the world; to settle down in your foggy England, drowse away your life as a country squire, growing too stout even for the hunt (sole amusement of that *triste pays*), or you will be forced into Parliament, condemned to spend the remainder of your days listening to the hum-drum orations of your port-fuddled aristocracy. The very thought of it *m'étouffe!*

N*

"Now, *mon chéri*, I would be ungrateful indeed did I not hold very dear your repeated assurances of attachment to my unworthy self; and I feel sure that I need not recall to your recollection a certain evening at 'Grantly,' and the pledge you then gave me of fidelity! I have it still, with the letter which accompanied it; and, although I prize it beyond all other possessions, should I not see you before this day week, I shall feel bound to convey it by trusty messenger to the hand of my successor, the Lady Florence Ellesmere.

"Accept, I pray thee, the assurance of my devotion.

"TA PAULINE."

CHAPTER VIII.

PERCIVAL TYRRELL TO ANNE OGILVIE.

"NEW YORK, ——.

"YOUR friend Martin Luther tells us, 'The human heart is like a millstone in a mill: when you put wheat under it, it turns and grinds, and converts the wheat into flour; if no wheat comes to it, it still turns; but then it is *itself* it grinds and slowly wears away.' So was it with me, until the arrival of that quaint little letter, from which I have ground much useful and pleasant knowledge, finding therein the germ of my 'staff of life' in all the future years. For, Anne, even in the coy shyness of your careful phrases I could see the true heart beating, and the little hand I have sought so long held out to me at last! Is it not thus we stand together? Nothing else in your gift would content me now; naught in the gift of the whole world would be able to purchase even *the hope* of such happiness from me!

"I cannot write love-letters; perhaps because I *feel* them. You tell me you are about to leave the family of the Countess d'Hauteville, and give me a new address. But you do not state wherefore, or what your present plans are. Of your future ones we shall talk together when I return to England, which will be before the 'Yule' is lighted or the mistletoe hung.

"I should like you to know this country, and my countrymen and women; not the cock-crowing, 'woman's rights,' 'man and brother' American; nor the jewelry-bedizened, Lindley-Murray-annihilating 'shoddy' of Continental touring; nor the irrepressible tobacco-chewing Yankee, who dins his 'reckons' and 'guesses' to the accompaniment of Yankee Doodle and Hail Columbia in a maddening fashion into one's *every* tortured sense; but, Anne, I should like you, with your deep-seeing eyes and your far-reaching comprehensiveness, to know this vigorous offspring of old Mother England. The America of Calhoun and Webster and Clay, of Longfellow and Hawthorne and Emerson and Irving; the America which your Chatham, who was said 'to know nothing perfectly but Barrow's "Sermons" and Spenser's "Fairie Queene,"' was wise and just and far-seeing enough to defend with his 'mighty' pen.

" How surprised you would be at the natural wonders of the country,—the enormous lakes, the mighty rivers, the prairie, and the forest! how amused at the 'learned ignorance' of its people! (Tocqueville says, 'There is no country so celebrated for so few men of *great* learning, and so few ignorant men, as America;') and how delighted would you be with some of those 'few' cultured ones in whom we take pride,—among our forty millions of educated people!

" How satirically you would handle our pet weakness,

conceit! (Inherited from our Puritan and Cavalier ancestry! for, although German, Celtic, Danish, and other blood has inevitably infused itself in our veins, we prefer to trace back all our small vices and foibles to the fundamental basis of our nationality. And any Englishman will recognize the transmitted tendency to a national vanity and a bombastic self-laudation.)

"Let us hope that this 'acorn in our young brows will not grow to be an oak in our old heads,' and so overshadow us with a mental and moral blight.

"We have a pretty society in New York; the men are rarely visible out of Wall Street, therefore they need not be mentioned; the ladies are of *jolie tournure,*—graceful, delicate, generally uninteresting; but one might apply to them the description of Russian society,—*de toutes les facultés de l'intelligence, la seule qu'on estime ici, c'est le tact;* for truly in *savoir-vivre* and gracious tact they have no rival. There is beauty, but little soul; brilliancy, but no depth; pedantry is abhorred, and the faintest shade of *blue* in one's hose is considered *mauvais genre.*

"Judge, then, how eagerly I shall watch for your letters; which, if they be (as they should) *part of you,* will alone satisfy my soul until I come to crown you 'My Queen!'

"PERCY TYRRELL."

CHAPTER IX.

DORA FAIRFAX TO RONALD BUCHANAN.

"RUE BERGÈRE, ST. DENIS, September 22.

"YOU reproach me with an 'undue reticence,' and 'a prim setting forth of events in the style of Goldsmith's "Vicar of Wakefield,"—matter of fact, but eminently unsatisfying,'—in my letters to you.

"How readily you discern, through the flimsy veil of language, the effort it costs me to write according to the dictates of those cold moralists,—Right and Reason !

"Only by the delight even these grim skeletons of letters give me each week, can I gauge the joy it would be to follow your command and write freely as I think.

"But the trivial details of my prosaic life, my daily walks with Marian and faithful Jacques, varied by sketching and botanizing, and the innumerable *contes* of our French Hercules (in which he always figures as the hero), are not brilliant materials for an entertaining correspondence, and my delicate health and rigorous seclusion afford no other.

"I dreamed last night of my dear father. So vividly did I see him smile and stretch out his arms to me, that all this day has been clouded by a new sense of loss and loneliness. It was sweet to me, even in a dream, to creep into the shelter of those fond arms, and lay my weary head upon the breast that pillowed it so often ; for, dear friend,

> " ' My feet are wearied, and my hands are tired,
>   My heart oppressed ;
> And I desire, what I have long desired,
>   Rest, only rest !'

Tell me, might not this dream have come to me as a messenger of peace? Is the 'sleep which He giveth His beloved' to be mine at last? Ah, my friend, when I awoke to the dreary *facts* of my existence, I cried out in despair for the sleep which knows no waking! Do not censure me. Your letter of yesterday convinced me overwhelmingly that *it would be far better for you* were I dead.

"I begin to wonder at the tenacity of life in my frail body. Marian is the pulse within my heart which keeps it beating. Were it not for her,—my precious one,—I could, like Mozart, with joy compose my own requiem,—

> "'The burden of my days is hard to bear,
>　　But God knows best;
> And I have prayed,—but vain has been my prayer,—
>　　For rest, for rest!'

"I fear you will be vexed with me for giving way to the sadness which sometimes colors everything with its dark shadow, but you will forgive me when you remember that it was on this day, one year ago, that my beloved father was taken from me.

"I have not been able to give singing-lessons to my pupils to-day, or to listen calmly to the chatter of my landlady; but, from early morning, Marian and I have been wandering through the forest (where Jacques served our frugal breakfast), and where the spirit of the dead seemed to whisper in the sighing of the wind.

" And now, looking out in the quiet evening from my window, I can feel thankful that *he* is at rest; that *his*

> "'Part in all the pomp that fills
> The circuit of the summer-hills
> Is, that his grave is green!'

"You will thank your sister for her loving letter to me. In a few days I will be more able to answer it. When the dear apparition which came to me last night shall have faded a little before the sunshine of these fair autumn days; when I have forgotten the sad hooting of an owl just outside my window, which has filled me with dire forebodings for weeks past; when, in short, I can feel that Lydia will not laugh at my morbid imaginings, and I have grown peaceful once more, I shall write and tell her how dearly I prize her friendship.

"Marian is well, and thanks you for the pretty English nursery-tales you sent her.

"DORA."

CHAPTER X.

RONALD BUCHANAN TO DORA FAIRFAX.

"WOODLAND PARSONAGE, Sept. 26, 18——.

"YOUR letter, breathing such hopeless sadness, such weary impatience of life, has undermined the resolution with which I had fortified my promise to you.

"*I must see you!* Lydia will follow me immediately if you are really ill, as I suspect from your letter. She will nurse and care for you most tenderly.

"I have not been able to write you before to-day. All the pain of these last three months seemed concentrated since those sad lines reached me.

"Keep up your courage, brave little Christian heart; let not the angel-wings droop which have borne you aloft over all your troubles without soiling the tiniest feather. In the dark hours when the waves threaten to overwhelm you, remember the reply St. Theresa made to those who compassionated her helplessness, her poverty, her loneliness,—'Theresa and two sous are nothing,' she said; 'but Theresa, two sous, *and God, are all things.*'

"RONALD."

As Dora, with hands trembling from excess of joy, folded and replaced in its envelope this promise of a happiness to which she had not dared to look forward, no shadow of misgiving darkened the brightness of that blissful anticipation during those first moments when the one thought absorbed her, that she would see Ronald once again.

For a brief space of time she sat feeding her hungry heart upon this hope,—her eyes full of a wistful tenderness, her hands lying with the dear letter idly in her lap. Presently her eyes fell upon those thin, transparent hands, and she noted, with a little sigh, their extreme attenuation. Her heavy wedding-ring had slipped almost off her slender finger, and, as she replaced it, a look of sudden pain marred the brightness of her face, while the bitter conviction forced itself upon her that, just in proportion to the joy which this letter seemed to pour into her desolate life, was the necessity urgent for her to brace herself to reject the happiness it offered.

"I cannot see him!" she moaned; "I cannot! It would only make everything more difficult, and—there is no use in disguising the fact—*it would be wrong*, and weak, and selfish. It must not be. And yet——" Great tears rolled down over the patient face and fell upon the fragile hands, while Dora fought anew with temptation the sorest which had yet assailed her.

Long before Marian had crept into the shadowy room, where the twilight had deepened into night, and nestled herself in the loving arms which seemed to hold her with a twofold tenderness, Dora had decided that she must avoid the meeting which awaited her in the next few days, even, if necessary, by flight.

CHAPTER XI.

THE yacht " Io" lies at anchor in the port of St. Malo, off the coast of France.

It is a superb night, the sea calm as a lake, gilded by the full radiance of the moon. Like a huge silver swan, the "Io" rests tranquilly on the golden waves, holding herself slightly aloof, like a proud young queen, from the crowded assemblage of more plebeian shipping, struggling for precedence at the mouth of the harbor.

Touched into quaint beauty by the moon-rays, the old fortified French town lay slumbering in the Rance's Mouth, although the ancient clock in the tower of the Cathedral had not yet sounded forth ten o'clock.

But there was little fashion in St. Malo, and the hard working "hewers of wood and drawers of water," and the net-makers, whose ideas never soared above marine tackle, were primitive in their hours, as in their tastes.

Strangers rarely lingered long here; after a glance at the house where Chateaubriand was born, and at the island where he lies buried, they were generally glad to take the *diligence* for the beautiful drive to Avranches and St. Lo, and to escape from the dreary streets crowded with squalid but cheerful specimens of the embryo sailor and fishmonger.

And yet the brilliant, courted Marquise de Courboisie had contrived to exist in this out-of-the-way old sea-port town, and her apartment on the first floor of the Hôtel de France was luxurious in its appointments as if situated in the Faubourg St. Germain.

There are women who seem to exhale an atmosphere of comfort, luxury, elegance, in which alone they seem able to exist, under all circumstances, abroad, as well as in their own sumptuously-appointed homes.

To their cultivated senses all ugliness is abhorrent ; it creates a physical distress, which is restless until tact and invention come to the rescue, harmonize colors, drape angles, tone down glaring deformities, cover, in short, with the impalpable veil of refinement those monstrous defects of taste in which the vulgar soul delights.

" *Chez moi*," to the belle marquise, meant comfort, and " *chez moi*" accompanied her wherever she moved; and so, when Dyke Faucett was ushered into her *salons* on this night of his arrival, he could scarcely realize, as he passed under the silken *portière* into the brilliantly-lighted suite of rooms, that he was not once more in Paris.

With a glance he took in the *ensemble*,—the delicately tinted walls hung here and there with a glowing Claude or a cool sea-view of Turner, the filmy-lace curtains; the luxurious *fauteuils*, the graceful tables covered with objects of art and *bijouterie* of all descriptions; the profusion of hot-house flowers, the tropical foliage and creepers, with here and there a gleaming statuette hidden amid the green.

And one other fact was patent to him at that first moment of entering.

With every accessory of gorgeous toilette, of velvet and lace, and jewels of unique design and variety, always according well with her brilliant style of beauty, never had Pauline looked so entirely irresistible as to-night, when she swept swiftly across the room with extended hands to meet him, in her black crape robe, which seemed to enhance the rich brune coloring of her complexion, and to render dazzling the dead whiteness of her shoulders, and the perfectly moulded arms, on which blazed diamonds set in black enamel.

No widow's cap disfigured the contour of the well-formed head, with its crown of raven hair bound simply with a narrow band of black-enameled gold clasped with a single brilliant (of a size and purity which could have founded an orphan asylum in that town swarming with the fatherless children of mariners, who, if they were not lost at sea, sometimes forgot to come back to their native town and interesting families).

In Pauline's eyes flashed the light of a great triumph, and her exquisite lips curved in a victorious smile as she drew Dyke Faucett gently down by her side on the *causeuse,* crying, joyfully, "*Allons! nous voilà ensemble enfin!* Are you not content, *mon cher?*"

How could he be otherwise, with her beautiful face before him, her silvery voice in his ears, her great diamonds flashing light all about her?

"'Truly yes, Pauline," he replied, looking his admiration; "and you are more bewitching than ever. *Comment!* is this the face of mourning and desolation you led me to expect?"

In a moment a pensive expression crept over her laughing features: she sighed heavily. "Ah, yes; you are right, it is very naughty of me to smile so soon; but, *que voulez-vous?* I *am* so happy, so glad to see you again!" And as she said this she caught up impetuously one of Dyke's gloves which lay beside his hat on a table, and pressed it to her lips.

Dyke laughed, while a wicked gleam came into his eyes. "What a child you are, Pauline, after all! Really, you must begin to put on dignity with your widow's weeds;

which, by the way, are excessively becoming.'' And then followed some more earnest talk ; talk all arranged beforehand on each side, and ending, as all such invariably does, in accomplishing precisely the reverse of what was anticipated.

Pauline had poured out, as she had intended, a recital of the various inducements she had to offer wherewith to tempt Dyke to break faith with Lady Florence, even at this late hour ; determined, at all hazards, that this should be the result of her machinations. But she had underestimated her attractions, or she had accredited Dyke with a higher sense of honor than he possessed.

At the conclusion of their interview she found *him*, figuratively, *at her feet*, utterly regardless of every claim upon him elsewhere.

And Dyke, who had parted with the proud high-spirited girl whom he had bound himself to marry with affectionate farewell and a promise to return to claim her hand on the 28th of that same month ; Dyke, who assured himself that it was only necessary for him to run over to the coast of France, see, and *reason* with this willful Pauline,—if needful, break with her forever,—that he might fulfill his engagement with his *fiancée* and thus please his guardian, Lady Florence, and himself; now, to his astonishment, caught himself actually pleading with and suing this beautiful creature with an income of one million francs per annum, as he had never sued before !

CHAPTER XII.

THE 28th of September dawned tearfully; over the lovely Isle of Wight drooped a misty veil, impenetrable to the sun's rays, even had they tried to pierce its foggy imperviousness, which they did not.

Great banks of leaden-colored clouds on every side; a depressing, drizzling rain falling upon the spirits of everybody, and extinguishing the faintest spark of merriment; the sullen roar of the breakers as they dashed upon the beach, and the scream of the sea-gull as he hoarsely threatened storm, added their melancholy influences to the bridal-morning of the Lady Florence Ellesmere.

In a long room, lighted at either end by great oriels, shrouded by pale-blue damask and lace, in a temperature which would have better suited the brilliant exotics which bent their fair heads in the chill rain outside on the balconies than the human lungs of this pale creature who shrinks closely to the open wood-fire in the soft, silken depths of a low easy-chair,—screening her delicate face with a feather screen from the heat, to which she gracefully stretches forth a pair of tiny embroidered *brodequins*, Lady Florence loses herself in conjecture.

Enveloped in a white cashmere *robe de chambre*, whose rose-pink lining casts a shade of color on the white cheek, the bride-elect awaits, languidly, the arrival of her bridesmaids and her mother, that the important toilet should be begun.

Of the appearance of the *groom* at the hour appointed for his return she had never for one moment entertained a doubt in her proud heart. At their parting he had taken her hand, and, looking full into her eyes, had said, gravely, "Florence, I need not ask you if you trust me thoroughly. You have given me the highest proof of that in consenting to be my wife. It is a great annoyance to me to leave you at this time, but it is out of my power to do otherwise. Do you believe me?" "Assuredly," she had answered, without one prick of conscience. Could it be possible that any man should *willingly* leave her during the last weeks of her engagement? She felt sorry for Dyke.

And then he took her in his arms, and kissed her cold cheek tenderly, whispering, "However long I may be detained, dearest, trust me! I may not return before the very day fixed for our wedding, but, Florence, my own, you will see me then, *if I live.*" She trusted him without the shadow of a doubt upon her tranquil heart, shielded by her suspicion-proof *amour-propre.*

And yet, to the uttermost capacity of her dwarfed sus-·ceptibilities, Florence loved Dyke Faucett; over her, as over all women whom he strove to fascinate, his influence reigned paramount. Had she not confessed in a calmly-measured speech and with quickly-beating pulses to her mamma, long since, that, undistinguished commoner as he was, without other title to renown than such as it accorded to the most *renommé* of carpet-knights, *she* preferred him and his simple name to a ducal coronet or a superannuated marquisate?

The earl and his countess dared utter no remonstrance, however. Their ambitious hopes writhed in the death-agony, for Florence, since her infancy, had ruled the household with a rod of iron, through the extreme delicacy of her constitution, which could not abide restraint or contradiction.

Sir Philip Standley had acted, too, with a munificent

liberality in the matter of settlements, and the *fiancialles* were formally celebrated in great state prior to the conclusion of "the season" and their adjournment to the Isle of Wight.

Listlessly she sat dreaming on in her cozy room; a slight shudder passing over her whenever she glanced through the windows at the dreary prospect without; a faint gleam of interest waking in her eyes when they fell occasionally upon the silvery sheen of satin and billowy waves of lace which were extended in bridal splendor upon her bed, awaiting the hour to strike when they should deck the statue-like face and form of the girl who looked white and cold and fragile as the waxen orange-blossoms which were to crown her haughty head.

Listlessly, without smile or blush, she greeted her cousins, who acted as bridesmaids, the Honorable Misses Somerville; languidly she held forward her cheek to her mother's eager caress; serenely she yielded herself to the hands of her maid to be prepared for the hymenial sacrifice.

Only for a moment a pink flush crept over her cheek, —when her mother, consulting every five minutes her watch, or the clock on the chimney-piece, whispered, "Have you received any letter or telegram from Mr. Faucett, my love? We have only two hours to wait!"

She answered, petulantly, "How absurd you are, mamma! How could Mr. Faucett possibly telegraph from his yacht, or send a letter, except, indeed, by a carrier-pigeon, which has not yet arrived?"

"I cannot conceal from you, my dearest," the countess went on, undaunted by the rebuff for once, "that I am anxious, very anxious; surely he should have spared me this uneasiness."

Lady Florence reared her head proudly, and replied, coldly,—"Pray keep your anxious fears to yourself, my dear mother; they are not especially gratifying or complimentary to me, and certainly utterly groundless.''

"Heaven grant it!" sighed her ladyship, gazing wistfully from the window, against whose pane now rattled rain in fitful gusts.

The guests were beginning to arrive; carriage after carriage rolled up and deposited its burden on the velvet carpet spread out through the garden, which separated the entrance of their villa from the road.

His lordship, the bishop of L——, who was to perform the ceremony, had retired to his apartment to invest himself in the robes of his office; ushers with white favors were bustling about, actively doing nothing; the bridesmaids had overlooked the trousseau, weighed it in the balance, and enviously found it—*not* "wanting." Dyke's gifts had been duly inspected, and their value appraised; those of the various friends and members of the family, rapturously admired.

Nothing now remained to do but struggle strenuously with the ten-buttoned gloves, striving to make their narrow proportions stretch over plump arms which never "tapered gently" since babyhood. Elderly spinsters gave the last surreptitious glance in the mirror to ascertain whether the tint of their noses had faded to a *rose-tendre*, and descended to the drawing-room, where they established themselves in the best position for witnessing a scene which they had been *too sensible* to enact in *propria personæ*.

Mothers of families ranged themselves where the grand *coup d'œil* would move them to sympathetic tears, each furnished with a large handkerchief, in a straw-colored hand, wherewith to stem the torrent of grief which invariably gushes forth! For although the British matron is proverbially imperturbable, and rarely relaxes into any demonstration of emotion, the solemnization of the wedding-service inevitably produces a lachrymose effect, even among those who are in nowise connected by ties of blood or affection to the bride.

But on this occasion the laced handkerchiefs were doomed to return in their pristine crispness to the pockets of those sadly-disappointed dames, and the patient spinsters, weary at last of waiting and craning their necks each time the doors of the drawing-room were thrown open to admit everybody *excepting* the bridal party, were fain to ejaculate their wonder and various surmises under cover of their opera-hoods, and in the shelter of their own broughams, wending their way steadily back to their respective homes.

For the hour fixed for the ceremony struck, and Dyke Faucett had not appeared ; a half-hour's grace had been accorded,—still no tidings ; people began to murmur and look significantly at each other. Another thirty minutes passed, and then Florence Ellesmere, surrounded by her bridesmaids and family in an upper room (her own the least agitated face among them all), calmly, and with a faint little laugh, raised from her head the snowy crown, saying, as she laid it aside, " There will be no wedding here to-day, my friends ! ' A laggard in love' is the one man of all others who can never wed with Florence Ellesmere ! It is all over, forever, between Mr. Faucett and myself. Should he kneel at my feet, this moment, he would have no other answer. And now, pray leave me ; I would prefer to be alone !"

There was not the slightest tremble in her clear voice, nor the suggestion of a tear in the cold blue eyes ; just a faint rose-tinge on the cheeks and a little curl about the delicate lips told of her deadly wound.

Silently they passed, one after the other, from the

chamber, one or two of them just pressing their lips in a mute sympathy to Florence's cheek, for which she made no other acknowledgment than the faint smile which still lingered on her face.

At last her mother alone stood beside her, with anguish written upon every feature. But when she attempted to take her child in her arms and solace herself by plentiful weeping over her stricken idol, Florence gently disengaged herself from the moist embrace, and said, without a quaver in her soft tones, "Mamma, you must go too; I wish to be alone;" and then, a little wearily: "Ah, if I could only convince you that this grief is *most humiliating* to me; that all is as it should be. My heart is not broken,—believe me! Ha! What can this be?" And with a sudden spring, which contrasted strangely with her words and her habitual languid grace, she reached the window, as a horse, hard-ridden, stopped suddenly before the door, and a man sprang to the ground, carrying in one hand a telegram.

White and breathless, but outwardly still, the poor girl stood like a statue of expectation, with eyes strained in their gaze, fixed upon the open door of her room, through which her mother had rushed, in uncontrollable impatience, to hear the news.

What an eternity of suspense lay in those few moments! how the pearly teeth clinched, and the delicate hand bruised itself in a frenzied clutch at the bronze quiver of a Cupid which held back the curtain from the oriel! And when, at last, steps were heard ascending the staircase, and Sir Philip Standley entered, with ghastly face and trembling hand, in which still rested the terrible message which had so shocked him, Florence drew herself up to her full height and awaited the crowning blow with majestic calmness.

But she had not dreamed of the truth. Treachery, dishonor, unpardonable forgetfulness or neglect, she could have met with a sublime scorn and an outward indifference; but when Sir Philip quietly answered her cold, authoritative "The *truth*, if you please, without reserve, and immediately," by placing in her hand the telegram he held crushed in his, and her eyes had glanced over its contents, there rang throughout that festively-garnished villa a cry so terrible in its anguish that in every heart it found an echo, from the stateliest dame among the guests to the tiniest page in the servants' hall.

As Sir Philip raised in his arms the slender figure in its gorgeous bridal-robe and laid her on the bed paler. than the pearls about her throat, his heart smote him for a too-ready belief in her coldness and apparent heartlessness.

He looked at her, lying there like a broken lily, and the vision of his dead love swam before his tearful eyes as he sank on his knees beside the bed, bowing his head with an irrepressible groan as that never-fading memory stirred in his heart with a newly-added bitterness of grief.

CHAPTER XIII.

THE sun was smiling serenely, bathing the rugged coast of France with its cheery glow; the white sails of the ships, the spars and the rigging, stood out clearly in the transparent atmosphere, while the gilt decorations of a gay little pinnace, which was being pulled into shore by four English sailors, glittered in the sunlight.

A few moments before the pinnace had put off from the yacht "Io," still lying somewhat aloof in solitary grandeur, a carriage containing a lady, closely veiled, and her maid, drove swiftly through the town of St. Malo to the point of embarkation on the wharf. There they soon transferred themselves, by the aid of the gallant skipper, and with many suppressed little shrieks of terror, to the exquisitely-appointed barge, and were pulled gently out towards the yacht, where, standing at the gangway to welcome them, they perceived Dyke Faucett. As she threw back her veil a beaming smile parted Pauline's lips, and she caught the hand he extended with a murmured ejaculation of delight, while Dyke, tranquil, pale and calm as ever, assisted her on board, and directed all things for her comfort and convenience.

While the yacht was getting up steam, and Pauline's maid was attending to the arrangement of those indispensable auxiliaries to a lady's toilette, and unpacking as much of the luggage as would be needed during a cruise of several weeks, her mistress, leaning on Dyke's arm, paced the snow-white deck, admiring everything with childish glee, clapping her hands and trilling forth musical laughter. And when he took her below, and she saw the luxuriously-fitted cabin, with its delicate frescoes, and its gold-colored damask divans and lounges, its innumerable mirrors, and its piano, its book-case, and card-tables,—all made of the beautiful wood mosaic,—and afterwards, when she penetrated still further into compartments, each furnished with the same magnificence, her delight knew no bounds.

Her own state-room, lined with white satin, carpeted with a great white bear-skin, with all its decorations in silver and pearl, enchanted her. No single thought of the proud heart of the woman for whom this had been designed in its bridal outfit crossed the mind of the triumphant Pauline, who had accomplished the sum total of her wishes the previous day, and married Dyke Faucett in the quiet little Church of St. Sulpice in that forlorn old sea-port town.

It was to save *ce cher* Dyke from a fate worse than death—his marriage with a woman he did not love—that she had consented to sacrifice the conventionalities and secure him from further persecution ; and so she had yielded to his persuasions, and they were together at last.

Then, for the first time in her life, Pauline almost learned the true taste of real happiness. Many of her little petulant ways left her ; she grew softer and gentler to her maid, and all about her,—under the influence of an unruffled content.

And Dyke also experienced a *bien-être* which had been foreign to him for some time : Pauline was irresistibly bewitching ; the sea was calm and the wind fair ; his cook was a *cordon-bleu*, and his conscience was numb ; what more could the gods bestow ?

And now they were out at sea ; the outline of the coast was fading from sight ; the green hills were no longer visible, and a soft autumnal haze settled down over the dark line by which, only, they could distinguish where France lay.

It was like a dream, Pauline said, so tranquil were the sea and the sky, and so still was everything. And when through the pale grayness of the evening the stars came out, and Dyke watched them mirror themselves in the sea, I wonder if a vision of the past glided before him, and he thought of *that long-ago*, when he *and another* had gazed together at these same stars, reflected in another sea ? If it did, he thrust it aside as he would have done a disagreeable insect, and in the lively chatter of Pauline, her witty repartee and caroling French *chansons*, he soon distracted his thoughts from all disturbing reminiscences.

Pauline had resumed her brilliant toilettes,—and never had Hebe herself looked more utterly beguiling than this beautiful creature, as she filled Dyke's glass with ruby wine during their *tête-à-tête* dinners and the delightful little suppers with which their *chef* regaled them; for in the glow of happiness which added to her beauty Pauline grew young again.

CHAPTER XIV.

Sunny days and starlit nights followed each other in swift succession, and out from the treacherous Bay of Biscay the "Io" emerged safely upon the broad bosom of the Mediterranean.

They stood one morning together, Dyke Faucett and Pauline, leaning over the taffrail, talking in low, musical murmurs to the accompaniment of rippling laughter, looking out on the sapphire-colored waves sparkling in the sunlight.

Never "since the morning stars sang together" had that deceitful Delilah of seas smiled more seductively than to-day, as she sunned herself, dimpling all over under the ardent kisses of faithful, unsated Phœbus.

Ah, fair, tideless sea!

> "Time writes no wrinkle on thine azure brow;
> Such as creation's dawn beheld, thou rollest now!"

blue and laughing in the sunshine of to-day, as when thy waves lapped caressingly the four great empires of the earth in their noontide glory (now, alas! standing grim and stark, like skeletons, amid the ashes of dead Ambition !),—clasping in fickle embrace the storied lands of classic lore; kissing as of old the blossoming shores of Ægina, of Piræus, of stately Corinth; coquetting still with the blooming triplets, Capri and her sisters. Are there no tears under those surface-smiles? and are thy briny depths not sometimes shaken with the sob of woe? When the zephyrs bring thee a sigh from crushed Attica, from snow-capped Liakura, or the plains of Marathon, or when a plaint from that vaster sepulchre of the majesty of Man—the East—reaches thee, dost thou not rise up in thy wrath and roar like a lioness robbed of her young, refusing consolation because *they are not?* Alas for thy whelps! Cruelly entreated have they been! In the ruins of Babylon, wild foxes, owls, and serpents make their habitation, while the cry of the bat and the cushat re-echoes in her temples; for the glories of past ages serve but as monuments to the vandalism of the warrior, as well as of the highly-educated Christian,—the history-grubber, the antique-robber, of the last centuries.

Did not a pair of rival painters deal less gently with the pride of Greece—the Acropolis—than did Philip, Xerxes, or the Venetian bombs?

Only one man, with a soul, could look upon the wrecks which strew this fair shore unmoved,—and he was a synonym for patience and had no definite ideas of art,—the patriarch of Uz.

But Pauline's joy-brimming eyes saw no spectres of the past to disturb the serenity of her blissful present, nor did she even try to look pensive while Faucett told her the story of Penelope, whose sad, questioning gaze had swept these same shimmering billows long ago, or pointed out to her the towering rock from which Sappho took her fatal leap. I fear she even felt somewhat bored when Dyke's adulation of herself was momentarily interrupted to show her the various objects of interest all about them. She did not care to see the island where Homer dreamed his grand old dreams with sightless eyes turned ever towards this murmuring sea; nor to hear how Virgil, drinking inspiration from its illimitable beauty, wrought out upon its shores his Æneid, and peopled every glen and cave and stream with nymphs and sibyls and nereids, centuries ago.

"And now the land where Tasso sung is silent," Dyke would conclude, "and only the song of the mermaid breaks the monotonous murmur of the waves, or perhaps the wail of the mariner whose trust has been betrayed by this treacherous sea, which has lured many a brave ship, many a fisher's *caïque*, to sudden doom."

"And these beautiful, cruel waves close over their nameless graves and leave no sign!" cried Pauline, shuddering. "Ah, Dyke, you terrify me!" And she glanced fearfully over the sun-lighted sea. Instantly she shook off the momentary depression, and, with a beaming smile, took up once more the thread of conversation.

"And what if these 'classic shores' yield us no more poets, do they not furnish us with an indispensable *hors d'œuvre*, the olive? And if those 'sacred groves' you speak of boast no more *temples*, I am sure it is from them you procure this delicious honey in the comb, which is my delight! *Que voulez-vous, mon ami?*"

And Dyke would be forced to smile at this utilitarian view of things and change the subject.

And now the sun is setting in sheets of lurid flame. Dyke and Pauline are pacing the deck together, arm-in-arm, feeling strangely happy; wondering a little at their own content; noting not the unusual oppressiveness of the atmosphere.

It was the last day of their cruise; to-morrow they were to enter port.

Through the stillness of the evening they could hear the whistle of the curlew as he flew over their heads, while the sound of a fish leaping from the water and falling back into it again was as distinctly audible. A faint veil of cloud dimmed the light of the stars, and towards the east there arose a dark outline against the sky.

Pauline had been gayer, brighter, more amusing than ever, all through that day; and now she broke forth with unwearying vivacity into the refrain of a *chansonnette* which was set to a charming little air of which Dyke was very fond.

> "'Jeunesse trop coquette,'

she warbled in the soft twilight,

> "'Ecoutez la leçon
> Que vous fait Henriette
> Et son amant Damon——'

Oh, Dyke! *What is that?*"

Abruptly the song was hushed as she crept closer to Faucett's side, fairly cowering with terror as a strange sound suddenly arose in the air. It seemed to her that the darkness all at once had spread over the twilight, and that all about them sounded threatening voices, muttering hoarsely, ominously, of danger to come! A moment she stood, and listened with awe-struck eyes, and then she clung to Dyke, crying out in French, "Why do you not answer me? What is this roar and sudden darkness?"

"It is nothing, *ma mie!*" replied Dyke, caressing her, while his eyes anxiously noted the quick-gathered clouds.

A sudden gust of wind now struck the yacht on the bows, causing her to stagger and reel for an instant. Pauline gave a little hysterical scream and hid her face on Dyke's breast.

"Do not be frightened!" he urged. "There is no possibility of danger in a yacht of this size, even if we *should*

O*

be in for a squall. You must come down below, *chérie,* and in the lighted cabin you will forget the storm outside."

Silently she allowed him to lead her down the companion-way to the cabin, where dinner was served, and where brilliant lights and the air of luxurious comfort for a moment seemed to dissipate her fears.

But only for a moment. Dyke poured out a glass of wine and held it towards her; and, as she took it, a hissing, bubbling noise sounded directly about the yacht, as if she had been suddenly plunged into a huge boiling caldron, and she rolled and tossed and pitched frantically for some minutes. The glass fell from Pauline's trembling hand and lay shivered amid the fragments of costly bits of Sèvres and crystal which, during this last convulsion of the sea, had been dashed off the table.

All traces of confusion in the cabin were quickly cleared away by the well-trained servants, who, with white, scared faces, found comfort in bustling about.

Pauline had thrown herself prone on a couch, and, with hands pressed tightly over her ears, was sobbing hysterically. Dyke, after directing her maid to bring a warm shawl to cover her mistress, and bidding her remain with her, mounted hastily to the deck.

The sky was now one entire black pall, through which an occasional flash of lurid lightning struck like a tongue of flame. All the winds of heaven seemed to be engaged in a wild warfare,—roaring through the black mountains of waves, sweeping before their fierce gusts the well-built, graceful yacht like an egg-shell on these hissing billows of foam.

Dyke Faucett, drenched to the skin,—for they were shipping seas every moment,—could scarcely make himself heard above the roar of the tempest, as he addressed the captain, a good sailor, and with some experience of these sudden, treacherous squalls for which the Mediterranean is noted. "Will it be serious, think you?" called out Faucett; and he was answered,—

"Cannot tell yet, sir. The wind may go down as suddenly as it rose." Then followed some orders to the sailors, and he resumed: "We are off a bad bit of coast here, sir. I am sorry you would not consent to remain out at sea to-day, but madame would not hear of it, and now the gale is driving us into shore; but, please God, the wind may veer at any moment."

"But the engines?" began Dyke.

"Fires out, sir; couldn't stand against these seas; our only hope is in the wind. I told you I didn't like those curlews flying about us all day."

When Dyke re-entered the cabin, his blanched face told its tale to the terrified woman, who raised her head as he knelt on the floor beside the couch and called her by name,—"Do not leave me again," she entreated, piteously. "Oh, Dyke, do not let me drown; save me! save me!" she wailed.

"Pauline, I can do nothing," he said. "We must hope for the best; perhaps at midnight the wind may change."

"Oh, why did I come?" she cried. "Why did I tempt you to bring me here on this cruel, treacherous sea? Oh, Dyke, I cannot die; I must not! I tell you you *must* save me!" And she started to her feet, and stood before him, in her satin and lace, with the jewels flashing in her ears and about her snow-white throat, with her soft, dark eyes wild with fear, and the crimson struck out of her lips with terror. And then broke over the deck a mountain-wave, and the yacht shivered and creaked in every timber, while the sullen roar of the waters was deafening.   Down on her knees Pauline sank with a shrill cry.

Dyke felt that they were going down.   He sat quite still, awaiting his doom.   And in those dread minutes, before the yacht righted herself and once more rode gallantly over the surging waves, there arose before this man a condensed panorama of his life.

Of the faces which passed in review before him, of the lives he had wrecked and the hearts he had broken, there was not one missing.   Of the wasted talents and the ill-spent years, of the heartless selfishness and the base in-gratitude, and the great mistake he had made of his life, he realized to the very uttermost extent in those dreary moments whilst he sat waiting for death, with Pauline lying crouched at his feet in merciful insensibility till the end.

Boom ! went the signal-gun of distress, but the hoarse voice of the storm drowned its sad call for aid ;—still the tempest raged with unabated fury.   The " Io" deserved the encomiums which had greeted her appearance every-where, by weathering the assaults of wind and sea for hours after another vessel would have gone surely to its doom.

Boom !   Boom !

And still Dyke Faucett sat there motionless, with one hand covering his eyes ; and still the book of his life lay open before his mental gaze and tortured him.   Now and again a low moan broke forth from his lips, as out of the crowded phantoms of the past the white, tender, pleading face of Dora, as he saw it last, stood distinct and clear as marble against the black background of his memories. Like the angel of Retribution she stood before him, with her sad, reproachful eyes fixed full upon his, murmuring always in his ear, " You did love me once, Dyke; you did love me then."

How differently would she have met this fate ! And he had cast her aside for this weak creature who lies at his feet faint from fear !

"Oh, God! Dora, turn your eyes away, or I shall go mad !"

CHAPTER XV.

THE morning dawned grayly. Fierce gusts of wind were still blowing, but rain was falling and the sea was growing calmer, sobbing sullenly like a child after a terrible fit of passion.

In spite of the weather, all along the coast people were swarming from all directions.

The demons of the storm had been wildly active on the sea over-night. Barrels, planks, bits of spars, were floating about, telling the story of the wrecks on that dread coast. And there, where the people crowd most eagerly, lies stranded on the rocks the saddest wreck of all,—the bruised and broken carcass of the beautiful yacht "Io," —from which is speedily being stripped every article of value, and from whose cabin have been removed at early dawn three bodies, drowned within a step of land.

The curé of the village had taken possession of the bodies, and, finding in Dyke's pocket-book full particulars of his guardian's name, address, etc., had sent immediately the telegram which was forwarded from Ellingham to the Isle of Wight, and which, on her bridal morning, struck with fatal cruelty the heart of Florence Ellesmere. So, even after his death, this man had power of evil !

With the exception of the cook (an obese Frenchman of the fatalistic school, who quietly awaited death amidst his saucepans), the bodies of Pauline, Dyke Faucett, and Célestine, the maid, were the only ones which escaped being washed away from the wreck. During the following day, the sea gave up the dead forms of the stalwart English sailors, who had spent their futile strength in battling with those angry waters, in a vain effort to swim to shore.

Lying in a ghastly row on the sandy beach, those noble-looking fellows, with wide-open eyes staring up into the blue heavens, whence the sun poured down its glory on the rippling, dancing waves, which scarce forty-eight hours ago had beaten the life out of their sturdy limbs and stifled the pulses of their brave hearts forever !

CHAPTER XVI.

Sir Philip Standley sat alone in his study at Ellingham Hall.

Beside him on the floor stood an empty dispatch-box with the name of his adopted son engraved upon a brass plate on the lid, and strewn over the table were piles of bills, letters, notes, receipts, unfilled checks, and the customary accumulation of a careless business man.

Patiently Sir Philip had gone over each document; methodically and neatly arranged in separate piles the paid and unpaid bills; he had laid the loose cash in a corner apart; he had glanced with a sigh over sundry French notes, redolent of *mille-fleurs* and the Quartier Bréda ; he had mastered the contents of sundry missives from the Marquise de Courboisie, bearing dates as late as the past month and addressed to the Isle of Wight ; and he had carefully laid aside a few letters written in a delicate, clear English hand, and signed, "Your loving wife,

Dora Fairfax Faucett," until such time as he could clear away this rubbish, which he felt was unworthy to be associated with *her* correspondence.

At length all was arranged; the French and English *billets-doux* had perished in the wood-fire which burned by Sir Philip's side; notes had been carefully made which might be useful, and a list of indebtedness stood ready with filled-up checks upon it. And then Sir Philip drew towards him the fair, clean pages on which Dora had poured forth her girlish fondness, her wifely devotion, her frenzied grief at Dyke's desertion of herself and child. These letters, dated Rome, Tours, and Paris, revealed the whole agonizing truth to him. This man, on whom he had wasted the entire affection of his nature, to whom he had transferred the whole-souled devotion which, had he been able, he would fain have bestowed upon Dyke's mother, had deceived him basely; through all those last six years he had been a living lie! "Pah! it makes me shudder to think of him, even though he is dead!" And Sir Philip laid the letters gently down, and paced the room in a wild tumult of grief, disgust, and indignation.

"And this poor girl,—this pure-hearted, high-spirited creature, whom he must needs crush under his merciless heel! Oh, Dyke, Dyke, what a curse did my beloved Constance leave behind her! May God have mercy on you, my poor boy!" And tears coursed down the old man's cheek as he sank again into his arm-chair, while the picture of a noble-looking child, with one arm thrown across the back of a superb St. Bernard dog,—with the sunlight bringing out the gold in his curls and lighting up the laughing blue eyes,—caught his gaze, hanging, as it did, directly over his study-table.

A long time Sir Philip sat dreaming, with his eyes fastened upon the fair boy who had filled his lonely heart, and gradually his anger fled, his feelings softened, and never again did a harsh thought of the dead cross his mind.

And then his thoughts turned to the living, and, taking up a delicately-tinted photograph of Dora, he studied her sweet face and graceful figure carefully. "She is a lady," he said to himself,—" thank Heaven for that, for she must be found, and immediately." He arose slowly, and, putting aside her letters in a locked drawer, pulled the bell.

"Has Burrows returned?" he inquired of the servant.

"No, Sir Philip. Ah, yes, there he is now, coming through the park. Shall I call him, sir?"

"Send him to me at once," answered his master.

A moment later, Burrows entered.

He was a small, wiry individual, with the face of a terrier, a clear brain, indomitable perseverance and energy, and a great power of holding on. By profession he was an attorney, by inclination he was factotum in the house of Sir Philip Standley, for whom he had a real respect and affection. He was honest and thoroughly trustworthy, and in Sir Philip's absences from home it was an understood thing throughout the establishment that Mr. Jonas Burrows acted as vicegerent. Strange to say, the servants liked him, and even Sir Philip's own man and the gray-haired steward, who had grown old and feeble on the estate which he now only nominally managed, were condescendingly cordial to him. For Burrows never put on any airs, and was kindly disposed towards everybody.

"Good-morning, Burrows. Pray seat yourself near the fire; this is cold weather for October. Did you return by the 10.30 train?"

"Yes, Sir Philip; I made no delay, knowing how anxious you would feel."

"Thanks. You saw—the bodies yourself?"

"I saw them, and recognized Mr. Faucett. There were several friends of the lady's who arrived before me, having been telegraphed by the hotel-keeper at St. Malo, where I believe the yacht lay for a time, and where they embarked. These gentlemen took possession of the bodies of the lady and her maid, and their luggage, some of which had been washed ashore. I believe they started for Paris last night."

"And you," asked Sir Philip,—"you fulfilled my instructions?"

"To the letter, Sir Philip. Mr. Faucett's remains are now at the Ellingham Station, and I am awaiting further instructions."

Sir Philip silently extended his hand and pressed that of the little attorney, whose shrewd gray eyes glistened with delight at this mark of approval.

"You will make all preparations for the funeral, if you please, Burrows," began Sir Philip, after a few moments, during which he had covered his eyes with his hand. "I should prefer it to be as quiet as possible, and to take place immediately. Can—can I see the body?"

"I think it better not, my dear sir; there is much discoloration, and—it would be a very painful sight to you now."

"Very well," replied Sir Philip, with a deep sigh. "And now, my good friend, leave me for a little while. You will find luncheon laid in the dining-room ; and afterwards I wish to consult you on another very important matter."

"And you, Sir Philip? Shall you not take anything? Let me send you at least a glass of port and a biscuit."

"As you please," answered the old gentleman, wearily. But when the glass of port and biscuit presented themselves, supplemented by a couple of delicate slices of cold fowl, Sir Philip mechanically regaled himself for the first time that day. And when little Burrows answered his summons, feeling immensely refreshed by his hearty luncheon, he found his patron looking far brighter and more business-like than when he had left him.

*   *   *   *   *   *   *   *

"We must employ detectives, Sir Philip; there lies your only hope of ever discovering this lady, who, you say, does not even bear her husband's name."

"No," answered Sir Philip, referring to one of the pile of letters scattered before him, in which poor Dora reproaches Dyke for this unwarrantable exaction,—"no, she goes by her maiden name, Fairfax. This last letter written in Paris, addressed to No. 10 Rue Royale, where Mr. Faucett was living at this date (September 2, 1870), —for I corresponded with him at that time,—comes from a street in the Latin quarter, Rue de Vaugirard, No. 7."

"And this is the last trace you have of her,—and just prior to the siege; I have very little hope, Sir Philip, but I shall do my very best."

"I am sure of it," answered the old gentleman, heartily. "And, Burrows, spare no expense; employ detectives; use the telegraph. Remember only this, she *must be found.* Justice must be done—if she lives! Shall you require these letters?"

"No, Sir Philip; I have made all necessary extracts, and now I must leave you, if you please, to arrange for the funeral to-morrow. To-night I go up to London, and before to-morrow mid-day you shall hear from the Rue de Vaugirard. Good-morning, Sir Philip. Ah, many thanks!" as his grateful patron pressed into his hand a well-filled check, and, rising, bowed him out as politely as if he had been an ambassador from a foreign court.

That night a telegram from London reached Sir Philip,

and proved to his satisfaction that the machinery was working already which was to atone for part of the evil done by his too fondly-trusted adopted son. It contained these words:

"Send the photograph of the lady by first express to No. —— —— Street, London, under cover to me. Collyers is hopeful of success; leaves to-night for Paris.

"JONAS BURROWS."

CHAPTER XVII.

"OH, mais oui, monsieur! I remember her perfectly, bless her pretty face; she rented two rooms of me, *au quatrième*, for herself and her father (poor old gentleman, he was killed, you see, sir, during the siege), and the beautiful little child. What has come to that angel, I wonder?"

"When was this?" broke in Mr. Collyers, impatient of the old woman's garrulity,—"in September last?"

"Yes, monsieur, the old gentleman was killed in September; shot down just in front of the Hôtel de Ville, where he was standing as peaceable as a lamb; and was just brought home by the young surgeon, as if he was his own son, sir, so tender was he with the body, which I helped to lay out; and I must say, a more beautiful corpse and a more natural I never——"

"*Voyons!*" again interrupted the detective, "do you see these?" And he took from his pocket-book a couple of gold coins. "You shall have these if you can give me two plain answers to two questions without *any more un-*

necessary talk.   How long ago did Madame Fairfax leave your rooms?"

"She left them and went to the English Ambulance Hospital about the first of October.   I know, because she came to me in July and she paid me for two months in advance, and when they had expired, Paris was besieged, —she could get no more money; and you know, monsieur, I could not let the rooms without pay, being a poor widow, and——"

"Did you ever see her after she left you?"

"No, monsieur, I never saw her again.   I fear she died of want,—she and the little one,—for they were both very delicate—and meat was dear; and indeed I have made my dinner of a rat-pâté, and been glad to get it——"

"*Tiens!*" broke in Collyers, dropping the gold pieces into her outstretched palm.   "Where does this English Ambulance find itself?"

"Ah, it is all broken up now, monsieur; it was only a temporary hospital during the war.   *Bonjour, monsieur, mille remerciments.*"   And she turned to re-enter the *porte-cochère*, leaving Mr. Collyers in a rather despairing frame of mind.   At that moment the *concierge* of the house opposite appeared in the gateway; at a signal from her neighbor she crossed the street; Mr. Collyers waited. Old Bénoît approached her cap-frills to those of her comrade, and whispered, "*Voici un milord Anglais;* he wants information concerning *cette pauvre petite dame* Fairfax.   He pays well, my dear."

Her friend took the cue instantly.   With a low curtsy and a suave smile she addressed Collyers: "*Pardon, monsieur;* but perhaps I may be able to assist you.   In my *appartement au cinquième* lodged Monsieur Buchanan, *monsieur!*"   Triumphantly she spoke, while her eyes glistened at the prospect of English gold.

"And who the devil is Buchanan?" quoth Collyers, mildly surveying her *appartement au cinquième* from the street, and trying thereby to deduce some important information respecting its former occupant.

"Monsieur Buchanan was the surgeon, sir,—the surgeon, and the *bon ami* of Madame Fairfax! He it was who took her to the Hospital, and who sent *me* to her constantly with food and wine, when we were all starving in Paris. He it was who, in saving a family from death in a burning house, was injured so badly that he was obliged to give up his practice and leave Paris. And he did not leave *sa chère amie* behind him. They went away a party of four, and the little child, *and I know where they went!*" She stopped suddenly, and closed her lips resolutely.

"This becomes interesting, *ma bonne dame,*" began Collyers, again having recourse to his well-supplied pocket-book. "Will you do me the honor of drinking a bottle of wine with your good man to my health?" And he handed her a glittering testimonial of his appreciation of her valuable *reticence.* "They went, you said, out of Paris?" he began.

"*Merci mille fois, monsieur!* Yes, they drove out to St. Denis, where I afterward sent part of Monsieur Buchanan's luggage; the remainder—his instrument-cases and books—I sent only last week to him in England."

"What street and number did you say at St. Denis?" queried Collyers, with note-book in hand.

" No. ——— Rue de la Bergère," replied the old woman.

"Thanks. I have the honor to bid you good-morning, mesdames!" And, saluting them profoundly, the *milord Anglais* jumped into the fiacre which awaited him, and directed the man to drive out to St. Denis.

En route he stopped at the telegraph-office, and sent the following lines to—

"Jonas Burrows, Ellingham, Kent:

"On the right scent. The lady lives,—interview her in half an hour.

"Collyers."

As the gentleman-like detective reseated himself in the fiacre, after dispatching the above bit of encouragement to England, he took off his hat, and passed his fingers through his crisp, sandy locks with a smile of complacent content on his mild physiognomy. He was most agreeably disappointed. This had looked a discouraging undertaking, seen from the other side of the Channel, only yesterday, and now here he had his bird in his hand already, all owing to his patience with the voluble old Frenchwoman; and he sank into a pleasant reverie, which was brought to an abrupt conclusion by the stopping of the fiacre at the door of a villa-looking house in a suburb of St. Denis.

He alighted, and smiling graciously at the neat *bonne* who answered his ring, he inquired for Madame Fairfax, who resided there. But the girl shook her head, and assured him that there was no lady of that name in the house at present; there *had* been an English lady, with her little girl and man-servant, but she could not say that the name was Fairfax; perhaps she had better call madame?

"Do so, *ma chère fille*, I beg of you; time presses, and I must have the address of this lady you speak of."

The girl retreated, and soon the proprietress of the villa appeared in her widow's weeds and cap. She invited the gentleman to enter, and, seated in her cosy parlor, she told him all she knew of the lady he sought.

"Madame Fairfax occupied rooms in my house during the past four months, and I had hoped to have kept her for the winter, but letters from England seemed to have troubled her somewhat, and she left quite suddenly, paying a fortnight in advance, although I did not wish her to do so, and left no address with me."

"Do you mean to say that you have no idea where she intended to go? Was there no address on her luggage? What train did she take?" asked the crest-fallen detective, eagerly.

"No, monsieur, her boxes had no address; and when I asked her where I should send her letters, she smiled very sadly, and said 'there will be no letters for me now,' and then she drove away in a fiacre, but where I know not."

"Was it one of the cabs from the station?" asked Collyers, desperately.

"Indeed, monsieur, I could not possibly say; they all look alike, and I, never dreaming that inquiries would be made, took little interest in it."

"Was it the servant who opened the door who went for the cab?" he asked.

"Oh, no; madame had her own man-servant who always attended to everything for her. Perhaps, sir, they have gone to England; her letters were all English," volunteered the kind-hearted landlady.

"Perhaps," assented the detective, dubiously. "I am under infinite obligations to you, madame," rising and bowing low, "and should feel grateful if you would send me word to this address, should any letters arrive for or from Madame Fairfax, or should you gain any information regarding her whereabouts."

Madame promised to do so, and, taking the card he offered, she bowed him out.

As he repassed the telegraph-office he stopped the carriage, hesitated a moment, and finally scrawled the following message:

"To Jonas Burrows, Esq., Ellingham, Kent:

"Bird flown,—all trace lost.   Believe her to be in Paris. If so, will find her.

"COLLYERS."

As the detective, feeling very hungry and somewhat discouraged, descended from his fiacre in front of Meurice's, a lady with a little girl were at the same moment alighting from an omnibus just before him.   Suddenly the lady gave a slight scream.   The child had slipped off the step of the omnibus, and would have probably been injured in the crowd of vehicles had not Mr. Collyers sprung forward, seized the little girl in his arms, and restored her to her mother, who waited in breathless anxiety on the pavement.

"Je vous remercie, monsieur!" cried Dora, pressing her darling to her bosom, while a sweet smile of gratitude lighted up her pale, sad face.

Mr. Collyers raised his hat, with a muttered "Il n'y a pas de quoi, madame," and entered the *porte-cochère* of the Hôtel Meurice, whilst his thoughts reverted to the puzzling question, "Where under heaven has that woman hidden herself?"

After an excellent *table-d'hôte* dinner, Mr. Collyers took a stroll on the Boulevard des Italiens, and finally dropped into the "Variétés," where he spent the *entr'actes* in conjecture and vigorously plying with questions a French detective with whom he had once been associated and whom he met at the entrance to the theatre.   The latter obligingly gave him all the information in his power, but strongly advised his returning to England, as it was more than probable the object of his search had left France. But there was something of the bull dog about Collyers. He had got the idea firmly rooted in his mind that Dora was in Paris, and he meant to find her *there*. Before he retired to rest that night, he had resolved to pay another visit to the elderly *concierge* who had rented her *appartement au cinquième* to the young surgeon Buchanan. He was far from despairing yet.

CHAPTER XVIII.

FROM DORA FAIRFAX TO AGNES OGILVIE.

"St. Denis, September 28.

"Agnes, I am wretched! My burden is too heavy for me to bear. You are right; I have been writing you with a feigned cheerfulness of late. How could I bear to cast a shadow on your joyousness? And now my strength is all gone, and I am sinking. I feel like a frail bark tossed on a wild, stormy sea. Another wave, a little stronger than the last, will wreck me utterly.

"For, Agnes, I am forced to leave this peaceful shelter in which I rested; I am obliged to go out once more into the great, troubled world, where I feel such a mere helpless atom in the great whirling rush of humanity. When this letter reaches you, I shall have left St. Denis forever.

"You will have guessed before my pen traces the words, dear, why I have thus resolved. You will feel with me, my strong, pure-hearted Agnes, that Ronald Buchanan and I have met for the last time in this life; and you, too, know well the anguish these words cost me. Never to see him again! never to hear that low, firm voice which always brought strength and comfort in its tones; never to see that noble, earnest face, those clear blue eyes, that kindly smile! Oh, Agnes, is this *sin?* Can it be wrong for me to love him, to reverence him, to pray for him in my loneliness, my desolation? If so, the God of Mercy who forgave much to her who 'loved much' will pardon me.

"What agony it causes me to fly from him!—for he writes me that he will come (he may be here any day, Agnes), and I have not courage to warn him that he will not find me! For I shall leave no address, and no one shall be told, save your dear self, in what corner of the wide world I will hide myself and Marian. There I will strive to live patiently until the end, which, please God, may not be far off; for now, Agnes, since your last dear letter brought me the blessed promise of your loving care for my little one, I feel that I can wait calmly, thankfully, with just the same

> ' Patience as a blade of grass
> Grows by, contented in the heat and cold"

until the day comes when I can creep into my mother's arms, in the land where the weary and heavy-laden are promised rest at last.

" Farewell, dear Agnes. Ah, what would I give to feel your loving arms about me! How often do I live over those dear, sad days in the Hospital!

> " ' When I remember something which I had,
> And which is gone, . . . and I must do without;
> When I remember this, I mourn, . . . but yet,
> My happiest days are not the days when I—*forget*.'

"Good-by again, dear. I will write you from our new home.

" DORA FAUCETT."

(For to Agnes alone had Dora confided her true name and the entire sad story of her life at last!)

The tears fell fast upon this letter as her friend perused

its sad lines, and when Dick gayly entered his wife's little sitting-room, shortly after, he found her weeping bitterly.

He threw himself down beside her on the lounge and took her little figure in his strong arms, whilst he half coaxed, half commanded her to "dry up those tears and not make a fright of yourself, my darling, for I have got some glorious news for you, Agnes, and you shall not hear it until I've seen you smile."

Agnes had some of a woman's weakness, although she was very nearly perfect, so she smiled instantly through her tears, crying, "What is it? Oh, do tell me! Is she coming here?"

"Now just listen to her!" cried Dick, apostrophizing an imaginary being in the background. "'Is she coming here?' Who?"

"Why, Dora, of course," replied Agnes. "Oh, Dick, I have had the most broken-hearted letter from her to-day! Dick, I must go to her, or she must come here; she is ill, and obliged to leave St. Denis, and—oh, Dick!" And, hiding her face on his broad chest, she sobbed again.

"All right, Agnes!" cried Dick, who never could abide hysterics. "Cheer up, my girl! Dora is all over her trouble now; that ras—that husband of hers is dead!"

"Dead!" exclaimed Agnes, starting to her feet with excitement. "Dead! Oh, thank God!"

"Pious," ejaculated Dick, "but uncomplimentary."

"Dead!" again exclaimed Agnes. "Can it be possible? How? When? Where?"

"One at a time, please," urged Dick; "I never was good at multiplication. It seems he was wrecked in his yacht, off the coast somewhere. The *Times* has a full account of it; here it is." And he drew from his pocket a copy and spread it out before Agnes, who, without glancing at it, went on :

"Oh, Dick, I *am* so glad!   Does she know it, do you think?   I will write to her at once; but," here her face grew troubled again, "where is she?"

"At St. Denis, to be sure," said Dick.

"Ah, no, she left there yesterday; but she has promised to write to me immediately.   Dick, *would* you mind sending to the post now? there may be a letter, you know."

Dick smiled.   "It would be useless, dear; there cannot possibly be another mail from France already.   See here, Agnes, if you will be good, and stop crying directly, I will do something towards finding your friend for you."

"How?   What can you do?   Oh, Dick, if she were only in England, safe and well, I should be content!"

"No, you wouldn't; even if she were here, and safe, you two would find something to wail over,—unless Buchanan were on the programme!   Now, I'll tell you what I shall do: I mean to run up to London to attend this great lecture on anatomy, and afterwards I shall take the train down to 'Scrooby' (that's where the brother-in-law parson holds forth, is it not?) and have a talk with Ronald, and tell him that the coast's clear at last!"

"Oh, you dear, blessed Dick!" cried Agnes, enthusiastically.   "How good you are!   When will you go,—to-day?"

"Don't be impatient;   I must have some cold pasty and a bottle of Bass before I can move, and then I shall catch the express up to town."

Agnes bustled about waiting on her beloved, packing a small valise for him, while bright smiles now chased each other over her sunny face.   Dick watched her, through half-closed lids, with an expression of serene content upon his honest features.

Presently there was a tap at the door of their sitting-room, and a blithe voice asked, "May I come in?"

As Dick sprang forward to meet her, Anne Ogilvie entered, carrying a light wicker basket filled with ferns and orchids from her little conservatory, wherewith she meant to "decorate the shrine of St. Agnes," she said, and forthwith commenced to arrange the exquisite specimens tastefully about the pretty sitting-room, which, with the rooms *en suite*, Anne had dedicated exclusively to the occupation of her brother and his wife,—"So that you can feel perfectly *at home*," she said, with her winning smile, to Agnes on that first day of her meeting with the bride. "A region where you and Dick can be all by yourselves when you choose, and where even *I* must be expected to be *invited* to join you sometimes." For Anne had taken Agnes to her heart not only outwardly, during those first hours together: she had so longed for a sister all her life, and now, here was one with whom she could find no fault. They suited each other admirably, and Dick was as happy as a king (in a fairy-tale!).

And when, after her husband had discussed the better part of a cold game-pie and gone off on his errand of mercy, Agnes and Anne sat cosily together in the pretty drawing-room, each occupied with needle-work, and Agnes recounted the story of Dora's life, she brought ready tears of sympathy from the deep-blue eyes of her eagerly interested friend.

"Something must be done immediately," concluded Agnes; "for, Anne, I feel sure she is dying; her letters lately have been so sad, so despairing!"

"I agree with Dick," began Anne, wiping her eyes, and drawing nearer to Agnes. "I think Mr. Buchanan will move heaven and earth to find the poor child—*now*, —and we must just sit at home, and wait patiently until he *does* find her, and then we will all strive to comfort her, and fill the rest of her life with joy and peace. Poor Dora! I never heard anything so sad, so pitiful!" And in her heart Anne wondered how she could bear to have had such a barrier as that which parted Dora and the man she loved, rise up between her life and that of the man who had brought "the gold and purple of his heart," and laid all at her feet. Her great wealth of happiness but made her pity more tender for the bare poverty of poor Dora's lot.

"If Percy were only here, with his clear, strong judgment and his dauntless energy, all would be well. He could tell us what to do, and would direct Dick's impetuosity, which may only alarm Dora and put her on her guard, and so farther out of reach. She doubtless has heard nothing of her husband's death, and may imagine he is seeking her!"

"Ah, Dick will be very careful not to startle her; he is not devoid of judgment, if he is a little impulsive," cried loyal Agnes; "and Mr. Buchanan knows her better than any of us, I do believe; *he* will be most guarded and indefatigable."

"No offense to Dick, darling!" laughed Anne, stooping forward to kiss Agnes's cheek; and then gravely again: "But should they find her and the little one, must they not come here, to us, Agnes?"

Her sister's eyes filled with grateful tears. "Oh, Anne, what joy that would be to me, and to Dora!"

"And to Anne," concluded the latter, with a smile.

And then they discussed the question of which room in the rambling old house would be most cheerful and comfortable for Dora, and how delighted Marian would be with an English poultry-yard; and what a blessed angel it was who had invaded the recesses of Anne's aged godmother's heart in her last days, and bestowed through her so cheery and delightful a home upon three as homeless and desolate creatures as the world contains !

And after they had talked over everything appertaining to their expected guests, Agnes delighted Anne's heart by counting up on her fingers the exact number of days which must intervene before the good ship " Java" should land her passengers at Liverpool, and bring into their joyous circle that one other link which (Dora found) would complete the golden chain of love which bound them all together.

CHAPTER XIX.

IT was a murky, foggy night in London ; the windows of the brilliantly-lighted shops, dripping with moisture, allowed little of their cheerful glow to brighten the hearts of the passers-by, or direct their slippery footsteps, while the gas-lamps at the street corners gave forth a blear-eyed and dejected twinkle. So thick was the fog, that had it not been for the glaring transparency over the entrance to Exeter Hall, Dick Ogilvie never would have recognized in the crowd pouring itself out after the great anatomist's lecture the form and features of the very man of all others he wished most to meet.

Ronald Buchanan's face, under the glare of a great green letter " A," looked wan and careworn ; and when Dick, pushing his way violently through the crowd, laid a hand on his friend's shoulder, he could not but feel struck by the languid, listless greeting which he received.

Linking his arm in that of Buchanan, he said, " I'm in luck, dear old boy, in meeting you by chance in this way.

I was just about to start for Scrooby, and you have saved me a day, and some impatience, by turning up at the very right moment."

Ronald looked surprised. "You were about to start for Scrooby?" he asked.

"Yes. Haven't you meant all those invitations you have extended to me?" smilingly asked Dick.

"Of course; you know that; but——"

"But what brings me down now? Well, we will just step in here and have a bit of supper quietly, and then I shall tell you some news which will gladden your heart, my boy! Gad, I can scarcely keep it!"

"You can tell me nothing I care to hear," answered Ronald, wearily, seating himself at a little table, while Dick gave orders for supper.

"We shall see," returned Dick, sententiously.

"And now, Ronald," began his friend, as the waiter bustled away. "Do you know where Mrs. Fairfax is?"

Buchanan started, and, leaning eagerly forward, said, in a low voice, "Is it about her? Can you tell me where she is? If so, for God's sake do not keep me in suspense!" His face grew wild and haggard as he awaited Dick's reply.

"I cannot," his friend answered, gravely. "Have you been to France? or how did you guess she had left St. Denis?"

"Yes. I have just returned from that fool's errand." Ronald spoke bitterly, and Dick sympathized thoroughly with his exasperating disappointment.

"Could you gather no clue from the people in the house of her probable destination at present?"

"None; I saw the landlady and all the servants about the place. Nobody seemed to know anything, excepting the fact that Dora's husband (the villain!) had tracked her to this place, but fortunately after she had been warned and fled.''

'' When was this? I had not heard anything of this!'' cried Ogilvie, astonished.

'' It was the day before I reached St. Denis (that is the day before yesterday), that this man called and demanded to see Mrs. Fairfax; but she was then out of his reach, thank God !''

'' Yes,'' said Dick, with an unusual solemnity for him. '' She was certainly out of his reach then, Ronald, for—the man was dead !''

'' What !'' exclaimed Ronald, starting to his feet and almost overturning the table in his excitement. '' What ! dead ?''

'' Yes, dead ! He was drowned in his yacht off the Mediterranean coast more than a week ago. You have seen it all in the papers, Ronald,—the loss of the ' Io', and its owner's death by drowning.''

'' And is it—can it be ?—Is Faucett the name of Dora's husband ? *Is it this man?*—whom I have met in Paris,—talked with, shaken by the hand ! to whom I owe the wreck of my whole life; *the vengeance which God has taken out of my hands now forever! Can* it be? Oh, Dick, this seems *too* improbable !''

'' True, nevertheless, dear boy. Come, sit down and take it quietly. There is something to be done now. We must find *the widow !*''

And now for the first time the joyful part of this sudden intelligence struck upon Ronald's comprehension. '' The widow !''

No more wrong, no more sin in loving her, no more flying from him, or speaking coldly to him. She was his now,—his own for evermore !

And Ronald's head bowed down until it rested on his

P*

clinched hands, utterly oblivious of Dick's presence, of place, of time, of *everything*, save the one great, joyful fact, that Dora was free at last !

Dick waited patiently. There was great depth of tenderness in his nature,—and his sympathy was very perfect.

When Ogilvie and Buchanan separated for the few hours which remained before the dawn, each felt certain in his heart that if Dora lived in this little world still, she surely would be found, right speedily.

Ronald slept during those precious hours, as he had not slept for months, with his head pillowed on the bosom of *hope* and the dream-angel whispering of joy to come.

CHAPTER XX.

THE next morning Dick and Ronald parted in exuberant spirits ; Ogilvie returning home, and Ronald going on to the parsonage to make a few preparations for another trip to the Continent which might possibly be prolonged, and to tell Lydia the news of Faucett's death and gain her counsel as to his own future movements.

A dozen miles to the south of Doncaster, on the great Northern Railway line, just at the junction of three counties, and bordering the fenny districts of Lincolnshire, lies the little village of Scrooby, where Paul Wyngate had established himself and his wife in a newly-built parsonage adjoining the ancient stone church, which had stood steadfast there for centuries.

Taking no note of the monotonous scenery through

which he was whirling at the rate of fifty miles an hour, and which had always reminded him of the flat and uninteresting country of Holland, Ronald, with hat drawn down over his eyes and with folded arms, leaned back in the cushioned seat of the railway-carriage, plunged in profound reflection.

When the train stopped, for a moment, on a wide plain, at a miniature station-house, with just a suggestion of a village in the distance across some rushy fields, Ronald barely woke up in time to escape being carried on beyond his destination.

Walking swiftly along the country-road bordered with poplars, with head a little more erect than usual, and his clear eyes filled with joyful light, he looked very unlike the pale, haggard, drooping figure who emerged in the foggy night from Exeter Hall only a few hours ago.

Such puppets are we all, responding accurately to the slightest wire-pulling; brain acting on physique, physique reacting upon brain. For, humiliating as it seems, not only does the body tremble and bow and sink under the influence of the mind, in abnormal conditions, until we are forced to acknowledge not only that grief sometimes kills (as in the case of Louis of Holstein, who yielded up the ghost as he knelt by his wife's dead body), or that joy can be equally fatal (as when Chilo, one of the seven wise men of Greece, died from excess of happiness in seeing his son gain the victory of Olympia), but also that the mental powers are direfully swayed by the amount of phosphorus in the bones, the action of the various vital organs, and the ganglionic centres!

Are not the judgment warped, the affections narrowed, the "milk of human kindness" soured, and the charity which cloaks infirmities shriveled up, when dyspepsia fastens its fangs upon its victim?

And how many cases of suicide, when the brain, reeling from its throne, clutches at the mysterious Unknown, have resulted from some cog in the wheel of internal machinery going awry?

And although

> "Men have died from time to time, and worms have eaten them;
> But not for love,"—

because that malady does not enter into the diagnosis,—it is not less true that the mental depression has so sympathetically affected the nervous and spiritual condition, that men *have* died, and women too, of love betrayed, dishonored, or rejected.

What are we, then, but puppets strung on the wires of circumstance, with hope, joy, conscience itself, centred in the *spinal cord?*

Lydia, clipping the dead leaves from the evergreen hedge inclosing the neat grounds about the parsonage, could scarce believe that this was Ronald who sprang up the steps before her with the gay lightness of a boy, calling out, in cheery tones, "Lydia! where are you, Lydia!"

"Here I am, Ronald. What has happened, dear, since you sent me that sad note yesterday?" she asked, coming through the window which opened from the study on the lawn.

Her brother came quite close to her, and, first stooping to kiss her soft cheek, he said, simply, "Lydia, my Dora is free! Her husband perished in the wreck of the yacht ' Io.' "

"Oh, Ronald! May God have mercy on his soul!" She closed her eyes a moment as though that prayer sprang from her heart.

" Can you guess how happy I am, Lydia? I wrote you how she had fled from me; but nothing on earth shall come between us *now!*"

"Take care, my darling," urged his sister, "do not speak so positively; leave everything in the hands of Him who has removed this great obstacle to your happiness and hers. All will be for the best in the end."

"I must go back to France immediately," he answered, only replying by another kiss to her earnest speech. "And, Lydia, should I find Dora ill, or should I want *you, will you come to me there?*"

"Certainly I will," she answered, cheerfully. "And now I must give you your letters and papers which have arrived since you left." She opened a drawer in the writing-table and produced a budget of medical journals and letters. Ronald glanced at them carelessly,—his thoughts were straying elsewhere,—and mechanically opened one with whose handwriting he was unfamiliar. He soon became absorbed in its contents, and his sister stole softly from the room. The letter was dated the previous day, and bore the signature of Sir Philip Standley.

"Oct. 10.

"To Ronald Buchanan, Esq.

"My dear Sir,—You will pardon my addressing you in order to gain information which I have been assured you will be able and willing to furnish, viz., the present address of the lady to whom you showed much kindness during the late troubles in Paris,—Mrs. Dora Fairfax Faucett.

"During the past week my agents have been employed in seeking her, to no avail, and I am now driven to accept the last expedient open to me, and beg your aid.

"Having ascertained that you were in correspondence with Mrs. Faucett (having obtained your address through the concierge of your apartments in Paris), I feel encour-aged to hope that through your instrumentality I may

soon have it in my power to receive the wife of my
adopted son and heir (had he lived), Mr. Dyke Faucett.

"To this end I ask your co-operation, and, hoping to
hear from you by return of post,

"I remain, sir,

"Very truly yours,

"PHILIP STANDLEY, Bart.

"ELLINGHAM HALL, KENT."

"And I thank God that I cannot give you the information you seek!" cried Ronald, excitedly, while he thrust
the letter away from him as if it had burned his hands.
"While she was wretched, forsaken by that villain,
lonely, ill, and desolate, her great relations could ignore
her existence, and leave her to perish with a broken heart
in a foreign land; but now, just as she is left free to turn
her sweet face towards me,—instead of hiding it away from
me,—these grand folks must step forward to claim the
widow of the heir! *But they shall not have her;* even
should I find her immediately, they shall never know it;
I will keep her safely; I will not let them hear from me.
Oh, Heaven! have I not suffered enough yet?"

These were the rebellious, angry thoughts which surged
in Ronald's heart, as he felt the keen anguish of losing
Dora a second time through the impassable gulf which
rank and wealth would create between the heiress of Sir
Philip Standley and the poor surgeon of a country-town.

"Could the mistress of Ellingham Hall stoop to the
village apothecary? She could scarcely deign to employ
his services save for the hirelings about her grand establishment! Ah, little Dora, I cannot let you go now; I
have waited too patiently for that." Thinking thus, he
drew towards him his letter-case, and indited a few concise lines to Sir Philip Standley, assuring him of his utter

ignorance of Mrs. Faucett's place of abode; tacitly declining to aid him in his search for her; politely but firmly giving Sir Philip to understand that no future information need be sought from him.

He signed and sealed this epistle, and then laying it on the rack where the letters for the next post awaited collection, he paced up and down the room, with a look of weary pain once more gathering about his lips and eyes.

Before very long he took his letter once more in his hand, looked at it lingeringly a moment, and then tore it across and tossed it into the fire.

" ' God and man and hope abandon me ! ' "

he muttered,

" ' But I to them and to myself remain constant!'

I have no right to decide for her; it seems that my love is growing selfish, and—I think only of my own pain. This shall not be. I will do all in my power to restore her to her friends, and leave the rest to—God !''

As if in answer to this resolution the servant brought in that moment the mid-day mail; and a few lines from Dick, written immediately upon his return home that morning, ran thus:

" Have this moment arrived, dear old boy, and Agnes greets me with the tidings that she has heard from Mrs. Faucett. She is well, and living in Paris, No. 13 Faubourg Poissonnière; has heard nothing of Faucett's death.

" Agnes leaves you to break the news to her, and joins me in good wishes for your happiness.

" Faithfully yours,

" RICHARD OGILVIE.''

And then Ronald took a fresh sheet of paper and wrote a courteous letter to Sir Philip, giving him the address of the woman he loved well enough to` sacrifice his own selfish longing to be the first to tell her of her altered prospects, and to stand quietly by and see her go out of his life into another which lay open to her,—far away— from him—and his small world.

When Lydia came in later, she saw in his face that he had fought a battle with himself—and *conquered;* and though she did not know the grounds of strife, she *felt* that he had won a victory over himself, and caressed him with loving words and tender hands. And then he told her all.

CHAPTER XXI.

"Oh, mamma! What is this? Look at this beautiful brooch!" cried Marian, jumping off the bed, where she had been extracting the contents of Dora's dressing-case, which contained also her only jewel which survived the siege,—the diamond pin which had belonged to her mother.

"Yes, darling," said Dora, taking the trinket in her hand, sadly; "put it away again carefully in its little case; and, Marian, replace all those things again and lock the box."

"Yes, mamma; but see, this mirror in the lid is loose, and, oh, mamma, here is a letter behind it! Don't you want to read it?"

"A letter?" cried her mother, stretching forth her hand from the couch where she lay resting after a long day spent in seeking pupils. "What letter can it be? Ah!" Almost with a sob she seized the yellow, time-worn envelope, still sealed as when her mother's hand last touched it. "I had forgotten it," she murmured, kissing it over and over. "I had forgotten all about it, and now here it comes back to me at the time when I am most sad, most desolate. Comes to me like a touch of my dear mother's gentle hand upon my weary head. Oh, mamma! mamma!" And the tears fell fast on the old faded lines as she broke the seal and opened its pages—with "To be opened only in case of trouble befalling you *after* your father's death" inscribed upon the outside :

"My life is waning, little Dora, day by day, and, as I let my eyes rest on your golden head, my one ewe-lamb (spared to us of all the flock !), I tremble at the thought of leaving you behind me. And yet I dare not murmur, knowing as I do that there is an Arm so loving and so powerful that, before *its* cherishing, the most tender mother's care grows impotent and vain. To its protection I confide you, Dora, happy in the knowledge that in your pure nature and innocent heart rests now no germ of evil. Oh, may they long be kept 'unspotted from the world' ! It is to aid you in doing this, my child, that I have refrained from offering the key which might open to your untried simplicity the great, false, tempting gates of the world; the world to which by birth you belong, and in whose gaudy, meretricious, treacherous enticements you will never find the inexpressible joy and repose which, in our humble home, where the sunshine of love has never been clouded for a day, have filled my heart to overflowing, and which, in this sweet, calm twilight of my life, while the shadows of night encompass me about, fill the air with angel voices, whispering of duty done, and the promise of life everlasting with the darlings who have 'gone before !'

"And you, and my beloved Vincent, will come to us there!   Ah, Dora, my crown of glory would be incomplete were *one* single jewel missing at the last great day!

"And so, perhaps through erring judgment, I leave you to live out your life in the primitive simplicity of your early childhood, with your dear father's approval and consent.

"God grant that the day may never come to you when you will feel authorized to read this letter!

"My strength fails me.   I will put, in few words, the knowledge of your father's antecedents, and my own, which may prove useful to you should your path grow too rugged for your tender feet.

"Your father is the only son of Marmaduke Vincent, of Maudley, Leicestershire.   We have never held any communication with either his family or my own since we left England,—forty years ago.   My marriage with a nobleman, whom I need not name, was thwarted almost at the last moment by my elopement with your father!   For this we were cut off forever from our own kin.

"I am the fifth daughter of Lord Laurence Vavasour, thus my maiden name was Marian Adelaide Vavasour.   My father's estate is encumbered, I believe; it lies in —— shire.

"My mother died when I was born.   My youth was a sad one; only one face stands out in my memory with an expression of kindness in it,—that of my godmother, Lady Marian Oglethorpe, of Oglethorpe Manor, Shropshire.   Should she live still when you open this letter— *go to her!*

"And now, my precious one, my hand is weary, and my sight grows dim.   To the loving Father, who is now stretching out His arms to me, I commend you, my frail flower, my lily-blossom, fit only to bloom in the garden of our Lord.

"Your Mother."

(Inclosed were a marriage-certificate and that of Dora's birth.)

As Dora concluded reading the tender words which fell like dew from heaven on the parched flower of her barren heart, Marian, who had been gazing at her with startled eyes since she had given up the terrible yellow letter, which seemed to contain cause for all these tears, now drew near to her mother's side, and, drawing her head down on her childish breast, poured forth a torrent of loving epithets; kneeling on the floor beside her, her head raised, and tears of sympathy in her bright eyes, she implored Dora to speak to her and tell her what that cruel letter held to distress her so. Dora caressed her, and strove to smile and explain the contents of the mysterious packet. So absorbed were they in conversation, that neither heard the door open behind them, or perceived the figure of a gray-haired gentleman, who stood quietly taking in every detail of the most exquisite picture he had ever seen, on, or off, canvas.

In a low chair, near the window, sat Dora, in an attitude of willowy grace which belonged to her,—a little languid, perhaps, in pose, but with a face instinct with life,—changing momentarily in expression. Against her black dress leaned a child with the head of an angel; liquid blue eyes lifted with adoring love to her mother's face; lips half parted showing pearly teeth between; a golden cloud of hair falling nearly to the ground as she knelt with head thrown back in eager listening. For Dora was telling her the story of her childhood in the great forest of Virginia (for her father and his bride had fled to America, and there built up their humble, happy home, unmolested by their indignant kindred, who looked upon them henceforth as *dead*); and as the sweet voice went on like a strain of music to which beautiful thoughts were set, the tears gathered in Sir Philip Standley's eyes, and he with difficulty restrained himself from stepping forward and taking the wife of his dead boy in his arms.

But her extreme delicacy was so apparent to him, so fragile she looked, he dreaded the effect of startling her even by his unannounced presence; and so he stole gently out of the still-open door, and, encountering a servant in the passage, begged her to carry his card to the lady in the little room beyond.

* * * * * * * * * *

When, after a couple of hours of quiet talk, Sir Philip stood holding Dora's hand in his, while he reiterated his request that she should be ready to accompany him home to England on the morrow, the sweet face raised towards him wore a bright flush of happiness, and the light of the glorious eyes shone through a mist of grateful tears.

He had told her all, not excepting Dyke's death,— lightly touching upon his reticence concerning his marriage, —breathing no word of his unworthiness; and Dora had wept, feeling shocked and pained that her child's father could never now hear her say, "*I forgive all.*" And then she had given Sir Philip her mother's letter, and they talked reverently of her, and of the omnipotent hand of Providence which had at last brought *him* this solace in his solitary old age. With Marian on his knee, and sweet Dora close beside him, the old gentleman looked happier and brighter than he had done for many a long year.

After the door had closed behind him, Dora, still radiant, drew Marian to her side, whispering, "My darling, God has been so good to me;" and then, falling on her knees, tried to pray for strength to bear this happiness meekly, through intermittent smiles and tears.

Oh, God of Strauss! God of Rénan! of Herbert Spencer, of Carlyle, of Emerson,—or of any of those others, "wise in their own conceit," to whom the name of Jehovah has become as unpronounceable as to the Israelite of old,—is it at the feet of any of your "strange gods" that Dora cast herself, in the first impulse of a gratitude which acknowledged the source from which sprang every joy and love?

Or was it from the great "Universum" of one of these Deity-creators, or the "Absolute," the "Ideal," of the other, or from the "Unknowable" of the rest,—who spend God-given brains in the vain effort to establish *a higher form of religion than that of Christ,*—that Dora (as a type of suffering humanity), in the dark night of her adversity, drew comfort and balm for her grievous wounds?

The mutilators of our beautiful faith, throned on the apex of their own sovereign intellectuality, which has submerged long since the weak emotions of the heart, offer nothing adequate in exchange for the marred and broken image they have desecrated; but, wrapped in an egotistic beatitude, they look down calmly from their heights upon the surging, throbbing sea of humanity beneath them, breathing over their heads and *out of their range of vision* their hazy intangibilities, their misty illusions, wondering, in their own sublime serenity, at the blindness of those who see not through their eyes.

In abstract theory, these men sparkle dazzlingly in the blue ether of an intellectual elevation *above the herd they lead;* some of them forming a constellation which threatens almost to extinguish the steady, tranquil, world-flooding light of the moon; others, brilliant satellites only, revolve around a larger planet of wider-diffusing radiance.

And their god *seems* a "very God" in his noble proportions, his grand attributes, his "spiritual essence" (than which nothing is more volatile); but, when the eyes rain tears, they are blind to the glitter of those far-off, unapproachable stars; and, when the heart is bleeding, it is surely only on the breast where the loved disciple's head rested, that *peace is to be found*.

And it was *there*, at the feet of the loved "Master" of Paul and Luke and John, that Dora's tears were wiped away; and there, also, did she cast herself in an involuntary impulse of grateful homage, which in His sight was more eloquent than words.

Marian stood by her, gently stroking her cheek with one little hand, while the other stole about her neck. Young as she was, this child had learned the true, sweet sympathy of *silence*.

As Dora knelt with her head buried in her arms, the past years returned to her with all their bright and bitter memories. She thought of her childhood in America, that joyous season which knew not a single cloud; of her life in Rome before she met Dyke Faucett; of her blind idolatry of him, and the subsequent breaking of her idol; of poor Trelawney's sad fate; of Agnes and her sisterly affection; and lastly, with a deep, hot blush, of Ronald Buchanan. "Would he ever forgive her flight,—would he understand it?" she wondered. "And if he did, and we should ever meet again—— But what folly is this? —that I, with my broken life, the wreck of what I was once, could ever dream again of love! Oh, that is all over, all passed away forever!

> "'Who can undo
> What time hath done?
> Who can win back the wind?
> Beckon lost music from a broken lute?
> Renew the redness of a last year's rose?'

Ah, it is all over for me!"

For Dora was very human and very womanly in her great new glory of happiness. She could not grieve for Dyke's death, although she reproached herself for the want of power to do so; she could not feel sorrowful about *anything;* she could not regret the past, and she dared not look far into the future which stretched now before her, wrapped in rose-colored clouds.

The evening came on imperceptibly, and Dora was startled when a clock in the neighborhood chimed forth six o'clock.

She hastily prepared and gave Marian her dinner, touching little herself,—so over-strained were her nerves that she felt no need of food. And then, giving the child some pictures to amuse her, she sank once more into a reverie, which was only broken by two little arms twining themselves about her neck and a sleepy whisper begging that Marian should be put to bed.

But there was no possibility of sleep for Dora that night; she paced the room in partial dishabille, with a restlessness upon her which almost amounted to fever. She unbound her luxuriant hair, and lighting with unscrupulous extravagance half a dozen candles, improvising candlesticks with fertile invention, she sat down before the two-feet-square bit of mirror which decorated her toilet-table and studied her own beautiful face with the critical eye of an artist. She was almost alarmed when she first caught the feverish glitter of her great lustrous eyes, and the deep flush which burned on either cheek, to which the faintest rose had been strange so long. At last she threw back the masses of hair from her face, and, still gazing at its brilliant beauty, opened her lips and caroled forth in the stillness of night, *to that face in the glass,* a few bars of a new " Ave Maria" she had been practicing that day; for song was as natural an expression of joy to her as to the little brown wren, who bursts into trills of melody, with plumage all "ruffled with the whirlwind of his ecstasies!" . . .

She wondered, as she suddenly checked herself, if her brain were giving way,—if she were mad! This was strange mourning for a widow of a fortnight! How wicked, how cruel, how selfish she was growing! she thought, as she extinguished part of the illumination, and bound up her tresses, growing pale and chilled as she did so, and concluding her unnatural emotions by a convulsive fit of weeping, which left her weak and weary,—too weary to make her preparations for departure, as she had intended to do, that night; too weary for anything but lying awake the greater part of it, thinking, dreaming, wondering! in a glad, restful consciousness, which was more refreshing than sleep, and which even the sighing of the autumn wind outside her *persiennes* had no power to sadden. For

> "Not all the whispers that the soft winds utter
> 　　Speak earthly things,
> There mingleth there, sometimes, a gentle flutter
> 　　Of angels' wings." . . .

CHAPTER XXII.

A CHEERY group of four was assembled in the cosy library at "The Oaks," where the leaping flame of the great wood-fire paled the soft light of the shaded lamp and brought out the scarlet of the holly-berries, which gemmed the evergreen garlands decorating with festive luxuriance every arch and angle and picture-frame in that crimson-glowing room.

How exquisitely the shining holly-leaves contrasted with the carved black-oak bookcases against which they were festooned, and how coquettishly peeped forth, here and there, the branches of the mistletoe! while the deep crimson of the curtains, shutting out of sight the storm outside, and the rich carpet of the same warm hue, seemed to fill the room with a smile of tranquil comfort.

It is Christmas eve. For a month past Anne Ogilvie and Agnes had been busy in the preparation of joyful surprises which would bring a tithe of the happiness in their full hearts to the desolate ones to whom even this merry season rarely brings good cheer.

And now the last button had been sewed upon the neat little suits (masculine and feminine); the last plum-pudding had been satisfactorily turned out; the last gallon of soup and the final form of jelly had been pronounced all that could be wished; and, a little tired, but most supremely content, Agnes and Anne rested from their labors, each in a great arm-chair, whilst Dick read aloud a legend from his favorite " Ingoldsby," and a low laugh occasionally issuing from the shadowy depths of another easy-chair not far from Anne's proximity revealed the presence of Percy Tyrrell, who made the fourth in this happy quartette.

" Gad!" exclaimed Dick, springing to his feet and flinging the book upon the table, " if ' Ingoldsby' isn't the jolliest book I've ever read, I would like to know where the other is!" Then stretching himself and yawning audibly, " Beg pardon! But do you girls know that the dressing-bell has rung? and if there is one thing that disturbs my equilibrium more than another, it is cold fish."

Laughingly they all scattered to dress for dinner; not, however, before Percy, detaining Anne by a look, after the others had disappeared, had whispered, "You have given me no Christmas gift, Anne, do you know it?"

"Certainly I know it; but why this impatience? No gifts are distributed before midnight. See what the morning will bring you!" she laughed.

But he would not be pacified or patient. "No, no; my Christmas gift is here, behind these lips. A promise, Anne,—a promise only, I want from you. Will you not give it me, darling?"

"And what is this promise you wish to extort from me?" she asked, demurely.

"Oh, Anne, you know it well; that a fortnight from to-day shall be our wedding-day! Shall it, little Anne?" He leaned forward eagerly, his deep eyes gleaming in the firelight, his face pale with suspense, his lips smiling.

Anne, looking at him, blushed, and then suddenly, shyly, stretched forth both hands to him, murmuring, "What can I say? You *will* have your own way." The last word was smothered in a tender embrace, from which Anne, extricating herself all blushes and smiles, began, with mock indignation, to reprove him.

"*And what were you doing just under the mistletoe?*" he cried out, with a joyous laugh, as she fled up the stair-case, looking like a sweet wild rose which had been gently ruffled by the wind.

One more *intérieure*, and then, dear reader, we will shake hands and wish each other God-speed.

A year and a half have passed swiftly away since the wreck of the "Io" and the subsequent alterations in Dora's life and prospects, and the earth has thrown off its dun-colored garments and re-clothed itself in the green mantle of spring.

All the country about Ellingham, whether over hill or

through dale, was lined by the blooming hedge-rows, where hawthorn, brier, and the wild rose form a tangled, compact, green wall, impervious to anything but the fox-hunters' rush, and which causes the English landscape " to blossom like the rose!"

And now the delicate perfume of the hawthorn-blossom fills the breeze, sweeping gently over the vivid green fields, where the blackberry with its colored flowers, the stone-bramble, and the spiked leaves of the holly, add their spring offerings to the sweet English hedge.

All about " The Hall" the young year wore her fairest aspect; never had lawn been rolled to smoother perfection; never had flowers bloomed in such wild profusion; never had the trees in the park worn such vari-tinted green in their foliage; and was water *ever* so limpid before, as this calm lake, on whose bosom rest great water-lilies, with their broad, beautiful leaves? So Dora asked herself, as she sat under the shade of the old cedars, watching Marian as she stooped to caress a proud peacock, who strutted with gorgeous feathers spread out in the sunshine; and as the gentle little girl failed to make friends with his highmightiness, Dora was about to recall her to return to the house, when two gentlemen emerged from a walk divided by shrubbery from the lawn and approached her.

Dora tried in vain to keep her dimples under proper control as she turned to greet Ronald Buchanan, whose arm was linked in that of Sir Philip Standley.

" We have come, my dear," began the old gentleman, "to suggest the propriety of your going within, as the sun has become somewhat overpowering since mid-day; and Ronald has confided to me the fact that he is perishing for a little music! Come, Marian, my pet; grandpapa and you will lead the way."

" What shall I sing?" cried happy Dora, improvising

a triumphant prelude, raising her beaming eyes to Sir Philip's face as he and Ronald stood eagerly waiting beside her.

"Sing the little Scotch ballad you were so fond of crooning through the long winter evenings; it begins——"

"Oh, I know!" she interrupted Sir Philip; and, striking a few lively chords, she began,—

> "'Where Cart rins rowin' to the sea,
>   By mony a flow'r and spreading tree,
>   There lives a lad,—the lad for me,
>   He is a gallant weaver!
>   Oh, I had wooers aught or nine,
>   They gied me rings and ribbons fine;
>   And I was feared my heart would tine,
>   And—I gied it to the weaver!'"

As Dora's voice, sweeter, fuller in tone than ever before, lingered over this last line, Sir Philip gently raised her chin with one finger until she was forced to look into his eyes, and then he said, "Ah, wicked Dora! to cheat me so; this is not the song you sang so often in the gloaming. Will you not sing that very one for me now?"

She drew his hand tenderly to her lips and kissed it, while her cheek grew crimson. "Yes, Sir Philip," she said, after a silent struggle; and after a plaintive little prelude, she began,—

> "'My heart is sair, I darena tell,
>   My heart is sair for somebody;
>   I could wake a winter-night
>   For the sake of somebody.
>   Oh, hon! for somebody!
>   Oh, hey! for somebody!
>   I wad do—what wad I not?
>   For the sake of somebody.'"

Her voice trembled slightly in the first lines, but before the old song ended she had forgotten her audience and everything but the sweet, quaint melody, which rang out unfettered by the faintest self-consciousness. And then, without moving, she glided into a stirring march from Saul, which she as suddenly abandoned, turning quickly around to where Ronald sat, still absorbed by the little Scotch ballad (Sir Philip had yielded to Marian's entreaty, and wandered off into the conservatories),—

"Ronald!" began Dora, timidly. "Will you be good enough to tell me what first induced you to call upon Sir Philip? Where did you meet him?"

"I met him for the first time in his study, here, at Ellingham, by his own invitation."

"Invitation? Were you not strangers, then?"

"Yes. It was in my power on one occasion to do Sir Philip a service; he did not forget it, and wished to tell me so. I was invited to come here; after some demur, I came."

"'After some demur,'—oh, Ronald!" remonstrated Dora.

"Yes, darling, after a great deal of very serious demur, during which I almost went mad; for, Dora, you see, I was then but a country surgeon, and you were lady of Ellingham Hall! And even now that this noble-hearted old gentleman has given me the stewardship of this vast estate, and treats me in all things as his son, I feel still at times a weight of obligation which——"

"Oh, foolish boy!" cried Dora, stroking back with loving hand the bonnie brown hair which had fallen over his broad brow, "do you not know that you help me to fill this great, lonely heart, which without love would starve to death? Sir Philip *loves and trusts you, Ronald;* and if you have given him those inestimable blessings, the power to love and trust *another human being implicitly,* your obligations are canceled forever."

31*

"Do you really think so, my beloved?" he asked, smiling. "Then what do you not *owe to me*, for with that power you have also invested me in fullest measure?"

Dora's reply was unheard, save by Ronald, and he told nobody!

Farewell, little Dora! We leave you now basking in the sunshine of happiness. May those beautiful eyes nevermore have their light quenched by tears! May those tender feet nevermore be blistered in the stony paths through which they walked so courageously in the past! We hope that

> "All is over now,—the hope and the fear and the sorrow;
>   All the aching of heart, the weary, unsatisfied longing;
>   All the dull, deep pain, and the constant anguish of patience;"

for the future years seem strewn with Love's fair flowers, and "in all the welkin is no cloud."

THE END.

Dorothy Fox. A novel. By Louisa Parr, author

of "How it all Happened," etc. With numerous Illustrations, 8vo. Paper cover. 75 cents. Extra cloth. $1.25.

"The Quaker character, though its quaintness and simplicity may seem easy enough to catch, requires a delicate workman to do it justice. Such an artist is the author of 'Dorothy Fox,' and we must thank her for a charming novel. The story is dramatically interesting, and the characters are drawn with a firm and graceful hand The style is fresh and natural, vigorous without vulgarity, simple without mawkishness. Dorothy herself is represented as charming all hearts, and she will charm all readers. . . . We wish 'Dorothy Fox' many editions "—*London Times.*

"One of the best novels of the season."—*Philadelphia Press.*

"The characters are brought out in life-like style, and cannot fail to attract the closest attention."—*Pittsburg Gazette.*

"It is admirably told, and will establish the reputation of the author among novelists."—*Albany Argus.*

How it all Happened. By Louisa Parr, author of

"Dorothy Fox," etc. 12mo. Paper cover. 25 cents.

"It is not often that one finds so much pleasure in reading a love story, charmingly told in a few pages."—*Charleston Courier.*

"Is a well-written little love story, in which a great deal is said in a very few words."—*Philadelphia Evening Telegraph.*

"A remarkably clever story."—*Boston Saturday Evening Gazette.*

John Thompson, Blockhead, and Companion Por-

traits. By LOUISA PARR, author of "Dorothy Fox." 12mo. With Frontispiece. Extra cloth. $1.75.

"Extremely well-told stories, interesting in characters and incidents, and pure and wholesome in sentiment."—*Boston Watchman and Reflector.*

"These are racy sketches, and belong to that delightful class in which the end comes before the reader is ready for it.

"The style throughout is very simple and fresh, abounding in strong, vivid, idiomatic English "—*Home Journal.*

"They are quite brilliant narrative sketches, worthy of the reputation established by the writer."—*Philadelphia Inquirer.*

"Very presentable, very readable."—*New York Times.*

The Quiet Miss Godolphin, by Ruth Garrett; and

A CHANCE CHILD, by EDWARD GARRETT, joint authors of "Occupations of a Retired Life" and "White as Snow." With Six Illustrations by Townley Green. 16mo Cloth. 75 cents. Paper cover. 50 cents.

"These stories are characterized by great strength and beauty of thought, with a singularly attractive style. Their influence will not fail to improve and delight."—*Philadelphia Age.*

St. Cecilia. A Modern Tale from Real Life.

Part I.—ADVERSITY. 12mo. Extra cloth. $1.50.

"It is carefully and beautifully written."—*Washington Chronicle.*

"A tale that we can cheerfully recommend as fresh, entertaining and well written."—*Louisville Courier Journal.*

Tricotrin. The Story of a Waif and Stray. By

"OUIDA," author of "Under Two Flags," etc. With Portrait of the Author from an Engraving on Steel. 12mo. Cloth. $1.50.

"The story is full of vivacity and of thrilling interest."—*Pittsburgh Gazette.*

"Tricotrin is a work of absolute power, some truth and deep interest."—*N. Y. Day Book.*

"The book abounds in beautiful sentiment, expressed in a concentrated, compact style which cannot fail to be attractive and will be read with pleasure in every household."—*San Francisco Times.*

Granville de Vigne ; or, Held in Bondage. A

Tale of the Day. By "OUIDA," author of "Idalia," "Tricotrin," etc. 12mo. Cloth. $1.50.

"This is one of the most powerful and spicy works of fiction which the present century, so prolific in light literature, has produced."

Strathmore ; or, Wrought by His Own Hand. A

Novel. By "OUIDA," author of "Granville de Vigne," etc. 12mo. Cloth. $1.50.

"It is a romance of the intense school, but it is written with more power, fluency and brilliancy than the works of Miss Braddon and Mrs. Wood, while its scenes and characters are taken from high life."—*Boston Transcript.*

Chandos. A Novel. By "Ouida," author of

"Strathmore," "Idalia," etc. 12mo. Cloth. $1.50.

"Those who have read these two last named brilliant works of fiction (Granville de Vigne and Strathmore) will be sure to read *Chandos*. It is characterized by the same gorgeous coloring of style and somewhat exaggerated portraiture of scenes and characters, but it is a story of surprising power and interest."—*Pittsburgh Evening Chronicle.*

Under Two Flags. A Story of the Household and

the Desert. By "OUIDA," author of "Tricotrin," "Granville de Vigne," etc. 12mo. Cloth. $1.50.

"No one will be able to resist its fascination who once begins its perusal."—*Phila. Evening Bulletin.*

"This is probably the most popular work of Ouida. It is enough of itself to establish her fame as one of the most eloquent and graphic writers of fiction now living."—*Chicago Journal of Commerce.*

Puck. His Vicissitudes, Adventures, Observations,

Conclusions, Friendship and Philosophies. By "OUIDA," author of "Strathmore," "Idalia," "Tricotrin," etc. 12mo. Fine cloth. $1.50.

"Its quaintness will provoke laughter, while the interest in the central character is kept up unabated."—*Albany Journal.*

"It sustains the widely spread popularity of the author."—*Pittsburgh Gazette.*

"*It is the Fashion.*" *A Novel. From the German*

of ADELHEID VON AUER. By the translator of "Over Yonder," "Magdalena," "The Old Countess," etc. 12mo.
Fine cloth. $1.50.

"It is one of the most charming books of the times, and is admirable for its practical, wise and beautiful morality. A more natural and graceful work of its kind we never before read."—*Richmond Dispatch.*

"This is a charming novel; to be commended not only for the interest of the story, but for the fine healthy tone that pervades it. . . . This work has not the excessive elaboration of many German novels, which make them rather tedious for American readers, but is fresh, sprightly and full of common sense applied to the business of actual life."—*Philadelphia Age.*

"It is a most excellent book, abounding in pure sentiment and beautiful thought, and written in a style at once lucid, graceful and epigrammatic."—*New York Evening Mail.*

Dead Men's Shoes. A Novel. By J. R. Hader-

mann, author of "Forgiven at Last." 12mo. Fine cloth.
$2.

"One of the best novels of the season."—*Philadelphia Press.*

"One of the best novels descriptive of life at the South that has yet been published. The plot is well contrived, the characters well contrasted and the dialogue crisp and natural."—*Baltimore Gazette.*

Israel Mort, Overman. A Story of the Mine. By

JOHN SAUNDERS, author of "Abel Drake's Wife." Illus-
trated. 16mo. Fine cloth. $1.25.

"Intensely dramatic. . . . Some of the characters are exquisitely drawn, and show the hand of a master."—*Boston Saturday Evening Gazette.*

"The book takes a strong hold on the reader's attention from the first, and the interest does not flag for a moment."—*Boston Globe.*

"The denouement, moral and artistic, is very fine."—*New York Evening Mail.*

"It treats of a variety of circumstances and characters almost new to the realm of fiction, and has a peculiar interest on this account."—*Boston Advertiser.*

In the Rapids. A Romance. By Gerald Hart.

12mo. Toned paper. Extra cloth. $1.50.

"Full of tragic interest."—*Cincinnati Gazette.*

"It is, on the whole, remarkably well told, and is particularly notable for its resemblance to those older and, in some respects, better models of com-position in which the dialogue is subordinated to the narrative, and the effects are wrought out by the analytical powers of the writer."—*Baltimore Gazette.*

The Parasite; or, How to Make One's Fortune.

A Comedy in Five Acts. After the French of Picard
12mo. Paper cover. 75 cents.

A pleasant, sprightly comedy, unexceptionable in its moral and chaste in its language. As our amateur actors are always in pursuit of plays of this character, we should suppose they would find this a valuable addition to their stock."—*Philadelphia Age*

The Old Mam'selle's Secret. *From the German of*
E. Marlitt, author of "Gold Elsie," etc. By Mrs. A. L.
WISTER. Sixth edition. 12mo. Cloth. $1.50.

"A more charming story, and one which, having once commenced, it seemed more difficult to leave, we have not met with for many a day."—*The Round Table.*

"Is one of the most intense, con- centrated, compact novels of the day . . . And the work has the minute fidelity of the author of 'The Initials,' the dramatic unity of Reade and the graphic power of George Eliot."—*Columbus (O.) Journal.*

Gold Elsie. *From the German of E. Marlitt, author*
of "The Old Mam'selle's Secret," etc. By Mrs. A. L.
WISTER. Fifth edition. 12mo. Cloth. $1.50.

"A charming book. It absorbs your attention from the title-page to the end."—*The Home Circle.*

"A charming story charmingly told."—*Baltimore Gazette.*

Countess Gisela. *From the German of E. Marlitt,*
author of "Gold Elsie," etc. By Mrs. A. L. WISTER.
Third edition. 12mo. Cloth. $1.50.

"There is more dramatic power in this than in any of the stories by the same author that we have read."—*N. O. Times.*

"It is a story that arouses the inter- est of the reader from the outset."—*Pittsburgh Gazette.*

"The best work by this author."—*Philadelphia Telegraph.*

Over Yonder. *From the German of E. Marlitt,*
author of "Countess Gisela," etc. Third edition. With
a full-page Illustration. 8vo. Paper cover. 30 cents.

"'Over Yonder' is a charming novelette. The admirers of 'Old Mam'selle's Secret' will give it a glad reception, while those who are ignor- ant of the merits of this author will find in it a pleasant introduction to the works of a gifted writer."—*Daily Sentinel.*

The Little Moorland Princess. *From the German*
of E. Marlitt, author of "The Old Mam'selle's Secret,"
"Gold Elsie," etc. By Mrs. A. L. WISTER. Fourth edition. 12mo. Fine cloth. $1.75.

"By far the best foreign romance of the season."—*Philadelphia Press.*

"It is a great luxury to give one's self up to its balmy influence."—*Chicago Evening Journal.*

Magdalena. *From the German of E. Marlitt,*
author of "Countess Gisela," etc. And THE LONELY ONE
("The Solitaries"). From the German of Paul Heyse.
With two Illustrations. 8vo. Paper cover. 35 cents.

"We know of no way in which a leisure hour may be more pleasantly whiled away than by a perusal of either of these tales."—*Indianapolis Sentinel.*

Folle-Farine. A Novel. By "Ouida," author of "Idalia," "Under Two Flags," "Strathmore," etc. 12mo Fine cloth. $1.50.

"Ouida's pen is a graphic one. and page after page of gorgeous word-painting flow from it in a smooth, melodious rhythm that often has the perfect measure of blank verse, and needs only to be broken into line. There is in it, too. the eloquence of genius."—*Phila. Eve. Bulletin.*

"This work fully sustains .he writer's previous reputation, and may be numbered among the best of her works."—*Troy Times.*

"Full of vivacity."—*Fort Wayne Gazette.*

"The best of her numerous stories '—*Vicksburg Herald.*

Idalia. A Novel. By "Ouida," author of "Strathmore," "Tricotrin," "Under Two Flags," etc. 12mo Cloth. $1.50.

"It is a story of love and hatred, of affection and jealousy, of intrigue and devotion. . . . We think this novel will attain a wide popularity, especially among those whose refined taste enables them to appreciate and enjoy what is truly beautiful in literature."-*Albany Evening Journal.*

A Leaf in the Storm, and other Novelettes. By "OUIDA," author of "Folle-Farine," "Granville de Vigne," etc. Two Illustrations. Fifth Edition. 8vo. Paper cover. 50 cents.

"Those who look upon light literature as an art will read these tales with pleasure and satisfaction."—*Baltimore Gazette.*

"In the longest of these stories, 'A Branch of Lilac,' the simplicity of the narrative—so direct and truthful—produces the highest artistic effect. It required high genius to write such a tale in such a manner."—*Philadelphia Press.*

Cecil Castlemaine's Gage, and other Stories. By "OUIDA," author of "Granville de Vigne," "Chandos," etc. Revised for Publication by the Author. 12mo. Cloth. $1.50.

Randolph Gordon, and other Stories. By "Ouida," author of "Idalia," "Under Two Flags," etc. 12mo. Cloth. $1.50.

Beatrice Boville, and other Stories. By "Ouida," author of "Strathmore," "Cecil Castlemaine's Gage," etc. 12mo. Cloth. $1.50.

"The many works already in print by this versatile authoress have established her reputation as a novelist, and these short stories contribute largely to the stock of pleasing narratives and adventures alive to the memory of all who are given to romance and fiction "—*New Haven Journal.*